BENJAMIN TATE

LEAVES OF FLAME

DAW BOOKS, INC.

DONALD A. WOLLHEIM, FOUNDER

375 Hudson Street, New York, NY 10014

ELIZABETH R. WOLLHEIM

SHEILA E. GILBERT

PUBLISHERS

http://www.dawbooks.com

First Printing, January 2012
1 2 3 4 5 6 7 8 9

COLIN SHOUTED A WARNING . . .

He could feel the power slipping outward from his grasp, glanced up to see shock and horror dawning on the faces around him. The crowd pulled farther back as tendrils of light began flickering up from the stone around him. As the light intensified, Colin scanned the area, noticing that the light curling upward around him was centered on one spot, one location.

He stepped forward, clearing the stone of the plaza in a wide circle. Then he fell to his knees, setting his staff to one side.

The light emerging from the ground came in sheets, rising like steam or mist.

Lifting the seed toward the sky with both hands, he released the power of the Lifeblood, the Confluence, and the White Fire inside him. It surged through his arms, into the seed, and the last restraints on the power locked inside it collapsed.

With a harsh cry, he drove the shaft of the seed into the stone before him, felt it pierce deep. Beneath his hand, the knot atop the staff writhed. The pale white bark split beneath his palm with a crack of splintering wood. He hissed and lurched away. Grabbing his staff, he continued backing up. White light licked up around him, flowed through him, touching and tasting, rising higher as the stone beneath his feet trembled. It recognized its creator.

The crowd gasped when the seed quickened and the sapling that sprouted from it shot skyward, higher than the tendrils of light, growing in the space of heartbeats, seeking sunlight. The sapling thickened, the bole of an immense tree emerging, its bark dark, nearly black, limbs thrusting outward from the trunk like spears, splitting, branching. The groan of stressed wood filled the plaza, punctuated by sharp cracks and sizzling, hissing pops. And still the immense tree strained upward. Roots pierced the stone at the trunk's base, and dove back underground, grinding the stone to dust as the trunk thickened and spread. Buds appeared on the thousands of branches, burst open between one breath and the next, thick silvery leaves unfurling. Colin stepped back once, twice, tilted his head so that he could see the branches reaching outward, obscuring the sky. . . .

DAW Books Presents
A bold new fantasy series from
Benjamin Tate:

WELL OF SORROWS
LEAVES OF FLAME

This book is dedicated to George,
who puts up with all of the geekery
with a mere shake of his head.

Acknowledgments

Most books require some blood, sweat, and tears from the writer, but this one asked that of my beta readers as well. They suffered through nearly six entire chapters of utter dreck until I finally realized that *it wasn't working* and started all over again. Those intrepid souls were: Ariel Guzman, Patricia Bray, Tes Hilaire, April Steenberg, David Fortier, Jake Philion, and Dan DeVito. Thank you for your patience.

Of course, after they beat it into shape, it got mauled by my editor, Sheila Gilbert. Once again, thanks for the insight and for pushing me to think beyond what I've already written and seeing the larger picture. The books are much better because of this.

Then there's the family—mother, brothers, sisters-in-law, partner, grandparents, and now nephews. Thanks for being there for moral support . . . and for a few sales as well. *grin*

And finally, thank you, readers. I hope you enjoy the book. If you'd like to find out more about me or my books, check out www.benjamintate.com. You can also find me on Facebook and Twitter (bentateauthor).

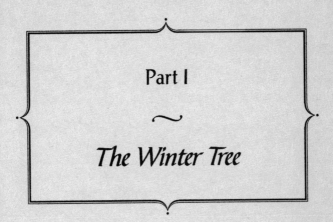

Part I

~

The Winter Tree

1

COLIN PATRIS HARTEN—known as Shaeveran by the Alvritshai, also called Shade—slid through the grasses of the plains, the world unnaturally still around him. He carried a cedar staff given to him by the heart of the forest, its power twining around and through him. A satchel hung from his shoulder, steadied by his other hand. He moved swiftly, head bent, time slowed around him but not halted. He was too exhausted to stop the flow completely, or to press beyond the barrier and into the past. He wanted to be at the Alvritshai stronghold of Caercaern before the end of night, and he'd already traveled far. He wasn't certain how much longer he could slow the flow of time to make the journey quicker. He'd grown in power over the last forty years—gained in strength as he used the Lifeblood to battle the ever growing threat of the Wraiths and the Shadows, and immersing himself in the cleansing heart of the White Flame and the healing waters of the Confluence—but there were limits.

And prices paid.

He was reaching the extent of his strength. He could hear it in his own ragged breathing, could feel it in the pounding of his heart and the humming of the world around him. Time pushed at him, tried to force him back into his natural state. But he wanted to reach Caercaern before the Alvritshai lords called the Evant for the last time and the lords dispersed to their own lands for the winter months. He *needed* to meet with them, to get them to accept the responsibility for what he carried in his satchel.

The survival of the Alvritshai—of all of the races of Wrath Suvane: Alvritshai, dwarren, and human—depended on it.

So he shoved the increasing pressure of time back with a grunt, felt it give beneath him even as a shudder of weariness passed through his chest. He ignored it, focused on the plains ahead, on the moonlit silver of the grasses and the brittle stars in the sky. Folds in the land appeared as shadows, and by the growing darkness he could tell that he was getting closer to Alvritshai lands. He walked upon dwarren lands now, on earth he'd traveled as a child over a hundred years ago, when his parents had abandoned Portstown for the unknown wilds of the grasses to the east.

Those unknown wilds had killed them—and everyone else in their ill-fated wagon train—except for Colin.

And Walter.

Colin frowned at himself and shrugged the disturbing memories away. It had happened a long time ago, in what felt like another world, another lifetime. Wrath Suvane had changed since then. The Accord he had helped establish between the three races had held, although tenuously, strained by the continued attacks of the Shadows and the work of the Wraiths to bring about the awakening of the Wells. The dwarren retained their claim to the plains, the Alvritshai the lands to the north and the mountain reaches of Hauttaeren, and the humans the coastal region.

The Shadows and the Wraiths maintained their hold on the forests of Ostraell.

But in the past forty years, all of the races had grown. The Alvritshai had branched out along the mountains, both east and west, carving new strongholds into their depths even though the encroaching ice sheets to the north continued to build, their original homeland still locked away beneath the frigid cold. The dwarren continued to survive beneath the plains in their extensive warrens, although they'd begun building stone and cloth cities at the mouths of the most prominent entrances to facilitate trade. Colin had passed one such city a few hours before, a caravan of twenty wagons headed toward its vast towers along the main road from the human province of Corsair. The humans had expanded the most, populating the coast at first, but spreading south and then east, along the sheer cliffs of the Escarpment that provided a natural boundary between dwarren and human lands. They'd spread far, although they had not yet reached the edges of the desert to the east.

But they would. The lords of the Provinces craved land and the resources that came with it. They'd succeeded in breaking free from the Court of Andover and the chokehold of the Families during the Feud, now ended. They'd seized the coast of the new world and held it in a firm grip, pushing the Andovans back. But they needed to retain that hold, and that required a strong presence in the New World.

Colin grimaced and shook his head. The affairs of the Provinces were not his concern at the moment. The expansion of the humans to the south and east had strained the treaty and relations between the three races, but the treaty had survived. That was all that mattered. The real threats were the Wraiths and the Shadows.

He hefted the satchel against his shoulder, felt the weight of it, reassuring himself that the three forged cuttings were still there, wrapped in muslin cloth for protection. He'd left the fourth cutting under the Faelehgre's protection, until he could determine what to do with it.

As he shifted under the satchel's weight, a light caught his attention in the distance.

He slowed, squinted to the northeast. At first he saw nothing, the urgency of reaching Caercaern on time pressing down upon his shoulders, but then he caught the light again—a familiar white light, incredibly bright.

He cursed and began running toward the light, even though he knew he was already too late.

He slowed as he neared and saw the scattering of wagons and bodies, his heart thudding hard in his chest, his throat threatening to close off. He sucked in air, tried to convince himself that he was short of breath because of the run and his exhaustion, but he knew better. The images of his own family's wagon train, trapped at the cusp of the Ostraell, sliced too keenly across his vision. He clutched at the front of his clothes with his free hand, found and gripped the crescent-shaped pendant that hung from his neck but lay hidden beneath the cloth, as all vows should be, even if those vows had remained unfulfilled. The edges of the crescent that cradled the empty blood vial bit into his palm and fingers and he focused on that pain, used it to push thoughts of Karen's lifeless body to one side. She'd died over a hundred years ago, on these plains, cradled close to Colin's chest. And she'd been killed the same way these people had.

Straightening, Colin moved into the shadows of the wagons, the cedar staff held out before him, even though he had not yet allowed time to resume. He paused at the body of a young girl, no more than twelve, crumpled to the ground next to the wheel of one of the wagons. Her face was tilted toward the moonlight, her eyes wide open, her skin unnaturally pale. No blood marred her body, but the Shadows killed without tearing skin or leaving gaping wounds. Their death was more subtle, and more horrific. Colin knew. He'd nearly experienced that death himself. If it hadn't been for the Faelehgre . . .

He stood, shoved aside that memory as well, and moved on to the next body. A man this time, without a mark on him but dead nonetheless. His sword was drawn, as if he'd tried to protect the girl, but it lay useless in the grass beside him. Colin hesitated over this man—so much like his father—then continued on, moving from body to body. Men, women, a few children—they were all dead, left as they had fallen. He circled from wagon to wagon toward the center, where the Faelehgre's light burned hideously bright, his chest tightening the closer he came. Horses, dogs, goats—everything living had fallen. The wagon train had had time to react—the typically scattered wagons drawn close for defense—but the travelers had all died nonetheless. Caught out in the open, they had possessed nothing that could have stopped the Shadows. Only one thing could have helped this close to the forest, this far from Alvritshai lands: the Faelehgre. And the one Faelehgre that had arrived had come too late.

Colin halted in the center of the death, where the pure white light of the Faelehgre shone at the heart of the shimmering folds of darkness of a Shadow. The body of a woman lay beneath them, curled protectively around a young boy, maybe five years old. Her face was buried in the crook of her arm, her tears of terror still wet on her cheeks. The night was too cool for them to evaporate.

The Shadow had been rising upward from its feast, the life-force drained from both the woman and the child, when the Faelehgre caught it. The anger the light had felt over the deaths still pulsed throughout the scene. It might have been able to repulse the attack on its own—it would have depended on how many of the Shadows had attacked, how well they were organized—but from what Colin could see, it hadn't. Its anger had been too great. It had sped between the wagon and shot to the heart of the Shadow as it rose, had pierced it in its fury, had killed it . . . and killed itself in the process.

Colin lowered his staff. He reached out a hand to touch

the light at the heart of the Shadow, but halted. Even with time slowed he could feel the coldness of the folds of darkness that made up the Shadow. He wondered briefly if he'd known this particular Faelehgre, suspected he had.

He let his arm fall back to his side. There was nothing that could be done here. The pulsing light of the Faelehgre would slowly absorb the darkness of the Shadow and then vanish. The wagon travelers were dead, and there were too many for him to bury or burn. Not if he was to make Caercaern before dawn. And his purpose in the Alvritshai city was to prevent attacks such as these, to protect the Alvritshai, the dwarren, and the humans from the Shadows. He needed to keep moving.

Gripping his staff tightly, binding his grief and sorrow and hatred close—a hatred that had survived undamped for over a hundred years—he struck out northward.

Caercaern and the lords of the Alvritshai waited.

Lord Aeren Goadri Rhyssal stood on the balcony outside his House rooms in Caercaern and stared out at the lightening horizon as dawn approached. Spread out on the stone terraces beneath him, the city had begun to come to life. The majority of Caercaern lay on these terraces, behind the stone walls of the fortress, although there were more rooms and halls carved out of the depths of the mountain behind him. Thousands of tunnels and hundreds of rooms, leading all the way through the Hauttaeren to the northern wastes, all abandoned.

Now, the Alvritshai had spread out onto the hills and valleys below, the forested peaks beginning to emerge into the light, covered in thick mist. The terraces of Caercaern proper weren't hidden, though, and he could see people beginning to fill the streets: errand boys racing from level to level; the White Phalanx changing shift; bakers and tavern keepers and merchants beginning to open shops or carting wares up to the wide plazas and open markets. He could see the round Hall of the Evant in the central marketplace, its thick colonnades shadowing the main building within. The stone obelisks of the Order of Aielan's temple rose into the graying light. And if he turned, he could see the rising levels of the main tower, where the Tamaell resided with his ruling House, the mountains of the Hauttaeren behind it, streams and falls cascading down its stone face, runoff from the snows that covered the peaks year round. The mountain range cut a jagged swath east and west, keeping the snows and the glacial drifts that had driven the Alvritshai southward locked in the north. But Aeren didn't turn to gaze along the mountains and their white peaks. They represented the past. He preferred to look out toward the future, toward the dense forests, valleys, and hills that stretched from here to the southern plains. Even now, he could see the spires and tiled roofs of buildings jutting up from the mists, emerging as the light increased.

The temple of the Order of Aielan began to chime utiern and Aeren glanced toward the east, where a thin arc of reddish-gold sun had slid above the horizon. Dawn.

He grunted and drew in a long, deep breath, tasted the chill bite of the coming winter, frigid against his tongue, then exhaled in an extended sigh as he heard footsteps behind him.

Arms wrapped around his waist and a chin rested against his shoulder. He drew in the scent of jasmine as his hands enfolded those at his waist, the body behind pressing up against his back.

"You should not be seen here, with me," he said. The words could have been a slap in the face—they had been, the first time he spoke them—but the tone had changed over time. Now they throbbed with humor, with the memory of that first unintentional slight.

"I know," the voice responded, the woman's breath tickling his ear and sending a tingling shiver down his neck and side. She pulled him tighter against her. "But you'll be departing for Rhyssal House lands in another few days, and I will be forced to remain here, alone. I'll take the risk, to be with you a few moments longer."

"And I'll be less alone in Rhyssal than you will be here?"

She snorted and pushed back slightly, Aeren taking the opportunity to turn around within the confines of her arms so he could face her.

Moiran, former Tamaea of the Alvritshai, wife of Fedorem and mother of the current Tamaell, Thaedoren, shook her head. "You will have Eraeth there to keep you company, as you always have."

"Eraeth is my Protector, so he does not count. You have Thaedoren."

Moiran's gray eyes narrowed. "He is my son, and Tamaell besides. He has no time for his mother."

"He listens to you more than you know. I've seen it in the Evant."

"He listens only when it suits him, especially regarding the Evant. And if the lords find out about us—"

Aeren silenced her with a firm, lingering kiss.

As he drew back, a reserved reply of unconcern ready, someone said, "If they find out, they'll be overjoyed, I'm certain. At least, most of them."

Moiran's arms slid away instantly and she stepped back from Aeren, both of them straightening, the formality that cloaked all Alvritshai—that formed the basis of their society—sliding back into place instinctively. Moiran clasped her hands and brought them to rest before her, even as her head rose to face the intruder, her eyes flashing with the authority of the Tamaea, an authority she ostensibly no longer wielded. Aeren simply let his arms fall to his sides, although he glowered into the weak shadows at the back of the balcony where he could barely make out the figure resting in one of the chairs tucked away beside the doorway.

"How long have you been there, Shaeveran?" he demanded.

Colin shifted forward, leaning into the light so that Moiran could see him. The brittle stiffness in her shoulders relaxed, although it did not completely vanish. The Alvritshai did not share their private lives with anyone. Not even old friends.

Colin nodded toward Moiran, then turned his attention to Aeren. "Since before you arrived. I know you enjoy the dawn." His voice hardened. "We have much to discuss before the Evant meets."

Moiran smiled, the expression tight with regret and understanding. Aeren had seen the smile often. She'd been Tamaea for far too long to protest when the Evant intruded on her personal life.

"I should return to my chambers," she said formally, nodding toward Colin, then Aeren, refraining from any form of affection although Aeren could see the impulse in her eyes.

When she'd left, Colin caught Aeren's gaze and raised an eyebrow.

"It's been forty years since Fedorem's death," Aeren said defensively.

"And Thaedoren? How is he taking it?"

Aeren hesitated. "He did not take it well at first, but it was impossible to keep it from him. The White Phalanx escort her everywhere after all, and they report to the Tamaell. Once he calmed down, an understanding was reached, more from Moiran's influence on him than my own. We have his blessing, his support, as long as we keep it from the Evant until the time is right for an official announcement."

"You don't think those in the Evant already know?"

"The Alvritshai keep their private lives ... private." He shot a warning glance toward Colin, who shrugged.

"Your private life is not my concern, although this may help my cause more than you know. If you are already allied with Thaedoren, if it is on the verge of a blood-tie—"

The loud thud of bootfalls sounded from the inner room and three Phalanx guardsmen led by Eraeth burst through the doorway, their cattan blades brandished. They halted abruptly as they saw Aeren standing at the balcony's edge.

"The Tamaea-rhen claimed—" Eraeth began, but spun, straightening into a fighting stance even as his blade settled dead center on Colin's chest. The other guards reacted as quickly, Aeren noted with approval.

A deathly silence hung over the crisp dawn air, four swords hanging motionless.

Then Eraeth's eyes narrowed. "You," he said, his voice a low rumble.

Colin smiled. "It's been a long time, Eraeth."

The tension held a moment longer, filled with emotions and things left unsaid. Aeren could sense the strange bond his Protector and Shaeveran shared in that tension, so rigid and carefully controlled, filled with sorrow and misplaced mistrust and an unspoken respect.

Eraeth finally lowered his sword with a grimace. With a curt command, the other three guardsmen lowered their weapons as well, then departed. Eraeth remained behind, after a short glance and confirming nod from Aeren, moving into a guardsman's position near the door.

Aeren shifted away from the balcony's edge toward Colin. "What brings you to Caercaern, in need of the Evant? You haven't been here in nearly thirty years. Is it about the Wells? The Shadows and the Wraiths? Have you managed to stop them?"

Colin stood, leaning on his staff. He appeared older than when Aeren had seen him last, but Aeren knew he could change his age at will. He wondered why Colin had chosen age over youth in this instance, what advantage it gave him.

"We both know that, even with the help of the Faelehgre, our chances of stopping the Wraiths from awakening the Wells would be . . . difficult. I've discovered that perhaps it shouldn't be done at all."

"So the Wraiths and the Shadows will be allowed to run free, to feed off of our people at will?" Eraeth couldn't keep the anger from his voice. Aeren tensed as well, thinking of all of the Alvritshai who had already died in their attempts to keep the Shadows from their lands.

Colin bowed his head slightly. "I have come up with another option. But it will require the help of the Order of Aielan."

Aeren straightened. "Lotaern has used the Order to gain power within the Evant, more power than I am comfortable with at the moment. He has used the threat of the Shadows and the Wraiths, and the fears of the lords and the Alvritshai, to consolidate his control. The Order has essentially risen to the level of a House. I do not think that allowing him control over something more—"

"I think you'll find that this may limit his control, rather than extend it. At least regarding the Shadows and the Wraiths. I cannot say how it will affect his political power within the Evant. That is . . . an Alvritshai concern."

Aeren frowned. "What is this other option?"

Colin's free hand moved to the satchel he carried at his side. "A way to counter the effects of the awakened Wells, to limit the range of the Shadows . . . and the Wraiths to an extent. A way to protect the Alvritshai from their threat."

Aeren stared at the satchel. He found it hard to believe that something that could save the Alvritshai from the Shadows and the Wraiths could be contained in such a small case.

He caught Colin's gaze. "How?"

~

Colin raised his head enough he could see through the heavy folds of his hood as he, Aeren, Eraeth, and the rest of the Rhyssal House Phalanx passed through the massive wooden doors of the inner chamber of the great Hall at the center of Caercaern's widest marketplace. He could see little through the opening of the cowl, had entirely missed the thick colonnades of the Hall and the magnificent stone carvings on the outside walls depicting Alvritshai in their daily labors and religious observances. But the interior was as grand. The Tamaell's platform stood on the far side of a wide area surrounded by circular arrays of desks and seats and tiered stairs leading down to a central oval. Alvritshai lords and their attendant guards, clerks, and aides filled the stairs, their conversations echoing loudly in the huge vaulted ceiling overhead. The desks were draped in thick folds of cloth of various colors, representing each of the Houses of the Evant, those colors mirrored in the banners arrayed against the rounded walls of the chamber and in the formal dress of everyone present.

Eraeth and Aeren led the Rhyssal House party down the stairs to the deep-blue-and-red-shrouded desk. Colin felt the eyes of the attendant lords register Aeren's arrival ... and then fall on the shrouded figure carrying a staff and satchel behind him. Beneath the folds of the cowl, he heard the sudden lull in conversation, saw the pinched frowns that flashed briefly across faces before gazes shot toward Aeren, toward the empty throne that graced the Tamaell's platform, then to their fellow lords to gauge reactions. Conversations resumed as Aeren reached his own seat and settled in, motioning Colin to a place on his left, Eraeth taking up position on his right. A flurry of activity ensued, as pages were sent to relay messages throughout the room.

Colin glanced around, taking note of the lords he recognized and a few he didn't. The fallout from Lord Khalaek's betrayal and murder of Tamaell Fedorem had been swift, the declaration that House Duvoraen had fallen occurring on the battlefield at the Escarpment after Khalaek had been banished and handed over to King Stephan and subsequently executed. House Uslaen had risen in its place, led by Lord Saetor, who stood near his white-and-gold-shrouded desk, back rigid. He looked uncomfortable among his fellow lords, even after forty years. Younger, and raised and trained to be part of the Phalanx, his ascension into the Evant had been unexpected, an honor placed upon him for his part in the battle at the Escarpment and his handling of Lord Khalaek's forces after the lord had been removed and his Phalanx placed under Saetor's command. The transition hadn't been entirely smooth—there were those loyal to Khalaek who had abandoned the House as Saetor seized control—but after Khalaek's betrayal had been exposed, backed by both Thaedoren and Lotaern's word, it had gone as smoothly as could be expected.

Saetor watched Colin intently, ignoring the flurry of messages that had accumulated on his desk. He was so focused that Colin shifted uncomfortably in his seat, then looked away, even though he knew Saetor could not see beneath his cowl.

His gaze fell on the other unknown lord, Orraen Licaeta, the son of Vaersoom, who had ascended in his father's place as the Lord of House Licaeta soon after the Escarpment, when Vaersoom had succumbed to the wounds received during the battle. Orraen was the firstborn and, unlike Aeren, had been trained to take his father's place since the day he was born. Aeren's elder brother had been groomed for the role Aeren now held. When he had been killed over the course of the war for the plains, Aeren had been forced to leave his studies as acolyte in the Order of Aielan and take control of his House.

Orraen reminded Colin of Khalaek. His posture was relaxed, his genial smile unforced as he moved among the gathering of the Evant, talking to lords and aides and, on occasion, their Phalanx guardsmen. Yet the hardness around his eyes never abated, and his actions — every gesture, every movement — were far too smooth, too slick and practiced. He appeared to have dismissed Colin, his back turned toward Aeren as he conversed with Lord Jydell, even laughing at something his fellow lord said. Jydell cast Aeren a contemplative look, and appeared at ease, but the way one hand twisted the sleeve of his shirt and his occasional glance toward Colin's shrouded figure revealed his concern.

Behind Orraen and Jydell, a few levels up the stairs, stood Lotaern, Chosen of the Order of Aielan. As if sensing Colin's gaze, even from beneath the hood, the Chosen nodded in acknowledgment, as if he knew who hid behind the cowl. And perhaps he did.

Before Colin had a chance to assess the rest of the lords, members of the White Phalanx filed into the room. Four appeared on the platform itself, arranging themselves around the main throne and the two smaller thrones set a pace back to either side. The rest filed in beneath the platform, carrying standards or spears, moving slowly, with formal, deliberate steps. The surrounding lords and their entourages began filtering toward their seats, conversations falling silent.

The White Phalanx halted, standing stock-still, waiting until the room had quieted before the two carrying the spears raised them and pounded their metal bases into the marble floor. The sound cracked through the chamber, and Colin started, even though he'd been expecting it. The procedure for the Tamaell's arrival had changed subtly since Colin had last attended the Evant, but the feel of the chamber — the simmering tension of predator and prey — was the same.

"Tamaell Thaedoren Ormae Resue," one of the standard-bearers announced.

Everyone in attendance stood as Thaedoren emerged onto the platform, followed by his mother, Moiran, and his brother, Daedelan. Colin's eyebrows rose. Both Thaedoren and Daedelan were dressed in the full regalia of the White Phalanx, including bracers on their arms and armor beneath the silky red-and-white folds of their House shirts. Daedelan had darker hair than Thaedoren, like his mother's, but even from this distance Colin could see they both had their father's green eyes. Both were tall and solidly built, although Daedelan was obviously younger, even with his face set in a serious expression. Moiran's gaze swept the room, lingering on no one, not even Aeren, but seeing all. She wore a dress that hinted at armor, the folds and cut more severe and serious than usual. No one spoke, but a rustle eased around the room as the rest noticed as well. Eraeth shot Aeren a questioning look, but Aeren merely shrugged.

Obviously, Thaedoren had prepared since they'd met with him that morning.

"Be seated," Thaedoren said, but remained standing as the chamber filled with the sounds of rustling cloth. Moiran and Daedelan took the two thrones behind him.

When everyone had settled, Thaedoren bowed his head slightly. "We have reached the end of another session of the Evant. I know that you are all looking forward to returning to your House lands in the next few weeks to see to their preparation for winter, and you will be able to depart as planned. But there is one last issue—one of extreme importance—that must be discussed before we bring the Evant to a close." Thaedoren turned toward Aeren and nodded respectfully. "Lord Aeren." He settled into the seat of his throne as Aeren rose.

Aeren hesitated, as if gathering his thoughts, then moved

out from behind the desk and claimed the oval floor beneath the platform. He caught each lord with a penetrating gaze before he spoke. No one sneered or scowled as they had during the first meeting of the Evant Colin had attended when Aeren had tried to speak.

Aeren's House had risen since the death of Fedorem and the battle at the Escarpment. And once his relationship with Moiran was revealed and a blood-tie established with the Tamaell, with Thaedoren . . .

Colin stirred in his seat. Even he, an outsider, a human, realized the power over the Evant that Aeren would wield then.

"The sukrael and the Wraiths," Aeren began. His voice was soft, but everyone in the chamber stirred. "We have all suffered from their attacks since before the Escarpment, since before Khalaek's betrayal of our people to the Wraith called Walter. Those attacks continue to plague us, the sukrael randomly taking lives within each of our Houses, attacking villages and towns, caravans and traders, sometimes destroying every living thing within a wide radius, every man, woman, child, and animal, their lives drained away, their bodies left where they fell. They ravage our lands, spreading out from the Ostraell forests as their power grows, as the Wraiths continue to awaken the sarenavriell that bind the Shadows. Lotaern, the Chosen of the Order of Aielan, has scoured the Scripts and used its knowledge of these creatures to train his warriors of the Flame to defend against them, but as we have all seen, those defenses are minimal."

At this, Lotaern rose in indignation. "The Order of the Flame has done everything in its power to stop these creatures! If not for the Flame, their attacks on Lord Saetor's lands would have been disastrous! They would have decimated the city of Touvaris at the edge of the Ostraell!"

Grumbles of agreement shot through the chamber, but

Aeren overrode them all. "And what is the situation now?" he demanded. "The Order of the Flame has a permanent presence in Touvaris. They patrol its borders with Saetor's Phalanx, using their powers and the Flames of Aielan to keep the sukrael at bay."

"And the sukrael *are* at bay."

"Barely. All that you have achieved is protection of one land at the sacrifice of another. The sukrael don't care about land or buildings or crops. They care only for life. They shifted their attention elsewhere, so while Touvaris lies protected by the Flame, they attack House Redlien, or Licaeta, or roam out onto the dwarren plains attacking our trade routes. And as their power grows, as their Wraiths continue to awaken the sarenavriell and expand their territory, the Order of the Flame is spread thinner and thinner and becomes less and less effective. You have already split the force to cover Licaeta's lands, those closest to the Ostraell. I know you have been discussing the use of the Flame in Lord Jydell's lands. How many warriors do you have in the Order, Chosen? Are there enough to cover all of the Houses, all of the Alvritshai borders?"

Lotaern's jaw worked for a long moment, his eyes blazing with anger, back stiff. "No," he finally said, the word low and grudging. "More warriors of the Flame are being trained as we speak, but there are not enough to protect all of our lands, all of our people."

Aeren nodded. "More warriors of the Flame should be trained, because the threat of the sukrael and the Wraiths is real. I meant no disrespect for the Order, and I—along with every lord present—am grateful for the protection that the Flame has provided from that threat so far. But we must be realistic. The protection the Flame offers will not be enough to cover us all. Not if the sukrael continue to grow in power and the lands they can hunt expand. We need something more. We need something stronger."

"What?" Lord Saetor demanded, standing abruptly, one hand pressed forward onto his desk. "We have done everything within our power. What more do you propose we do?"

Colin rose, even as Aeren turned toward him. Every gaze settled on him as he moved forward, Aeren falling back as he took the center. He moved slowly, the butt of his staff thumping softly onto the marble floor. Tension escalated as he positioned himself before the Tamaell's platform. A murmur ran through the room, and from the corner of his eye he saw Saetor shove back from his desk. He couldn't see Lotaern, but he knew the Chosen well enough he could imagine the frown that darkened his face. He had wanted to include Lotaern in the meeting with the Tamaell, to plan how they would present the proposal, but Aeren—and later, Thaedoren—had felt it better that they catch him unaware. They didn't want to give him the opportunity to turn this proposal to the Order's advantage. And after what he'd seen and heard since his return, he found he agreed with their fears. The Order *had* gained in power, had grown, had created its own Phalanx with the Flame. He could feel the weight of its presence even here, not just in Lotaern's inclusion in the Evant, but in how the Flame had been used to infiltrate the Phalanx of at least two of the Houses. Those members of the Flame would have influence on the caitans of the Phalanx they were there to help, and those caitans could influence their lords.

But all of that political maneuvering was Aeren's concern, not Colin's. He only wanted to stop the Shadows and their attacks, and keep the Wraiths from destroying what the Alvritshai, dwarren, and human races had managed to build over the last hundred years here on the plains of Wrath Suvane.

Whether the Alvritshai agreed to it or not.

Raising both arms, he pulled back his hood as he said, "I have a solution."

A gasp of recognition echoed through the chamber, immediately followed by outcries of shock, of awe or derision, even a few curses. Colin didn't flinch, kept his gaze locked on the Tamaell's expressionless face, on his dark green eyes. Thaedoren let the Evant's outcry rise and fall, but before he could speak, Lord Peloroun—Colin would recognize the lord's sneering voice anywhere—snapped, "You have a solution? What of your promise to stop the Wraiths from awakening new Wells? What of your assurances that you could halt the spread of the territory the sukrael could control? Why should we listen to you when none of your promises before this have been fulfilled?"

A few other lords barked agreement, but everyone quieted when Thaedoren stood, anger flaring across his face. "We will listen because of the debt that we owe Shaeveran after his actions at the Escarpment. Without him, without his intervention, the armies of the Provinces would have slaughtered us all." His gaze latched onto Peloroun's. "You know this, Peloroun. You were there. You fought King Stephan's men, know that they were out for blood, that nothing short of an order from their king could have stopped them. And Shaeveran convinced their king to give that order."

Peloroun leaned back, but the heat in his eyes didn't abate. "Yes, I was there. I remember."

Thaedoren's eyes narrowed at the disrespect that still tinged Peloroun's voice. "Then let him speak."

Colin waited until Thaedoren glanced toward him and nodded, then turned toward Peloroun directly. "I had intended to stop the Wraiths from awakening the Wells, but I've discovered that would not be in the best interests of either the Alvritshai or the dwarren."

A low murmur rose. Peloroun scowled.

A low throb of anger pulsed through Colin, warmed his blood. "Since the Escarpment, I *have* battled the Shadows and the Wraiths. I have traveled these lands in search of them, in search of the Wells that they seek to awaken, using the information gleaned from your own Scripts, given to me by your Chosen. I've fought to the heart of forests, to the depths of mountains, to swamps and ancient ruins, all in an attempt to stop the Wraiths from awakening any more of the sarenavriell. And I have the scars to prove it!" He shucked back the sleeves of his robes and exposed his arms, exposed the black mottling that marred his skin, like ink, trapped beneath the surface, pooling and shifting and swirling back and forth. The lords gasped, drew back at the sight, most whispering to each other as he turned so that all could see, even as his own stomach roiled in revulsion. He did not rip open the robes to expose his body, where the hideous black marks scored his chest, shoulders, and back. All of the damage done during his attempts to stop Walter and the other Wraiths at the few Wells he and Lotaern had managed to discover. Every moment spent near the Lifeblood contained within those Wells made the stains upon his skin grow, the Wells themselves eating away at his soul, altering him inexorably.

"This is what I have suffered for your protection!" he roared, holding up his arms. "This is what I've done to help you!"

"And yet you have achieved nothing," Peloroun spat.

Colin dropped his arms, strode purposely toward Peloroun's seat, gathering power around him as he moved. He felt a twinge of satisfaction when Peloroun flinched as he came to a halt two paces away, staff held to one side.

"I've discovered that the Wells hold the key to the entire balance of power on the plains. I've discovered that all of the freakish storms that rage across the grasses, all of the occurrences of Drifters, of what you call the occumaen, are the result of the imbalance of the Wells themselves. The reason that I have failed to halt Walter and his fellow

Wraiths from awakening them is because if I do, then the storms and the occumaen will continue to worsen. We cannot halt the awakenings. The imbalance of doing so may tear the plains apart."

"But the sukrael," Lord Daesor protested. Colin turned toward him, recognized the son who had taken over Barak's position after he'd been killed on the battlefield at the Escarpment. "If we allow the Wraiths to awaken the Wells, then the Shadows will have free reign over all of Wrath Suvane."

"Not," Colin said, "if we have another way to protect ourselves from them."

He reached into the depths of his satchel and drew forth one of the seeds wrapped in muslin. Pulling the cloth free, he held up what looked like a scepter—a length of wood the size of his forearm, with a gnarled knot at one end larger than his fist. The shaft was sheathed in pale white bark, like that of a birch or beech tree, smooth beneath his grip but marred in places with black cuts, as if branches had once sprouted from the shaft but had been sheared off. Power pulsed through the wood into his palm as the muslin fell free, awakening the power of the Lifeblood within him, stoking the flames of the White Fire and swelling the waters of the Confluence in which he had immersed himself. It surged through his arm, tingling across his skin, and for a long moment he thought it would consume him beneath its weight, that it would overwhelm him here, within the Hall of the Evant, which would be disastrous. But he'd been carrying the seeds for far too long. One for each of the three races—Alvritshai, dwarren, and human. One each for them to guard and protect. And a fourth protected by him alone, its location secret from everyone.

He turned toward Lotaern, whose entire body stood rigid with tension. Colin wondered if he could sense the immense power straining to break free from the seed, wondered if he could see the power that poured off of Colin's skin in waves now that he'd touched the seed directly. Like the Wells, the seed had been awakened by that touch. He had little time left now.

"What is it?" Lotaern asked, and everyone shifted restlessly at the brittle fear in his voice.

"It is a gift," Colin said, and even he heard the power throbbing in his voice, threatening to break free. "A gift I give to the Alvritshai people to protect them from the sukrael—the Shadows—and from the Wraiths as well. No longer will the Flame be forced to provide the sole protection from their attacks. When this power is released, it will cast a mantle over Alvritshai lands. It will cloak the Alvritshai people with a barrier that the Shadows and Wraiths cannot pass, a barrier that the Alvritshai people will not be able to see. But this protection comes at a price. It has boundaries. Within its protection, you are safe; venture outside and you will be within the Shadows' grasp. And it will require care and protection of its own. Neglect it, and it will fail."

"And what do you ask in return for this protection?" Peloroun asked.

Colin turned toward the Tamaell, ignoring the lord. Peloroun did not wield the greatest power here; the Tamaell did. "Nothing. Nothing, except that you continue to honor the Accord established at the Escarpment. Will you accept this gift? Will you accept its protection?"

His voice cracked and broke with the strain of containing the seed. It wanted release, its need surging in Colin's hand. He ground his teeth together, willed Thaedoren to accept as the Tamaell, as they had planned that morning.

"This is something that should be discussed by the Evant!" Lotaern shouted. "At length and in depth. What Shaeveran wields, what he holds in his hand—" he shook his head. "I can feel its power. We must be careful. It is dangerous, more dangerous than anything I've witnessed before."

"I agree with the Chosen," Peloroun cut in. "We do not know what kind of power he holds. We should allow the Order of Aielan to investigate it, to confirm its intent."

"Your lands aren't the ones being attacked," Lord Saetor replied, an edge to his voice. "If it were your people dying beneath the sukrael's darkness—"

Lords rose from their seat, some in protest, others arguing to accept the gift, the tumult rising. Colin felt his arm beginning to tremble and lowered his hand, cradling the seed close to him. Anger lashed through him, and disgust. He should never have brought the subject before the Evant, should have known that the decision would not be reached easily, even with the Tamaell's support. He and Aeren had hoped that the Evant would seize the chance for protection without question, but there were still too many within the council who did not trust Aeren or Colin, even after the events at the Escarpment. They had assumed Lotaern would support them, even though it ate away at his newly won power with the Evant. They had assumed that he would see the benefits of freeing his warriors of the Flame for other purposes, and that it would more than likely fall to the Order to care for the seed.

"Fools," Colin muttered under his breath, glaring around at the cacophony of noise, the power of the seed pulsing with his own blood. "All fools."

The power would not wait for the Evant to come to a decision. It had already been awakened.

He turned toward the platform, caught the eyes of the former Tamaea. She reached out and touched Thaedoren's arm, the Tamaell's gaze shifting from the bickering lords to Colin.

His lips pressed into a thin line as they regarded each other—

Then he nodded.

Colin moved, not waiting for the Evant to be called to order. Permission had been granted; the wishes of the Lotaern and the lords no longer mattered. He headed for the stairs, saw a blur of blue-and-red motion out of the corner of his eye, Eraeth and four other Rhyssal Phalanx surrounding him a moment later. But they didn't impede him. Two darted forward and cleared a path up the stairs to the hall's inner doors, Eraeth motioning the waiting Phalanx there to open the chamber. They scrambled to draw the doors back, even as Colin heard Lotaern shout out a warning from behind them.

Colin and his escort spilled out through the main stone doors of the Hall, past the thick colonnades, and into the blinding sunlight of the marketplace. The clamor of the Evant became the roar of thousands of Alvritshai vying for attention or haggling for a bargain, the plaza packed with hawkers, carts, tents, and animals. Alvritshai in the conical hats of commoners wove through the makeshift paths toting baskets and bundles, stopping to inspect wares or chat with friends and family. Children dashed between bodies, and messengers and pages darted through every opening as they rushed to deliver their notes.

Colin halted on the edge of the morass of people, Eraeth coming up beside him.

"Where?" the Protector asked bluntly.

Colin drew in a deep breath, felt the power of the seed building, drawing upon the life-force of the crowd around it. He wouldn't be able to control it much longer. But the seed couldn't be placed just anywhere. It had to be within the walls of Caercaern so that Thaedoren and the White Phalanx—and Lotaern and his Flame—could protect it.

But it needed room. Lots of room.

"The center of the plaza," he rasped. Eraeth shot him a

questioning look, but he shook his head. "There's no other choice. We don't have much time."

Eraeth barked orders, the Rhyssal Phalanx closing in tighter around him, and then they plowed into the crowd.

Eraeth drove straight toward the center of the plaza, ignoring the cries of protest as the Phalanx shoved people out of their way. At the heart of the group, Colin struggled with the seed, its pulse now locked into his heartbeat, threading through his body and drawing on his own power. He could taste its urgency, frigid and silvery, like snow, the sensation coursing through his skin, making him shudder with cold. Eraeth glanced back, caught the look on his face, then barked new orders. The Phalanx broke through the center of a tent, cloth ripping as tables were knocked aside and pottery crashed to the ground. They tipped over a cart laden with melons, nearly trampled a gaggle of old women, who shrieked and scattered like hens, and then Colin could hold the power within no longer.

He shouted a warning toward Eraeth, even as the Phalanx drew back from him. He could feel the power slipping outward from his grasp, glanced up to see shock and horror dawning on the faces around him. The crowd, Eraeth and the Phalanx included, pulled farther back as tendrils of light began flickering upward from the stone around him. As the light intensified, Colin scanned the area, saw that they'd nearly made it to the fountain, noted the discarded blankets and abandoned tables of merchants, then noticed that the light curling upward around him was centered on one spot, one location.

He stepped forward, thrust a tarp from a collapsed tent aside with his staff, bared the stone of the plaza beneath in a wide circle, the seed clutched to his chest with one arm as he worked. Then he fell to his knees, setting his staff to one side.

The light emerging from the ground came in sheets, rising like steam or mist. On the far side of the veil, Eraeth and the rest of the Phalanx were herding the Alvritshai in the plaza back, farther away from Colin. The Protector met Colin's gaze for a brief moment, then broke the contact as more Phalanx arrived in the varied colors of the other Houses. Colin caught sight of Aeren, Peloroun, Lotaern, the latter two looking furious, and behind them all, Thaedoren. The Tamaell broke through the widening circle of Phalanx, stepping close to the swirling light.

Then the urgency of the seed pulsed deep into Colin's chest. He gasped at the intensity, felt his body shudder in response.

Lifting the seed toward the sky with both hands, he released the power of the Lifeblood, the Confluence, and the White Fire inside him. It surged through his arms, into the seed, and the last restraints on the power locked inside it collapsed.

With a harsh cry, he drove the shaft of the seed into the stone before him, felt it pierce deep. Beneath his hand, the knot atop the staff writhed. The pale white bark split beneath his palm with a crack of splintering wood. He hissed and lurched backward, stumbled on the detritus left behind by the market vendors, but caught himself. Grabbing his staff, he continued backing up. White light licked up around him, flowed through him, touching and tasting, rising higher as the stone beneath his feet trembled. It recognized its creator.

The crowd gasped when the seed quickened and the sapling that sprouted from it shot skyward, higher than the tendrils of light, piercing upward, growing in the space of heartbeats, seeking sunlight. The sapling thickened, the bole of an immense tree emerging, its bark dark, nearly black, limbs thrusting outward from the trunk like spears, splitting, branching. The groan of stressed wood filled the plaza, punctuated by sharp cracks and sizzling, hissing pops. And still the immense tree strained upward. Roots pierced the stone at the trunk's base and dove back underground, grinding the stone to dust as the trunk thickened and spread. Buds appeared on the thousands of branches, burst open between one breath and the next, thick silvery leaves unfurling. Colin stepped back once, twice, tilted his head so that he could see the branches reaching outward, obscuring the sky, stretching out over the crowd below.

That crowd stood stunned, the Phalanx no longer trying to usher the gathered Alvritshai backward. Some had bolted and were thrashing their way through those too awed to move. Even the lords of the Evant and the Tamaell had stilled, gazing up in wonder at a tree nearly five times as large as any tree they had ever seen before. It would take twenty men, hands linked, to encircle the trunk alone.

Colin bowed his head. Weariness seeped through him, enveloped him like a warm blanket, sapped his strength. He turned, moved through the fading white light, the ground reabsorbing it. Behind him, the groans and shudders of the tree's birth eased, replaced by the calming sigh of wind through thousands upon thousands of leaves. Silver leaves, even though the bark of the tree was the color of deep, earthy loam.

He halted before the Tamaell, Thaedoren ripping his gaze from the sight to look down upon him.

"The Alvritshai are now protected from the Wraiths and the Shadows," Colin said, and his voice shook with exhaustion. "I give you the Winter Tree."

Part II

~

The White Wastes

2

COLIN STARED DOWN at the knife.

The blade was about five inches long, the handle only four, handle and blade all one piece, shaped from a length of wood shorter than his forearm. The wood had been given to him by the heart of the Ostraell forest—the same forest that held the Well and the Faelehgre and had once been the prison of the Shadows—but unlike the staffs the forest had gifted him in the past, this had simply been an unshaped, yet living, part of the forest. He could feel the forest when he touched it, could feel the pulse of its heart when he ran his hands down its length. It throbbed with an inner life, with a power that even he, after all of the decades he'd spent in the city of Terra'nor and all of his searches throughout the lands of Wrath Suvane, did not understand. It was the power of the spirit of woodland itself, of the trees, smelling of the acrid inner bark of a cedar after the outer layers had been stripped away, tasting of bitter sap and damp moss.

And it was one of the few substances he knew of that could harm one of the Shadows.

His gaze hardened and he placed his hands on either side of the knife to keep them from trembling.

He sat at a table in the center of a meeting chamber of

the Order of Aielan, at the heart of Caercaern. His staff leaned against the back of the chair beside him. Ancient tapestries depicting scenes from the Alvritshai religious Scripts lined the walls, a few small tables set beneath them at odd intervals, surrounding the large central table where he waited for the arrival of Lotaern and a few other members of Aielan's Order. One of the acolytes had already been sent in search of the Chosen, the youth's eyes widening when Colin blurred into existence in what, a moment before, had been an empty corridor.

Colin smiled as he remembered the expression on the youth's face, but the amusement was fleeting. He shouldn't have startled the boy, but he'd needed to find Lotaern as quickly as possible and he'd been too exhausted to conduct the search himself. The acolyte had recognized him after a moment and had led him to the meeting chamber to wait while he searched for the Chosen.

Now, as Colin sat and waited, he suddenly wished he'd asked the acolyte to bring him something to drink, perhaps something to eat. He didn't know how long he'd spent within the depths of the Alvritshai catacombs, in the heart of the mountain, but this last excursion might have been days, maybe even weeks. He found that he lost his sense of time too easily now, especially when he was working alone.

Yet, he thought, *perhaps this particular project was finished.*

He reached out to touch the knife, but his hand paused above it. He could feel it even so, could feel the multiple energies within it, mingling with each other. Flames from the numerous sconces that lit the room flickered on the bright sheen of its wooden blade, the gloss a consequence of the process he'd used to shape it.

He let his hand fall back to the table.

The shaping had been . . . difficult.

Colin stood at the edge of a room within the dead city of Terra'nor, sweat dripping from his nose, his chin. He held metal tongs before him, stared into the seething red-orange-white embers of the forge. A misshapen form of heartwood rested on the floor before him. He'd already destroyed three pieces by attempting to carve them with a knife, had intended to make another attempt with this one until Osserin had found him.

The gift of the heart of the forest can not be carved with so blunt an instrument as another knife, the Faelehgre had murmured, light flaring in agitation, as if this were obvious. *The life-force that inhabits the heartwood—that gives it the power to affect the Shadows as if they were made of cloth, instead of passing through them like other weapons—will die as soon as any regular knife cuts too deeply into the grain. You must find another way.*

And then the light had drifted off.

So Colin had set up the forge. It had taken him days to build it, days more to stoke the fire to its current intense heat. If the heartwood couldn't be carved, then perhaps it could be molded and shaped, like metal.

The fire would never be hotter.

"Now or never," he said to himself.

Reaching down with the tongs, he lifted the heartwood up and thrust it into the heart of the bed of coals, sparks whirling upward as flame rose with a hiss. Pain prickled his skin as the embers landed against his exposed face, but he held the tongs steady, gasping as the heat stole his breath and burned his throat and lungs. He pulled the heartwood out, noted the scorch marks along its sides, felt the pulse of the forest still residing within. Yet the wood hadn't softened; he could sense it through the tongs.

"Too soon," he hissed through clenched teeth, and thrust

it back into the inferno. He counted slowly in his head, removed it again, the wood beginning to char, thrust it back with a curse.

The third time he pulled it from the coals, it burst into flame. As he stumbled backward in surprise, he felt the life-force inside it die. Before he could drop it, before the disappointment of this new failure could sink in, the length of wood hissed and then exploded, like the boles of trees at the heart of a raging forest fire.

He cried out, dropping the tongs as he protected his face and lurched out into the white ruins of the city surrounding the Well. The coolness of the forest air seered his lungs as harshly as the heat inside the forge, and he fell to his knees. He bellowed at the sky, his clothes flecked with smoking splinters of the heartwood, his chest constricted with raw frustration.

Osserin and the other Faelehgre found him there, head bowed forward where he knelt, sobbing. They calmed him down and after he tried the forge again with the same results, he gathered another length of wood from the heart of the forest and traveled to Caercaern, to speak to Aeren.

The Lord of House Rhyssal held the heartwood in his hands, turned it in the firelight of his inner chamber. He ran his fingers over the reddish wood, flecked with striations of burnt yellow and ridged like bark. "Have you taken it to Lotaern?" he asked.

Colin grimaced. "It's one of the reasons I've come, to see if he has any insights into how to mold it. But since my arrival with the Winter Tree and the disastrous gathering of the Evant that ended with the planting of the Tree in the marketplace, he and I have barely spoken."

A smile touched Aeren's lips as he set the heartwood down and rewrapped it in the cloth Colin had carried it in.

"He did not appreciate the responsibility of the Tree being thrust upon him, no. But he has managed to wield the unexpected responsibility to his advantage. My expectation that it would deter his rise in power in the Evant was, perhaps, incorrect."

"What has he done?"

Aeren glanced up, one hand on the supple cloth that now covered the heartwood. Behind him, Eraeth stood near the entrance to the chamber. "You haven't been following the events in Alvritshai lands since the quickening of the Tree?"

"I've been busy, Aeren, trying to balance the awakening of the Wells, battling the sukrael in the lands not protected by the Seasonal Trees, battling the Wraiths."

"Battling Walter, you mean."

Aeren frowned at the interruption of his Protector, Eraeth's voice barely a murmur. But then he focused on the bundle nestled among the stacks of papers and other detritus of the maintenance of a House of the Evant. "Is that who this is for? Walter?"

"For all of the Wraiths and the Shadows," Colin said, and heard the defensiveness in his voice. He sighed. "But yes, this is for Walter."

"It's been seventy-two years since the battle at the Escarpment and the signing of the Accord. Walter and the Wraiths have caused little problem since the planting of the Trees thirty-three years ago."

"Not here on Alvritshai lands, or where the other two Seasonal Trees hold sway, but outside of their influence . . ." Colin shook his head. "Walter and the Wraiths are only biding their time. The Trees were not meant to last forever."

"How long *will* they last?" Eraeth interjected.

Colin shrugged. "I don't know. I suspect hundreds of years, or longer, because of the Lifeblood they are imbued with. But we will need a way to defend against the Shadows and the Wraiths no matter when the Trees fail."

Aeren's eyebrows rose. "And this has nothing to do with Walter and what happened between the two of you?"

Colin said nothing, his brow creasing in irritation. For a moment, he felt the wooden bars of the penance lock across his neck, biting into his wrists. He felt Walter's foot connecting with his stomach, Walter's arm pressed into his throat, choking him.

The memories caused his hands to clench into fists.

Aeren sighed, and Colin saw Eraeth nod knowingly. "Eraeth, have someone bring us some wine, perhaps some bread and cheese."

Eraeth moved to the door as Aeren motioned Colin to the balcony. They stepped out into the night air, chill even though it was nearing summer. Nights in Caercaern were always cold, and the temples of Aielan had rung the chimes for cotiern hours ago. Colin moved to the edge of the balcony, hands resting on the lip of stone, and glared out over what he could see of the tiered city. The streets of the third tier were empty, only a few windows glowing softly with lantern light. From the second tier, the Winter Tree cleaved the cloudless night, its silver leaves shimmering in the moonlight. Colin kept his eyes on the Tree, a new wall surrounding the marketplace where it had been planted.

"Does this mean that you won't help?" he asked. His breath fogged the air with bitterness.

"No. You and I both know how dangerous the sukrael are, how deadly the Wraiths. But I will not help you out of any need for vengeance. I'll help because, as you say, the Wraiths and the sukrael—including Walter—have not vanished. They will return at some point to plague us. You are letting your personal feelings blind you. I can see the tension in your shoulders, in your stance."

Colin's hands gripped the edge of the stone hard enough he could feel grit scraping free beneath his fingers. He drew in a deep breath . . . and then exhaled sharply, releasing the stone and pushing back from the edge, trying to calm himself. He caught Aeren's gaze where the Lord stood in the half-light coming from the inner room and shook his head with a troubled smile.

"You're right. I've been working on the heartwood and practically nothing else for too long. I've lost myself to the effort, the failure upon failure. . . ."

"You are too hard on yourself. You've done more than expected in our efforts to fight the sukrael and the Wraiths. You brought us the Winter Tree—even if the gift was unexpected and, perhaps, unwanted by some. And you've managed to halt the preternatural storms that plagued the plains, as well as the occumaen, by balancing out the power of the Wells."

"None of that has solved the real problem. It's only bought us time."

Before Aeren could answer, Eraeth appeared behind him, accompanied by a servant with a platter of wine, bread, and cheese. Aeren motioned for the servant to set the platter to one side and then dismissed him. He poured each of them a glass, Colin raising his wine and drinking without really tasting it, still thinking about the heartwood, about Walter, about the Shadows.

Aeren joined him at the balcony, stared out at the Winter Tree, then said casually, "Perhaps you need a different kind of fire for this heartwood . . . a different kind of forge."

"Like what?" Colin muttered in frustration.

"What about Aielan's Light?"

In the confines of the meeting room within the Order of Aielan, Colin grunted and shook his head. It had taken him a moment on that chill night over forty years ago to understand that Aeren did not mean the metaphorical Light that the Alvritshai used as a representation of Aielan, but the literal white fire that lay in the depths of the Alvritshai mountains of Hauttaeran. Every acolyte of the Order of Aielan must at some point immerse themselves in the white flames hidden in the catacombs and halls that riddled the mountains behind Caercaern before they could become true members of the Order. Aeren had done so before the deaths of his father and elder brother had forced him to ascend as Lord of his House and give up his ties to the Order. Occasionally, he wore the pendant that signified his passage. Colin had entered the white flames himself in the years following the Accord, after studying the Scripts of the Order as if he were an acolyte himself, although he had never officially been part of the Order. He couldn't become a true member, since he wasn't Alvritshai.

But he should have thought of Aielan's Light on his own. After all, he'd used the white flame to create the seeds that had become the Seasonal Trees. He'd only immersed the seeds in the flame then, so that they could absorb some of the properties of the fire itself, so that they'd be imbued with its power and be more resilient and harder to destroy. But attempting to wield the flame, to use it as a tool to shape the heartwood. . . .

He hadn't known if it had ever been attempted, hadn't known if it could even be done.

But if it could be done, then Aielan's Light would be perfect. A natural flame, but completely unlike the fire of a blacksmith's forge. It would not burn like the fire of a forge; it would not incinerate the heartwood or cause it to explode. It was a fire like the power already resident in the wood he needed to mold, alive and somehow prescient.

It was a fire under the control of Lotaern, the Chosen of the Order.

As if the thought had summoned him, the door to the meeting room opened and Lotaern stepped into the room, followed by two members of the Order of the Flame, the

guardsmen taking up positions on either side of the door as
Lotaern halted at the edge of the table. The stylized white
flame of the Order stood out on the chests of the two
guardsmen, signifying they were members of the Order's
internal Phalanx. Lotaern wore the robes of the Chosen, a
subdued dark blue, flames stitched into the sleeves and collar. He carried no visible weapons, but both guardsmen
rested hands on the pommels of their cattan blades. All
three were tense, but it was the weariness in Lotaern's
bearing—even though the Chosen stood tall, back
straight—that caught Colin's attention. He appeared tired
and worn, and with a start Colin realized that he had to be
nearly two hundred years old. No. Two hundred was too
young. If Lotaern had been the Chosen when Aeren was
merely an acolyte, it meant that Lotaern had to be closer to
two hundred and fifty. Perhaps more.

And for the first time, Colin saw that age, as if it had
been draped around his shoulders like a blanket. The
changes since the Accord and the planting of the Winter
Tree were subtle, yet striking. Wrinkles had appeared
around his eyes and mouth, breaking the usual smoothness
of Alvritshai skin, and his dark hair had lost some of its
sheen, appearing dull and somehow brittle. It suddenly
struck Colin that he had not thought the Alvritshai would
age. Aeren and Eraeth, Moiran and Lotaern, had been such
a constant part of his life since he emerged from seclusion
near the Well that he'd assumed they'd remain with him
forever, unchanged.

The fact that they wouldn't, that eventually even the Alvritshai he knew would die—as all of his human acquain-
tances had—hit him like a sharp jab to his heart. It left a
deep hollow in the center of his chest, a coldness upon his
skin.

Lotaern stirred, and Colin shoved the sudden pall of
loneliness aside. He stood slowly, his hands resting on the

table on either side of the knife for support. He still felt weak and wasn't certain he was strong enough to reach his staff without stumbling. He didn't want to show such weakness in front of Lotaern.

"I did not realize that you were in Caercaern," Lotaern said, and even the timbre of his voice was raspier, although it still throbbed with the power he had accumulated for the Order over his lifetime.

"No one knows. Not even Lord Aeren."

Lotaern's eyebrows rose in surprise. "Then why have you come?"

Colin shifted back, lifting his hands from the table, testing his strength. As he did so, Lotaern's gaze dropped to the knife.

He drew his breath in sharply and locked eyes with Colin. "You've been down to the cavern, to Aielan's Light. Without my knowledge."

"You gave me permission to seek Aielan's Light in my studies whenever necessary."

Lotaern's eyes narrowed. "So I did. But that was over forty years ago, when you first arrived with the request."

He began moving around the edge of the table, the two warriors of the Flame shifting uncertainly behind him. When they started to step forward, he waved them back in irritation. The anger and guarded tension in his shoulders fell away as he approached, replaced with a blatant curiosity, but he halted a few paces away, even though Colin could see the urge to reach out and touch the knife, to inspect it, in the way he clutched his hands at his waist, as if restraining himself. It was the same curiosity that had overcome Lotaern's wariness the first time he'd approached him about the heartwood. His anger over having the responsibility of the Winter Tree thrust upon him had faded with the challenge of molding the heartwood, although it hadn't completely vanished.

"I thought we'd decided that Aielan's Light was not enough," he said. "Every attempt we made to mold the wood—by either of us—caused it to crack as it was re-shaped. How did you manage to overcome that?"

"I didn't know how to at first," Colin said, watching Lotaern closely. "And then I realized what we were doing wrong. We were treating the heartwood as if it were inanimate, merely a block of wood waiting to be molded. Carving it, forging it like metal, even shaping it with Aielan's Light—all were attempts to manipulate it with tools. But it's not inanimate. It's a living thing. Attempting to work it with something as primitive as a tool literally caused it harm. Even Aielan's Light cracked its skin. It has no blood, so cannot bleed, but the effect is the same as if we had cut ourselves open from groin to throat. The heartwood could not survive the trauma."

Lotaern frowned down at the knife. "So what did you do? How could you shape it as a living thing without harming it?"

Colin turned away, grabbed his staff, comforted by the life-force he felt pulsing through the wood. "It required the knowledge of the Faelehgre, the Lifeblood, and the cooperation of the dwarren."

Lotaern looked up, startled. "The dwarren? How could they have been of help?"

Colin closed his eyes at the taint of derision in Lotaern's voice. He'd been expecting it, although he'd hoped that enough time had passed with the Accord in place that emotions would have changed.

Except that the Alvritshai were long-lived. Unlike the dwarren and humans that lived today, Lotaern had been at the battlefields of the Escarpment, had lived during the vicious attacks that had preceded it, Alvritshai and dwarren killing each other over a misunderstanding and a territorial dispute about lands and the plains. Lotaern had had family and friends killed by the dwarren. Such memories were hard to forget.

He sighed. "The reason the heartwood was cracking during the molding process was because it couldn't heal itself fast enough under the changes we were requiring it to undergo. I needed a way to keep it alive long enough that it could heal itself after I shaped it. The Faelehgre suggested I immerse it in the Lifeblood, to prolong its life, but even though the wood is alive, the Lifeblood did not affect it the same way as it affected me or the Faelehgre. It absorbed some of the Lifeblood's power, making it hardier, but it still cracked and died during the shaping process. I suspect that the reason the forest surrounding the Well is as . . . aware as it is, is because of the Well. The trees have absorbed the Lifeblood's power over time, which is why the Lifeblood did not affect the heartwood as expected—it already contains some of the power of the Well. I needed something different.

"So I went to the dwarren to ask them for access to the Confluence."

Lotaern stilled. "The ruanavriell?"

"Yes."

"And they allowed you to see it? They allowed you to use it?"

The dwarren guarded the Confluence with a religious zeal that transcended even clan lines. If the Confluence were threatened, all clan rivalries were forgotten. It was their most closely guarded secret, one that Colin knew the Alvritshai had been attempting to discover for hundreds of years. The sons of the Houses of the Evant were once sent into the plains to search for the Confluence as part of their Trial, their initiation into the House. They were sent to find the Confluence's source, and could not return until they'd obtained a vial of the rose-tinged healing waters. Most of those on their Trial found an offshoot of the Confluence, a river or stream or pool of the water tinged pink by the heart of the Confluence, but none of them had found the true source. None that had survived their Trial anyway. Colin had met Aeren during his Trial, and Aeren had given the vial he'd gathered to Colin's father to help heal one of the members of the wagon train.

With the signing of the Accord by Tamaell Thaedoren, the Trials and the search had ceased, at the request of the dwarren and in the interest of forging peace. Now, the location of the Confluence could be easily surmised by the conflux of the four linear rivers that divided the dwarren plains into quarters ... but how to access the Confluence was still a secret. It lay underground, in the labyrinthine depths that only the dwarren knew and controlled.

Colin met the avid interest in Lotaern's eyes and said, "Yes. As with the Order, I studied with the dwarren shamans, learned about their religious beliefs, learned of their gods—Ilacqua and the four gods of the winds—and their vow to protect the Lands. Perhaps if the Alvritshai spent more time learning of their ways, the dwarren would be more accommodating."

Lotaern frowned at the reprimand, but ignored it, motioning toward the knife. "And the effects of the Confluence— of the ruanavriell—worked?"

"With time, yes."

Lotaern reached for the knife, but halted with his hand hovering over its handle. "May I?"

Colin caught the barest hint of annoyance that he had to ask, but nodded.

Lotaern lifted the blade lightly, treating it as if it were fragile, although it had the heft and weight of a normal dagger.

"Careful," Colin said. "It's sharp. Sharper than a normal blade."

Lotaern frowned, then touched the edge of the blade

lightly with one finger, wincing as he drew it away, a thin line of blood already welling up from the cut. He held his injured hand to one side and let the blood drip onto the table until one of the watching guardsmen produced a small square of cloth and handed it to him, shooting Colin a dark glare.

"I warned him," Colin said to the guard, his voice soft, although his hands clenched on the staff.

"Yes, you did," Lotaern muttered. He pressed his finger into the cloth, but did not let go of the knife, turning it in the light of the sconces, examining the handle, the double-sided blade, the sharp point. He glanced toward Colin. "Why a knife and not a sword?"

"The length of wood given to me was not heavy enough for a longer blade. And I thought starting with something smaller would be better, until we knew if it would work."

"How long did it take to forge this?"

"What day is it? What year?"

Lotaern looked up, eyebrows raised. "The fifth of Iaen, third quarter, the five hundred and eleventh year since the Abandonment."

Colin thought for a moment. "Then it's been seventeen years."

Lotaern's mouth opened, but no words came out. They stood staring at each other silently, until Lotaern finally closed his mouth and grunted. "Why does it take so long?"

"Because the heartwood must be submerged long enough for the Confluence's waters to penetrate to the wood's core. This knife took twelve years. It will take even longer if we attempt the molding of a sword or anything larger. And then, before I could mold it with Aielan's Light, it had to dry.

"About a month ago, I returned to the Hauttaeren, to the fires below, and I began to craft this."

"You've been down in the Halls for a month and none of the acolytes or members of the Flame were aware of it?"

"Yes."

Lotaern glared at the Alvritshai who'd given him the now bloody cloth for the cut on his finger. The guardsman shifted uncomfortably, bowing his head slightly. Colin suppressed a small smile as he shifted his grip on the staff. He could sense the animosity radiating from the man, although he wasn't certain why the member of the Flame felt he was a threat.

"Perhaps we need additional guardsmen surrounding Aielan's Light," the Chosen said in a leaden voice, and the guardsman nodded imperceptibly.

"You shouldn't fault the Order of the Flame," Colin said. "I can remain hidden if needed."

"Yes, but you are not the only one with those powers. As we learned before, with the unfortunate Benedine, the Wraiths can hide in our midst as well."

"Not with the Winter Tree in Caercaern," Colin countered, then cursed himself for bringing up the touchy subject.

"Ah, yes. The Winter Tree. I've often wondered how the Tree protects us from the Wraiths—men and women like you, who have drunk from the sarenavriell—and yet appears to have no effect on you at all."

Colin almost didn't answer, Lotaern's tone carrying an edge, some of the anger over not being consulted about the Winter Tree before its introduction to the Evant seeping through. "I created them," he finally said. "In some sense, they are a part of me. And unlike the Wraiths, I have not fully embraced the Well. It hasn't affected me to the extent that it has changed them." He thought about the stain of the Shadow that swirled beneath his skin beneath the outer robe and the shirt beneath. Creating the Seasonal Trees—and now the knife—as well as trying to establish a balance between the awakened Wells had taken its toll.

"I see." Lotaern considered for a moment, long enough

for Colin to begin wondering what he was thinking, but then he dropped his gaze back to the knife.

"Molding the knife is one thing," he said, then set the blade back down onto the table between them. "But it doesn't address the real question."

"Which is?"

Lotaern looked up. "Does it work? Can it be used against the sukrael? Can it kill one of the Wraiths?"

Colin straightened. "Short of testing it on myself, there's only one way to find out." He thought about what Aeren had said on the balcony decades ago, about the dark understanding he'd seen in Eraeth's eyes, about Walter.

"And do you know where the Wraiths are?"

Colin shook his head. "No. The Faelehgre have still not determined how to track them, or the Shadows, except through the news of those who have been attacked by them."

Lotaern stilled and frowned. "I thought—" he began, then halted and murmured, almost to himself, "No, you wouldn't know, would you? You've been within the mountain for the last month."

"I wouldn't know what?" Colin asked.

Lotaern moved away from the table, toward the two guardsmen and the door. "When the acolyte said that you were here, waiting for me, I thought you'd come for a different reason." He motioned to the head guardsman, returning the bloody cloth at the same time. The moody guardsman nodded and stepped out into the corridor beyond, and for the first time Colin thought that perhaps the tension he'd felt from Lotaern and the guards of the Order of the Flame came from something other than the strained relationship the Chosen and he maintained.

The Chosen turned back. "Follow me. Vaeren will escort us to the top of the temple. There's something I need to show you."

Colin hesitated only a moment, suddenly uncertain and uneasy. He retrieved his satchel, removed a swath of finely made chain mail, the links so small it was nearly cloth, wrapped the wooden knife in the metal folds, and tucked it away.

Vaeren and the other guard were waiting in the outer corridor and began moving as soon as Colin appeared. Members of the Order of the Flame stepped out of their path as they wound through the corridors, climbing stairs until they'd reached the main level of the temple of Aielan that stood in the center of Caercaern. The groups of Flame fell away, replaced by the scurrying acolytes in training in the temple, and still they ascended flight after flight of stairs, passing through corridors that Colin had never seen even during his years of study. The members of the Flame looked apprehensive, but the acolytes merely appeared curious.

"Where are we going? What is it that I need to see?"

"Wait," Lotaern said. "We're almost there."

The wide stairs leveled out, a set of doors at the far end of a narrow hall. Vaeren outpaced them, reaching the doors with enough time to open them just as they arrived at the threshold. A gust of frigid air, tasting of winter and the snows of the mountains, blasted through the opening and bit into Colin's skin, passing through his robes as if he were naked, and then he followed Lotaern out onto the roof of the temple into the darkness of night. The Chosen didn't pause, moving across the stone roof toward the building's edge, his own robes flapping about his feet, his only concession to the cold the hunch in his shoulders. Snow that had fallen earlier blew across his path in a fine dust as Colin followed, staff in hand, satchel flung across his back. Behind, Vaeren and the other guard produced lanterns and came after them, the light reflecting warmly off of the roof, although the lanterns created no real heat against the chill.

When he reached the edge of the building, Colin stared down into the wide plaza in front of the temple, the arc of stone obelisks rising into the night beneath him. Flurries blew back and forth, lifted up by the wind from the few drifts of snow that remained from the recent storm. Lantern lights dotted the cityscape to either side outside the plaza and in the first tier beneath them. From this vantage, Colin could see the base of the Winter Tree over the wall that had been built around it, its leaves thrashing in the wind, its length towering above him, even though the marketplace where he'd planted the seed stood on the far side of the city. It had grown since the planting, and even though he had created the Tree, had crafted the seed using the power of the Lifeblood and Aielan's Light, its sheer size awed him. He stared up at its branches, the uneasiness Lotaern had evoked crawling across his skin as he searched it for damage, for flaws, assuming the Chosen had brought him to the roof so that he could see the Tree. But he saw nothing wrong, felt nothing wrong, although he'd only be able to tell for certain by touching the Tree itself.

He turned toward Lotaern in confusion. "What is it? I don't see anything wrong with the Winter Tree. It appears healthy."

Lotaern shook his head. "It isn't the Winter Tree. As far as I know, it's fine. The Wardens—the acolytes assigned to its care—have reported nothing amiss."

"Then what did you bring me up here to see?"

Lotaern nodded toward the south and east, toward the night sky, where the stars on the horizon were blotted out by what Colin assumed were clouds. Colin shifted position and moved down the edge of the roofline, staring into the distance. Neither Lotaern nor the two guards followed him. He watched the horizon intently, his fingers growing numb as the wind gusted into his face, but he saw nothing.

He had just begun turning toward the Chosen in irritation when something within those clouds flickered. Lightning flared, arcing from cloud to cloud, their contours harshly and vividly exposed, the sky beautiful for the space of a heartbeat before plunging back into darkness.

Colin sucked in a sharp breath, waited for the rumble of thunder though he knew the storm was too distant for them to hear it, even as horror crawled its way down into his chest. He straightened and turned toward Lotaern. "That's not a natural storm," he muttered, loud enough to be heard, even though his voice felt weak.

"No, it's not. You see why I am concerned."

"Yes." Colin turned back to the darkness that blotted out the sky. Even as he watched, more lightning streaked from the clouds, flashing a preternatural purple. Like the storms that had scoured the plains before and after the Accord, that had plagued the dwarren and the Alvritshai alike for decades.

Until he'd balanced the power of the Wells and the storms had stopped.

"Someone has upset the balance of the sarenavriell," he said, stepping forward as he angled his staff across his body protectively.

"That was our thought as well," Lotaern said from behind him. "It's why I thought you'd come."

"No. I knew nothing of this." He searched the storm, as if he could find answers there. Then he spun toward the Chosen, glancing toward Vaeren and the other member of the Flame. Anger had begun to build, creeping through the shock and sudden clench of his gut. "But it isn't possible."

"What do you mean?"

"It isn't possible! I spent nearly thirty years finding those Wells and adjusting them so that the power had stabilized."

He began to pace, the frigid wind and the numbness of his fingers forgotten, his brow creased in furious thought.

"And the Wraiths can't upset that balance somehow? They can't adjust what you did?"

"No! I placed wards around all of the Wells, not just for the Wraiths and the Shadows, but to keep everyone else away from them as well. Their power is too dangerous, too deadly. I didn't want anyone stumbling onto one, drinking from it, becoming like me, like the Wraiths. The Wells are protected!"

"None of those wards have failed?"

"I would know. They are tied to me, linked to the Life-blood, to the sarenavriell. Even if one had failed, most of the Wells are within the boundaries of the Seasonal Trees. The Wraiths couldn't approach them."

"Most, but not all. How many are outside the Trees' influence?"

Colin paused, drew in a deep breath to steady himself, said, "Three. Only three."

Lotaern nodded. "Then you'll need to verify that the wards on those three are still intact and that the Wells haven't been altered in any way. Maybe the Wraiths have found a way around your wards. Or maybe something else has occurred."

Colin straightened, back prickling at the tone in Lotaern's voice, the hint of condescension. The words rang with command, as if Lotaern were ordering him to act, as if Colin were one of his acolytes.

"Such as?" he asked, an edge to his voice.

The guards caught the hint of warning. They stiffened.

Lotaern ignored it. "Perhaps you haven't found all of the Wells yet."

Colin wanted to scoff, his shoulders already tensing, but he was forced to let the anger out with a ragged exhalation. "You helped search the Scripts for the locations of the sarenavriell. You know how exhaustive that search was."

"Yes. But the sarenavriell existed long before the Alvritshai appeared in these mountains. It's possible that the locations of some of them remained hidden, even from our ancestors, those who wrote the Scripts in the first place."

Colin nodded in grudging agreement, then turned back to the storm, watching the ethereal purplish lightning light up the skyline. The storm appeared to be moving southwest, out toward the plains and dwarren lands. He frowned. With effort, he shoved his irritation with Lotaern aside. He needed to focus on this new problem, on what it meant and how to solve it.

"When did you first notice the storms?" he asked after a long moment.

"A little over two weeks ago."

Fingers aching with the cold, Colin moved across the roof toward the doorway. He heard the Chosen, Vaeren, and the second guard following, the light of the lanterns spilling his shadow out in front of him.

"What do you intend to do?" Lotaern asked as they entered the warmth of the Sanctuary, the guards closing the doors behind them.

Colin began massaging his hands as the Chosen took the lead and they descended into the halls and corridors of the Sanctuary proper. "First, I intend to get warm," he said, snapping his hands briskly to increase the blood flow. "Then I intend to visit Lord Aeren."

He smiled at Lotaern's irritated glance.

The irritation did not taint the Chosen's voice when he spoke. "And the storms?"

Colin's smile faltered. He hated to admit it, but Lotaern had been correct. "I'll have to verify that the Wells have been untouched, as you said."

They reached the main corridor, the central chamber of worship for the Alvritshai and its acolytes opening up before them, its cavernous heights lit with thousands of candles. The chamber smelled of oil and smoke and incense, and echoed faintly with the scuffing of sandals from acolytes moving through the corridors and hallways above.

Lotaern paused, then said, "You won't do it alone. You'll have an escort of the Order of the Flame with you."

3

"I DON'T NEED AN ESCORT," Colin protested.

"But you will have one."

Colin's eyes narrowed and he straightened inside the foyer of the Sanctuary, conscious of the two members of the Flame standing behind Lotaern and the acolytes kneeling in prayer inside the ritual chamber to one side. As he adjusted his grip on his staff, Vaeren surreptitiously shifted his hand to his cattan.

"I can travel much faster without them," he growled.

The Chosen nodded. "I realize that, but there are more important things at play here now than speed."

"Such as?"

"Such as the knife that you carry." Lotaern did not drop his gaze from Colin to the satchel slung across his chest where the knife rested, wrapped in chain mail, but Colin tensed anyway. "That knife may be the only weapon we have against the Wraiths, the only object that can kill them. It cannot be lost. If you travel alone and the Wraiths find you . . ." He let the thought trail off, then added, "We cannot allow it to fall into the Wraiths' hands."

Colin's knuckles turned white and with conscious effort he forced himself to relax. He'd spent the last one hundred and twenty-seven years since the Accord more or less alone.

He'd traveled the land, worked with the Alvritshai, the dwarren, the Faelehgre, searched for the Wells and created the Trees, but almost always by himself, isolated, withdrawn from the world. Even the time spent with Aeren, Moiran, their son Fedaureon, and Eraeth eventually ended, the Lord of House Rhyssal drawn into the politics of the Evant, Moiran focusing on their new son and the Ilvaeren and the economic stability of the House. Colin had found himself visiting them far less often than immediately after the Accord, preferring the seclusion of the Ostraell and the white ruins of Terra'nor.

But Lotaern was correct: the knife had to be protected, guarded. Entrusting it to one person, even himself, could not be allowed. His isolation would have to end, unless he gave the knife to someone else, and that he would not do. Not until it had been tested and proven effective. Not until another weapon like it could be made.

And not until Walter was dead.

His shoulders slumped, although he let his anger darken his face, allowed his reluctance to tinge his voice. "Very well," he agreed. "I'll allow an escort of the Order. No more than four, I'll want to travel as swiftly as possible. And they will follow my orders only."

And if the need arose, he could always abandon them. They could not hold him prisoner, could not contain him.

He saw the same thought flicker through Lotaern's eyes, but the Chosen turned to Vaeren. "Assemble the group. You'll lead, but use only members of the Flame. Take whatever you feel is necessary from the Order."

"I'll want to take Siobhaen." When Lotaern hesitated, Vaeren added, "She's the best warrior you have, the most skilled with the Light."

Lotaern grimaced. "Very well."

"Also Boraeus and Petraen."

The Chosen's eyebrows rose. "Both brothers?"

"The two work well together."

"Fine. Send word and have them gather here by dawn."

"No."

Both Lotaern and Vaeren turned toward him in surprise. Colin knew it was petty, but he didn't like the sudden loss of control he felt. "If you want me to have an escort, assemble it now. I'll give you an hour."

"There's no reason—" Lotaern began, but Colin halted him with a look.

Vaeren nodded, sent his fellow member of the Flame off in search of the two brothers, then gave Colin a threatening glance before stalking off into the depths of the Sanctuary, leaving Lotaern and Colin alone.

Colin watched his retreating back. "He doesn't approve of me."

"He doesn't revere you, as so many within the Order do, acolytes and Flame alike. He sees you as a threat to the Order, to me."

"Do you?"

Lotaern met Colin's gaze, held it for a long moment. "You are not Alvritshai, not part of the Evant, and you have your own motivations, your own agenda. But the greatest threat you represent is that you are . . . unpredictable."

Colin smiled. "Thank you."

"That was not a compliment."

Colin turned away from Lotaern's scowl and moved into the depths of the main chamber. One of the acolytes looked up from his prayers at the scuff of his feet on the flagstone floor, then reached forward, rubbing his fingers in the soot that had stained the low stone pedestal beneath the wide bowl, spillover from when the bowl was filled with fire. He smudged the soot onto his cheek beneath his eye, as Colin had seen Aeren do so long ago, when he'd first met Lotaern. Then the acolyte rose and drifted from the chamber.

Colin moved to the edge of the bowl, where the acolyte

had knelt, and stared into the empty depths. The scent of oil was stronger here, as if it had leached into the stone of the basin. The contours of the room amplified the sounds surrounding him, but blurred them as well. He heard murmurs from the depths of the Sanctuary as acolytes conversed, the scuffle of feet, and the flutter of wings from a bird trapped in the upper reaches of the chamber.

He glanced up and caught sight of the bird as it flitted from one of the stone-carved arches above to another, settling in a corner niche, its brown coloring blending into the gray of the stone.

"I never intended the Winter Tree to be a burden," he said suddenly, his voice louder than he expected in the depths of the room. "I thought you'd welcome the protection it would bring the Alvritshai from the Shadows. I thought I'd have your support."

Behind, he felt Lotaern still, then shift forward into the chamber. In the eighty-odd years since Colin had arrived with the Winter Tree's seed in hand, they had rarely spoken of that day in the Evant. Even while working on the knife with Aielan's Light they had carefully skirted the topic.

When the Chosen finally spoke, his voice was guarded. "I did welcome the protection, as did all of the acolytes and the Order of the Flame. The years without it, with the sukrael attacking Alvritshai lands, were horrible. The Flame and Phalanx did their best to protect the Alvritshai, but the sukrael were too difficult to track and attacked at random, without warning. The Phalanx could not harm them, their swords useless, and so they were relegated to evacuating towns and villages and cities when necessary, or diverting the sukrael with their own lives. And the Flame . . ."

He'd moved into the periphery of Colin's sight, and Colin saw him shudder. "I went there with them, of course. We tried to use Aielan's Light against them, and it worked to some extent. The Light burns them, harms them. But to be effective we needed to prepare, which meant we needed to know where the sukrael were going to attack ahead of time. If we arrived after the attack had begun, the sukrael would simply flee before we could bring Aielan's Light to bear." He shook his head, mouth pulled down in a grim frown. "It was hideous: the loss of life, the panic of the people within the sukrael's hunting ground, the uncertainty. The Order couldn't offer anyone solace."

He turned to look at Colin directly. "You brought them solace with the Winter Tree. You allowed them to return to their land and resume their lives. But the way in which you brought the Winter Tree." His face tightened with anger. "You should have brought it to me. I should have been the one to present it to the Evant. Its power obviously fell within the domain of the Order, not the Evant, not Lord Aeren nor the Tamaell. I should have been given time to plan, to find the best location for its planting. It should never have been placed in the center of Caercaern, in the marketplace!"

Colin's gaze had dropped from the bird toward Lotaern. He didn't like the assumption of authority he heard in the Chosen's voice, nor the fact that Lotaern felt his authority rose above that of the Tamaell. "The placement in the marketplace was a mistake. I did not realize that it would quicken so fast."

"That doesn't matter now. It was planted in the marketplace, and has since been walled off, the plaza now a garden sanctuary maintained by the Order."

Controlled by the Order, Colin thought. Aeren had told him how Lotaern had sealed access to the Tree from the Evant, how he'd established Wardens to care for it even as the Flame guarded it and kept it from the Alvritshai, all with the sanction of the Evant, most of whose lords welcomed and feared the Tree's power at the same time. It had become another way for Lotaern to control the Alvritshai, and through the lords, the Evant.

If Lotaern expected Colin to apologize for bringing the Tree to Aeren first, or to the Tamaell, he would be disappointed.

They heard Vaeren's approach, his boots thumping through the chamber, moving swiftly, accompanied by the footfalls of another. Both the Chosen and Colin turned as the caitan of the Order of the Flame appeared in the foyer, his gaze flickering with irritation before he caught sight of them near the bowl. He and the woman, Siobhaen, approached, both dressed in the armor of the Flame, wrists banded with metal, the heavy cloth over their chests emblazoned with the stylized white flames of Aielan, boot heels harsh on the flagstone floor, although Colin noticed that Siobhaen's tread was much softer than Vaeren's. Siobhaen's long black hair was pulled back into a braid behind her head and she caught Colin with a sharp, searching glare, her light brown eyes flicking up and down once. Colin felt as if he'd been sized up and dismissed in the space of a heartbeat and straightened in indignation. Her features were narrow, made more severe by having her hair pulled back, but softened by small silver earrings.

Vaeren had changed into different armor as well, something more suited to traveling long distances. His hair had been tied back with a length of leather. "I've ordered the acolytes to bring horses to the main plaza for us, readied with supplies," he said, ignoring Colin completely.

Before Lotaern could answer, two more members of the Flame appeared. Dressed like Vaeren, they came up behind the caitan and nodded toward Lotaern formally. The Chosen had straightened, assuming the mantle of his power. They were younger than Vaeren, but obviously related, their eyes the same dark gray.

"Is everything prepared?"

"No," Siobhaen said. "Not yet. There is still one more thing to do."

When the brothers shot her a curious glance, she moved toward the bowl, knelt on one knee, and lowered her head. Colin could hear her murmuring beneath her breath.

When he looked up, he caught the brothers rolling their eyes. Vaeren gave them a look and with sudden solemnity they both knelt.

A moment later, Siobhaen reached forward and smudged soot along her cheek, the two brothers following suit. Then all three rose.

"Now we are ready," Vaeren said.

The entire group moved to the main entrance, acolytes pulling open the doors as they approached. Gusts of winter air pushed through, and Colin hoped that the acolytes had thought to include warmer clothes in his own set of supplies. Even as he thought it, one of the acolytes stepped forward and presented him with a second satchel. Inside, he found clothing of an Alvritshai cut and the Order's colors, a bedroll, bowls and utensils, and other assorted tools for the road.

He pulled the clothing free. "I'll need to change," he said to Vaeren and Lotaern.

The Chosen motioned him away. As the acolyte showed him to a room, he and Vaeren spoke to each other quietly, too low for Colin to catch.

A few minutes later, he joined the Order of the Flame outside in the Sanctuary's plaza, the stone obelisks surrounding them on all sides. The Alvritshai clothing fit, even though Colin fidgeted with its unfamiliar cut, a little too tight in the shoulders for his taste.

Lotaern had just finished a blessing, the Flame members rising. He turned to Colin as they mounted the waiting horses. "Find out what's causing the storms, Shaeveran."

Colin didn't answer the command, merely swinging up

into the saddle of his own horse. He remembered when the Alvritshai had been afraid of horses, when he and his family had first ventured onto the plains and met Aeren and Eraeth.

The Chosen backed away, his acolytes following him into the protection of the door's alcove, away from the wind.

"Why are we leaving in the middle of the night?" one of the brothers asked, barely above a whisper. "Couldn't this have waited until morning?"

The other brother shrugged.

Colin turned to Vaeren.

"Where to first?" the caitan asked. "Rhyssal House lands to see Lord Aeren?"

"No," Colin said. "To the Winter Tree. I need to verify that the Trees have not been affected."

Vaeren's eyebrows rose in surprise, but he nodded.

They wound their way through the darkened streets of Caercaern, lit sparsely by lanterns or candlelight from high windows, Colin tugging the sleeves of his shirt down over his hands against the chill. Vaeren took the lead with Siobhaen, the two brothers trailing behind. Only a few Alvritshai were out at this hour, hurrying from one spot of warmth to another, bundled up and hunched into their clothes. No one paid them any attention. Most windows were dark, but a few of the shops they passed, mostly bakeries by the strong smell of bread that drifted from them, showed chinks of lantern light. In a few hours, the streets would be bustling with the thousands of Alvritshai that lived in the city, thronged with pull-carts and wagons, the citizens dressed in the loose clothing and conical straw hats of commoners. He glanced toward the third tier, where most of the lords kept their own houses when the Evant was in session, then higher to where the Tamaell resided in the highest of the tiers, towering over the city, but the buildings were lost in the darkness. Then he turned his attention south. The storm he had seen from the top of the Sanctuary had moved too far away to be visible.

Ahead, Vaeren and Siobhaen slowed and he shifted in his saddle, looking up to where the Winter Tree towered above them. They'd reached the wall that surrounded it, had stopped at one of the gates. Vaeren spoke to the Warden who responded to his knock on the heavy wooden door.

The door opened and they ducked through the stone arc of the wall into what had once been Caercaern's largest marketplace.

Colin remembered what the plaza had looked like the first time he'd been here with Aeren and Eraeth. It had stretched nearly the entire width of the tier, had been twice as long, the colonnades of the Hall of the Evant on the far side appearing distant. And it had been packed with people, tents, wagons tilted onto their sides, blankets spread onto the wide flagstones, and tables of every variety of produce and goods imaginable. It had taken Aeren and his escort nearly an hour to work their way across to the Hall.

Now, the entire area had been transformed to deal with the Winter Tree. The flagstones had been ripped up and soil carted in and packed down to allow for a garden. Trees had been planted on the outer fringes near the wall, but as soon as they stepped inside, Colin could see that only grass grew beneath the shadow of the Winter Tree's branches, the lowest of which were too high to be reached even by ladder. The Tree obscured the Hall of the Evant, and in the darkness beneath it Colin could barely make out the wide trunk and its gnarled roots. But he could hear the wind in the branches above, thrashing in the leaves, and he could see where the Wardens had established crushed stone paths beneath those branches, winding out and around sculptures of stone and statues, benches and small basins of water.

The gate closed behind them, the Warden who'd opened it appearing nervous. Vaeren turned toward Colin. "What do you need to do?"

"I need to touch the Tree. And I'll need some time."

He nodded, then turned to the waiting Warden. "We'll leave the horses here. Fetch us lanterns, and inform the head Warden that we'll be at the bole."

The Warden scurried off; without a word Siobhaen dismounted and headed toward the center of the gardens, the rest following suit.

The branches of the Tree closed in overhead almost immediately, the thrashing of the leaves muted to a soothing rustle. Wood creaked and groaned, but the deeper they moved beneath the Tree's massive protection, the fainter those sounds grew. The metallic taste of winter tinged each breath, mingling with the acrid and earthy smell of bark as they drew nearer the bole.

Halfway to the trunk, a group of five Wardens arrived with lanterns, the footing becoming treacherous as roots began to break through the earth. The procession— strangely formal now—edged through the roots as they grew more and more tangled, increasing in thickness until they were the width of Colin's thigh. A moment later, they reached the base of the Tree.

They stood on the root system and stared up into the latticework of branches above, barely within the reach of the lantern's light. Colin could see the awe of the members of the Flame as they searched the heights, could feel the Tree itself pulsing beneath his feet. He drew its scent in with every breath. The Wardens were unaffected, waiting calmly to either side.

"Wait here," Colin said. He could have reached down and touched the Tree through the roots at his feet, but he wanted to be closer, nearer to its heart. He left his staff behind, waved away the offering of one of the lanterns, then began climbing the roots in front of him. The satchel proved an annoyance, but he hadn't wanted to leave the knife it held behind. He clutched the dry, dark bark, and scrambled higher until he'd moved beyond the lantern light, until the bole shot skyward before him. The scent of the Tree enfolded him here, the air no longer chill with winter, as if the Tree were generating its own heat, like that generated by peat in a bog. He settled into position, then reached out and placed both of his hands against the rough bark of the bole and closed his eyes.

The essence of the Tree wrapped around him instantly. Like that of his staff or the heartwood given to him by the Ostraell, it throbbed with life, but this was a thousand times more powerful. It overwhelmed him instantly and drew him in, recognizing him, his taste. He may have gasped; he couldn't tell, his awareness of the outside world and his body subsumed by the sudden sensations of the Winter Tree itself. Wind lashed at its branches, tossing the leaves to and fro, the trunk swaying beneath the tumult. Far beneath, the roots dug deeper and deeper into the earth and stone of the mountain, reaching for underground streams and the nutrients of the soil; reaching also for the heady pulse of power that Colin recognized as Aielan's Light deep within the mountain. The Tree sensed that power, strained for it, recognized it as a part of itself.

All of those were outside influences. In its heart, at its core, Colin settled into the surge of sap, the fluid rush of the Tree's life. It enfolded him with warmth, with a shuddering, coruscating sensation of motion, smothering him from all sides. He let it course through him, reveled in its amber strength, its power tinged with the white of Aielan's Light and the rose of the Confluence, and then he stretched out along that power and tested its reach. He searched for flaws, for signs of disease or weakness, reaching farther and farther, to the fringes of the Tree itself, stretching out beyond the confines of Caercaern, out into the surrounding lands where the power of the Winter Tree held sway. The farther from the Tree he roamed, the weaker that power became, but he didn't sense any damage.

Then, near the edge of the Tree's influence, out well beyond the shadow of the mountains, he felt the touch of the Winter Tree's siblings. To the southwest, on the plains, he tasted the sugary sap of the Autumn Tree, planted outside the human city of Temeritt; to the southeast, the golden savor of the Summer Tree flooded his senses from the central plains of the dwarren, beyond the Ostraell. He explored their tastes for a long moment through their connections to the Winter Tree, searching them for damage as well. He couldn't be as thorough from such a distance, but he could not sense any disease, and so he drew back, pulled himself back to the heart of the Winter Tree, back to Caercaern. He allowed the flow of the Tree's life to soothe him for a long moment, then separated himself from its embrace, not without effort, and back into his own body.

He sucked in a sharp breath as a wave of dizziness enfolded him, his heart thudding hard in his chest. A moment later he felt the bark of the Tree pressing into his forehead, and he pulled back. He sagged down to his knees, and as he sank, he turned, letting his hands fall to his sides.

The sun had risen. It streamed down through the branches on the outskirts of the Tree, the area around the bole still shrouded in darkness, the leaves and branches above too thick to allow the light to penetrate here. He could see the lanterns of the Warders below, could see the members of the Flame as well. They appeared distant. He hadn't realized he'd climbed so high.

One of them pointed toward him and he heard a faint shout, filled with concern. Two of the Wardens began making their way frantically up the roots.

"I'm fine," he called out and waved, but they didn't slow.

He watched them ascend, not moving, not knowing if he could move. His arms hung at his sides, hands pooled in his lap where he sat. The life-force of the Tree throbbed through his back. He felt distant and lethargic.

"Shaeveran!"

He glanced down, saw one of the Wardens scrambling up the last stretch of root to his position. The youth's face was wide with panic and fear and Colin suddenly remembered what Lotaern had said back at the Sanctuary, that most of the acolytes and the Flame revered him.

"So different from the reactions of my own kind," Colin muttered to himself. He hadn't journeyed through human lands in decades. His name was legend there as well, but tainted by fear and suspicion. At least along the coasts.

"Shaeveran! Are you all right?" The youth reached Colin and fell to his knees, one hand on Colin's shoulder, the other checking for damage. His fingers brushed Colin's forehead and came away sticky with blood. He must have scraped his head against the bark of the Tree without realizing.

The Warden frowned and dug in his pocket for a cloth.

"I'm fine," Colin said, pushing the cloth away in irritation as the Warden dabbed at his forehead. "I'm just . . . exhausted. I shouldn't have spent so much energy on the Tree after working with Aielan's Light."

The second Warden arrived. "Is he hurt?" he gasped, out of breath from his climb. This Warden was older, his face red from exertion, but his tone was more practical.

"He says he's simply exhausted, but he's bleeding—"

"It's just a scrape," Colin said, then gathered himself and rose, using the Tree behind him for support. "We should rejoin Vaeren."

The older Warden scanned his forehead, then nodded. "Very well."

They descended. Colin regained his strength as they

climbed down, although he did require the Wardens' help at one treacherous point where the roots were nearly vertical for a stretch; he didn't want to risk expending energy shifting into a younger form. By the time they'd reached the pooled lantern light of Vaeren's group, he'd recovered enough to glare when Vaeren demanded, "What happened?"

"Nothing. I overextended myself, but I'm fine." He reached for his staff, took strength from the life-force pulsing inside as he gripped the wood.

"And the Tree?" Vaeren glanced toward the thick bole before them, expression tight with concern.

"The Trees are fine. Whatever is causing the storms hasn't affected them at all. They're still protecting the Alvritshai, dwarren, and human lands from the Wraiths and the Shadows."

Everyone, including the Wardens, relaxed perceptibly. The young Warden heaved a sigh of relief and muttered a prayer of thanks to Aielan.

"Then what next?"

Colin began moving back toward the gates, picking his way carefully through the tangled roots, using his staff for support.

"Now," he said, grunting as his foot slid stepping down from one rounded knob to another. The others followed him, spread out to either side. "Now we see Lord Aeren."

He clutched the satchel containing the knife to his side as he said it. He didn't trust Vaeren and the Flame. He didn't trust Lotaern.

Which meant he needed someone in the group on his side.

~

It was winter, so only the Tamaell resided in Caercaern. The rest of the Lords of the Evant had withdrawn to their own

House lands, to ride out the winter months in the confines of their own homes. Including Aeren.

Vaeren led the small group down from the heights of Caercaern into the surrounding hills and woodland, the outer wall of the city falling away and obscured by trees almost instantly. For a brief moment, Colin stared back at the expanse of Caercaern. Sunlight glared off the white-gray stonework, off the intricate architecture, the subtle lines of the buildings slanting inward and up, giving the impression that the entire city was somehow stretching toward the heavens. The Winter Tree reached for those heights as well, its leaves of silver flickering brightly as they were riffled by the breeze. Behind, spray from the many cascading falls behind the city drifted and sparkled, catching the light and refracting it into rainbow prisms.

When it became obscured, Colin turned back, the forest shading the stone roadway. He'd traveled Alvritshai lands many times, but only recently with time slowed and never with a horse. He already felt aches and pains emerging in his thighs and backside from riding, but he found the people crowding the roadway with their carts, herd animals, and families more annoying.

"Do you hate us so much?"

He turned, startled, to find Siobhaen watching him intently from one side as they pressed their horses through the throng of people on the tail end of the road that angled up to Caercaern. It emptied out onto the wide main east-west road, where the traffic appeared to be flowing more smoothly, but here at the junction it was chaos.

"I don't hate the Alvritshai," he said. "If anything, I'm more comfortable with the Alvritshai than the dwarren. Certainly more than with my own race, who have willfully forgotten me."

Doubt crossed Siobhaen's eyes. "It would not appear so,

the way you were frowning at the common people." She waved toward the morass of people and animals below.

"I wasn't frowning in distaste. I was frowning in annoyance. If I'd been traveling alone, I would have slowed time, slid past everyone, and been five miles distant in the time it's taken us to move the last hundred feet."

She considered him for a long moment, expressionless. "You should be more careful what emotions you show. Some might misinterpret them." She glanced around at the rest of the members of the Flame, the two brothers arguing with each other twenty paces back, Vaeren ahead waiting impatiently for a cart to move out of his way. "Could you stop time for all of us?" she asked, turning with a raised eyebrow.

He smiled warily, wondering how much Lotaern had revealed to the Order about his powers, how much Vaeren, Siobhaen, and the two brothers knew. "It doesn't work that way. I'd have to be touching all of you, to carry you along with me, and while I've grown in strength the last hundred and twenty-odd years, I'm not sure I'd be able to handle all four of you." He thought back to the time he'd saved Moiran from the occumaen on the plains, and the time he'd taken King Stephan back to witness his father's death in order to end the battle at the Escarpment. "It could tear me apart."

"I see." She did not try to hide her disappointment. With a sigh, she nudged her horse forward, taking advantage as an empty space opened up to one side.

Half an hour later they were on the main road, headed at a much swifter pace to the west.

Toward Rhyssal House lands.

Eight days later, they emerged onto a ledge, the road curling around a promontory of stone, offering a view of the valley and lake below. At one end, the lake reflected the slate-gray clouds above, a narrow swath of water that widened like a teardrop, embracing a stone hillock. Lord Aeren's manse sat on top of the hill overlooking the lake, the tiered levels wider and flatter than most of the buildings they'd passed on the journey here, enclosed by a low wall.

The town of Artillien spread out across the base of the hillock, a single path leading up to the lord's house from the fair-sized collection of buildings, larger than most of the towns and villages they'd passed through in the rest of the House lands, but not the largest. Below the town, filling nearly the entire breadth of the wide valley, were fields now covered in the feet of snow dropped by the two storms that had passed through in the last eight days. The hills and trees all around were cloaked with the most recent fall.

Distantly, they heard the chimes of the town's temple to Aielan declaring terciern.

"We should reach it before dusk," Vaeren said. Without turning, he asked, "Will Lord Aeren be expecting us?"

Colin shook his head. "No, but he'll welcome us." He couldn't keep the anticipation from his voice. It thrummed through his arms, stuttered in his heart; he hadn't seen Aeren or Moiran in what felt like ages.

Dociern had already rung, the thin winter sunlight fading from the sky, when Colin knocked on the heavy wooden doors banded with iron at the Rhyssal House gates. His breath fogged the air in the lantern light as he waited, the temperature dropping quickly as the sun set. Inside, he heard movement and a moment later the door creaked open, one of the Rhyssal House Phalanx glaring out. The man's gaze raked Colin, taking in his staff, his cloak, and the horse Vaeren held behind. It paused as he noted the white flame emblem of the Order.

He stiffened slightly. "Who calls on the Rhyssal House at this hour?"

"Tell Lord Aeren, Lady Moiran, and Fedaureon that Colin Patris Harten and an escort of the Order of the Flame are here to see them."

The man's eyes widened and he whispered, "Shaeveran," under his breath, pulling back slightly. Then he regained his composure and motioned them inside stiffly. "Lord Aeren welcomes you, of course," he said. "You can leave your horses here. They will be attended to shortly. Allow me to escort you to the main house."

They stepped into a courtyard lined with ornamental trees now leafless but laced with white snow, branches weighted down so heavily that some touched the ground. A wide path had been cleared, splitting almost immediately as one arched off toward the stable yard, the other leading toward the main entrance to the manse. A second guard rang a bell set inside a small enclosure to one side and two additional Phalanx and two servants appeared from the direction of the stable. The servants took charge of the horses, the two Phalanx remaining behind to man the entrance.

As soon as they entered Aeren's manse, the Phalanx guard caught a passing servant and issued orders. The man bowed formally, shot a glance toward Colin, then darted into one of the halls and vanished. Colin scanned the inner room, the paneled walls carved with intricate garden scenes, lanterns hung from the heavy wooden ceiling beams overhead. The floor immediately inside the entrance was stone for easier cleaning of snowmelt and mud from boots and shoes. The stone gave way to wood in the hall on the far side. A table sat to either side of the entrance, one containing some type of potted shrub pruned into the shape of a windswept tree, its roots clinging to moss-covered stone, the other holding a collection of blown glass vases. Banners in the blue and red of Rhyssal House hung on the wall above them, the wings of an eagle—the House sigil—embroidered in gold on the split field.

A moment later, he heard footsteps coming from the left. Moiran appeared, dressed in Rhyssal House colors, smiling broadly. "Shaeveran! What an unexpected surprise!" Her gaze shot toward Vaeren and the rest of the Flame standing awkwardly behind Colin and creases appeared in her forehead between her eyebrows, the evidence of the frown there and then gone in the space of a heartbeat. Her gaze locked with his, and he saw the question there even as she said, "And you've brought guests. From the Order."

The only outward indication of the sudden tension in the air was the stiffening of the Phalanx member who had escorted them to the manse from the gate.

"Yes. There is news from Caercaern. This isn't a social visit."

Moiran's head bowed, strain tainting her smile. "That doesn't mean we can't enjoy it." She stepped forward and hugged him, hands on his shoulders as she drew back. As with Lotaern, Colin noticed the small signs of age on her face, the lines around her eyes, the dullness of her hair. The lantern light even glinted off a few strands of gray. "It's been too long," she said, and squeezed his shoulders before stepping back.

It was more emotion than the Alvritshai usually allowed themselves to share in public.

More formally, she turned to include all of the Order. "A light meal is being prepared. If you wouldn't mind leaving your bags, they'll be taken to rooms being made ready for your stay. Servants will show you to the kitchens." She turned to Colin. "Lord Aeren is waiting in our private chambers."

Servants appeared behind her as Vaeren and the others shrugged out of their satchels and cloaks. They gathered the supplies together and vanished down the opposite hall, Colin keeping the satchel containing the knife across his shoulder.

Siobhaen and the two brothers were led away by another servant, but Vaeren remained at Colin's side, daring him to protest. Moiran's eyebrow rose in question, but he shook his head slightly in warning.

She led them to one of Aeren's outer rooms. A fire blazed in the hearth, the room warmer than the entrance, the soft light glowing on the many glass objects strewn around the room on tables and desks and amidst more carefully trimmed plants and small trees. A large desk took up most of the central area, the wide top littered with books and papers and spent quills and ink bottles. Another desk off to one side was draped with blue-and-red cloth and held a single fat white candle in a gold basin, surrounded by a dagger, a sword, a locket with a fine silver chain, and the pendant Colin recognized as the sign of Aeren's successful completion of his studies as an acolyte at the Sanctuary.

Aeren sat in one of an array of chairs around a low table and stood as Moiran arrived. His smile didn't falter at all when Vaeren entered behind him, although he folded his hands before him.

"Colin, it's good to see you. You know Eraeth, of course," he said motioning toward his Protector, who stood as always to one side. Eraeth's gaze had settled on Vaeren, the two watching each other silently. "And my son, Fedaureon, along with his Protector, Daevon."

Daevon nodded formally, darker and broader of shoulder than Eraeth, with the same deadly stance all of the Phalanx used. But when Fedaureon rose from his seat beside his father, Colin had to stifle a gasp, his eyes widening. "Fedaureon?"

The young man—young by Alvritshai standards—smiled and stepped forward to take Colin's hand in a human handshake. "Yes, Shaeveran, it's me."

"You've . . . grown."

Fedaureon laughed and motioned toward the chairs

spread around the low table as servants appeared carrying decanters of wine, glasses, and platters of food. "It's been nearly twenty-five years since you last saw me," he said. "I'm not surprised I look different. Sit. My father and I were discussing the Evant and current trade negotiations with the Provinces and Andover. We could use a diversion."

Aeren frowned as everyone settled and when Fedaureon took his seat beside his father Colin glanced back and forth between them. Fedaureon looked like a younger version of his father in every respect except the eyes; he had Moiran's green eyes.

"He looks like you when I first met you on the plains," Colin said with a tight smile to Aeren. The smile broadened when Eraeth snorted. "A slightly older version of you."

"There is a resemblance, yes," Moiran muttered. "Please, eat, drink. Your travels must have been harsh with the recent storms. Was the snow troublesome? Were the roads kept clear?"

"For the most part," Colin said. "We had no serious trouble, it was merely—"

"Annoying," Vaeren interjected.

No one reached for the food; they were all waiting for Colin, he realized.

He took one of the small plates on one of the trays and began with a few slices of the smoked meat he recognized as gaezel from the plains, ladling a spicy sauce that smelled of oranges over it. As soon as he started, the rest leaned forward for their own trays.

"I was going to say it was merely an inconvenience," he said dryly. "I should introduce my traveling companions. Vaeren is caitan of the Order of the Flame. The others are Siobhaen, Boreaus, and Petraen, also members of the Flame."

Aeren nodded to Vaeren. "Welcome to Rhyssal House."

"Thank you for your welcome and your hospitality,"

Vaeren answered. "May Aielan's Light guide your House to prosperity."

"It has." Aeren's gaze drifted to Colin. "So what brings you to Rhyssal at this time of year, and with such company?"

"The sarenavriell."

Aeren, Moiran, and Eraeth stilled. Fedaureon and Daevon looked confused. It was not what they had expected.

Moiran was the first to move, reaching to pour some wine, but it was Aeren who spoke.

"The sarenavriell?" His voice was troubled. "I thought the Wells had been stabilized."

"I thought so as well. For that matter, they may still be stabilized."

"What makes you think otherwise?"

"Do you remember the storms on the plains?"

"They are impossible to forget. They were violent, their winds harsh, driving the rain so hard it felt as if it would scour your skin raw. And the lightning was . . . unnatural. Wicked. The thunder growling in your chest."

Colin shuddered, recalling the viciousness of the storm that had caught the wagon train as it fled from the dwarren. He caught Aeren's eyes and saw the same memory reflected there.

Fedaureon stirred. "What are you talking about? What storms?"

Aeren shook his head. "You would not know. The storms had been part of the plains since the arrival of the Alvritshai south of the Hauttaeren Mountains. The dwarren say that they were always part of the plains, as far back as their shamans can remember. But in the years before the Accord, the storms began to grow in intensity."

"The number and size of the occumaen as well," Moiran added. A shiver ran down her arms as if she were chilled, and her gaze met Colin's, her eyes sad.

"Yes. The occumaen also became more prevalent. Shaeveran thought that the storms and the occumaen were the result of the awakening of the Wells by the Wraiths. He thought their actions were causing an imbalance, and that the storms and the occumaen were the side effects."

Colin nodded. "After the Accord, I intended to see if I could correct the imbalance and stop the storms, but the attacks of the Wraiths on Alvritshai and dwarren lands grew too intense. I spent years trying to help the two races fight them, before finally realizing that something more drastic needed to be done. I created the Seasonal Trees so that the threat of the Wraiths and the Shadows would be halted, and after their seeding I focused my attention on the stability of the Wells. It took thirty years, and I lost count of how many times I faced the Wraiths and the Shadows, but I achieved a balance."

"And the storms stopped," Aeren said. "The occumaen faded. There hasn't been an instance of either since you were born, Fedaureon."

"Until now," Vaeren said, and Aeren, Eraeth, and Moiran turned toward him.

He stood, his stance formal, as if he were addressing Lotaern in the Sanctuary, or the Lords of the Evant in the Hall. "Over a month ago, one of the acolytes from an outer temple on Uslaen House lands arrived at the Sanctuary with word of such a storm that ravaged the town the temple served. The Chosen did not believe him and sent a party of the Flame to verify the account. Since then, numerous reports of the storms have been drifting in from Redlien, Ionaen, and Licaeta, as well as Uslaen. A missive was sent to the dwarren shamans, the reply received two weeks ago. It appears a resurgence of the storms has been reported across the breadth of the plains. The occumaen as well. When Shaeveran appeared in the Sanctuary, we thought it was because of the recent activity."

"But I hadn't heard of the storms," Colin said. "I was in Caercaern for a different reason." He picked up the satchel he'd placed on the floor near his feet and removed the fine chain-metal cloth that held the knife. Aware that Vaeren frowned down at him in disapproval, he set the cloth on the table between the trays of food and then opened its folds.

The reddish-yellow color of the knife appeared to glow in the flickering firelight. Aeren and Fedaureon leaned forward, Eraeth and Daevon stepping away from their respective corners. Moiran leaned back with a frown.

Aeren shot Colin a hard look. "Does it work?"

"Does what work?" Daevon asked. "What is it?"

"It's a knife that I believe will be able to kill one of the Wraiths. A knife that should be able to kill the sukrael."

"Should?" Eraeth asked sharply.

Colin glanced up with a small smile. "It hasn't been tested. Yet."

Eraeth's eyes narrowed, and Colin could see the sudden urgency in his expression. He wanted to test the blade himself, but he made no move to pick it up. None of the Alvritshai did.

"I found Lotaern to inform him about the knife," Colin said, sitting back. "That's when he took me to the Sanctuary's roof and showed me one of the storms on the horizon. I told him that I would investigate, but Lotaern felt that an escort was necessary."

Aeren said nothing, but Colin knew that both he and Eraeth heard what he had not said. The knife lay between them, although neither of them glanced toward it. After a moment, Aeren nodded, the gesture almost imperceptible.

"That does not explain why you came here," Moiran said into the silence.

"No, it does not. The problem with our theory that the stability of the Wells has been altered is that I placed wardings on all of them, to keep the Wraiths away as well as everyone else. None of those wardings have been disturbed. The Seasonal Trees protect all but three of the Wells from interference by the Wraiths and Shadows, but Lotaern feels that the Wraiths have found a way around the wardings, and so, with my escort, we are going to these three Wells to see if they have been touched or if the wardings have been tampered with."

"And where are these three Wells?" Aeren asked.

"Do you have a map?"

Aeren motioned to his son, who stood and began sorting through the papers on the large desk, Eraeth and Daevon moving over a moment later to help him.

"The Wells are outside the influence of the Trees, obviously. One of them lies far to the south, beneath the lands settled by the Provinces," Colin said as they waited. He felt Vaeren listening intently. He wondered yet again what his orders from Lotaern were, but shrugged that aside. "The second lies to the west, across the Arduon, in Andover."

Aeren's eyebrows rose in shock. "I had not realized there were sarenavriell in Andover."

"Neither had we," Vaeren said sharply, anger threading through his voice. Colin assumed he meant Lotaern and the Order. The fact they had not known was strangely satisfying.

"There is only the one, as far as I know," he said.

At the desk, Daevon and Eraeth had halted their search at this revelation, but Fedaureon cried out and pulled a sheaf of papers from a stack. He sorted through them as he came to the table, while Moiran moved the trays of forgotten food to one side to make room.

"Here," he said, setting down a map of the Hauttaeren Mountains and Alvritshai lands. Each of the eight Houses were marked with different shades of color, Caercaern and the major cities black dots with swirling script, black lines marking roads and trade routes connecting them. Everyone,

Moiran and the Flame included, Eraeth looking over Aeren's shoulder, leaned forward as Colin perused the map to orient himself.

"And the third," he said, turning the page toward him and pointing, "is right here." He glanced up, met Aeren's gaze squarely. "In the White Wastes."

4

"**T**HERE ARE ONLY TWO ROUTES northward to the lands that we abandoned," Aeren said, sitting back in his seat as the shock of Colin's revelation slowly wore off. "We can travel through the halls beneath Caercaern, or we can travel to the coast and take a ship up around the coastline, hoping for a break in the ice that would permit landfall. I'd not recommend the ocean approach."

"And returning to Caercaern will add another week or more to the trip," Vaeren said with a scowl, turning on Colin. "Why did you have us travel here if you knew we were going to be turning back? We could have sent a message by courier. We could have summoned Lord Aeren to Caercaern if it were that important. Aielan's Light, we didn't need to come here at all!"

"There is another way," Colin said.

Vaeren straightened. "What do you mean?"

"I spent a large amount of time reading the Scripts in search of any hint about the locations of the Wells, and during that time I read much of Alvritshai history as well. Once, the Alvritshai dominated the entire region above the Haut-taeren, from the coast to the northern arctic sea, the mountains to the glacial ice to the north. There are more halls within the mountains besides those behind Caercaern, and there are passes through the Teeth that we can use to reach them.

"One of those passes, called Gaurraenan's Pass, is here," he pointed to a region of the mountains beneath where he'd indicated the Well lay. "It's secluded in the reaches above Nuant House lands, but it is still accessible. Once we reach its edge, we can travel to the far side of the Hauttaeren through the ancient halls beneath."

Vaeren stared at the map for several moments. "How long do you think it will take?"

"It depends on the storms and the snow, of course, but we should be at the Well within two weeks."

Vaeren met his gaze, his expression hostile. "You planned this from the beginning. Why didn't you tell the Chosen?"

"Because he did not need to know."

Vaeren's face darkened, his hand tightening on the hilt of the cattan at his side. Colin thought he'd confront him there, in front of Aeren and the rest, but instead he turned to Moiran. "Lady Moiran, if you would have someone escort me to my rooms, I'd like to retire for the night. The journey from Caercaern has been long and tiring."

Moiran stood with a slow, formal grace. "Of course. I'll show you to your rooms myself."

Moiran led him from the room, leaving Aeren, Colin, and the others alone. Aeren waited until he heard their bootfalls die out before he frowned. "It does not appear that you are on good terms with the Order."

Colin laughed. "Lotaern is still angry over what happened with the Winter Tree. He feels I should have brought the seed to him first, that it was obvious the Tree's powers fell under the Order's mantle, not the Tamaell's."

"But that happened over eighty years ago," Fedaureon protested.

"This isn't truly about the Tree," Aeren said.

Daevon answered Fedaureon's confused look. "It's about the knife," he said, nodding toward where it still sat on the table. They all looked down at it.

"I still don't understand."

Aeren reached forward and, with a wave of permission from Colin, picked it up. He frowned as he held it and Colin wondered if he could feel the power of the forest pulsing through it. He'd passed through Aielan's Light, so perhaps he could. Then Aeren handed it to Eraeth, who hefted it in one hand, testing its weight as Lotaern had done.

"Colin came to the Alvritshai with an object of power once before and he used that object without Lotaern's fore-knowledge. The Chosen does not like to be surprised. He likes to be in control. If Colin had come to him with the Winter Tree, he would have used the Tree against the Evant, to gain even more power. The fact that Colin brought it to me, and then to the Tamaell, meant that he could not use it to his immediate advantage."

"He adapted quickly," Eraeth muttered.

"He did," Aeren agreed. "Even though the Tree was never initially under his control, he's gained control of it using the lords' fears. For all intents and purposes, the Tree is now part of the Order. He's walled it away from the people and uses it as a symbol of the Order's strength."

"That was never its intent," Colin grumbled.

"No, but that is how it's been used. And now you bring to Lotaern another object of power. One that does not have the same visual strength as the Winter Tree, but—if you are correct—is more deadly. The Tree merely protects us from the sukrael; the knife may be able to kill them. If Lotaern can show that the Order holds the power to rid the world of the sukrael forever . . ."

Fedaureon nodded his head in understanding. "The Alvritshai commoners will band around him even more. They'll see him as a savior of sorts."

"He wants the knife. He may even need the knife," Aeren said. "The Winter Tree has been in Caercaern for over eighty years. The awe over its creation and its power has faded. For those that live in Caercaern, it has already become commonplace. Only those outside of Resue House lands find it striking. And those that have been born since it was planted, like Fedaureon, have never known a time when the Tree was not in Caercaern, protecting them. When they begin to take their places in the Evant, Lotaern will lose even more of his power, more of his control."

"It's already begun," Eraeth added. "Both Houdyll and Terroec ascended in their fathers' places after the introduction of the Winter Tree."

Colin stared at the knife in Eraeth's hands and grimaced. "I should never have gone to him after forging it, should never have revealed its existence to him."

"You worked with him in its creation. It was only natural for you to take it to him."

But Colin knew what Aeren would not say out loud: that Colin had once again ignored the changing world around him, that if he had only looked he would have seen how Lotaern had lost power in the Evant and he would have known that sharing the creation of the knife would be a mistake.

He caught Aeren's gaze and said, "You are too forgiving." Then he frowned, shifted forward. "Why does Lotaern seek this power? The Order is already equivalent to a House, from what I saw in the Evant years ago. Hasn't he achieved enough?"

Aeren sighed and shook his head. "Once, before the threat of the Wraiths and the sukrael, I believe the Chosen would have been content with what he has now, but not any longer. I think he believes that the Wraiths and the sukrael are a trial, sent by Aielan to test us, to bring us all back beneath her Light."

"He may be right," Eraeth said.

"Yes, but he believes our failure to eliminate the Wraiths is because we are not showing enough faith—in Aielan, in the Flame . . . in the Chosen. He believes the Lords of the Evant, and the Tamaell in particular, have fallen short of Aielan's regard. He believes that it is Aielan's will that the Order rise up and seize control, that only then can we defeat the Wraiths and the sukrael."

"With himself as Chosen."

Aeren nodded. "He thinks the war with the Wraiths is a religious war, and that only with the Order in power can the Alvritshai prevail."

"I would think he would welcome my help then," Colin muttered, "since I have brought him the Tree, and now the knife."

"And have a human be the savior of the Alvritshai?" Eraeth scoffed. "He has reserved that role for himself."

Moiran returned, trailing a few servants who began clearing out the remains of the food, leaving the wine. "Are the members of the Order situated?" Aeren asked.

"I have placed them in the farthest corner of the house, on the second level. They will have a spectacular view of the lake."

Aeren smiled. "And be as far from this discussion as possible."

Moiran sat down beside Colin. "I have no idea what you are insinuating," she said innocently. "Now, what did I miss?"

"We were discussing Lotaern."

"He wants the knife, to solidify and regain some of his lost power within the Evant," Moiran said succinctly. At Fedaureon's annoyed look, she added, "I was the Tamaea of the Evant at one point, Fedaureon. I know how power works and is wielded." Then she turned to Colin. "But the caitan asked an important question: Why did you come here? Even using the pass and the halls beneath the mountain, you did not need to come to Artillien."

Colin could hear in the tone of her voice that she already knew the answer and did not approve. Taking a deep breath, he caught and held Aeren's gaze and said, "I need reinforcements. I was hoping—"

"No." Moiran stood as her voice cut across Colin's, so she could glare down at Aeren. "You are a Lord of the House of Evant. You will not traipse off to the White Wastes."

"It's winter. Anything that would require the attention of the Lord of House Rhyssal can be handled by its heir."

Moiran crossed her arms over her chest, ignoring the way Fedaureon perked up in his seat. "It is winter, yes, which means that the White Wastes will be as dangerous and as deadly as at any other time of the year. And it is not the heir's responsibility to care for the House."

"But it will be."

Moiran did not immediately respond, but she did not move either. Colin shared a glance with Eraeth, who still held the knife. Fedaureon had shifted forward and now sat on the edge of his seat, his head bowed, eyes on the ground, although Colin could see the tightness in his shoulders. Daevon regarded his charge with a slight frown of disapproval. The tension in the room was awkward and strained.

Then, in a quiet voice that throbbed with suppressed emotion, Moiran said, "I have already lost one husband to the Evant and the protection of the Alvritshai. I do not want to lose another."

Aeren stilled, a frown darkening his face, and then he stood as well, reached forward to grip Moiran's shoulders. She tensed, met his gaze with head tilted upward, mouth set. "Fedaureon can handle the House, especially with you and his Protector here to guide him. And I will not be venturing out alone. I will have Eraeth with me as my Protector, and members of my own Phalanx."

Moiran pulled out of his grasp, reached down to take up the last decanter of wine, but halted before Eraeth, the Protector stiffening. "Bring him back to me."

Then she left, the room silent except for the crackle of the fire. Slowly, the tension bled from the room, until Fedaureon finally stirred.

Before he could speak, Aeren said, "Never defy your mother like that, Fedaureon."

"Not if you value your life," Eraeth muttered, then he placed the knife back onto the metal mesh of the cloth. Colin folded it up and packed the knife away in his satchel.

"Do you expect trouble from the Flame?"

Colin shook his head. "Not immediately, no. The only reason I think Lotaern allowed me to leave Caercaern with the knife in my possession is that it hasn't been tested yet, and he knew it would be nearly impossible for him to take it from me and keep it. But I'd feel better having you and Eraeth by my side, rather than only members of the Flame." He stood, caught Aeren's gaze. "There's no need, though, if you'd rather respect Moiran's wishes. I can handle it myself."

Aeren shook his head. "I agree with you. We cannot allow Lotaern to take control of the knife. I can't say he'd use it as we fear, not with certainty, but if there's something I can do to keep that possibility from occurring, then I'll do it. And what I said was true. Fedaureon is more than capable of handling the House while I'm gone."

"Then how long do you need to prepare?"

Aeren smiled. It made him appear twenty years younger. "I can be ready to leave before midday tomorrow."

~

"Shaeveran is on the move," Khalaek reported. Around him, the other Wraiths—six in all, dwarren and Alvritshai—stirred, but Khalaek kept his eyes fixed on the human, Walter, the ostensible leader. Khalaek could barely keep his lip from twisting in derision at the thought, but without Walter—without the Lifeblood—he would have died on the battlefields of the Escarpment, a sacrifice made by Thaedoran to the human king in order to solidify the peace Accord. Khalaek's hatred of Thaedoran overrode his contempt of Walter . . . at the moment. He could wait.

Walter held his gaze unflinchingly, but Khalaek did not back down. "Where is Colin headed?"

"To Lord Aeren's estates. He has likely already arrived."

"Lord Aeren is a friend. Are you certain Colin knows what we have started?"

"He knows. He spoke to the Chosen before departing, and is escorted by the Flame. He must know of the imbalance."

Walter smiled, and Tuvaellis—one of the other Alvritshai Wraiths, a woman—said, "You do not seem disturbed by this."

Walter chuckled. "I'm not. Colin was bound to notice that something was amiss eventually. I doubt he realizes exactly what, as yet."

"Should we alter our plans?" Arturo asked. He was dwarren. The beads and feathers strewn throughout his beard, and the chains running from the rings in his ears to the one in his nose, proclaimed him a clan chief; the oily darkness swirling beneath his leathery, wrinkled skin claimed him as Wraith.

"No." Walter moved to a chunk of crystal set to one side, part of what had once been the ceiling of the immense room where they had gathered. Other shards of crystal littered the room on all sides, surrounding an open pit in the center of the room. On top of this crystal rested a small wooden box, polished to a fine sheen. He picked up the box, turned, and handed it to Tuvaellis. She gripped the handles on both side, but Walter did not let go. "You understand the importance of this? The human forces in Andover in the old continent must not be allowed to aid the Provinces here in the new, nor the Alvritshai or dwarren. This will guarantee that they are otherwise occupied. If you fail. . . ."

"I will not fail." Tuvaellis' tone was mildly offended.

"Very well. You should depart now. Our contact in King Justinian's Court will be waiting for you."

Tuvaellis nodded as Walter released the box. She tucked it under her arm and blurred away. Walter turned toward Arturo and Khalaek. "Begin gathering your forces. They will need to be ready to move shortly."

"Are you certain Shaeveran will not cause problems?" Khalaek recalled what the human had done to their plans at the Escarpment.

"By the time he figures out what our true goal is, it will be too late." Walter caught Courranen's gaze, Khalaek's fellow Alvritshai straightening where he stood. "Besides, I do not intend to leave him as a loose thread. You know where he will head once he learns of the imbalance. Courranen will be waiting for him when he arrives."

~

Colin, Aeren, and their entourage left the seat of the lord's House at midday, Moiran and Fedaureon standing at the entrance to the main house surrounded by Daevon, the Rhyssal House Phalanx, and a few servants. More Phalanx held the gates open as Colin, Aeren, Eraeth, and the rest mounted their horses and situated their satchels and packs, then turned to go. Vaeren and the rest of the Order were already waiting restlessly to one side, the caitan of the Flame's expression disgruntled and impatient. He flicked the reins of his horse as Aeren spoke to his own caitan, then the man stepped back and Aeren motioned toward the gates. The Lord of Rhyssal House turned back once to nod toward Moiran and his son, and then they were through the gates and headed down to Artillien.

"Do you want me to call them back?" Colin asked as Vaeren and the rest of the Order charged ahead, taking the lead. "I am, ostensibly, their leader, and we are on your own lands."

Aeren smiled and shook his head. "Let them posture. I'm secure enough in my own power as Lord of House Rhyssal, even with an escort of only three Phalanx." Eraeth coughed meaningfully and Aeren smiled, adding, "And my Protector."

They reached the town of Artillien, and the Alvritshai on the streets stopped to stare as the Order of the Flame passed by. A few waved toward Aeren, the lord nodding in their direction. They skirted the marketplace, swept past the temple of Aielan, one of the acolytes outside pausing as he brushed snow from the stone window ledges. He genu- flected toward the Flame, Siobhaen returning the gesture.

Then they passed outside the town into the fields be- yond. Sunlight broke through the layer of clouds, blazing harshly on the snow, and Colin raised one hand to shade his eyes. To the left, the lake gleamed a deep blue, riddled with waves from a brisk wind from the west. As soon as they cleared the outskirts of the town, Vaeren picked up the pace, taking them west along the road as it curved around the water. The wind struck Colin full in the face, burning his skin raw, until they reached the shelter of the cedar and pine trees beyond.

After that, Colin pulled up the hood of his cloak and settled in for the ride, nearly everyone else following suit.

~

They rode for three days, angling northwest as soon as the roads allowed. On the fourth day, they entered Nuant House lands, the maroon-and-gold House colors supplanting the blue and red of Rhyssal. Away from Aeren's lands, the lord received more piercing looks and second glances, but it was the Order that caught and held nearly everyone's attention. The only connection the commoners had to the Order was through their acolytes in the local temples. Seeing the Order of the Flame passing through their village caused a stir. More than one acolyte emerged from his temple to offer the group a place to rest and refresh before continuing on their journey. Vaeren rarely accepted, except when Siobhaen caught his attention and murmured something for his ears only. On these occasions, Siobhaen spent most of her time within the temple, kneeling before the small basins that mimicked the large one in the Sanctuary back in Caercaern. The acolytes would hastily fill the basin with oil, perform a short ritual, and then light the basin so that Siobhaen and the other members of the Flame could pray before it. Always at the end of her prayers, Siobhaen would remove a pouch from her satchel and toss something into the flames, the acolytes in attendance gasping as the fires in the basin burned a harsh, brilliant white. Then she'd run her fingers through the soot beneath the basin and mark her face before rising, the others often doing the same.

"She's solidifying their ties to the temple," Aeren said at the third such temple, even as he genuflected while the flames were burning white.

"What do you mean?" Colin asked. He knew the ritual she performed, had studied it in the Sanctuary before being allowed to pass through Aielan's Light beneath the mountain. It was a simple enough rite, one used to calm the observer, to center them so that the problems they faced might be made clearer. It was one of the basic rituals of the Scripts, although it did not require the basin actually be lit, and the addition of the white flames generally only occurred at significant bondings or rituals.

As the white flames died, returning to normal, the acolytes murmuring to each other in awe and excitement, Aeren turned away, his brow troubled. "She's using the rit-

ual and the white flames to remind the acolytes of their ties
to the Order, their ties to Lotaern and the Flame. There's no
need for the theatrics otherwise. These acolytes all trained
in the Sanctuary at one point. She's reminding them of their
time in Caercaern, of their loyalties.

"And these acolytes will spread that to the common
people in this area."

"But why does Lotaern want them to remember?"

Aeren shook his head. "I don't know. But I've learned
through the course of the years that Lotaern does nothing
without a purpose. He feels he's going to need the commoners' support for something soon. Siobhaen did not stop at
any of the temples before you reached Artillien?"

"No. Why? What are you thinking?"

They watched as Siobhaen and the others circulated
among the gathered acolytes and villagers who happened
to be in or near the temple when they arrived.

"I'm wondering what changed in Artillien that prompted
them to begin this . . . little campaign," he finally murmured.

"We need to find out," Eraeth said.

Colin thought back to his first conversation with Siobhaen, on the road down from Caercaern, when she thought
he despised the Alvritshai. "Perhaps we shouldn't isolate
ourselves anymore." When Aeren and Eraeth looked at
him, he added, "We've separated ourselves into two groups:
the Flame and Rhyssal House. For the last few days we've
eaten separately, traveled separately, even slept in separate
rooms or sides of the outposts. We need to mingle more."

Eraeth grimaced in distaste, while Aeren's eyebrows
rose. "They haven't been overly friendly toward us since
Artillien."

"And we haven't been overly friendly toward them. The
distrust is mutual."

One of Aeren's Phalanx coughed lightly and they turned
to see Vaeren approaching. The caitan nodded, the rest of

the Flame preparing to depart behind him. "We are finished here."

"Very well," Aeren said.

Vaeren hesitated and frowned, as if he sensed something hidden in the tone of Aeren's voice, or in the slightly awkward silence that had settled over the Rhyssal House contingent. Then he shook his head and turned, motioning the Flame outside.

They reached an outpost near dusk, the wayside stop nothing more than a stone hut a few paces from the road tucked into a niche beside a stream of snowmelt, its wooden roof covered in dark green moss beneath dangling cedar branches. Colin scanned the mountains, a hand shading his eyes, the sun a burnt orange glow to the west. He called out to where Vaeren and a few others in the group were refilling their waterskins. "We'll stop here for the night."

Vaeren stood, looking toward the setting sun. "We could make the next village, perhaps even the next outpost."

Colin shook his head. "We're close to the pass now and it's getting dark. We'll have to leave the road tomorrow, after leaving the horses in the village."

Vaeren eyed him for a long moment, suspicion touching the corners of his mouth, but then he waved to the other members of the Flame, who had begun to remount. "Unpack your saddlebags. Boreaus, hunt us something decent to go with what the acolytes gifted us at the last temple. Petraen, gather some wood for a fire. Siobhaen, take care of the horses."

All three hesitated, trading confused looks, but the two brothers shrugged and hauled their gear from their horses before handing the reins to Siobhaen. Boreaus drew a short bow from a cylindrical case, leaped the small stream, and vanished into the woods to the north. Petraen headed in the opposite direction, scrambling up a small embankment before the trees claimed him.

Aeren dismounted at Colin's side. "Is there another reason we're stopping early?" he muttered under his breath as he began working at the ties of his bags.

"We need to learn more about Vaeren and the Flame. I'd rather do it on this side of the mountains, where the weather is calmer and the terrain is decent, than in the White Wastes. If we reach the town, the Flame will join the acolytes in the temple and we'll lose our opportunity."

Aeren grunted in agreement, then passed a silent command to Eraeth.

The Protector turned immediately toward where the other three Phalanx members were unsaddling their own horses. A moment later, two were headed off after Petraen, the third stringing his own bow as he followed Boreaus. Eraeth himself drew their horses closer to where Siobhaen had already begun combing the Flames' horses' flanks. She gave him one hard, suspicious glance as he began pulling saddles from the Phalanx mounts' backs, then resumed her work.

Vaeren had vanished inside the stone hut.

"I'll go check on Vaeren," Colin said.

Aeren nodded. "And I'll join Eraeth and Siobhaen with the horses." He muttered something under his breath as his own mount snorted and stamped its foot against the stone of the roadway. One hand brushed the animal's neck in a long soothing motion.

The lord caught Colin's look. "Why are you smiling?"

"I was just thinking about when we first met on the plains. You shied away from our horses then. You were terrified of them."

Aeren's eyebrows rose. "They were strange and terrifying beasts. And I was young."

Colin shook his head, then grabbed his staff from his own mount and headed toward the hut.

As he ducked inside, Vaeren looked up from where he used a branch to clean out a fire pit sunken into the middle of the hut. "Whoever used this last left in a hurry," he said as he pulled charred ends of sticks and thicker branches toward him. "But they did leave behind some firewood." He pointed with the branch to one side, where wood had been stacked. His eyes never left Colin.

"That should make Petraen's job easier." Colin scanned the rest of the hut. The roof was steep, to keep the snow from piling up too heavily. Smoke would be funneled from the fire pit up to a hole shielded against the weather at the top. The rest of the rounded interior was mostly bare, a few stone benches that could be used as sleeping pallets against the walls. There were no windows, only the main entrance and a covered hole in the floor against the back wall for the disposal of garbage and waste. The stale smell of smoke and musty dampness cloaked the small room.

"It's not much of a wayside," Vaeren said.

Colin caught and held his gaze. The undertone in the caitan's voice suggested that they could find better accommodations in the village. "It will suffice for tonight," he said. Then he knelt down and began dragging the black, sooty remains of the previous fire from the pit.

After a moment, Vaeren helped him.

They worked in utter silence, Vaeren studiously ignoring him as they scraped the last of the dead coals from the hollow that reminded Colin of the rounded depressions in the middle of the dwarren keevas, where they held their most serious consultations. The silence became strained, itching at Colin's back, until he finally sighed and asked, "What House are you from?"

Without looking up, Vaeren said, "I am a member of the Order of the Flame. I am associated with no House except the Order."

The caitan said it as if by rote, and Colin grimaced. He knew that acolytes of the Order renounced their ties to their previous Houses. Their allegiance was given to Aielan and the Order, their previous House abandoned, although erasing those ties completely was impossible.

"I meant, what House were you originally from?"

Vaeren glanced up at that, his brow creased, as if he were trying to determine why Colin would ask, what his ulterior motive might be. But finally he answered, "Uslaen."

"Lord Saetor's House, Khalaek's caitan before Khalaek was banished and his own House declared fallen."

"Yes," Vaeren said shortly. His shoulders stiffened, his soot-greased hands clenched hard on the branch he now held defensively before him. "What of it?"

Colin sat back, surprised by his reaction, by the sudden tension in the room. "Nothing. A simple question, nothing more."

Vaeren watched him intently, then visibly forced himself to relax, letting his held breath out in a long sigh. "I . . . apologize," he said, his voice rough. "I should not have reacted so . . . forcefully."

Colin brushed the apology aside with one hand. "No offense was taken. But I'm surprised. Khalaek and his House were destroyed over a hundred years ago. I thought the ascension of the new House had gone smoothly, that the emotions of that time would have been laid to rest by now."

Vaeren sneered, the expression twisting his face for a moment, then gone, replaced by a troubled brow. He busied himself with the fire pit, drawing the last of the coals close enough to be retrieved.

"Alvritshai have long memories," he said finally. "I was part of Khalaek's House before his betrayal, proud to be Duvoraen. I wore the black and gold of the Phalanx on the battlefield at the Escarpment, fought for Khalaek there and before."

Colin silently adjusted his estimate of Vaeren's age. "You must have been newly risen into the Phalanx to have been at the Escarpment."

"Yes. I was only thirty-three, had been part of the Duvoraen Phalanx for barely a year. When the Evant announced Khalaek's betrayal, when they declared him khai and banished him. . . ." Vaeren paused to stare off into the distance, his face open and easy to read. Colin could see the young Alvritshai soldier he had been, could see an echo of the shock and disbelief that young warrior had felt.

Then Vaeren's face hardened with pain and the anger of the betrayal, and Colin again saw the warrior of the Flame he had first seen in the Sanctuary.

He turned to face Colin. "It felt as if Khalaek had betrayed me personally. I was young; I was newly risen to the Phalanx. It crushed me. And I was not the only one that felt lost and adrift after that."

"But the Evant declared the rising of House Uslaen almost immediately, appointed Saetor as the new lord and gave all of Duvoraen's lands and people over to him."

An echo of the sneer returned. "You can't declare a new lord and House and expect the people to follow so easily. I'd been part of Duvoraen for decades, had been raised to serve Lord Khalaek, been trained to protect him, to revere the black-and-gold uniform, to live under the Eagle's Talon." Vaeren stood abruptly, brandishing the branch, the fire pit between them. "I couldn't do it," he muttered, the sneer seeping into his voice. "I couldn't shrug the Duvoraen House mantle aside so easily. I couldn't simply vow to serve Uslaen after all that I'd done, after spilling my blood for Duvoraen on the battlefield. The Lords of the Evant should not have expected that of us."

"Even though Khalaek had betrayed you, betrayed all of the Alvritshai?"

"That was only what the Lords of the Evant claimed," he said sharply, but his conviction faltered even as he said it, the branch he wielded lowering. "I didn't know what to believe. Neither did anyone else within the Phalanx. None of us understood, but we all know of the games the Lords of the Evant play."

Colin held Vaeren's gaze. "They needed stability. For the treaty with the humans and the dwarren."

Vaeren's glare hardened. "And I needed time to adjust, to come to terms with Khalaek's betrayal."

Colin shifted where he sat. "But you said you were part of House Uslaen when I asked."

Vaeren snorted with derision. "I was. Duvoraen had fallen; Uslaen had risen in its stead. The Evant declared me Uslaen. No one can claim to be of House Duvoraen anymore without the risk of becoming khai themselves, of being shunned by everyone, being cursed or spat upon. Duvoraen is dead. But I couldn't stay with Uslaen, couldn't pretend to a vow to Saetor that I'd never made, not in my heart."

"So you joined the Order."

"Yes. I joined the Flame. What better way to deal with the betrayal of Khalaek and the Evant than to remove myself from them altogether? Nearly a hundred of the Duvoraen Phalanx fled to the Order after the Escarpment. Hundreds of others abandoned Uslaen completely."

Colin frowned. "They shifted to another House?"

Vaeren shook his head with a grim smile. "They left. They vanished, departing in the night, abandoning their watches, their posts. They became khai-roen, a self-imposed exile. They could not serve under Saetor, could not serve under any lord at all."

Colin felt a shudder pass through him. The fact that hundreds of Alvritshai had simply left their House and lands behind, had vanished, disturbed him deeply. He understood being disillusioned, understood feeling betrayed by your own people—the refugee families who'd fled Andover nearly two hundred years ago before the onset of the Feud, families like his own, had been betrayed by the Proprietors in New Andover. That betrayal had driven Colin and his family onto the plains, had ultimately killed them all.

All except for Colin and Walter, and neither of them were exactly human anymore.

He reached across with his right hand and massaged his left arm, where beneath the sleeve of his shirt his skin was mottled black with the poison of the Wells and their Lifeblood. It was an old habit, one that he'd thought he'd broken. With a disgusted wince, he snatched his hand away, glanced up to find Vaeren watching him intently.

"Where did they go?" he asked, his voice harsher than he'd intended. "Where are the Alvritshai who abandoned Uslaen now?"

Vaeren shrugged. "No one knows."

The unease Colin felt sank deeper into his chest. He held Vaeren's gaze a moment longer, then motioned with his soot-stained hands toward the fire pit and the wood. "We should get the fire started."

Ten minutes later, he stepped from the hut as a thin, white smoke began to drift from beneath the small aperture in the roof. Aeren, Eraeth, and Siobhaen were still grooming the horses, Aeren talking quietly with Siobhaen, although it didn't appear Siobhaen was participating much. Eraeth shot Colin an irritated look and shook his head slightly. At the same time, a burst of laughter echoed from the woods south of the road. Petraen and two members of Aeren's Phalanx approached, ducking under the low-hanging branches of the trees, arms laden with firewood. All three were chatting amiably, Petraen grinning as he related some story about his brother and himself stealing apples from a neighbor's orchard.

"—and then Boreaus took off as if Aielan Herself had lit a fire under his ass, leaving me behind with the sack of apples," Petraen said as Colin stepped to one side, allowing the three into the hut. "I scrambled as fast as I could, but the sack got caught on the rail fence and I couldn't get it free. The next thing I knew the overseer's hand dug into my shoulder and jerked me back—"

The door to the hut closed, cutting off the words.

Colin looked down at his blackened hands, then moved toward the stream to one side, stepping over the smoothed rocks to the water's edge. He shoved back the sleeves of his shirt, ignored the swirling darkness that seethed beneath the exposed skin on both arms, and plunged his hands into the water with a sudden sharp breath. The frigid water numbed his fingers immediately, but he scrubbed at the greasy soot nonetheless.

"That won't come off with water."

Colin drew his hands out of the water and shook them vigorously, snapping his fingers in an attempt to get the blood flowing again. "I'm used to having darkened skin," he said, drying his hands on the cloth of his shirt, leaving black smudges behind. Eraeth's eyebrow rose at the comment, but he said nothing. Colin motioned toward Siobhaen and Aeren, the two tying the horses up near the hut. "No luck with Siobhaen?"

Eraeth grimaced. "She responds to your questions, but she reveals nothing. She's too guarded."

Another bout of laughter, muted by the hut's walls, broke through the gurgle of the stream.

"At least one of the Flame has opened up," Colin said.

"Vaeren revealed nothing?"

"More than I expected, actually. He's originally from House Duvoraen. He joined the Order rather than become a permanent part of Uslaen."

"Many chose that path after the Escarpment and the banishment."

"He also claims that many Alvritshai abandoned their House and lands altogether."

The Protector shifted awkwardly, then said grudgingly,

"It's not something that is spoken of. No lord wants to admit that the members of his House would rather choose exile than to serve beneath him. And most Alvritshai refuse to speak of the khai-roen at all. I'm surprised Vaeren mentioned it."

Colin began climbing the rocks back to the roadway, Eraeth reaching forward to pull him up the last stretch. "I think Vaeren nearly chose that path for himself."

Petraen emerged from the hut and gave a shout, catching their attention as both Boreaus and the last Phalanx appeared, the Flame with a few squirrels held by the tail, Aeren's guardsman with a rabbit and some type of fowl.

"Looks like we'll have fresh meat tonight," Eraeth said.

They headed toward the hut as Aeren and Siobhaen joined the returning hunters. Petraen clapped his brother on the back and took the squirrels from him, the two settling in near the stream with the rest of Aeren's Phalanx to gut them for roasting. Siobhaen sent the two brothers a sharp look of disapproval as they bantered with the Rhyssal House men, but they pointedly ignored her. After a moment, she shook her head and entered the hut.

"They don't act like Alvritshai," Colin said, keeping his voice low, his eyes on the two brothers.

Eraeth grimaced. "They are more Alvritshai than you realize. You've dealt mostly with the Lords of the Evant and their Phalanx. The lords are more rigid and formal than the commoners, and more guarded with their emotions. And the Phalanx are trained to formality, since they will be serving their lord and representing the House. The commoners are much more . . . relaxed."

Colin smiled. "I see."

Eraeth scowled. "They're still more respectable than you humans!"

"Who's more respectable than humans?" Aeren asked sharply. He'd waited for them at the door of the hut as they approached and now shot Eraeth a look similar to the one Soibhaen had given the brothers earlier.

Eraeth drew himself up stiffly. "No one is more respectable than humans, Lord Aeren."

Aeren glared at him with suspicious reproach, then nodded. "Very well." He gave Eraeth one last look, then pushed through the hut's door and inside.

Vaeren and Siobhaen had already split the room into two sections, the saddlebags of the Flame on one side, room for the Rhyssal House on the other. Vaeren had prepared the flames for spits, the fire crackling, embers fluttering upward as he tossed on another few branches. The smell of smoke had permeated the entire hut, the heat driving out the musty dampness of the stone.

Aeren, Eraeth, and Colin began settling in on the Rhyssal House side, laying out pallets on the stone benches, Eraeth sitting, legs crossed beneath him, and removing his cattan. He began cleaning the blade with a soft cloth, Vaeren watching from the far side of the fire. Siobhaen removed a small dagger and whetstone, the scrape of metal against stone echoing harshly in the small hut. The rest of the group returned, Petraen and Boreaus bearing dinner already on spits. They set them over the fire, Petraen retrieving the bread they'd been given and handing it out, Boreaus turning the spitted animals.

The enticing scent of roasted meat filled the room, thick and heavy, making Colin's stomach growl. He took the bread from Petraen as he passed and bit into it. He leaned back against the stone of the wall and closed his eyes as he chewed, listening to the schick of Siobhaen's dagger, the banter between Petraen and the rest of the Rhyssal Phalanx, the softer conversation between Aeren and Eraeth.

Then, when the sounds and smells and warmth had almost lulled Colin into a light sleep, the flutter of a pipe broke through the general noise.

Colin opened his eyes to find Petraen sitting across the fire from him, the pipe drawn to his mouth, his fingers playing lightly over the holes down its length. He ran through a series of runs, the pipe's sound hollow and playful, lower in tone than Colin would have expected. At the spit, Boreaus shook his head and sprinkled some kind of herb onto the charring meat. The fire sizzled as grease dripped from the carcasses.

Warmed up, Petraen hesitated, then launched into something more serious, the tune vaguely familiar.

Siobhaen stopped sharpening her dagger, set it aside, and began singing.

Colin shifted forward as her voice and that of the pipe drowned out the fire and the cooking meat. The tale of how Aielan's Light had guided a grieving young woman to her lover's side on an ancient battlefield, only to find him still alive though gravely wounded, unfolded slowly, hauntingly.

When the last notes faded, the woman having saved her lover's life, everyone in the hut sat motionless, staring at Siobhaen. Colin's heart ached with the woman's struggle, but nothing rivaled the shock he felt and saw on the others' faces at the raw emotion that had been in Siobhaen's voice. This was not the Siobhaen that Colin had known on the journey to Artillien, or the days since.

"That was excellently sung," Aeren said quietly, breaking the silence.

Siobhaen tensed, as if suddenly realizing what she'd done. Colin thought she would draw the mantle of the hardnosed Order of the Flame about her again, withdrawing herself from the group, but instead she relaxed, her shoulders dropping.

"Thank you," she said, nodding toward Aeren with a small smile. "Alfaen's tale has always been one of my favorites."

"Because Aielan guided her?"

"No. Most of the songs of the battles and times before the Abandonment of the northern reaches are about death and grief and loss. This one is different. She finds Torrain alive, in time to save him."

They considered this in silence, and then Boreaus swore, lurching forward to grab one of the spits and jerk it from the fire before one of the blackened squirrels could slide into the flames. He hissed as the heat seared his hands, shifting the hot spit from one hand to the other until it cooled enough he could tear a piece of the meat off and taste it.

He grinned. "Time to feast."

He began slicing chunks free and handing them out, Vaeren moving to grab the second spit. Colin nearly moaned as he bit into the succulent meat, juice dribbling down his chin and through his fingers. He began sucking his fingers clean when he suddenly noticed everyone watching him, Vaeren with thinly veiled disgust, Petraen and Boreaus with grins.

They were all eating meticulously, almost formally, picking the bones clean with their fingers or the blades of small knives, even the two brothers. No juice dripped from their chins, although it did glisten in the firelight on their fingers.

Colin slurped his last finger clean noisily. "I refuse to be anything but human," he said.

Vaeren glanced toward Aeren and Eraeth, both with studiously blank faces. "I don't understand why you associate with him."

Eraeth shrugged. "He has his uses."

Aeren smiled as Colin gaped in mild affront, but then his face turned serious. "You said we were close to the pass. I have never heard of this pass, nor of this tunnel into the Alvritshai halls beneath the mountain. Caercaern was supposed to be the only path from the northern reaches to the south over the Hauttaeren Mountains."

Everyone turned to Colin. "The Tamaells since before

the time of the Abandonment have kept the secret of this one entrance well. It has a rather dark and deadly history. I found mention of it in some of the oldest records in the Sanctuary, in journals and pages that nearly crumbled apart in my hands. I'm not even certain that Tamaell Thaedoren knows of it."

"The secret has been kept from even the Evant?" Aeren asked with a frown.

"As far as I can tell. Its purpose, and what it was used for, is not something that the Tamaell or the lords of that time would have been proud of."

"What was it used for?" Vaeren asked bluntly.

Colin shifted where he sat, frowning as he thought back to reading those pages, sitting in the depths of the Sanctuary's archives, surrounded by thousands upon thousands of dusty books and loose sheaves of writings. "It was carved out of the mountain in an attempt to betray Cortaemall, the Tamaell of the time."

One of the Rhyssal Phalanx gasped. "But Cortaemall was one of the most revered Tamaells of that age!"

Aeren nodded thoughtfully. "Which is perhaps why what happened at the pass has been suppressed."

"Tell us what happened," Vaeren said.

Colin hesitated. Even though there were no windows, he could sense that night had fallen, that it was already late. "It's a long story."

"You had us stop early," Vaeren countered.

Colin sighed. "Very well." He leaned back against the wall and gathered his thoughts as one of the Rhyssal guardsmen rose and left to check up on the horses outside. The frigid night air gusted into the hut, set the flames of the fire flapping, but no one stirred even when the guardsman returned.

"Gaurraenan's Pass was named after a Lord of the Evant," he began, letting his voice lower as he shifted into a more comfortable position. "A lord with ambition and patience. He wanted his House to rise within the Evant, wanted to become Tamaell."

"Like Khalaek," Eraeth interjected.

Colin turned in surprise, but Eraeth wasn't looking at him. The Protector was watching Vaeren, the caitan of the Flame gazing down at his hands where he sat against the wall across the fire with a frown.

"Yes, but Cortaemall had been Tamaell for a long time and was loved and revered by the Alvritshai. Living in the halls beneath Caercaern, Cortaemall held dominion over all of the northern reaches. The Alvritshai prospered beneath his hands, the area that we now call the White Wastes producing enough food for the hundreds of thousands of Alvritshai that lived there. The great glaciers were far to the north, and the lands abounded with streams and springs, the growing seasons were long, the plains and lakes and forests teeming with herds of deer and antelope, with rabbit and fowl, and with the shaggy beasts called bison.

"Gaurraenan saw no support within the Evant for his ambitions, but as I said, he was a patient man. He knew there was no way to convince the other lords that Cortaemall should be overthrown, knew that the only way to seize the Evant and rule was through subterfuge. He began to ingratiate himself with his fellow lords, rising slowly but surely through the ranks of the Hall of the Evant, closer and closer to the Tamaell. But he knew that no matter how high he rose, he could never become Tamaell with Cortaemall and his sons in power. That's not how the Evant and the ascension of the Tamaell works. Cortaemall's House must fall before a new House can ascend. And so he began the tunnel.

"Within the depths of his halls within the Hauttaeren, he discovered a warren of natural caverns that led to the southern side of the mountains. He decided to finish those tunnels, giving himself passage to the south, and so hired hundreds of masons and miners to widen the passages near his own halls and carve out an exit on the far side, all under the pretense of building a new manse on the flatlands beneath his mountain stronghold. And he built that manse, using the stone from the mines. But the real purpose was the tunnel, wide enough to carry his Phalanx and their supplies southward and up to the pass. None of the other lords would suspect him of tunneling to the south. Everything the Alvritshai needed was there in the northern reaches, and the mountains were too difficult to navigate, the tunnels beneath Caercaern—the only known routes southward—were controlled by Tamaell Cortaemall. The glaciers had not yet begun to creep into the northern reaches to force the Alvritshai off of their lands.

"So Gaurraenan carved his own path to the south, with the intent to take his Phalanx through the tunnels into the southern lands, skirt the mountains, and then back into the depths of Caercaern through the back entrance in secret. He could attack Cortaemall from behind, catch his Phalanx and his House unprepared, kill Cortaemall and his entire family—his wife, daughter, and sons—and ascend in the Evant to take his place."

Vaeren was shaking his head. "It wouldn't work. The southern entrance to Caercaern would have been closed and sealed from the inside. Gaurraenan would never have been able to open the doors from the south."

"There are always those within the House who will betray it and their lord," Eraeth said quietly. "For wealth, for position, or for simple spite."

Everyone shifted uncomfortably, but Colin simply nodded. "Gaurraenan found a few within Cortaemall's Phalanx who were willing to open the seal of the southern portal."

Petraen huffed in disbelief. "Betrayed by his own Phalanx?"

"It was a different time, remember," Aeren said. "The Houses were much larger than they are now. There were more Alvritshai then, at least ten times as many as there are now. The Phalanx of each House was larger as well. The caitans and the lords of the Houses would not have been familiar with the individual members of their own Phalanx, not as they are now. I wonder more how Gaurraenan kept his tunnel secret. Building the manse was a nice subterfuge, but what of the masons and miners who built the tunnel? One of them would have said something."

"Gaurraenen had them killed. As soon as the tunnel was finished, his Phalanx slaughtered them beneath the mountains. Those who worked on the tunnels had lived there since the tunnel was begun. None of them saw the light of day again. Gaurraenen blamed their deaths on a collapse, and ceased construction on the manse immediately out of respect, although it was nearly finished by then."

Petraen scowled as he reached forward to lay another chunk of wood on the fire.

"So what happened?" Siobhaen asked. "We all know Cortaemall wasn't killed by Gaurraenan."

"No, he wasn't." Colin closed his eyes. He sat in silence for a long moment, absorbing the heat from the fire, feeling the chill embedded in the stone at his back, the scent of roast meat still thick in the air. "The reason Cortaemall was so revered, and remained in power for so long, is because he wasn't stupid." He opened his eyes, caught Siobhaen and Vaeren watching him closely. "He knew what Gaurraenan intended, knew of his pretense with the manse, of his tunnel, of his betrayal."

Siobhaen flinched and looked away, troubled. Vaeren's eyes narrowed, creases appearing above the bridge of his nose.

Colin let his gaze drop. "After years upon years of gathering influence within the Evant, rising to its highest ranks, the southern tunnel now complete, Gaurraenan finally felt ready to become Tamaell. He sent word to his contacts within Cortaemall's House, and prepared his Phalanx for the long march to the southern pass. They left at the end of autumn, after the Evant had been called to a close, but before the snows would make traveling the pass with an army at his back impossible. When they finally emerged from the dark depths into the pass, they found it free of snow, the southern lands waiting for them. Gaurraenan took this as a sign, a good omen, and so he marched east. The weather held, and emboldened, he pushed on to the southern entrance of Caercaern.

"It was nothing like the Caercaern of today. There was no city, no walls and tiers and marketplaces and halls. It was simply a tower, where the Sanctuary now sits, on a ledge of stone that jutted out from the side of the mountains behind, a ledge barely large enough to hold two thousand men. On the first day of winter, with dark clouds beginning to emerge from the west, Gaurraenan and his men scrambled up the slopes to this ledge, and found the doors to the entrance at the base of the tower firmly closed. Nailed to those stone doors with iron spikes were the men of Cortaemall's Phalanx who'd betrayed him, the men Gaurraenan had bribed into opening the seal to let him in.

"When he saw this, Gaurraenan felt true fear in his heart for the first time. He'd planned so well, been so patient—he'd thought nothing could go wrong. But seeing the Alvritshai nailed to the doors, seeing their dried blood staining the stone, his confidence shattered. Panic gripped him. He turned to order his Phalanx back to his own halls, back to the pass and the tunnels and safety—

"But it was already too late. From the height of the ledge, from the base of the tower, he turned to find Cortaemall and his House Phalanx emerging from the dense forest below. Ten thousand strong, against Gaurraenan's six thousand,

Gaurraenan realized that Cortaemall meant for there to be no survivors.

"There was only one chance of escape: the passage he had carved beneath his own House.

"Gathering his forces, he charged Cortaemall's men before they could completely organize on the field below, surprising the Tamaell by giving up his advantage on the heights. Cortaemall had thought Gaurraenan would keep hold of the tower and defend the ledge to the last man. He had not planned on Gaurraenan fleeing. But he met the charge and when Gaurraenan gained enough ground to retreat to the west, Cortaemall hounded him with his own men the entire length of the Hauttaeren Mountains. It was no true battle, only skirmishes as one force caught up with the other before it could break away. Thousands fell, on both sides, as Gaurraenan's flight grew more and more desperate. But Cortaemall was relentless, outflanking his army, ambushing them in close valleys, hitting them as they forged rivers and streams, harrying them without end. Until finally Gaurraenan reached the pass that led to his tunnel. He could taste the safety of the passage, even though the pass was now choked with snow. He could smell the darkness of the stone depths of his own halls.

"But Cortaemall was waiting for him. He'd brought the remains of his army, still seven thousand strong, to the pass. And as Gaurraenan and his men broke at the sight of the tunnel entrance—so close—Cortaemall fell upon him.

"It was a vicious battle, Gaurraenan driven mad by desperation, Cortaemall murderously calm. Blood stained the snow of the pass a bright, gaudy red in the pale sunlight of that winter's day, and then the snow and blood churned to mud, trampled as the battle surged back and forth across the narrow valley. Gaurraenan arrived at the pass with only three thousand men remaining, and a thousand of those died within the first hour. The rest were whittled down to a mere five hundred, then a hundred, until those that were left were surrounded completely by Cortaemall's Phalanx. And they were still a thousand paces from the tunnel entrance.

"When Gaurraenan realized he had gained no ground and that the fight was hopeless, he raised his sword high and ordered his men to stop. The battle ground down into silence, and Cortaemall walked across the bloody field toward where Gaurraenan stood. The two stared at each other for a long moment, Gaurraenan exhausted, beaten, Cortaemall's eyes filled with rage. And then Gaurraenan gasped, 'I concede. I surrender.' He threw his sword to the ground at Cortaemall's feet and collapsed to his knees, too weakened to stand.

"Cortaemall stood silently over him, breathing heavily, his face unreadable except for the rage.

"And then he raised his sword with both hands and severed Gaurraenan's head from his body."

Shock filled the eyes of the Flame and those in Aeren's Phalanx.

"Gaurraenan had surrendered," Colin said into the stunned silence. "Cortaemall should have honored that surrender, seized Gaurraenan's House and declared it fallen. He should have banished Gaurraenan, exiled him to the glacial wastes farther north, or abandoned him in the southern lands. It was the honorable thing to do.

"But he didn't.

"Beheading Gaurraenan might have been overlooked, but Cortaemall went even further." He saw Siobhaen shaking her head and thought about her song, about why it had been her favorite, but he continued on. "Cortaemall ordered the hundred that had stood with Gaurraenan on the field in that pass beheaded as well. And then," he said leaning forward, "he took his remaining Phalanx through the tunnel and into the heart of Gaurraenan's House and he slaughtered every man, woman, and child that he found there. He rid himself of Gaurraenan and the stain the lord had made of his House completely.

"He declared Gaurraenan's House ora-khai. He forbid any Alvritshai to speak of it, or its members, for all time."

5

"**D**O YOU KNOW WHAT ora-khai means in Al-vritshai?"

Colin glanced to where Aeren rode beside him. It was an hour after dawn and they were nearing the last village before the group would need to break away from the roadway and begin the ascent to the pass and the halls beneath the mountain. After he'd told the story of Gaurraenan and his House the night before, neither the members of the Flame nor the Rhyssal House had felt the need to converse any longer. They'd all turned in, wrapping themselves in blankets, most of their faces troubled. Colin had stayed awake long after the rest had fallen asleep, and none of them had slept well, tossing and turning on their stone pallets. Colin had kept the fire lit all night, throwing on a log or branch at odd intervals.

He hadn't been able to sleep either, knowing what they would walk into the following day, knowing how it would affect him.

He shrugged his unease aside and addressed Aeren's question instead. "It means 'forgotten.'"

Aeren nodded. "I have to admit that it's not a term I've heard used before, because we have another word for forgotten. But ora-khai," he shook his head grimly, lips pressed tight. "It means more than simply forgotten. Khai means banishment or exile. Adding the ora in front of it means not only banished but purged—from sight, from voice, from thought, from memory. Eradicated as completely as possible, from every facet of life.

"Cortaemall must have been truly enraged to have declared not only Gaurraenan but his entire House ora-khai."

"Enraged," Colin said mildly, "or insane."

Aeren shot him a black look. "Perhaps both," he finally said grudgingly. "The Alvritshai have been raised to believe that Cortaemall was its greatest Tamaell since the dawning of Aielan's Light. It is hard to accept that what you say actually occurred."

"It did," Colin said sharply. "I know it did."

He was hoping he could control what had happened before, that neither Aeren nor the Rhyssal or Flame members would notice anything wrong at all.

When they reached the village, they left their horses at a stable yard, Aeren paying for their keep until their return, even though the Alvritshai—older even than Aeren—nearly fell prostrate at the feet of Vaeren and the rest of the Flame, offering up his services to Aielan. The caitan managed to keep him standing, and through the heavy bowing and genuflecting and muttered prayers learned where in the village they could find clothing and footwear more suited to traveling through snow.

Once provisioned, huddled now in fur-lined jackets with additional layers packed away in their satchels, the group continued west down the road, the woman who'd provided the jackets watching them while shaking her head in consternation.

Hours later, Colin abruptly halted, a prickling sensation coursing down his back. Squinting, he stared to the north, up into the reaches of the mountains, where the jagged, snow-covered peaks gleamed white in the sunlight, the sky free of clouds. The land sloped upward at a gentle angle away from the road, but he could see where it steepened before the tree line, a fold in the land jutting up before leveling out and vanishing behind the rocky side of the mountain.

"Here," he said to himself, his voice soft. He tensed, felt a sheen of sweat on his forehead that didn't come from exertion or the overly-warm jacket, caught the flicker of a shadow out of the corner of his eye, an impression of a figure there and then gone.

He shuddered and turned to find that the rest of the group had halted.

He motioned with his staff. "There. The pass is up there." They looked, faces skeptical. "You can't see the pass itself," he added. "It's hidden behind the outcropping of the mountain. And the entrance to the hall is above the tree line."

"In the snow," Vaeren said.

"Yes. We should climb until we reach the tree line, then make camp. We can get to the hall before nightfall the following day if we leave early and aren't held up by the weather."

No one responded, but a moment later Vaeren motioned toward Colin to take the lead.

It was not yet dusk when they reached the edge of the tree line, although the temperature had dropped sharply. The climb had been steep, the Rhyssal House guards and the two brothers scouting ahead to find the easiest path. The ground was covered with a dense fall of needles, kept free of the worst of the snow by the hanging branches of the cedars. After the first hour, large outcroppings of rock began to cut through the earth, like bones, riddled with moss and lichen. After reaching the tree line, Vaeren and Aeren sent the others out to find game and wood for a fire, while they searched for a suitable flat section of ground for a camp. One of the plinths of stone was wide enough to serve the purpose, once they brushed it free of the nearly foot-deep snow. Eraeth and Siobhaen began collecting heavy boughs, laid down on the hard stone for use as pallets.

Colin stared up toward the pass, still hidden behind a ridge of the mountain, as the others returned with freshly killed rabbit and enough wood to last the night. As their voices rose into the falling dusk behind him, a chill pressed against Colin's skin. He shuddered, then heard someone approaching from behind.

Aeren moved up beside him. "You've been apprehensive all day," he said, looking up through the last of the trees at the heavy fields of snow. "What's bothering you?"

"Nothing that you or the others need be concerned about."

"But there is something?"

Colin dropped his gaze from the pass. He didn't want Aeren or the others to worry, but clearly he hadn't been able to hide his fears as much as he'd thought. "There was much death on these fields of snow, on this ground. That much pain, that much dark and brutal emotion, leaves . . . a taint, an echo."

"I've passed through Aielan's Light," Aeren said. "Lotaern always said it was because I was more sensitive to Her powers, Her workings, than others, so the trial was easier for me. But I've sensed nothing here."

Colin half grunted, half laughed. "I've drunk from the Well. It demands a different kind of price. But I passed through here once before, alone, and survived. I don't expect it to be any more difficult this time."

"Then you should return to the fire. The rabbit is almost done."

"Boreaus does know how to roast a rabbit," Colin said with a false grin.

~

They awoke to a bitter chill the next morning, mist rising up from the valley below in thick sheets. Colin urged everyone to bundle up against the cold and they all donned heavy boots and their fur-lined coats. As soon as they were ready, he led them to the edge of the tree line and into the drifts of snow beyond.

It took them most of the morning to reach the base of the outcropping of stone that cut off the view of the pass, everyone struggling at first, quickly learning the best way to maneuver through the waist-deep snowbanks beyond. They followed in single file behind Colin, who tried to trample as clear a path as he could to make it easier. The worst part was closest to the base of the outcropping, where the land sloped up at its steepest angle. No one spoke, except for soft curses beneath their breath or the occasional cry or grunt as they lost footing. By midmorning, the mist had burned away completely and the sun reflected harshly off the field of white. Vaeren and some of the others tied a thin cloth over their eyes to keep from being blinded.

Colin spent most of the morning darting glances left and right at the slightest movement or shadow. He could feel time pressing up against him, could feel the events of the past gathering, as if they sensed him, knew that he was susceptible to them. But every shadow, every flicker of movement, every half-caught sound turned out to be a cloud overhead, the flutter of a bird's wing as it took flight, or his own imagination. By the time he reached the outcropping of stone and rested one hand flat against the pocked granite, he was cursing himself for creating the tension that strained in his shoulders.

And then he rounded the edge of the outcropping, the jagged plinth of rock towering above him, its peak covered in snow, and found a man waiting.

The Alvritshai stood twenty paces away, his lean face darkened by a vicious frown. Dressed in full leather battle armor emblazoned with intricate leatherwork, he stood with arms crossed, one hand hanging above the pommel of his sheathed sword. His cloak billowed in a nonexistent wind in the lee of the rock, his hair blowing back from his face. As Colin drew up short, one hand still against the frigid rock to one side, he noted that the Alvritshai was taller than those he knew, the heraldry and armor more archaic, even the bone structure of the man's face subtly different.

But what struck him the most was the palpable anger he felt on the air and saw in the man's eyes. He drew in a sharp breath, unconsciously brought his staff forward and across his body defensively.

They stared at each other. Distantly, Colin heard the faintest echo of swords clashing, of men screaming. Behind, he heard Eraeth and Vaeren gasping as they drew nearer. The sounds of the battle escalated, someone roaring in rage, and behind the lone figure Colin suddenly caught a shudder of movement. A thousand men surged forward. A battle cry rose into the chill winter air. Pennants snapped in a harsh wind as thousands of feet churned the snow-covered fields of the pass into mud—

"What is it?" Eraeth said at Colin's side.

Colin blinked and the vision of the past vanished, the Alvritshai lord who had stood watching him with such anger and hatred gone. The snow where he had stood was untouched.

Colin exhaled, the sound harsh, but not as tortured as Eraeth's own breath. Vaeren didn't fare any better, coming up on the other side. They both stared out over the wide field of snow that had opened up before them, the mountains rising to either side, but dipping down in a shallow saddle of land between two of the peaks—a saddle that hadn't been visible from the valley below.

"It's the pass," Colin said, motioning with his staff.

Eraeth frowned out at the expanse, then back at Colin.

"There was something more," he said. "You looked troubled when I approached."

Catching the Protector's gaze, Colin realized Aeren had told him of their conversation the night before. A part of him was irritated, but he should have known.

"I'm fine."

Eraeth looked doubtful, the rest of the group gathering behind them. Vaeren merely said, "The weather's held, but I'd rather be inside before the storm hits."

"What storm?" Petraen asked.

"The one some of us can taste on the air," Siobhaen answered.

"It'll hit before dark," Vaeren added, then turned to Colin. "So where's the entrance to these halls?"

Colin pointed unerringly to where the snow drifted up the side of the peak to their left. "Up there, near the far side of the pass. I'm certain we'll have to dig it out. The drifts there are deep."

"If it's on the other side of the pass, why can't we simply descend from there rather than use the halls?"

"Because the route on the far side is too treacherous to risk in winter, or even spring. Especially with a storm coming."

Vaeren grunted, then pushed away toward the pass. The slope here was gentler, making it easier to plow through the snowpack.

Colin watched silently as the majority of the group ranged out ahead of him, no longer single file. He waited for the figure to return, for the echoes of the battle to reassert themselves, but nothing happened. Yet he didn't relax.

"So it's started?" Aeren asked. He'd stayed behind with Eraeth.

"Yes. It's not as bad as I'd feared it would be." He caught Aeren's gaze. "But I'm certain it will get worse before we've reached the other side."

Without waiting for a response, he sank his staff into the snow ahead and stepped forward.

Clouds began to rush in overhead, heavy and black and threatening. The taste of the storm had changed into a prickling weight on the air, but Colin ignored it as he searched the edge of the pass for the telltale markings on the stone of the mountain that would indicate where the stone had been mined. In the end, it was an echo of the past that led him to the correct location, the snow high enough to cover all evidence of the tunnel's mouth. But the snow couldn't hide the stream of Alvritshai warriors in ancient armor as they slaughtered the last of Lord Gaurraenan's men, then formed up in solid ranks before the opening and marched inside. Colin shuddered, a wave of sickening heat passing through him, like that of a fever. He shoved the sensation away as he pointed with the staff and said, "There. Dig there," then spent some time regaining his composure. He waved Eraeth's concerned look away curtly.

Snow had begun to fall—light and fine—by the time they'd dug enough to reveal the top of the tunnel's entrance. No intricately carved mantle or steps marked it; Gaurraenan hadn't been interested in art or architecture. The rock around the door was rough, chisel marks plain, smoothed only by the elements. Twenty feet wide, the door itself was a single stone, its face also rough, without markings, but Colin knew it was finely crafted. As soon as it was free, he stepped forward to where Vaeren inspected the crack between door and mountain, the others clustering behind him.

"How do we open it?" Vaeren asked. One hand brushed lightly across the door's surface.

Colin smiled. "We push. It isn't locked or warded or sealed. Gaurraenan never expected to use it more than once, and Cortaemall sealed the halls from the far side to keep the Alvritshai in the north out. He didn't feel the need to seal this side."

"But it will take all of us to move a door of this size!" one of Aeren's Phalanx exclaimed.

"Gaurraenan was practical, but not stupid. The door is weighted. I would never have been able to come this way the last time if it weren't. We only need to get it started."

Colin set his hands to the door, Vaeren and a few others following suit, even though Colin could have done it himself, and then they shoved, hard.

With a hiss, the ice that had formed between the door and the mountain cracked, showering them with fine crystals, but then the heavy stone began to shift, grating against dust and debris on the floor on the inside as it moved. A gust of air blew past Colin's face, smelling of cold granite, dry and ancient, and something deeper, something darker, like fresh blood. He glanced around to see if anyone else had noticed it, but all of the Alvritshai were leaning forward, peering into the darkness beyond. Vaeren actually stepped forward to the edge of the weak light, his hands on his hips, then turned back.

"We'll need the torches."

Colin stepped out of the escalating winds of the storm and stood beside Vaeren as the guardsmen scrambled to unpack the torches. The smell of fresh blood grew stronger inside the entrance and Colin swallowed against rising nausea. Vaeren watched him as he stepped out beyond the light, frowning as he vanished into the darkness. The guardsmen searched for him, shifting uncomfortably, then stilled when Colin spoke.

"I've been here before, remember?" Colin said, humor coloring his voice. "I know the tunnel proceeds straight for about a hundred feet, then begins to slope downward. We won't reach the first set of stairs for another hour."

Vaeren scowled.

Behind him, light flared as one of the torches caught, harsh yellow flame flickering in the gusts from the doorway.

Two more followed, the darkness receding enough to reveal Colin.

"We'll need to move swiftly if we want to have enough torches left for the return trip," he said.

The halls were empty, barren, and uninteresting for the first day, the tunnel carved from the rock with no attention paid to aesthetics or elegance. It had had a single purpose: to take Lord Gaurraenan's Phalanx to the southern edge of the mountains. That purpose could be seen in the sharp edges of the cut stone, in the crudeness of the stairs as they descended, in the abrupt change in the path as the ancient quarrymen ran into impediments and obstructions in the mountain itself. At one point the tunnel veered away sharply, curving around a wall of what appeared to be ice, but was actually some kind of crystal, veined in blues and greens that glowed in the light of the torches. Clear in places, it almost seemed as if something were moving deep within the crystal, although no one could tell if that were true or if it were simply shadows caught by the refracting light. Later, the tunnel opened up into a huge cavern, circling a wide pit on one side, the entire room smooth, as if it had been hollowed out by running water. When they reached the far side of the immense room, they found a waterfall emerging from a crack in the granite near the room's ceiling, the snowmelt pouring down and across the floor to the open pit, where it vanished in another fall. They forded the stream, the stone on either side slick with hoarfrost and ice, and entered the tunnel on the far side.

The smell of blood wavered as they moved, sometimes strong enough Colin nearly gagged, at other times fading so that he barely noticed it. It became obvious he was the only one who sensed it. As in the pass, he caught flickers of Tamaell Cortaemall's men as they made their way along the same path. They'd camped in the enormous cavern, their fires flaring in the darkness to either side of Colin's small group, the phantom light highlighting the ancient Alvritshai warriors' angular faces in sharp relief. Colin felt their presence against his skin, the same shudders he'd felt in the pass coursing through his body as they moved through the insubstantial camp. Sweat broke out on his back, prickled in his armpits and on his neck, but he tried to shrug the sensations aside. When he'd traveled this way before, over sixty years ago, the resurgence of these events hadn't been so powerful. He'd caught glimpses of the battle in the pass, heard the clash and screams of the fighting, smelled the blood and death on the air. But inside the tunnel, he'd sensed nothing until he'd reached the bridge across the underground river and the halls of Gaurraenan's House on the far side.

That's where the slaughter had truly begun, where the hatred and death had scarred the stone enough to leave a permanent echo.

When they passed beneath an intricately carved arch—Alvritshai words etched into the stone high above in a style and form long dead—a draft of wind blew from the tunnel ahead, carrying with it the stench of slaughter.

Colin gasped, drew in another breath unconsciously, then gagged and staggered to the side of the tunnel, nearly collapsing. Through the sound of rising screams, he heard someone cry out, heard scrambling feet, and then he was surrounded, someone holding his arm. He realized he'd bent forward at the waist and knees, his entire body trembling.

"What is it?" someone barked—Vaeren or Petraen, he couldn't tell through the echoing shouts from the tunnel ahead. "What's happening?"

"It's worse than I thought it would be," Colin gasped. "Far, far worse."

"What do you mean? What's worse?"

Colin looked up into Aeren's face, the lord kneeling in front of him. But it hadn't been Aeren who spoke. Eraeth was the one holding his arm, keeping him from slipping to the floor entirely. "They're dying," he said, his voice weak and shaking. "I can hear them dying."

Aeren frowned, glanced toward Eraeth.

"What's he talking about?" Vaeren demanded. He stood behind Aeren, arms crossed over his chest as he glared down at them all uncertainly. The rest of the Phalanx and the Flame clustered behind him, the torches held high.

Colin tried to straighten, managed to rise using Eraeth's help. He met Vaeren's eyes, drew a few breaths to steady himself, then said harshly, "When I came through here before, I could see what had happened in the past. I could see Cortaemall's slaughter of the House of Gaurraenan. I could smell it, hear it, practically taste it. Back then, I managed to force myself to continue. But this time. . . ." He drew in a ragged breath. "I can already smell the carnage. I can already hear the screams of the dying. And we haven't even reached the bridge that leads into the main halls yet."

"Are you saying that we're surrounded by spirits? That the Gaurraenen dead are waiting for us?" The derision in Vaeren's voice held the faintest tinge of fear. Some of those behind him shuffled and glanced down the black tunnel ahead of them, drawing closer to the torchlight.

"No," Colin said, setting his staff on the floor for support and pushing away from the wall. After a moment, Eraeth let Colin's arm go, but he didn't step back. "These aren't ghosts. They aren't reenacting the past. *What I'm seeing is the past.*"

Vaeren stepped back from the vehemence in Colin's voice, his eyes widening, even though Colin trembled as he spoke.

"I didn't realize that was how it worked," Siobhaen said into the awkward silence that followed.

Colin glanced toward her. "It isn't." He frowned, his eyes ranging over them all. "Normally I control where I am, how far back I go, what I want to see. But since the battle at the Escarpment, there have been places where I've seen the past without willing it. Usually places where there were many deaths, but also where something incredibly painful or horrific occurred."

"But why since then? Why not before?"

Even though it was Siobhaen who spoke, Colin turned to Aeren. "I think it's because I've spent so much more time with the Well. Its taint has spread. I can feel it sinking deeper inside me."

Someone muttered, "Shaeveran," but no one else spoke.

Aeren rose and caught Eraeth's gaze, his look troubled. "So what do you suggest? Should we turn back? You are the only one who knows the way through the halls of Gaurraenan's House."

"No," Vaeren barked. "We are not turning back." At Eraeth's glare, he stiffened. "It would add weeks to the journey!"

Before Eraeth could respond, Colin cut in. "Vaeren is right. We can't turn back. I don't know what the return of the storms to the plains means yet, but we can't afford to waste any time finding out. Not if they are already as violent as they seemed from the roof of the Sanctuary." He drew himself up, squared his shoulders. "I survived this once before, I can survive it again." At the looks of doubt, he scowled. "I was caught by surprise. I wasn't expecting it to happen this soon. I wasn't prepared. But now I'm on my guard."

He wished he felt as confident as his voice sounded. He could still smell the blood, its taint slick in his throat. The screams had died down slightly. But he knew it would be rougher once they were within the halls.

Everyone hesitated. But then Vaeren said, "Let's move."

They struck out again, moving faster than before, Colin trying to breathe shallowly as he suppressed the urge to gag. He tasted bile at the back of his throat, but swallowed it down. Aeren and Eraeth stayed close, the others split both ahead and behind. As they drew closer to the end of the tunnel and the bridge that crossed the underground river that marked the boundary of the Alvritshai halls, the air thickened and grew dense. The screams from ahead grew louder. Sweat sheened his face as he fought against the echoes, against their intrusion into the present that only he could see. The tremors that passed through his body increased, as if he were locked in the throes of a fever.

A moment before they emerged onto the landing of the bridge, he drew in a sharp breath. The tunnel's walls were splashed with blood, the dark reddish sprays glistening in the torchlight, dripping down the stone. Alvritshai guardsmen lay on the floor on all sides, wearing the ancient armor of House Gaurraenan, their throats slit. They'd been caught by surprise.

Then the tunnel ended, and Colin drew up short. Vaeren and Siobhaen were already halfway across the bridge, the light of their torches illuminating the far walls.

The river coursed through a massive cavern that stretched out to either side before narrowing into a low passage, the water churning just beneath the ceiling where it narrowed. But the roar of the water wasn't enough to drown out the sounds of battle coming from the numerous openings on the far cavern wall. Balconies, windows, and doors had been cut into the stone, some of the openings connected to each other by stairs and walkways jutting out from the main wall. The massive bridge—at least forty feet wide—arched out over the raging waters and drove into a doorway twice the size of the one they'd used in the pass to enter the tunnel. Unlike the tunnel's entrance, these doors were finely crafted, chiseled into a pointed arch at least fifty feet high, the stone carved into many smaller arcs, all reaching from the center of the door to the sides. The doors stood open, one slightly wider than the other.

Bodies were strewn everywhere—on the landing, along the bridge, and in the doorway. Colin saw where they had fallen, their blood pooling and flowing along the floor, faces staring up into the torchlight from the lanterns and sconces that lit the bridge and the wall of windows and balconies beyond. Shadowy figures played along the walls in that light as the fighting raged in the halls and corridors beyond.

But he also saw what remained of the bodies now—the armor that appeared collapsed, the body inside it decayed, nothing left but bones. The stone beneath was stained black where the blood had dried and flaked away.

"They didn't burn them," Aeren said. The anger in his voice startled Colin out of his paralysis. "They didn't release them to Aielan's Light. They left them here to rot. No wonder you can still see them, can still feel their pain. They were never returned to Aielan!"

"Cortaemall had declared them ora-khai," Colin said. "They no longer deserved Aielan's Light."

Aeren shot him a vicious glare. "These people were innocents," he spat.

"Not in Cortaemall's eyes." Colin swayed where he stood, light-headed. He sucked in a sharp breath and caught himself. He motioned Aeren and Eraeth forward. "We should move. Vaeren is already at the main door."

They ran across the bridge, Aeren's escort following behind, dodging the scatter of the long dead. Colin tried to stay clear of the blood as well, tried not to look at the men as he passed. But the stench—

He shook his head to clear it and charged through the massive doors.

Inside, it was worse. Bodies were piled everywhere, not just guardsmen, but women and children, cut down where

they stood, thrown against walls, into corners, thrust out of
the way. Occasionally, a warrior in blue-tinted armor lay
among the dead, one of Cortaemall's men, but for the most
part the dead wore the armor of Gaurraenan, or the casual
dress of the time, women with lots of drapery and hanging
folds to their dresses, the men with boots and loose pants
and shirts embroidered down the lengths of the arms and
legs. In the close confines of the corridors and halls, the reek
was cloying, enough that Colin breathed through his mouth,
one hand raised to his face. His eyes began to water, but he
raced forward, taking the lead even as Vaeren, Siobhaen,
and the others in front slowed. He felt the urge to brandish
his staff as the sounds of fighting grew louder and closer,
but he swore to himself and kept moving. He couldn't ignore the fact that the dead around him were growing
fresher. Blood had not pooled and settled yet, was still seeping from new wounds. As they passed door after door, he
caught glimpses of Alvritshai fighting each other out of the
corner of his eye, heard women shrieking, men bellowing,
children crying. He drew his sleeve across his sweaty face to
clear his eyes, noticed that some of the bodies on the floor
to either side were now moving, not yet dead. One Alvritshai reached out as he passed, blood bubbling from his
mouth; another sucked in air through a stab wound in the
chest, hand clutched over his heart, attempting to keep the
wound closed.

And then they lurched down a widening stairwell and
out into a grand hall.

Columns rose from floor to ceiling, thick and etched with
hundreds of names and dates and deeds, a history of House
Gaurraenan. The walls were lined with massive tapestries,
interspersed with banners and paintings, urns and statues.
The marble floor was coated with blood, bodies everywhere. At the far end of the hall, where three thrones stood,
the level of the floor rising toward them in wide steps, the

Cortaemall were battling a large force of the Gaurraenan Phalanx.

Even in the one swift glance, Colin could see the fight was hopeless. There was nowhere for the Gaurraenan to retreat to, nowhere for them to run. Their desperation was as thick on the air as the stench of death.

"Aielan's Light," Vaeren breathed at Colin's shoulder.

Colin blinked, and saw the hall as it stood now, littered with the remains of thousands of dead. The tapestries were gone, the statues and urns broken. The columns containing the history of the House had been mauled, two damaged so badly they'd shattered, chunks of stone scattered around the jagged stump of the base.

Reality wavered and the past reasserted itself, a woman's scream rising to echo through the chamber. She cowered near one of the thrones, the guardsmen of the House surrounding her. Another woman stood beside her, a band of twisted gold in her hair, her stance regal, her clothes too fine and elegant to be anything but a noble's. The Alvritshai warriors fought savagely to protect her, but she did not flinch from the carnage. She glared out over it, her eyes filled with contempt.

Gaurraenan's wife, Colin realized. The Lady of the House.

Her gaze turned toward him and something inside Colin's stomach seized. He gasped, clutched at his gut, leaned forward over the pain, even as fresh tremors coursed through his body.

"Eraeth!" Vaeren shouted.

Hands grabbed both of his arms beneath the shoulder, tried to raise him upright, but new pain shot through his body.

"We have to stop," Aeren said from somewhere to Colin's left. He could no longer see any of the group, could only see the past, the dead and the dying, the blood and bodies. He could feel their hands, but he couldn't see them. He could barely hear them.

"No," he hissed through clenched teeth. He waved with his staff toward the mouth of the corridor across the long stretch of the hall, then realized they wouldn't be able to see it, not with their torchlight. He could only see it because the entire hall was lit with the burning sconces of the past. "There. Go there."

They didn't hesitate. Lifting him up between them, Vaeren and Eraeth hauled him across the hall, his feet dragging on the floor. He gasped as another wave of pain swept through him, sucked in a ragged breath, heard Siobhaen demand harshly, "What's happening to him? Look at his arms! It looks like he's fading, as if he isn't really there!"

And then they were through the hall, into the corridor beyond, but the pain didn't stop. It escalated and he gasped, "Get me out. Get me out before it catches me completely." Pain lanced through his arms and legs and he cried out, the cry ending in a moan, but he suddenly realized what was happening, why it was so painful. He'd been wrong. He'd thought the past was intruding on the present, that it was surging forward. But it wasn't. The past was trying to drag him back, trying to pull him there, into the horror, into the miasma of death. Somehow, it had become a riptide, an undertow, trying to suck him down into the blackness that Cortaemall had visited upon the place. That's why they could see him, why they reacted to him—the lord in the pass who had glared at him, the lady in the hall. He was actually there. He was caught between the past and the present and it was ripping him apart.

Horror spread through him at the realization and he frantically clawed toward the present. He was nearly completely caught in the past now; he could see nothing of the present, only the carnage of the halls. Even as Eraeth and Vaeren dragged him forward, he saw three Cortaemall Phalanx butchering a mother and two children, all three cowering at the base of a wall, the woman's hands raised imploringly even as the cattans fell. Two more chased a group of servants down a side hall, cutting them down from behind, the women shrieking as they ran. Colin's gorge rose as he tried to draw back, but the only reference he had was the insubstantial hands that pulled him along the corridor.

The hands.

Instead of reaching for the present, he focused on the hands holding him upright, closed his eyes to the death and destruction on all sides, tried to shut his ears to the sounds. He drew in a ragged breath, slowly, through his mouth, and pulled himself toward the pain in his arms and armpit where Eraeth and Vaeren gripped him so tight he could already feel his arms tingling where they'd cut off the circulation. He pushed through that growing numbness, enfolded himself in it, and felt the past receding, the shouts and cries of the hunted in the halls of Gaurraenan growing fainter. Through the prickling of his arms, he heard Aeren commanding the rest of his Phalanx to move faster and realized he hadn't been able to hear them at all a moment before. Hope surging in his chest, he pulled the tingling closer, strove toward it with every beat of his heart, used it as his lifeline to the present. The past began to pull away, but he could feel its greedy undercurrent still attempting to draw him down into its depths. He mentally kicked at it, as if he were truly trapped underwater and struggling upward toward light and air. He felt the pressure of the undertow in his chest, squeezing—

And then, the past wrenched free and he gasped, even as he heard the rest of the party cry out in triumph. Brittle, frigid wind slammed into his face and he sucked it in sharply and opened his eyes. The death grip on his arms and shoulders relaxed.

They stood on an outcropping of stone carved into the

shape of the prow of a ship, stairs descending the sides of the mountain on either side, the steps barely visible through the drifts of heavy snow and layers of ice. Two stone statues—Alvritshai in robes and regal poses, arms stretched out and down in benediction toward the remnants of a huge city on the hills below—stood at the height of the stairs.

Colin tried to gather his feet beneath him, to support himself, but he had no strength left. He collapsed to his knees, the frigid air burning into his lungs. It stung, felt as if it were slicing through his chest, his heart, but he breathed it in deeply, using the sensation to push away the last remnants of the past and anchor himself in the present. He sobbed, felt tears burning cold against his cheeks and at the corners of his eyes.

"We're here," he gasped. "We made it." He sucked in one more deep breath, then murmured, "Welcome to the White Wastes," before the present overwhelmed him and he sagged forward into unconsciousness.

6

COLIN WOKE TO WARMTH.

He gasped and jerked upright, tendrils of a nightmare pulling away from his mind like tentacles, retreating back into the depths of the darkness. He groaned and settled back down, aches coursing up and down his entire body. Without moving, he surveyed the firelight dancing with shadows on the stone ceiling overhead and the wall at his side. The fire crackled, out of sight, but he heard nothing else. No movement, no voices. He breathed in the scent of the fire's cedar smoke, the lingering sizzle of fat from some animal cooked over flame, and beneath all of that the sharp taint of cold.

"The city," he whispered to himself. "We've made camp in Taeraenfall."

"We have."

Colin flinched away from the voice, regretted the motion as a muscle in his neck spasmed. He rubbed at it with one free hand as he turned and glared at Aeren. "I didn't think anyone was here."

Aeren smiled. "I'm the only one at the moment. The others are out hunting, or trying to find more wood for the fire. The White Wastes are well named. Nearly everything is covered in foot upon foot of snow. There are few trees, mostly firs and cedars, but there is game — snow hare and squirrel, some fowl, lynx and bobcat."

"And wolves."

Aeren nodded at the warning in Colin's voice. "We've heard the wolves, but for now they are keeping their distance."

Colin grunted and swung his legs off the raised platform they'd used as a pallet. He moved slowly, then began massaging his legs and shoulders. "How long have we been here?"

"Two days. When you collapsed at the top of the stairs above the city, we nearly made camp there. But it was too exposed, and no one wanted to risk taking you back inside the shelter of the halls. We spent the next day descending to the city and searching for a suitable place to make camp. When you didn't recover the following day, we began hunting."

"I can smell something roasted."

Aeren rose and rounded the fire, set in the center of the floor and surrounded by stone pillaged from the ruins. He dug in a pack and produced a grease-stained cloth.

Colin's stomach growled as Aeren made his way to his side, uncovering half of some type of bird, the skin charred black and crackling. "We saved you some," the lord said, handing it over.

Colin didn't hesitate. He ripped a wing from one side and bit into the meat. "Cold," he said as he chewed, "but I don't think I've tasted anything as good."

"Boreaus does have a talent with cook fires."

Aeren watched Colin intently as he ate, his brow furrowed. Tension prickled along Colin's shoulders, but he ignored it until he'd picked the bones of the fowl clean. He sucked the grease from his fingers, then leaned back against the wall with a sigh. His entire body still ached, but the pain had receded.

He caught Aeren's gaze, held it. "What do you want to ask?"

Aeren considered for a moment, then: "What happened back in the halls, in the mountain?"

Colin wasn't certain how much he should tell him; Aeren—and Eraeth—could do nothing to help him. But he'd known them a long time. They were the only family he had left, the only people who cared for him. They deserved an answer.

He sighed again, looked toward the fire. "When I came through the halls before, I caught echoes of what had happened, what Cortaemall had done to Gaurraenan and his House. I thought at the time that I was merely seeing events as they transpired in the past, that the emotions of the time had scarred the stone of the mountain in some way and because of the Lifeblood I could see those scars."

"But that's not what is happening," Aeren said when he paused.

Colin smiled grimly, gave a dark chuckle. "No. I don't think so anymore."

"Then what is it? It was obviously worse this time. And it was more than what you could see or sense. You were being affected by it. At points while we were dragging you out of the hall you appeared almost . . ." he groped for a word, settled reluctantly on, " . . . transparent. Eraeth said that he nearly lost his grip on you, not because he wasn't holding tight enough, but because you simply weren't there."

"Because I wasn't there."

Aeren's eyebrows rose.

Colin stood in frustration, began moving about the room, working strength back into his muscles as he talked. "I originally thought that the events of the past were somehow intruding on the present, but after what happened this time, I think it's the reverse. I think that somehow—

between my use of the Lifeblood and the atrocity of what Cortaemall's men did to Gaurraenan's House—somehow I was being drawn back to those events, forced back there, rather than me using the power of the Well to take myself back as I did at the Escarpment. It was like a massive current, pulling me back to that time. And I know I was there, because the people of that time—Gaurraenan and his wife—they both saw me. They did not know who I was, but they saw me, reacted to me. For brief moments, I was there. Or part of me was, enough that the effort to keep myself here, in the present, and the current trying to draw me back were beginning to tear me apart. If you hadn't dragged me from the hall, I don't think I would have survived. I would have ended up back in the time of Gaurraenan and Cortaemall, more than likely would have been killed during the massacre, since they would have had no idea who or what I was."

Aeren shook his head. "You cannot die, remember? You may have been drawn back to that time, but you would not have died."

Colin thought of the knife he'd created and wondered. "If I had been drawn back there and survived, I'm not certain I could have come back on my own. I may have been trapped there, forced to live through the past five hundred years or more." He shuddered and halted, his hands held out to the warmth of the fire. He suddenly felt cold.

"You may have to face that yet," Aeren said quietly. When Colin glanced up with a frown, he added, "We'll have to return through the hall again eventually, to get back to the southern side."

Colin grimaced. "I was trying not to think about that. I'll deal with that when the time comes."

Aeren nodded as if he'd expected that response, then glanced down to the fire himself, still frowning.

Colin abruptly straightened. "There's something else.

Something more than what happened to me within the mountain that's bothering you."

Aeren hesitated, then reached for two of their heavy jackets, handing one to Colin before shrugging into his own. He motioned Colin toward the entrance to the room, then followed him.

Colin felt the bite of the cold even through his jacket as he ascended the short stair he found beyond, the warmth of the fire vanishing as he rounded a corner. He emerged onto a roof, the building the group had chosen for shelter near the edge of the city. The mountains rose to the south, the massive stone steps that led to the ledge and the entrance to Gaurraenan's halls half obscured by blowing snow, even though the sky overhead was a clear, vivid blue. Colin spun where he stood, Aeren moving away from him as he took in the undulating rooftops of Taeraenfall stretching out on all sides, their flat tops dusted with snow and thick with ice. Evidence of the ravages of time were everywhere, nearly two-thirds of the roofs collapsed, a few of the buildings merely piles of rubble covered with a deep layer of snow. The streets between were heavily drifted. But there were still details in the stonework that stood out—peaked arches stretching over some intersections, finely etched lintels and windowsills, a richly decorated balcony.

Farther to the north, rising above the city at the top of a hill, lay the mansion that Gaurraenan had built using the stone quarried from the mountain as he dug out his tunnel. Some of the exterior walls—built low for aesthetic reasons, not for defense—had crumbled, but the manse itself appeared mostly intact from this distance. Wind blew sheets of loose snow across the vista, but Colin could see the hills as they descended to the plain he knew lay beyond. A wasteland of snow and ice now. If the day had been calmer, he knew he would have been able to see the nearest of the glacial ice packs that were grinding steadily southward.

Eventually, they would reach Taeraenfall, and then the city—and nearly all evidence of the Alvritshai's northern empire—would be destroyed.

He stepped up to Aeren's side at the edge of the rooftop, blinking at the glare of the sun on the mostly white landscape, his exposed skin already raw from the gusts and chill.

"All of the Alvritshai know of their origins here in the north," Aeren said, raising his voice to be heard. "We tell our children stories of our time here, although most of them now come across as legends, rather than histories. But I was an acolyte in the Order. I've read many of the Scripts, know many details that those outside of the Order do not. I know enough of the history of the Alvritshai to know that *that* is not natural." Aeren pointed toward the far distance, northwest of their position.

At first, Colin saw nothing, but the wind came from that direction and made it difficult to see, cutting inside the hood of his jacket. He brought one hand up to shield his face and eyes—

And saw what Aeren must be talking about. He felt his entire body stiffen, his breath caught in his throat. He struggled against the paralysis for a moment, then exhaled harshly, his lungs burning with cold as he sucked in another lungful of air and stepped close to the edge of the roof.

Far to the northwest, lights danced across the frigid wastes. Like the sheets of snow being picked up and blown across the city, the blue-and-green light wavered and drifted across the landscape, rippling and coruscating into deep purples and lighter greens nearly verging on yellow. And like the flames of the fire in the room below, or the mists on the southern side of the mountain, the colors rose and curled, licking toward the sky before fading into nothing.

Colin watched for a long moment, Aeren standing silently behind him. Then he said, "They're like the aurora borealis, the lights you can sometimes see in the night sky here in the north."

"Aielan's Nightdance, yes." Aeren took a step forward. "Except this is not part of the night sky. This is on the ground."

"Have you been watching it the last few days? What have you seen?"

Aeren shrugged. "Nothing extraordinary. It moves across the landscape, both day and night. Sometimes it fades into nothing and for hours the horizon is clear. Other times it has appeared in multiple locations. It's only come to within an hour's walk of the edge of the city, but none of us have risked investigating it in person."

"No." Colin shook his head. Even watching the mysterious lights from this distance, he could feel the back of his neck and shoulders prickling. The lights reminded him of the coruscating colors he could see in the occumaen when he slowed time, and remembered vividly how deadly that rippling phenomenon had been to those who were caught in it. Moiran had barely escaped, with Colin's help. Most of her entourage had not been so lucky.

He shuddered and turned toward Aeren. "Without a closer look, I can't be certain . . . but I think it has to do with the Wells again. It's like the occumaen and the storms on the dwarren plains. We should keep our distance."

"Does it mean that whatever is happening to the sarenavriell has gotten worse?"

"I don't know. These lights could have been here before, and they could have been worse. There's no way to tell. But I don't like it. We need to find the Well as soon as possible. Something is happening, and if it isn't the Wells. . . ." He let the thought trail off. If it wasn't the Wells causing the disturbances, then he didn't know what it could be.

"We can leave as soon as the others return, if you've recovered enough to travel," Aeren said.

Colin shivered as a stronger gust of wind cut through his jacket and touched his skin. "I can manage. Right now, let's get off of this roof and out of the cold."

~

They left the city behind without stopping, skirting the manse and entering the low hills beyond, Vaeren taking the lead and setting a harsh pace. A day later, they emerged from the forest onto a flat that had once been grassland but was now tundra, the grasses sparse, the frozen earth reduced to bare stone in places, the harsh wind keeping it nearly free of snowfall.

Colin raised his hands to shield his eyes from the worst of the wind as the rest of the party pulled out additional clothing to wrap around exposed skin. To the west, the strange sheets of pulsating light that Aeren had shown him from the rooftop in Taeraenfall danced across the flatland, angling north, but still too close for comfort. He slowed time for a moment, to see what the lights looked like, but they didn't appear any different. Perhaps larger, their influence spread out farther, but nothing else significant. Even at this distance he could feel the weight of the power behind them, could catch a taste of the Well, as well as a scent of the dwarren's Confluence.

He'd turned his attention toward the north, where he could see the ominous ice wall of the glaciers—a lighter, ephemeral blue than the washed-out color of the sky near the horizon—when he felt someone grip his arm.

He thought it would be Aeren, was surprised to find Siobhaen staring at him, concern etching her face.

"You . . . faded," she said. "Flickered."

He smiled in reassurance. "I'm fine. I was checking on the lights, trying to see what they were like with time slowed. It wasn't what happened back in Gaurraenan's halls."

Siobhaen's shoulders relaxed and she nodded, stepping away. Colin caught Aeren watching from a distance and shrugged.

A moment later, Vaeren stepped forward. "How far away are we? Where exactly are we headed?" His voice was muffled by the heavy scarf wrapped around his face.

"You can see the glaciers on the horizon, but they're deceptively distant. We'll be there in approximately two or three days, depending."

"Depending on what?" Vaeren asked suspiciously.

"Depending on whether we run into any trouble, such as wolves, or those strange lights, or a storm." Colin shrugged. "After that, it will likely be another day or so until we reach the Well."

"I don't understand how the Well could have been so close to where we used to live and be mostly unknown to us," Siobhaen asked. "We only found references to it in the Scripts. There was no mention of it in the folklore of the time, except in passing. How could it have remained hidden from us? Why wouldn't we have used its power back then?"

"You're assuming that the Well itself contained the Lifeblood back then. It didn't. This is one of the Wells that Walter and the Wraiths reawakened recently. In fact, I think this is the Well that the acolyte Benedine found in his research, that he located for Lord Khalaek."

"How do you know that?" Vaeren asked, tightness in his voice at the mention of his previous lord.

"I saw the rough map that Benedine passed on to Khalaek's aide. Even though I couldn't read the writing at the time, I remember the details of the topography."

"But you said that Khalaek refused to give Walter the information at the Escarpment. How did Walter find out about the Well?"

"Does it matter? He found it, and awakened it." He glared off into the distance, thinking about Walter and the knife wrapped in chain mail in his satchel. "Be careful," he finally said. "And keep your eyes out for game. There are rabbits and such on the tundra, but they are few and far between. If you get a shot, take it."

Then he grabbed his staff and led them onto the flat.

They halted that evening in the lee of a stand of rock, what had once been a watchtower at the corner of two intersecting roads. Heavy cobbles could still be seen, but the continual upheaval of the lands as water froze and thawed over the seasons had buckled and broken many of them, the cracks filled with brown grass. Throughout the night, they heard the howls of distant wolves.

The wind died the following day, the snow it carried settling back to the ground. The sky was cloudless, a vivid wintry blue. Both the Flame and Aeren's Phalanx spread out, searching for game as they moved, but Colin retained the lead, Vaeren close behind him. They were forced to stop early, the shimmering lights that the Alvritshai had begun to call iriaem—ghost lights—skating across the distance between them and the glaciers. The huge wall of ice now filled the horizon, stretching away on either side, even though Colin knew that it was still at least half a day distant. He frowned at it nonetheless, and at Aeren's questioning look said, "It's closer than it was thirty years ago."

The wolves returned that night, close enough that Petraen removed his pipe and began to play, tentatively at first, then louder, as if in competition with the howls from the darkness. Boreaus built up the fire, even though they hadn't brought much wood from the forest with them; no one halted him. Colin watched the iriaem in the distance, the hackles on his neck prickling, his hands closing on the haft of his staff, even as the group broke out in uneasy laughter behind him. He massaged the wood, felt the intricate grain beneath his palm and fingers, felt the life-force inside, but the wolves didn't approach, and the lights that danced on the flatland never drew near. The rest of the party settled down, the Phalanx taking the watch tonight.

An hour after the iriaem faded into the distance to the east, the real aurora borealis—Aiean's Nightdance—appeared in the skies above. Colin watched the much grander and somehow more mysterious lights at the Phalanx member's side, neither one of them speaking.

The next morning, the entire group was somber, the somewhat relaxed attitude of the night before gone as they focused on Colin. Blades were kept within easy reach, ready to be drawn. It took a moment for Colin to realize why: they'd be reaching the glacier's wall and no one knew what to expect.

"Let's go," he said, and then struck out.

No one responded, and everyone stayed close, on guard. Colin felt their wariness crawling across his back as he walked, tried to shrug it away. But he didn't know what to expect either. He only knew that the wards he'd set in place the last time he'd been here were still active and undisturbed the last time he'd checked. Yet he still felt uneasy

The glacial wall approached slowly, looming higher and higher into the sky, cracked and ragged at the edges, like a rocky shoreline. To either side, huge chunks of ice had broken free and plummeted to the tundra below. A ridge of stone and dirt and other debris had been plowed up at the base of the cliffs, while high above they could see a layer of fresh snow, the ice an iridescent blue beneath it in the sunlight.

The cliffs reminded Colin of the stone Bluff on the plains far to the south and he shuddered. He didn't have fond memories of the Bluff.

Near midafternoon, he noticed the Order and the Phalanx getting edgy, their unconscious defensive group tightening up, their faces tense, hands resting more and more on the handles of their cattans.

Then Petraen halted sharply and half drew his blade, crying out in warning.

"What is it?" Vaeren snapped from behind Colin, his own hand on his blade.

To the side, Eraeth and one of the Phalanx scanned the horizon where Petraen had focused, Boreaus in a half crouch . . . but Petraen was already relaxing. He let his blade slide back into its sheath, frowning as he shook his head and straightened.

"It's . . . nothing. I thought I saw something."

"What?" Vaeren demanded, stepping forward. "Where?"

Petraen motioned with one hand toward the base of the ice face. "Movement to the west, near that collapsed section. I caught it out of the corner of my eye. But there's nothing there."

Everyone considered the scattered chunks of ice he'd indicated, Boreaus rising slowly from his guarded crouch, until Colin said, "It might be the ward."

"What do you mean?" Eraeth asked. He kept glancing toward the debris.

"We're close enough to the ward for it to begin affecting all of you. It's placed on the ice wall."

"So the Well is close?" Vaeren moved forward as he spoke, out ahead of Colin, searching the wall of ice as if looking for the Well itself.

"No, but the entrance to the cavern that will take us to it is." He moved to Vaeren's side, but spoke to the entire group. "Stay here. You're all already on edge, if you get any closer, it will only get worse as the ward takes hold of you. I'll go see if it has been disturbed or tested in any way, then come back to retrieve you once I've taken it down."

He didn't wait for their response, but headed straight toward the nearest section of the glacier and what looked like a solid wall of ice. But it wasn't solid—that was an effect of the ward. He could see the layers of the ward as he approached, the air growing colder as he passed into the shadow beneath the immense glacier, ice closing in around him. Long ago, he'd thought the Bluff was immense, but this was staggering. He could no longer see the top of the ice cliff, even leaning backward and staring straight up, but he didn't try. He focused on the ward instead, on the illusion of solidness that he'd placed over the entrance to the cavern. Nothing seemed to have disturbed the threads of power he'd laid down at its center. The knot he'd used to tie it off was still secure.

He stood back, glanced toward where the rest of the group huddled on the open tundra watching him, then back to the walls. Grunting, he began to follow the threads that spun out from the central knot, checking each one carefully as he moved, first right, then left.

Nothing. No thread was out of place, no tie touched. As far as he could tell, no one had attempted to pass the ward, and he knew this was the only approach to the Well. He'd made certain of that before he'd left.

Reaching forward, he pulled at the knot in the center and watched the entire ward unravel, the threads relaxing and settling back into their natural shape. As they did, the ice wall in front of him shimmered and collapsed, revealing the gaping mouth of a cavern. Someone from the group behind shouted as it happened, even as Colin felt the tendrils of tension that had radiated out from the ward and set the rest of the group on edge release.

He turned and motioned Vaeren and the others forward. As Aeren and Eraeth approached, he said, "The ward was intact and untouched. No one has been here, as I said back in Caercaern. But we should check the Well itself, in case Walter or the Wraiths found another way in. There wasn't one thirty years ago, but the glacier is moving. Something may have cracked or crumbled, opening up another entrance."

"Are you saying the Well is *inside* the glacier?" Petraen asked, eyes wide.

"Not originally, but it is now."

"How is it that the glacier didn't destroy it?" Siobhaen asked, stepping forward up onto the ridge of debris that had been ground up from the glacier itself and looking into the dark hollow of the entrance. The winter sunlight didn't penetrate very far, but it was enough to see that the cavern walls were smooth, as if the ice had melted and refrozen.

Behind her, both Vaeren and Eraeth motioned for the others to break out torches.

"The Well generates its own heat. When the ice began to encroach on the Well, the glacier itself melted around it." A hissing whoosh and the stench of oil filled the air as the first torch was lit, followed by a second. Colin motioned Vaeren forward as he continued. "At first, the Well's heat merely carved out a chasm through the ice, like a hot knife slicing through butter. But as the glacier grew and ground its way farther south, it became too large. It covered the Well, the heat carving out a hollow inside it. We're at the end of that hollow now."

"How do you know this?" one of the Phalanx guardsmen asked.

Colin smiled and caught the man's eye. "I went back and watched it happen."

They entered the tunnel, the heat-smoothed walls of ice closing up around them. Now that Vaeren knew where they had to go, he ranged out ahead of them, torch held high to light the way. The ground beneath was mostly level, like the tundra outside, covered with rock and grass that had shriveled and dried after being closed off from the sunlight. As within the Gaurraenan's halls, Colin felt the weight of the ice above pressing down on him, although unlike the stone of the mountains, this weight sent shivers of cold down into his back. The torches blazed off the ice walls, shimmering against the smooth surface or refracting oddly where the immense weight of the glacier had caused the ice to crack or shatter as it moved. Occasionally, large chunks of ice had broken free and fallen to the ground, but nothing significant enough to block their path.

They paused to rest twice at Aeren's insistence, Vaeren anxious to keep moving, pacing even as the rest groaned and settled against the ice wall or, like Petraen, threw themselves flat on the ground. Boreaus passed out cooked meat he'd saved from the last few roasts. Without the sun, they couldn't tell how much time had passed. When Aeren called a halt for sleep, Vaeren shot him a dark glare and drew breath to protest, but a soft yet sharp word from Siobhaen kept him quiet.

Colin tried to rest, but couldn't. Lying flat on the rough ground, he stared up at the darkened ceiling of ice. The Lifeblood tingled through his skin, even though they were still distant. He could taste it, like leaves and ice and earth all mingled together on his tongue. It pulsed in his blood as well. In the dimness of the small fire they'd kept burning, he reached up and pulled the sleeve of his shirt back and looked at the swirling black stains that wound around his arm, like oil beneath his skin. If he concentrated hard enough, he could sense it shifting around within him, down both his arms, tendrils of it reaching into his chest.

It had gotten much worse after the Escarpment, no matter how much he tried to keep it at bay, no matter how long he stayed away from the Well or kept himself from drinking the Lifeblood. The need to create the Trees and then his obsession with the knife . . . they had both taken their toll.

He dropped his arm, then rolled onto his side, startled when he looked across the fire and saw Siobhaen watching him, her brow creased with a frown. She turned away as soon as she caught his gaze, troubled. He thought about moving to speak with her, since it was obvious neither of them could sleep, but he hesitated and eventually rolled away from the flames to face the darkness of his shadow against the ice wall.

He slept fitfully, the Lifeblood seething inside him.

7

"**W**E'LL REACH THE WELL TODAY," Colin announced when they woke, the others packing up what little they'd taken out the night before. He noticed they kept their cattans free, their clothing loose. Here inside the cavern, they didn't need the heavy clothes to keep the harsh wind at bay and so were dressed in layers mostly to protect against the cold. "Stay near me at the Well. And don't drink from it, don't even touch it." He pulled back his sleeve enough for everyone to see the black marks, heard one of them suck in a sharp breath, another whisper "shaeveran." He caught all of their gazes with a hard glare. "It will change you, even with a touch."

Then he spun and led them down the tunnel. Everyone stayed close, and everyone was on edge. Colin drew their tension around him like a cloak, his focus on the Well, on what he would find when he reached it.

He nearly gasped when, from the darkness ahead, he saw a faint flicker of bluish light.

"What is it?" Vaeren spat behind him. Only then did he realize he'd halted in his tracks, that he stood with his staff angled defensively before him.

Eraeth and Aeren came up on his left, Siobhaen to the

right. He motioned to the faint glow with his staff. "There shouldn't be any light."

Both Vaeren and Eraeth reached for their cattans. They shot each other annoyed glares.

"What does it mean?" Aeren asked.

"The light comes from the Well. It means that something has definitely disturbed their balance. This happened before, when Walter and the Wraiths began awakening the Wells the first time."

"So it doesn't mean that someone is at the Well now."

"No. But someone has been to one of the Wells somewhere and manipulated it."

"Back in Caercaern, you said that none of the Wells have been touched," Vaeren said.

Colin frowned at the harshness in his voice. "I said none of the Wells that we know of have been disturbed."

Vaeren's eyes narrowed at the distinction, but before he could say anything Eraeth broke in.

"Vaeren, Siobhaen, and I will take the lead," he said, "Colin and Aeren the center, the rest behind. We'll use the torches until the light ahead is bright enough we can see without them."

He didn't wait for an argument, simply stepped forward, drawing his cattan. A moment later, Siobhaen and Vaeren joined him, their own blades bare, moving cautiously but quickly. A short time later, Eraeth motioned for the torches to be doused, their bearers grinding them into the soil and smothering their flames with their feet. The bluish light filled the tunnel, and as it grew, Colin picked out a faint pulse to its glow. The pall of the Lifeblood fell across him, heavier and heavier the closer they came, throbbing in his skin in time with the light. His grip tightened on his staff and his heart quickened, falling into the same rhythm.

The tunnel widened, the ceiling reaching away at a slow slope. Eraeth increased the pace, the group fanning out.

And then the tunnel ended, expanding into a huge chamber, the ceiling of ice rising into a massive dome. The ground rose slightly, the wind-torn grass of the tundra giving way abruptly to trees. Water dripped down from the heights in a slow, steady fall of rain, and as they stepped forward to the edge of the forest, they could feel the heat pressing forward, damp and humid against their faces. Colin wiped the wetness from his face with one hand, saw many of the others doing the same. The rain pattered against the wide, flat, copper-colored leaves of the trees as they entered the grove, runneling down the smooth edges and dripping from the sharp yellowed tips. Within twenty paces, Colin's hair was plastered to his forehead, water seeping in under the edge of his clothing and settling uncomfortably against his skin. He noticed the others pulling at the collars of their shirts and shrugging their shoulders as they adjusted to the annoyance.

They continued forward, the forest silent except for the rainfall, the white-barked trunks of the trees slipping by on either side. The Phalanx and the Flame had circled Colin and Aeren and were scanning beneath the foliage, swords bared, but they saw nothing.

After a long moment, and at a backward, questioning glance from Eraeth, Colin said, "It should be just ahead."

Ten paces beyond, the land rose in a steep ridge, the boles of the trees falling away as it flattened into a circular stone plaza.

The Well stood in the center, its edge rising from the flat stone to waist height. There was nothing else in the plaza, although when he had been here last, Colin had found evidence of other structures built on top of the stone, their foundations still visible as outlines on the surface. The strange trees surrounded the plaza on all sides, their branches draping over the edge of the platform in places.

"How can there be trees?" Aeren asked. He whispered,

but his voice breaking the near silence still made some of the Phalanx start. "No sunlight can reach down here."

"The Well," Colin said, moving out from the edge of the platform toward its lip even as he spoke. "The Lifeblood keeps them alive."

The group reformed, Colin drawing up to the edge of the Well to stare down into the depths of the perfectly flat water, the bluish light washing up over his face, the rest hanging back. He could taste the Lifeblood now, wanted to reach out and drink it down, feel its coolness in his mouth, slipping down his throat and suffusing his body with warmth. The need was an ache. When he reached one hand forward, it trembled. He stared at it, the skin pale, nearly translucent, the marks that had pulled free of the cover of his sleeve a hideous black in contrast.

"I need to see if I can find out what has happened through the Well," Colin said. "I won't be aware of what's happening around me as I work."

Eraeth immediately ordered the rest of Aeren's Phalanx to spread out, halfway between the Well and the trees. Vaeren grudgingly did the same, sending Siobhaen, Petraen, and Boreaus to join them. Both Vaeren and Aeren remained close to Colin, who turned his attention completely on the Well and the pulsations of light.

With a small sigh of regret, he leaned forward and dipped his hand into the water, bringing it to his lips. He drank as little as possible, enough to connect him to the Well and no more. The tingling cold fire of it burned as he swallowed.

He leaned forward onto the stone lip, then closed his eyes and sank to his knees at its edge, as if in prayer in one of Diermani's churches. He nearly crossed himself in reflex—shoulder, shoulder, heart, waist—but halted the gesture mid-motion with a small smile and a shake of his head.

Then he sank into the Well.

He dove deep, through the pulsating light and into the depths, even though he knew his body remained behind, at the lip of the Well, protected by Aeren and Eraeth and the others. He followed the Lifeblood, followed its taste of leaves and earth and snow, deep and deeper, until the flow that fed this Well emptied out into a vast reservoir of Lifeblood, a lake of power far beneath the surface of the earth. A lake that spread southward, beneath the lands that the Alvritshai had once claimed as their own, beneath the mountains. It grew shallow in places, deeper in others, was blocked by pillars of earth and stone and rock through huge sections of land and narrowed down to channels in others. He followed those channels, wove his way along them, rising to the surface through streams whose mouths were the Wells that had been discovered over the past few hundred years, Wells like those in the Ostraell at the heart of the dwarren plains. At each Well, he checked his wards and found them intact, so he kept roaming, reaching out along additional channels, along less familiar routes, searching for something that was different.

As he skirted the edges of the Lifeblood beneath the dwarren's easternmost lands, he found it.

The flow of the Lifeblood had changed, the currents eddying in new directions. He felt them drawing him eastward, pulling him with a strength greater than any he'd felt before. He let himself be drawn along this new direction, felt himself funneled into new paths, ones that had not existed thirty years before. But as he was swept along, he realized that they *had* existed thirty years before. He felt the age in the rock, felt the hunger of the stone as the Lifeblood coursed through it, speeding eastward. These passages had been here long before the dwarren claimed the plains, long before the Faelehgre had built their city around the Well and been caught and transformed by it. These channels that now seethed with the Lifeblood had been closed off some-how, blocked.

And someone had released that block.

That was what had upset the balance of the Wells. That was what had caused the return of the ethereal storms on the dwarren plains, and the occumaen and iriaem of the White Wastes.

Walter.

Colin's heart seized in his chest and he suddenly realized that the current dragging him eastward had increased, stronger now than it had been before. He began to struggle against it, fought his way back toward the west, felt a mo-ment of pure panic as he thought the current had gotten too strong. As he struggled, he reached out to the east with thin tendrils, tried to determine where the new channels ended, because he suddenly knew that that was where he would find Walter, where he would find the Wraiths. He sensed further branches of the Lifeblood, far beyond the edges of dwarren lands. He snaked more tendrils east, followed as many of the paths as he could, but they all led toward the same location, toward the same central source.

Then, at the edges of his senses, stretched so thin he thought he would snap, he caught the faint vestige of an-other reservoir, another lake of Lifeblood so vast he gasped. His strength fled, and for a moment he lost his struggle against the current and was dragged toward that vast sea buried deep beneath the land.

A vast sea that had recently been awakened.

He snatched the tendrils back to himself, gathered them close. He couldn't spare anything for a further search, for further answers. The currents of the Lifeblood had him, were increasing as they drove him toward that sea. He needed everything he had to push against it, to force him-self through the churning flow. Surging forward, he strug-gled back through the formerly blocked channels, his progress increasing with every step forward as the strength of the current decreased, until he roared from the opened mouth of the passage and back onto familiar ground.

He paused to gather his strength, knew that his body back at the Well would be trembling, perhaps had even fallen from the lip of the Well itself. But he spared a moment to search the edges of the dwarren plain for other breaches leading to the sea he'd discovered. He found three, each drawing Lifeblood toward the sea as the two sources connected.

Then he shot northward, back to the Well, back to his body. As he traveled, his rage grew.

Walter had found another source of power. He'd opened up the paths to the east, had awakened the sea beneath, was drawing on it even now, had been drawing on it for decades. There was no other explanation. While Colin had been fumbling with creating the knife, Walter had already been moving forward, working outside the influence of the Trees. He'd thought there was nothing that Walter could do, that he'd accounted for everything by warding the Wells and protecting the Lifeblood.

He'd been so stupid!

The rage nearly blinded him to the taint in the taste of the Well as he approached the north. He caught it at the last moment—a bitterness, like sap. The taste startled him with its acridness, but it wasn't in the Well itself. It was approaching from the south, from the direction of the tunnel through the glacier.

And he recognized the taint.

He dove into his body, tried to seize control of it even as he felt it slip from the lip of the Well with the force of his return, even as he felt seizures race through his arms and legs. He tried to speak, heard Aeren cry out to Eraeth, heard Vaeren swear harshly. He opened his eyes, the bluish glow of the Well too bright, blinding him. He couldn't breathe, his chest heaving, and he broke out in racking coughs as he rolled onto his side.

"Shaeveran!" Aeren barked. "Don't try to talk. Breathe in deeply. You're only making it worse."

"Wra—" Colin wheezed, but his chest contracted and he hacked dryly into the damp, rain-slicked stone of the plaza. The coughing sapped his strength, already drained from his battle with the currents of the Lifeblood.

"What is he trying to say?" Vaeren demanded. "What did he find out?"

"I don't know," Aeren said, his voice calm, although Colin could hear the tension beneath.

"It sounded like Wraith," Eraeth cut in tersely.

Colin nodded, drew in another ragged breath, then gathered enough strength to snatch Eraeth's arm and drag him in close. "Shadows are coming, with a Wraith. Through the tunnel."

Before he finished, someone screamed, a horrid, high-pitched sound that cut off before it was finished.

Eraeth and Vaeren lurched back from Colin, Eraeth ripping free of Colin's grasp. Colin rolled to the side, coming to rest on his shoulder, his view of the trees in the direction of the tunnel's mouth clear.

One of Aeren's Phalanx had fallen, the blackness of a Shadow writhing over his form in frenzied ecstasy. Before anyone could react, four more Shadows flowed out of the forest, two falling on another of Aeren's guardsmen even as he swung his sword. He fell with a curse that cut into a shout and then silence. The third Phalanx member scrambled backward, falling back to Petraen's side, his breathing harsh as he moved.

And then the Wraith stepped from the trees.

Colin's heart leaped with a malice and hatred so fierce he half rose, resting his weight on one arm. He reached for his staff with the other, even as weakness passed down through his body in a wave. For a long moment, all he saw was Walter, the boy who had bullied him with his gang in the streets of Portstown, the man he had become in the forests of Ostraell as he drank from the Well and became a Wraith beneath the Shadows' hands. Colin thrust himself up, using the staff as support, before sagging back against the lip of the Well as the Wraith advanced, flanked by the two remaining Shadows.

When the Wraith drew an Alvritshai cattan, Colin's hatred faltered.

He blinked away his rage, caught himself. This wasn't Walter. This was one of the other Wraiths, an Alvritshai by the weapon and the stance. Too tall to be human or dwarren.

But advancing steadily.

"What do we do?" Petraen shouted, an edge to his voice. He, Aeren's remaining guardsman, and Boreaus were the closest.

"Retreat. You can't fight them. Your cattans are useless," Colin said, his voice unnaturally calm. "Only I can fight them."

He turned and dipped his free hand into the Well, drank deeply, felt the power of the Lifeblood seethe through him even as he reached into his satchel, pulling forth the chain mail of the quickened knife. He shrugged out of the satchel, dropped it and the chain mail cloth to the ground as he stepped forward, out in front of Vaeren, Eraeth, and Aeren, knife in hand. Siobhaen had backed nearly to their position. She shot a glance toward him as he passed, her eyes wide with fear, but her jaw set.

"Hold them off," she said softly. "Hold them off long enough for me to call Aielan's Light." Then she spun and sprinted back to the group around the Well.

"Petraen, Boreaus," Vaeren shouted. "Fall back now!"

Eraeth repeated the order, Aeren's guardsman answering immediately.

The two members of the Flame hesitated, the Wraith nearly upon them, the Shadows—all five of them— spreading out to either side, beginning to encircle them. Only when Vaeren cursed did they relent, backing away sharply, their useless blades held out protectively before them.

Colin took their place, staff in one hand, the knife half-hidden in the other.

The Wraith halted. Like Walter in the parley tent at the Escarpment, it wore a cloak, the hood drawn up to conceal its face. But even as it began to speak, it reached up and drew the hood back.

Colin didn't recognize the Alvritshai beneath. His pale skin was mottled with the same blackness that covered Colin's arms, only much darker, writhing around his eyes and nose, across his angular cheeks and sharp jaw. His black hair was tied back with a length of cord.

"We knew you would come," he said, his voice rumbling. "We waited for you. Outside. But you are too late. We are already moving, our armies already in motion. This is merely the removal of an . . . annoyance."

He didn't wait for an answer. With a single gesture, he motioned the five Shadows forward, even as he raised his cattan and swung, quicker than Colin had expected.

Colin caught the blade with the staff, crying out as he staggered backward beneath the blow, the wood unwieldy with only one hand; it was meant for a two-handed grip. But he didn't dare drop the knife, even though he wasn't certain it would work as he expected. As he blocked the Wraith's first blow, he swung the knife out sideways, catching one of the Shadows across its center. His hand tingled with numbness, but he felt grim satisfaction as the wooden knife caught in the substance of the Shadow and ripped across its length. The Shadow screamed, the sound shattering the stillness, shivering beneath the skin, the tatters of its two halves falling backward to the ground like cloth as its death cry faded.

The sudden death caused the Wraith to pause in shock. Taking advantage, Colin shoved his blade aside and swung with the knife toward the Alvritshai's throat.

The Wraith blurred, reappearing a step back, out of reach. "You have a new toy," he spat, his voice no longer laced with confidence.

"And I intend to use it."

Colin slowed time, even as he spun, bringing his staff up and around, catching one of the Shadows with its end as it reached for him, shoving the knife toward another. But the Shadows were created by the Lifeblood, were a part of its power. They sensed his movement, even with time slowed, and reacted, seething back out of reach. The staff caught one and flung it to the side unharmed, the knife blurring through nothing. But Colin was still moving, stepping to the side, swinging for the Alvritshai Wraith as he dodged beneath the flowing blackness of the Shadows. The group whirled and danced, time slipping back and forth as each plied the powers of the Lifeblood in an effort to find an advantage. The Shadows were restricted, only seeming to sense Colin's movements as he slowed and sped up time; they couldn't maneuver through it as he did. But the Wraith—

The Wraith was like him, touched by the Well yet not completely transformed. Colin blocked the Shadows with the staff as much as possible, tried to keep the knife in reserve for the Wraith as the Alvritshai blurred back and forth, his cattan flashing in the pulsating blue light of the Well. At the same time, Colin forced the group back toward the trees and away from Aeren and the others. He had no time to spare a glance in their direction, not with four Shadows and the Wraith dodging in and out of his defenses.

He found himself completely on the defensive. His

strength was gone, drained by his search within the Well and by two nights of little sleep. The Lifeblood he'd drunk had sustained him so far, and he would pay the price for that, but the Wraith and the Shadows weren't exhausted. They were merely wary of the knife, streaming away from his slashes as he fought. That wouldn't last long.

He needed to end this. Now.

When one of the Shadows reached for him, he swung the staff up sharply, catching its folds and thrusting it up and out, ignoring the attack from another Shadow to the left. He could sense the Wraith coming in from the right, could feel the blade slicing through the air near his back. But instead of spinning away from it, toward the Shadow, he turned toward it.

The blade caught him in the side, sliced in deep, the pain instant, searing across his vision with a white haze. He screamed, felt blood gurgling at the back of his throat, but he drew the arm carrying the knife up and drove it down into the body of the Wraith he could barely see, drove it deep into the Alvritshai's neck. The blade sliced cleanly through flesh, grazed the Wraith's collarbone, skated across the bone's ridge to the hollow below the throat, then slipped free.

The Wraith roared, staggering away, the cattan in Colin's side pulling free with a jerk. Blood splashed across Colin's face as he lost his balance and fell to his hands and knees. Pain shivered up his arms, lanced up his legs, but he held onto the knife, to his staff, his fingers crushed. His own hot blood sheeted down his side and dripped from his shirt, but he ignored it, thrust back onto his haunches, bringing the knife up with shaky arms.

The Wraith had staggered back, a ragged wound from the side of his neck to the bottom of his throat gushing blood between the hand clamped to it. He stared at Colin in horror, tried to speak, but couldn't, the wound across his throat too severe. With his free hand, he brought his cattan up, then stumbled backward three more steps before collapsing, the cattan clattering to the stone.

Colin caught the flicker of the Shadows to either side, all four hanging back as if uncertain what they should do.

But then five more emerged from the trees and moved up onto the plaza.

Colin exhaled sharply, nearly sobbed. Dropping the staff, he reached to clamp a hand around the wound at his side, his body wavering where it stood. He had no strength left. He couldn't even raise the arm that held the knife.

Behind, through the haze of pain and exhaustion that clouded his mind, he caught the soft drone of a chant as it reached its end. He frowned, the words vaguely familiar.

And then he remembered what Siobhaen had said.

He felt the power of Aielan's Light shuddering through the earth beneath him, felt it rising upward. He gasped as it reached the surface and white fire bloomed from the stone, seething up in slow unfurling flames in a ring around the Well at Colin's back. It hovered there, burning without any visible source, and then it began to advance.

Colin sucked in a harsh breath as it touched him, passed through him, closing his eyes as he felt it burn deep inside him, breaking down all of his defenses, searing away all of his pretensions, licking through his core, touching his heart, his soul, judging him. But he had experienced this once before, at the center of Aielan's Light in the heart of the mountains beneath Caercaern. There, the fire had been more intense, had consumed him completely. This was a mere shadow of that Light.

It passed on, left him behind as it advanced on the Shadows. They writhed, their forms flaring left and right in uncertainty.

Then the fire halted. Colin heard shouting from behind, heard Siobhaen cry out in a strained voice, "I can't! I can barely hold it where it is now!"

And then a wave of nausea folded over him. He wavered, light-headed, tried to remain upright but couldn't.

He slumped to the side, hit the stone with jarring force and rolled halfway onto his back, pain raging from his side. He screamed again.

Through the fog of pain, he heard more shouting, heard the scramble of feet. Faces loomed over him—Aeren, Eraeth, Petraen, others—and then they grabbed him by the arms and legs, hauled him upright with a wrench and dragged him back toward the Well. He could feel the pulse of the Lifeblood coursing through his body, sensed Aielan's Light through the stone beneath him. His vision wavered in and out, a film of yellow passing over his eyes, throbbing with his heartbeat.

Voices. He blinked, found himself on the ground at the base of the Well. Aeren ripped his shirt away from his side, swore, barked to his only remaining Phalanx member, "Cloth! We need to staunch the wound!"

The guardsman scrambled for the packs. Eraeth stood over his lord, his blade drawn, his gaze cast outward, his mouth pulled down in a dark, vicious frown.

His grip tightened on his cattan. "Don't," he said, his voice black with warning. "It isn't yours. It was never yours."

At the tone of his voice, Aeren's remaining guardsman turned, then dropped the pack he held and drew his blade, stepping up on Colin's other side.

Colin frowned in confusion—

And then gasped, a hollow of anger and disbelief opening up inside his chest, flowing outward, shoving away the haziness of the pain.

The knife. He'd dropped the knife.

Teeth gritted, he rolled onto his side, Aeren reaching out to support him with a sharp look. But he ignored the Alvritshai lord, glared instead toward Vaeren, the caitan of the Flame flanked on either side by Petraen and Boreaus, all three with cattans drawn, the quickened knife in Vaeren's other hand. Neither Petraen nor Boreaus wore the easy, friendly grins Colin had seen around the campfires on their trek to the Well. Their faces were deadly serious, their eyes cold.

Siobhaen knelt to the left, near the Well, facing the white fire that still blazed in a circle around them all, the Shadows writhing back and forth along its length. Her face was slick with sweat, her hair plastered to her skin. Lines of strain etched her eyes and cheekbones, turned down the corners of her mouth.

"It was never his either," Vaeren said, holding the knife carefully. His gaze shot toward Colin. "It belongs to the Order."

"To Lotaern, you mean," Colin said.

"To all Alvritshai! It can help us destroy the Shadows, the Wraiths. That is how Lotaern intends to use it. He should never have let you keep it, never have let you take it from the Sanctuary and risk losing it to them."

"Lotaern will not use it for the good of the Alvritshai," Aeren said, his voice calm. "He will use it only to further his own purposes."

Vaeren scowled. "And you would use it otherwise, Lord of the Evant? Forgive me if I feel better with it in the hands of the Order and the Flame."

Petraen stepped forward with the chain mail cloth. Vaeren sheathed his cattan, taking the cloth and wrapping the knife quickly, tucking it into his satchel. Eraeth made a move forward, but Petraen and Boreaus followed suit, halting him before he'd managed a single step. He growled low in his throat.

Vaeren smirked, drawing his cattan again. "Siobhaen, let the Light go. It's time to leave."

There was a moment of silence, and then Siobhaen said, "No."

Vaeren shot her a dark look. "Let it go! We have the knife, and Shaeveran's staff. We can fend off the sukrael ourselves."

Siobhaen glared. "But they can't." When Vaeren merely straightened, she added, "He is Shaeveran. He risked his life for us at the Escarpment, he has protected us since then, provided us with the Winter Tree, fought for us here, and he is no condition to protect himself or the others now. *I will not leave them to the sukrael.*"

Vaeren's eyes narrowed as the two stared at each other and the silence stretched.

Then Vaeren scowled. "Petraen, Boreaus, we're leaving." He motioned to the two, Petraen shooting Siobhaen an uncertain glance, but the three backed away, eyeing Eraeth and the other guardsman warily as they did so. When they were twenty paces distant, they turned and raced along the edge of the ring of white fire.

Siobhaen's shoulders slumped, but the determination in her face did not fade.

"Should we follow them?" Eraeth asked tersely. His hand flexed on the handle of his cattan.

Aeren looked down at Colin.

"No," Colin rasped, allowing Aeren to lay him onto his back again. "Let them go."

"But the knife—" Eraeth began.

"I can get it back!" Colin choked on blood at the force behind the words, at the anger that seethed in his chest. In a quieter voice, he added, "Lotaern won't hold the knife for long. He knows this. I can take it whenever I wish."

"Not if you don't recover," Aeren said harshly. He motioned toward the guardsman, who resheathed his blade and grabbed the pack again. He drew out clothing, Aeren picking through it, stuffing a shirt to Colin's side and pressing hard.

Colin moaned, as Eraeth finally lowered his cattan. The

caitan glanced toward Siobhaen. "How long can you hold the fire?"

She grimaced. "Not long enough. Not if the sukrael don't leave."

"Tighten the circle," Colin said through clenched teeth. Aeren had begun tying the shirt to his chest with strips of torn cloth. "Bring it closer to the Well. It will be easier to manage."

Siobhaen nodded, closed her eyes in concentration. Colin felt a surge of power through the earth, but the sensation was distant. The adrenaline over the loss of the knife was already fading. He could feel his arms beginning to tingle, the weakness pressing in on him from all sides. The light-headedness had returned.

"And then what?" Eraeth asked, frustration tainting his voice.

"And then," Colin said, darkness closing in fast now, weighing him down, drawing him into its vastness so fast he couldn't finish.

But he heard Aeren say from far away, "Then we wait."

Part III

~

The Thalloran Wasteland

8

"**W**ILL HE SURVIVE?"

Aeren looked up at Siobhaen from where he sat feeding wood into the fire. Eraeth and Hiroun, his only remaining House guard, had gone in search of game outside, through the cavern's tunnel. They'd left that morning, after waking to discover that the Wraith's body had vanished. They'd left it where it had fallen so that Shaeveran could look at it when he woke, burning the two Rhyssal House Phalanx who had died the day before instead.

Now, Aeren wished they had tried to take care of the Wraith as well.

Because of that, and because of the betrayal of Vaeren and the other Flame members, Eraeth had not wanted to leave Aeren alone with Siobhaen. But Aeren had insisted. They needed food. Boreaus had taken nearly all of it with his pack, along with most of the torches and a few other supplies. They didn't need torches now, not with the pulsing blue light of the Well illuminating the entire cavern of ice, but they would once they attempted to return through Gaurraenan's halls.

He stared at Siobhaen as she stood over Shaeveran, a frown touching her face. A thin layer of anger seeped through his voice as he answered her.

"I've seen him survive much more serious wounds."

She turned toward him. "Then why hasn't he woken?"

"I never said he would recover quickly. It took days for him to recover at the Escarpment. Most would have died, even with immediate attention from the healers. This one is not as serious, but it should still have been fatal."

"But there must be something more we can do. Have him drink from the sarenavriell. Something."

"The sarenavriell is what keeps him alive, but it also taints him. It's what is causing the darkness beneath his skin. Having him drink might help, but it would also hurt him. He has tried to break free of it." Aeren paused, brow furrowing. "I have seen him grow younger before, and that has helped heal his wounds, but only because the young heal faster, their bodies more resilient. His wounds do not vanish as he grows younger. And changing his age would require effort and energy I don't think he can spare at the moment."

Siobhaen didn't answer, the lines etched into her forehead—lines that had been a permanent fixture since the attack by the Wraith and the Shadows—deepening. Her arms were crossed over her chest, her shoulders stiff. The stance of a member of the Phalanx: mostly relaxed, although still mildly defensive.

Aeren waited, placing another branch onto the flames before him.

Finally, she asked, "Why does he do it? Why did he risk himself to save us? He must have known we intended to take the knife at some point."

"He's known since you left the Sanctuary in Caercaern."

"Then why?"

Aeren considered the pale form before him, thought of the darkness that he'd seen swirling beneath his skin when he'd redressed the wound. A shocking amount of darkness. "Because he is a good person."

When Siobhaen merely scowled in disbelief, he asked, "Why did you stay?"

"To hold Aielan's Light steady."

"To protect us. You didn't need to do that. You could have let the Light go, joined Vaeren and the others as they fled."

"And left you to the sukrael?"

Aeren raised an eyebrow. "Vaeren left us."

Siobhaen stiffened, her eyes blazing. "I am not Vaeren." Under her breath, she said, "He should have left the staff at least."

"He only cared about the knife, about returning it to the Chosen."

"It was what we were sent to do."

"And yet you stayed."

"Because we weren't told to sacrifice Shaeveran ... or you ... in the process!"

Aeren nodded. In a casual voice, he asked, "What does Lotaern intend to do with it?"

Siobhaen spun toward him. "I stayed, but that does not mean I intend to betray the Order. The Chosen is trying to protect the Alvritshai. He's trying to save us."

"From what?"

"From the Wraiths! From the sukrael!"

"But we are already protected from them. We have the Winter Tree. Lotaern doesn't need the knife for protection. He wants it for some other purpose."

Siobhaen's eyes grew troubled. She bit her lower lip, gaze drifting to one side, thinking.

Aeren would have pressed her further, but Shaeveran moaned.

Both of them turned instantly, Aeren rising from his place at the fire and stepping to Colin's side. Colin opened his eyes, blinked at the strange light, then caught Aeren's gaze.

"What happened?" Colin's attention flicked to Siobhaen as she knelt on his other side, then back. "I don't sense Aielan's Light. Where are the Shadows? Where's the Wraith? Where are the others?"

"Vaeren, Petraen, and Boreaus left with the knife, your staff, and most of the packs two days ago. The sukrael stayed a little longer, but fled when Aielan's Light did not fail. We think they went after Vaeren. Siobhaen released the Light a short time after that and collapsed."

Colin rose onto his elbows. "Where is Eraeth and the other guardsman?"

"Hiroun and Eraeth burned the others yesterday and are now hunting on the tundra."

Colin reached for Aeren, gripped his shoulder, his eyes wide. "You burned the Wraith?"

"No. We left the Wraith alone. No one wanted to touch him." He hesitated, then added reluctantly. "Apparently he wasn't dead. The body vanished while we rested. None of those on watch saw anything, it was simply gone."

Colin slumped, his hand falling from Aeren's shoulder. Conflicting emotions raced across his face—hatred, shock, grief—finally settling on resigned anger. "He should have died. The wound was fatal. The knife doesn't work."

Siobhaen jerked in surprise. "What do you mean it doesn't work?"

Colin laughed bitterly. "It didn't kill the Wraith. It should have, but it didn't. Vaeren betrayed us for nothing."

"But it did work against the sukrael," Aeren said. "The pieces of the one you sliced apart are still there, although none of us could touch them. We could feel a coldness tingling in our fingers when we drew close."

Colin sighed. "I'll take care of them." He reached for Aeren again, motioning with his hand. "Help me up."

"Your wound—" Siobhaen began, but Aeren grabbed Colin's hand and pulled him into a seated position. Colin gasped, hunching forward, his hand going to the bandages at his side matted with dried blood.

With his other hand, he gestured again to Aeren. "All the way."

Aeren frowned in disapproval. "Do you want something to eat?" he asked as he pulled Colin into a standing position, then supported him as he gained his balance. "We saved you some of the rabbit."

Colin's breathing came in rasping heaves, but the human swallowed and shook his head. "No," he gasped, then coughed. "No, the Shadow first."

He staggered toward where the Shadow had fallen, arm still pulled tight to his side. His footsteps faltered, but gained strength as he moved, his back straightening. Aeren watched with trepidation, waiting for him to collapse, but when he reached the place where the Shadow had fallen, the lord drew in a deep sigh and released it slowly.

"Is he always this stubborn?" Siobhaen asked curtly.

"Yes," Aeren said with a thin smile, thinking back to the battle at the Escarpment. "Especially when he's hurt."

They watched in silence as Colin knelt and inspected the remains of the Shadow closely. He frowned, then searched the surrounding area until he found a small stick. He tried to lift the strange folds with the end of the stick, but it merely passed through the clothlike material as if it weren't there, as the sukrael passed through blades when they attacked. Colin cursed, the meaning clear even though Aeren was too distant to catch the words, then dropped the stick and carefully picked up the skin of the Shadow with his bare hands, his face twisted in distaste.

He rose and headed straight for the Well, tossing the pieces of the Shadow into the clear waters where they floated for a moment, then began to sink and dissolve. Aeren and Siobhaen joined him as the last vestiges of the Shadow drifted into nothing in the depths.

"I thought it would pass right through you, as it did with the stick," Siobhaen said softly.

Colin grimaced. "One of the advantages of being shaeveran."

Siobhaen swallowed, her shoulders tense. "Did it hurt?"

Colin turned to meet her gaze, stepping back from the Well. "It burned," he said, then glanced toward Aeren. "Now, where's that rabbit?"

~

Colin ate, and then returned to rest, his face pale and drawn. At one point, Aeren thought he had a fever, his forehead shiny with sweat, although it was hard to tell with the perpetual drip of water from the cavern's ceiling. When Siobhaen brought a cloth chilled with a chunk of ice, Colin frowned in his sleep, muttered something about a Well before slipping away again. Siobhaen shot Aeren a questioning look, but he merely shrugged.

Eraeth and Hiroun returned a day later, carrying a brace of snowy white hare, Hiroun holding his arm awkwardly at his side.

"What happened?" Aeren said as he took the meat, passing half to Siobhaen, whose nose wrinkled in distaste even though she complied.

Eraeth answered as they began preparing them for the fire. "Wolf. Larger than any wolf I've ever seen, and colored gray to fade into the snow. We think it could smell the blood of the hare and tracked us as we made our way back to the tunnel. It attacked last night, managed to get a hold on Hiroun before we wounded it enough so it retreated."

At Aeren's concerned look, Hiroun said, "It will heal."

Eraeth nodded toward Colin. "Has he woken?"

"Briefly. Long enough to take care of the remains of the Shadow and eat. But he's still recovering."

"We can't wait much longer," Eraeth said. "Not if we

want to have any hope of catching up to Vaeren and the others and retrieving the knife."

"We don't need to retrieve the knife."

Hiroun started at the hoarse voice, and then everyone turned as Shaeveran raised himself to a seated position, leaning on one arm.

"What do you mean?" Eraeth barked. "Of course we need to retrieve the knife. They stole it!"

Colin shook his head, then grimaced as he pushed himself to his feet and joined them at the fire. None of the Alvritshai offered to help. "The knife is unimportant now."

"You learned something from the Well," Aeren stated.

Colin settled in near the fire. "Walter and the Wraiths have been busy."

"What do you mean?" Siobhaen asked this time. "We haven't heard or seen anything from them for nearly thirty years. Since the Winter Tree, our only reports of altercations with them have been from those who dare to venture outside the Seasonal Trees' influence."

"We haven't heard from them because they've been working far to the east, out past the dwarren's borders, where none of the three Seasonal Trees' power can touch them."

"What have they done?" Aeren asked.

Colin remained silent for a long moment, staring into the fire while Eraeth spitted one of the gutted and skinned rabbits and set it to roast over the flames. Hiroun had already done the same for one of Siobhaen's.

"I think he's awakened another Well," he finally said. "And by the force of the currents in the Lifeblood, by the way it's altering the channels, it's large. Bigger than any of the Wells I've located within the lands of the three races here in New Andover. That's why the storms over the dwarren plains and Alvritshai lands have returned, and why they seem so much more powerful so quickly. And that's why there are lights on the tundra here when there are no reports of such lights in the Alvritshai Scripts. Whatever Walter has awakened, it's completely upset the balance of the Lifeblood. We need to find out what he's done and repair it if possible. The theft of the knife is nothing in comparison."

Eraeth scowled and twisted the end of the spit viciously. Fat sizzled in the fire beneath.

"Are you certain it's Walter?" Siobhaen asked.

"It must be. I know of no one else who would even attempt such a thing."

The small group considered his words in silence, while the rest of the rabbit was cleaned and readied for the spit.

Finally, Aeren said, "Then we must go east, to see what Walter and the Wraiths are trying to accomplish. And to stop them."

Colin was already shaking his head. "No. I can't allow it. Moiran will not allow it."

Aeren stiffened where he sat. "Moiran does not decide the fate of the Rhyssal House, or its lord."

Colin smiled. "I'm certain she'd disagree. But it doesn't matter. I need you in Caercaern, watching Lotaern. The knife may be unimportant, but whatever Lotaern intends to do with it isn't. You need to remain behind to contend with him."

"So you intend to travel east on your own?" Eraeth asked.

"If necessary." As Eraeth drew breath to argue, he added, "But no. What Walter has done has happened on the edges of dwarren lands, and whatever he intends to do, it will affect the dwarren first. I intend to seek the dwarren's help."

Aeren frowned. "You would trust the dwarren over the Alvritshai, over me?"

"Not over you or Eraeth or Moiran. But over Lotaern and most of the Lords of the Evant . . . yes. The dwarren have accepted me since the Escarpment, and in many respects they are better equipped to deal with the Shadows and the Wraiths. Their shamans are powerful."

"So is the Order, so are the acolytes," Siobhaen added defensively.

Colin frowned at her, long enough that her stiffness faltered. "Perhaps. But the dwarren have made a ritual of hunting the Shadows and the Wraiths, of killing them. They form war parties called trettarus to hunt them down. If I am going to search the Wraiths out, I'd rather have the shaman-blessed dwarren warriors at my side."

Siobhaen appeared stung by the mild rebuke, her eyes narrowing in anger.

"You can't travel to them alone," Aeren said. "Not in your condition. What about the humans? They have lands close to the east as well. You should contact them, see if they are willing to help."

Colin snorted in disdain. "Those in the Provinces would not help me. I am nothing but a legend to them. No one who remembers me from the Escarpment is still alive, and those in power now are too caught up in the politics between the old continent and the new. The Feud may have ended, and the Provinces freed from the Court and the Families back home, but there are still ties binding them together. I doubt King Justinian would recognize me if I showed up in his Court, let alone trust me enough to give me aid."

"I will accompany you to the dwarren lands, and beyond."

Siobhaen's announcement shocked them all, Aeren rocking back where he sat as if he'd been pushed, Eraeth merely going still with a suspicious frown.

"I thought you'd want to return to the Sanctuary," Colin said carefully.

"After defying Vaeren? I'm not certain what kind of welcome I would get."

"You don't answer to Vaeren," Eraeth said tightly. "You answer to the Chosen."

"But Lotaern listens to Vaeren, more so than most." Siobhaen met Eraeth's glare and didn't flinch.

Aeren didn't trust her either, not after what had happened with Vaeren, and not after what he'd seen Siobhaen do in the temples as they made their way northward, but he said nothing when Colin said, "Very well."

But he intended to have words with Colin when neither Siobhaen nor Eraeth would overhear. He didn't like how she'd inserted herself into the group, didn't like how intrusive it felt, no matter that she'd stayed to protect them from the sukrael. He had the entire trip back to his House lands to convince Colin to leave her behind, and to accept a contingent of Rhyssal House guards as well.

"It may be moot," Eraeth muttered, his voice nearly a growl. "We may catch up to Vaeren and the others before we reach Gaurraenan's halls."

Siobhaen glanced away abruptly, but it was Colin who answered, taking one of the spits from the fire, the rabbit glistening in the light, the meat charred. The smell had permeated the area and Aeren's stomach rumbled. Meals had been lean the last few days as they awaited Eraeth's return.

"We won't run into the other members of the Flame," Colin said succinctly, then tore into the meat, hissing as the hot fat seared his fingers. He still stuffed a piece of the rabbit into his mouth.

"Why not?"

"Because Vaeren isn't headed back to Gaurraenan's halls. He's headed to the chambers beneath the mountains behind Caercaern. Isn't he, Siobhaen?"

She sat completely still, eyes narrowed at Colin, who ignored her, focusing on his meal. Hiroun had taken his own rabbit and was eating it as well, while Eraeth had rescued both his own and Aeren's from the flames.

Finally, Siobhaen murmured, "That is true."

Perhaps he wouldn't need to warn Colin about trusting Siobhaen after all.

"Are we returning the same way, or are we risking Gaurraenan's halls again?"

"I doubt that Lotaern would allow us entrance through the corridors beneath Caercaern. Tamaell Theadoren would demand it, but we have no way of contacting him to make the Chosen open the doorway. We'll have to risk returning though the tunnel and pass." Colin glanced up. "Don't worry. I don't plan on being conscious when we pass through the halls."

"Then how are you going to make it through the tunnels?" Eraeth asked.

Colin grinned around a mouthful of greasy rabbit. "I expect you to carry me."

Tuvaellis reached up to tug at the cowl that shadowed her face from the sailors, prostitutes, and vagabonds that crowded the wharf and docks along the north end of Corsair. Her hands were gloved, to cover the swirling darkness of the sarenavriell that roiled beneath her skin, but she could not force herself to stoop to hide the difference in her height from the humans on the docks. Her lips pursed in distaste as she glared out at them, scurrying to and fro, laughing raucously or shouting from the ships tied up along the entire length of the northern shore for as far as she could see. She had never been to Corsair, the human capital of the Provinces, but Walter had told her to expect . . . chaos. He'd smiled as he warned her, but he had not mentioned the squalid stench, the reek of fish and sweat and shit that she'd encountered as she'd made her way down from the more civilized streets and inns closer to the massive walls of the keep beneath the towering spire called the Needle.

She glanced toward the Needle, careful to keep her face in shadow. Out of all of Corsair, which sprawled from the heights of the cliffs at the mouth of the inlet down across both shores of the wide swath of blue-black water between, to the river that fed the inlet to the east, the Needle was the most impressive building she had seen. It rivaled some of the Alvritshai's own masterpieces, even some of those that had been abandoned in the northern wastes. Impossibly thin, reaching to a height that she could not judge against the backdrop of the clouded winter sky, and built of a pale white stone that had weathered into a yellow tinged with pink, she could not fathom how the weakling humans had managed to construct it. At its apex, during storms and at night, a light flared from the blackened windows to warn ships of the rocks beneath the cliffs of the narrow corridor that gave access to the inlet and protected the city from the harshest of the Arduon Ocean's winter storms. Even now, wind thrashed in the pennants at its height, the clouds streaming eastward above it, although here at the docks everything was calm.

The palace beneath the Needle was coarse in comparison, a gray stone monstrosity that had been constructed around the base of the lighthouse and had grown over the years without any clear shape or form. Like the rest of the city, Tuvaellis thought, letting her gaze drop to the houses beneath the palace walls, spread across the hill where it sloped down to the waters of the inlet. At least beneath the palace there was some attention to form, the streets laid out in a pattern interrupted only sporadically by a plaza or park or fountain out-of-place with the rest of the natural order. But once her eyes reached the ramshackle streets of the commoners bordering the water, both on the north end and the south, all the way to the mouth of the river. . . .

"Chaos," she muttered under her breath and scowled.

A laborer, carrying a crate across one shoulder, jostled

her and her hand fell to the small dagger at her side, hidden beneath her gray cloak. The man barked a harsh, "Out of the way!" as he continued down the dock to a waiting ship. Tuvaellis considered killing him. She could feel the dagger cutting into his throat, could smell the spill of blood, could almost taste it. She'd kill him and be gone before his body hit the dock, and all anyone would see would be the blurred flicker of a figure in a gray cloak. . . .

The temptation was nearly too much, but she restrained herself, glanced toward the harsh glow of the sun hidden behind the layer of clouds, then back to the crush of bodies on the dock, searching.

Her contact was late. Had he been held up in the palace? Would he have sent a runner if he had?

No. He wouldn't risk it. He'd come himself or not at all.

Even as she thought it, she spotted Matthais' figure among the crowd, working his way toward her. His blond hair was easy to pick out among the mostly darker browns and blacks of the dockworkers, but it was the cut of his cloak—gray, like hers—that set him apart. That and his girth. Nearly all of the commoners at the dock were thin, although most had wiry muscle; Matthais was twice their size. Tuvaellis wondered why he had chosen to meet her here, at the docks, when it was so obvious that neither one of them fit in.

Matthais smiled as he drew closer, but the smile did not reach his eyes. He regarded her with an intensity she found surprising, cold and harsh and much more intelligent than she had expected.

"Excuse my lateness," he said as he drew up in front of her, his gaze passing swiftly over the area. They had met at the end of one of the docks on the wharf, the ocean lapping at the supports beneath them, the press of the day workers on all sides. Yet Tuvaellis felt that Matthais' single glance had picked up every detail around them, from the men and women who plied their wares to the wharf cats that twisted among the commoners' feet. "King Justinian had business that I could not excuse myself from easily, not without drawing undue attention."

"And meeting here, at the wharf, will not draw enough attention?" Tuvaellis asked snidely.

Matthais grinned. "Not from the men and women who matter. Besides, I was told you needed a discreet ship, sailing for Andover immediately. One whose captain would not question who his passenger was, nor ask any bothersome questions during the passage across the Arduon. Such ships are to be found here."

"And you have such a ship?"

"The *Mary Gently*, a trading ship set to leave for Trent in Andover at the next tide."

Tuvaellis straightened where she stood and scanned the ships within sight, noting the *Mary Gently* tied to the dock two lengths down. Her lip curled up at its size and shape. Not one of the larger traders, it had only two masts, had not been freshly painted in the last year, and showed some weathering. But its deck was clean and the sails appeared properly stowed. The crew appeared clean as well, more so than some of the ships at berth near it.

"This was all that was available?" she asked. Crew loaded barrels of what looked like salted fish into the hold as she watched.

"Unless you wish to risk one of the larger, more conspicuous, traders."

She turned at the hint of annoyance in Matthais' voice. Her eyes narrowed at the arrogance in his eyes. "You would be wise to remember to whom you speak, Councillor." She tilted her head enough that he would see the black-marked skin of her chin beneath the cowl.

Matthais' jaw clenched in anger, not fear. "And you

would be wise to remember that I am the one in a position to influence the King."

Tuvaellis lowered her head and wondered if perhaps Matthais had outworn his usefulness here in Corsair. But the plan had progressed too far for him to be replaced. They would never be able to get as close to the King in the time required, and she doubted they would be able to turn anyone else within Justinian's ranks.

Besides, Matthais was not her problem. Let Walter deal with him. She was to handle Andover.

"This will do. When does it depart?"

"According to the harbormaster, within two hours."

"I will need to retrieve my . . . possessions."

"Then do so, quickly. The captain has already been paid. He will care little if you are not aboard when the ship sails."

Tuvaellis almost snarled as the councillor spun and began making his way back through the crowd, her hand gripping the handle of the dagger inside the shield of her cloak. She had expected him to help her, or for him to make arrangements. Now it would be up to her.

She scanned the docks again and picked out a pair of rough-looking pickpockets she'd noticed earlier. They looked everywhere but at her as she approached, tried to sink back into the wall behind them, blend into the general background. Dressed in little more than rags, she wondered how they had fared that morning. The docks were not the best place for thieves; the dockworkers carried little on them, at least until their shifts were done.

The younger of the two tried to bolt when she was three steps away, but she caught the focus of the older one by holding up a silver mark in one hand.

The boy's eyes widened, then narrowed in suspicion. The younger boy halted after taking ten steps, but hung back, wary.

"What you want?" the ruffian asked, sidling to one side, preparing to run.

Tuvaellis smiled beneath her cowl. "I need help loading a chest aboard a ship."

"That's all?"

"That's all." The coin, stamped with the crude image of Justinian, was within the ruffian's reach. All he had to do was snatch it and run. Not that he would make it far.

She saw the intent in his eyes, saw it die. His head lowered and he looked away guiltily. "Is not worth a silver," he said.

"It is to me."

He glanced back at her, then toward his friend, who cast him a questioning look.

He reached for the coin, but Tuvaellis let it slip back into her hand. "After."

The ruffian scowled, but motioned toward his companion.

She led them through the streets without looking back, confident that they followed, although they kept out of her reach and to the sides of the streets, ready to flee at any moment. As they moved, the younger carried on a whispered, fervent conversation with his elder, shaking his head and frowning, but the eldest finally growled and barked a harsh order. The youngest fell silent after that, but kept his eyes locked on Tuvaellis as they moved.

They reached the inn where she had stayed the night before and she motioned the two up to her room, ignoring the quizzical looks of the innkeeper. A moment later, the two ruffians were hauling the trunk down the stairs, one on each end. It wasn't a large trunk, perhaps three hands long, two deep and two high, but it was heavy. Tuvaellis carried her own satchel.

By the time they'd made their way back to the wharf, the two ruffians were cursing the awkward trunk and shooting her scathing glances. She paused at the end of a dock, then found the *Mary Gently* and halted before the man at the end of its plank. The two boys plunked the trunk down behind her.

The sailor eyed her, then the two boys. "What do you want?" he asked.

Tuvaellis straightened slightly and the man's eyes widened. He drew back, clutching the manifest he held in his hands closer to his chest. His white, wispy hair blew around his head; his beard was scraggly and rough.

"I am your passenger."

He ran a hand over his unshaven face. "There's no mention of these ... boys."

"They're here to deliver the trunk to my room, that is all."

The man still hesitated, but finally motioned up the ramp. "Very well. I'll take you to your quarters."

She followed as he stumped up the ramp, then down a short ladder into the depths of the ship. The two thieves spat and argued as they navigated the steps and the narrow corridor beyond before depositing the trunk at the door to what would be her quarters for the next month or more.

"This is where you'll be stayin'," the sailor muttered, motioning to a room barely large enough to hold her and the trunk. A cot folded down from one wall beneath a set of cupboards. A chamber pot sat in one corner. The only interruptions to the monotony of the wood were the worn but polished metal clasps and hinges on the cupboards and the latch to her door. "The mess is down the hall, food served at the bell. You can eat it there, or bring it back here. And I'd suggest you stay off the deck as much as possible. No need to give the crew ideas, what with a woman aboard and all."

Tuvaellis smiled in the shadows of her hood. "The crew does not worry me."

The sailor shook his head. He clearly didn't agree with his captain about bringing a passenger aboard, especially a woman.

The older of the ruffians coughed surreptitiously and gave her a meaningful look.

She frowned, then remembered the coin. Taking it from the folds of her cloak, she tossed it to him. He snatched it out of the air with ease, cast one last greedy look back, then he and his young companion made for the deck.

"You'll only encourage them," the sailor growled.

She didn't answer, simply stared at him until he fidgeted uncomfortably and cleared his throat. "The *Mary Gently* will be leavin' with the tide. We're only waitin' for a last shipment of spices to arrive."

"Very well."

He hesitated a moment more, then harrumphed, stepped carefully around her trunk, and vanished into the corridor.

Tuvaellis lowered the cot and tossed her satchel on it, then stared down at the trunk in the doorway. It was made of oiled wood—oak and ash—polished to a high sheen, its corners fitted with brass accents. The oak had been stained a dark brown, the inlaid ash paneling left its natural color. Two thick leather handles had been pinned to the ends for easy carrying; there were no marks on the trunk.

Tuvaellis knelt down beside it and rested her hand on the top. Even through the wood and the layers of protective cloth, she could feel the pulse of the object nestled inside, the object Walter had given her so many months before. She closed her eyes, her own heartbeat slowing and falling into sync with what was within. It lay silent, but she could sense the potential with which it had been imbued, taste the power it held wrapped in its innocuous form.

They had tried to transport the Shadows across the Arduon, but none of them had survived. They could not sustain their forms over such a large expanse of water, their dissolution occurring even with the foundation of the ship beneath them and the crew to feed upon. So they had turned to politics, attempted to incorporate their own among the ranks of the Families and the Court. But unlike the Provinces, the Families were too closely knit, the opportunities sparse. They had only managed to gain a foothold with the Church of Diermani, a powerful entity within Andover, more powerful than it had ever been since the Rose War, but still not one of the Families of the Court. And they had only gained a foothold at best.

But a foothold would be enough.

Tuvaellis stood, rounded the trunk, then knelt and shoved it across the plank floor to a position under the cot.

If they could not influence the Court, and could not corrupt the highest levels of the Church, then Andover would have to be dealt with in a more drastic manner. It could not be left unattended, could not be left capable of aiding the Provinces, the Alvritshai, or the dwarren.

And it had fallen to Tuvaellis to take care of the matter.

9

DEEP WITHIN THE HAUTTAEREN MOUN-
TAINS beneath Caercaern, two acolytes stood before the solid stone doors of the inner halls, their
eyes glazed with boredom. There were no ceremonies
scheduled for the day, nothing that would require the Chosen or a covey of fellow acolytes or any members of the
Flame to descend into the depths of the ancient halls. Certainly nothing that would require them to open the door
that had been carved from two massive slabs of granite, the
scenes on each—one depicting a lost location of the northern reaches during summer, leaves fluttering on a warm
breeze; the other the same scene held in the icy throes of
winter, the trees skeletal—worked in such detail that neither acolyte dared to touch them. The two had compared
notes on the Sanctuary's activities when they'd first arrived
and relieved those who had stood guard before them, had
stared at each for a moment, then sighed and settled in for
a long watch. With nothing scheduled, they would be guarding the doors for the next eight hours, with nothing to do
but stare into the darkness of the corridor beyond the slew
of lanterns that lit the room.

"I don't understand."

Caera shifted uncomfortably. The acolytes that guarded

the doorway to the inner halls were supposed to remain ritually silent. They weren't supposed to converse.

But she'd already suffered four hours of silence.

Reluctantly, she said, "What don't you understand?"

A tension in Thaddaeus' shoulders relaxed, as if he thought he'd be reprimanded for speaking. Both of them remained standing in place, at ease, but backs straight, their leather armor hidden beneath brown robes, ceremonial staffs held before them, butts planted solidly on the stone floor of the corridor. Neither glanced toward the other.

"Why we're here. The formality of it. No one is coming down to the inner sanctum today. The Chosen and the others know that. So why send two acolytes? We could be doing something else, something important."

"Such as?"

"Research. Study. Contemplation."

"Perhaps that is what we are supposed to be doing now. Contemplating. In silence."

Thaddaeus fell silent, rebuked. Caera raised her head slightly, stood a fraction straighter.

Then broke the silence five minutes later. "What are you contemplating?"

Before Thaddaeus could answer, a hollow booming sound filled the wide chamber where they stood. Both acolytes stiffened and shot each other terrified glances as the echoes faded down the corridor that stretched out before them.

"I think it came from behind us," Thaddaeus said, his voice weak and thready.

Caera turned and looked at the massive doors. The two scenes—summer and winter—were split down the center by a border a hand wide. Near chest height, two huge bronze rings had been set into the stone, used to pull the doors open when one of the Sanctuary's many ceremonies required descending into the mountain depths to Aielan's

Light, or when one of the acolytes required access to the ancient Alvritshai halls for their research.

Thaddaeus reached forward to grasp one of the rings before glancing toward Caera in uncertainty. She shrugged.

The hollow boom echoed again through the corridor and Caera was gratified to see Thaddaeus flinch. Then he pulled on the bronze ring, the counterweighted door opening smoothly but slowly.

From the depths beyond, three members of the Flame stepped forward, two torches raised to ward against the darkness.

The leader's eyes latched onto Caera and she started.

"I am Vaeren Tir Assoum, caitan of the Order of the Flame. I need to speak to the Chosen immediately."

As Aeren, Eraeth, Colin, Siobhaen, and Hiroun crested the last ridge before the descent into Artillien, the first of the town's bells began ringing, announcing their lord's arrival home.

Aeren shook his head, his face set as a lord's should be as he contemplated his holdings, the winter sun harsh on the water of the lake, the Rhyssal House banners flapping over his manse, but Colin could see the twitch in his cheek below his eye as he tried to control his relief over being home. If Siobhaen had not been here, he thought the lord might have actually smiled, but her presence had put a strain on their entire journey back through the mountains and to Rhyssal House lands. Neither Aeren nor Eraeth trusted her, so both refused to relax in her presence.

"One of the House towns or outposts must have sent word ahead of us," Eraeth said, edging his horse ahead of Aeren, "to alert them to our arrival."

"As they should," Aeren said stiffly. But then Aeren

sighed and let a small smile peek through. "Perhaps they will have a feast waiting for us."

Eraeth merely grunted, although his horse snorted and stamped the stone roadway as if in anticipation. Hiroun grinned.

"I could use a feast," Colin said. He shifted in his saddle, trying to relieve the pressure of his wound. He'd wanted to drink from the Well in order to speed up the healing process, but he'd drunk more in the last few weeks than he had in the last few decades and didn't want to allow the taint of the Well to spread any more than necessary. But the pain had slowed them down. "And a night of complete rest in a real bed."

"I, as well," Siobhaen said.

The tension between her and those from Rhyssal tightened as she spoke, but Aeren simply nodded toward Artillien, where more bells had joined the first and they could now see activity within the manse overlooking the lake. "It will be good to see Moiran and Fedaureon," Aeren murmured, then nudged his horse over the rise.

They rode through the town without halting, shouts rising from those they passed, slowing only as they reached the roadway up to the walls of the manse. The gates were open, Rhyssal House Phalanx waiting to either side to take their horses, but Aeren's gaze locked onto his wife and son where they stood on the steps of the manse. Colin hung back, beside Siobhaen, as the lord dismounted, Eraeth close behind, younger guardsmen leading their horses away as Aeren strode up to the landing.

"House Rhyssal welcomes home its lord," Moiran said with a bow of her head. She could not keep the smile from her face, nor the warmth from her voice.

"And its lord is glad to be home," Aeren said with a broad grin. He nearly laughed, but caught himself. A small crease of concern etched his brow briefly as he gazed at

Moiran, and with a closer look Colin realized why. Moiran had aged while they were gone. New wrinkles touched the skin around her eyes and mouth, making her face look drawn and tired.

Fedaureon had aged as well, although in a different way. He stood straighter, shoulders back, his face full of eager vitality.

Moiran's gaze swept through the remaining three members of the party. "Where are the others—caitan Vaeren and the rest of the Flame?"

Aeren immediately sobered. "Much has happened, none of which we can speak of here."

Moiran nodded. "I have had a meal prepared. We can discuss everything in the confines of your study. Fedaureon, accompany your father. I'll see to the rest of the guests."

She motioned Fedaureon and Aeren forward, Eraeth and Daevon trailing behind, Fedaureon speaking to his father in a hushed voice almost immediately. The last Colin saw of them, Aeren had frowned. Then they were lost to the shadows beneath the portico.

Moiran moved down the steps and clasped Colin's hands. "It is good to see you return, old friend." Her gaze slid toward Siobhaen, and Colin suddenly realized that he and Hiroun had positioned themselves to either side of her, as if they were guarding her, hemming her in.

"It's good to be back, although I won't be staying for long. I don't believe you were formally introduced to Siobhaen before."

Moiran's hands tightened their hold, "No, but I remember her. Welcome, Siobhaen."

Siobhaen bowed her head. "Aielan's Light upon you and your House."

Moiran caught Colin's gaze, brow furrowed in consternation. But she had been the Tamaell's wife for far too long to ask questions she knew he could not answer here.

She led them into the manse, but slowly, and Colin suddenly realized she was giving Fedaureon and Aeren time to talk. They passed through the halls to Aeren's study, where a table had been set, already laden with trays of fruit and cheese and a decanter of wine. Servants were removing extra place settings, laid out for Vaeren and the others, Colin assumed. Aeren, Eraeth, and Fedaureon were at the massive desk, papers scattered before them, Aeren scanning them with intent. Moiran frowned at them, but motioned Colin, Siobhaen, and Hiroun toward seats, even as the first steaming tray of food arrived.

Aeren looked up as the robust aroma of roasted meat and vegetables filled the room, then dropped the missive he'd been reading. "We can discuss this later," he said to Fedaureon, even though he remained troubled.

Fedaureon began to protest, but at a look from Daevon, he became silent.

The entire group seated themselves, Moiran and Aeren at each end of the table, as more platters began to arrive. Aeren nodded to Fedaureon to formally bless the food in Aielan's name, and then the group began serving themselves from the heaping trays.

For a long moment, no one spoke, Moiran's eyebrows rising in shock as those in the party ate as if ravenous. Colin grunted at his first bite of the roasted pheasant, flavored with a sauce containing rosemary and other herbs. Servants poured wine and hustled to replace empty platters, bowls of a creamy squash soup appearing, with some kind of spice that left a mild burn on the back of the tongue. But as soon as the initial hunger for something besides fire-roasted rabbit eaten with fingers had been slaked, Aeren asked, too casually, "So what has occurred in my absence?"

Colin felt a moment of surprise when Fedaureon straightened in his seat, washing down a bit of meat with a swallow of wine before he began. Moiran had always given the reports in the past.

"Winter harvests went well. We have an excess of wheat from the central and eastern fields. I've allocated most of it for use in the Ilvaeren, the rest for trade with the Provinces. Nearly half of that is already on its way to Neaell, to be stored and shipped south in the spring."

"And I have already contacted some of the other ladies of the Ilvaeren regarding the portion we have kept," Moiran said. "I believe that we can use the grain to garner some decent concessions regarding our own future needs."

Aeren nodded, then motioned toward Fedaureon with his knife. "Continue."

Fedaureon launched into a further accounting of some of the early winter harvests, a nervous tightness around his eyes relaxing as he spoke, as if he'd expected Aeren to be disappointed with the decisions he had made while they were gone. But Aeren said nothing, questioning him occasionally on his reasoning, or offering up a different point of view, but never actively countering any of the decisions his son had made. Colin did notice that none of the discussion concerned anything that would be of interest to Siobhaen or the Order of Aielan; both Fedaureon and Aeren were obviously still aware of her presence. Watching Fedaureon, Colin caught moments—an expression, a gesture—when he reminded him so strongly of Aeren as he had been when they'd first met on the plains that he winced.

Moiran reached forward and touched his arm, drawing his attention away from father and son, then said in a soft voice, "I shocked Fedaureon a little while you were away. Until recently, we've been including him in the decisions made for the House, both in the Evant and the Ilvaeren, but the final decisions have been ours. When Aeren left for this little adventure," her voice was tinged with the disapproval she'd voiced before they'd departed, "I decided that it was time Fedaureon received a taste of what making the decisions himself would be like."

"And?"

"He fared . . . well."

Colin grinned. "Meaning he didn't make the decisions you or Aeren would have made."

"Not on all counts, no. But that is to be expected. He is not Aeren, and I do not expect him to be. One day the House will be his. He will learn from his mistakes."

Colin's heart faltered. He could not conceive of the Rhyssal House without Aeren as its lord. At the time they met on the plains, Aeren had been the younger of two sons, there for his Trial, with the expectation that his brother Aureon would ascend and take over the House on their father's death. But since then, since Colin's emergence from the Ostraell and his transformation into Shaeveran by the Well, Aeren had been the House's lord.

The fact that this would change, that it was inevitable, disturbed him enough he set his knife and fork down, suddenly no longer hungry. He reached for his wine instead.

"And it doesn't bother you?"

Moiran looked surprised. "That he will learn from his mistakes?"

Colin smiled. "No, that one day the House will be his."

She chuckled, shaking her head before looking Colin in the eye. He didn't know what she saw there, but the smile on her lips faltered and she straightened, one hand reaching for his arm again. "Colin, I have served as the Tamaea, whose sole purpose aside from leading the ladies of all of the other Houses in the Ilvaeren was to raise the heirs to the Alvritshai throne. I spent nearly all of my life preparing Thaedoren and his brother Daedelan for their rise to power. This role didn't change when Fedorem died and I was bonded to Aeren. Only the scale. I've spent the last thirty years preparing Fedaureon to take Aeren's place." She squeezed his arm. "You, of all people, should be aware of how time changes everything."

"Yes, I am. And yet you and Aeren have been the one constant presence in my life since I returned from drinking from the Well."

Moiran frowned. "But we will die, Shaeveran. You know that."

"I know it, but that does not mean I have accepted it."

Moiran searched his face a long moment, concerned. Eraeth sat to one side, listening to Fedaureon and Aeren's conversation intently, although he'd been watching Colin and Moiran. Colin couldn't read his expression, but when he turned aside, a troubled look passed over the Protector's face. His gaze paused on Siobhaen, then dropped to consider Aeren before growing distant with thought.

Eventually, the conversation and focus on food died down, everyone settling back in their seats with glasses of wine close by, a mood of satiation and contentment settling over the room. The tautness in Fedaureon's face and body had released, and even Colin felt some of the stresses of the harsh travel falling away. He slumped in his chair, adjusting his position as pain shot up from his mostly-healed side. Silence settled, broken only by the crackle of the fire in the hearth and the occasional heavy sigh.

Until Hiroun yawned. The Phalanx guardsman had nearly nodded off where he sat twice already, his head lowering, eyes slowly closing, before jerking up at the last minute.

Aeren smiled and Moiran chuckled.

With a significant glance toward her husband, Moiran rose and said, "I think we should allow our guests to retire for the evening, Fedaureon. They have returned from a long journey and, so I've gathered, will be leaving us again shortly."

"Not all of us," Colin said.

Her eyebrows lifted, but she said nothing. Fedaureon stood as the rest rose as well, all except Aeren and Colin.

"Hiroun," Moiran said, "if you could escort Siobhaen to her quarters, I'll see that the rest of the rooms are prepared."

Siobhaen nodded. "Thank you, Lady Moiran. It has been a pleasure being a guest of your House."

The two left, Hiroun leading Siobhaen, although she could not have been unaware of the second guardsman who fell in behind them both. Colin expected Moiran and Fedaureon to depart as well, but they both stayed. As servants began clearing away the plates and serving trays, the relaxed atmosphere died and Colin suddenly realized that he would not be retiring to his rooms as early as he had thought, not based on the looks that fell on him from Aeren and Fedaureon. Eraeth, strangely, did not want to face him. But Moiran picked up on the tension in the room and settled back into her seat.

"It seems there is still something left to discuss," she murmured, then motioned for a servant to bring another decanter of wine.

"So it would seem," Colin said, and let some annoyance creep into his voice as he leaned forward, "although I'm not certain what it could be."

"It's Siobhaen," Fedaureon blurted.

"More specifically, the Order of the Flame and Lotaern," Aeren added.

A thread of anger began niggling its way up from Colin's stomach. "We've already been over this on the return trip. More than once. You cannot come with me and Siobhaen to the east." He turned on Fedaureon before the boy could speak, the youth already drawing breath, "And neither can you!"

Moiran stiffened in her chair, a small motion but one that sent ripples through the room. "You will not go wherever it is you're planning to go, Aeren. Not this time. You or Fedaureon."

The finality in her voice rang through the room like the clear tones of a bell.

"He knows that, Moiran. We've already discussed it. I thought we'd agreed."

Aeren shook his head. "That was before I knew what has been happening since we left."

Colin shot a glance at Moiran, saw her frown. "What's happening?"

"Remember on our way to the Hauttaeran Mountains how Siobhaen and the other members of the Flame were stopping at nearly every temple, ostensibly for prayer and reflection?"

"Yes."

"It wasn't just Siobhaen and Vaeren," Eraeth said, his voice low.

"What do you mean?"

Aeren hesitated, caught Moiran's gaze, then motioned toward Fedaureon.

The youth leaned forward. "Approximately twenty days after you left, a member of the Order of the Flame along with a few escorting acolytes arrived in Artillien. They were welcomed at the temple in the town below, of course, and once we heard of their arrival we informed them that Lord Aeren was not present, but invited this member of the Flame and his party here to the manse nonetheless."

"We were politely but firmly refused," Moiran interjected.

"We sent out House guardsmen to inquire in the surrounding area, including the adjacent Houses of Baene and Nuant. There are dozens of these groups in all three House lands, moving from temple to temple, staying longer in the larger towns and cities."

"What are they doing?" Colin asked.

Moiran shook her head. "Nothing except what the Order has always done for the people. They are performing services. More often than usual, and perhaps with more precision and dedication, but nothing out of the ordinary."

"Nothing that we can use to force the members of the Flame and their escorts to withdraw," Aeren said.

"And that is precisely the reaction that we've heard from the other ladies and lords we've sent messages to," Moiran said. "The continued presence of the Flame—even a single member—makes everyone uneasy. Their actions are unsettling. We want them to withdraw, to return to Caercaern—"

"But they've done nothing that will allow us to request it of Lotaern."

"And worse, the people have been flocking to the temples to see them, to see the rituals performed with all of their subtle nuances, with the flare of Aielan's Light in the fires at the end and the sprinkling of the waters over those crowded into the hall." She shook her head. "They are there for the spectacle, for the relief of the winter boredom now that the last of the harvests are in and the snows are heavier, and yes, some are there for true religious reasons, but it doesn't matter why they are going. What matters is that they are being drawn in. I fear they are being seduced."

Fedaureon had fallen silent as his mother and father went back and forth. Colin felt badgered on both sides, Aeren to his left and Moiran to his right, even though Moiran had been speaking mostly to Aeren, her eyes watching him, not Colin.

Aeren drew in a deep breath. "After all of this activity, and after what happened at the Well with Vaeren, we cannot trust Siobhaen, regardless of the fact that she stayed at the Well to uphold Aielan's Light to save us all. That sacrifice may not have been a sacrifice at all; it may have been planned."

Colin's eyes widened. "You think that Lotaern knew that

the Wraith and the Shadows would be there? That he knew I'd be incapacitated and he rigged it so that Siobhaen could gain our trust? You have more faith in Lotaern's abilities than I do."

"You said yourself that you knew of Lotaern's intentions to gain the knife before you even departed from Caercaern," Eraeth countered.

"Yes, but I do not think he had a specific plan for how to do that. He sent Vaeren and Siobhaen and the others with me so that *if the opportunity arose* they could retrieve the knife. I didn't expect the opportunity to arise, but Vaeren seized the moment when it did."

"And now Lotaern has the knife and is obviously using the Flame for something else throughout Alvritshai lands. Yet you insist on traveling to the dwarren with a woman who is a potential traitor and with no protection."

Colin smiled coldly. "You don't think I can handle her on my own?"

"You have to sleep at some point, Shaeveran," Eraeth said.

The use of his Alvritshai name cut off Colin's bitter response. After a moment of silence, he said, "You may be correct about Siobhaen. But as Moiran has pointed out, you and Fedaureon are needed here, to protect Rhyssal House interests in Caercaern and to protect its lands. You cannot allow the incursion of the Flame through Alvritshai lands to go unchallenged. You'll have to go to Caercaern. Which means Fedaureon will have to remain here to watch over your House and lands. There is no one else I would trust to accompany me and Siobhaen."

Aeren frowned at the blunt summary, at a loss for words. Fedaureon glanced toward his father, uncertain of what to say, then to Daevon.

Then Eraeth said, "I will go."

Colin would have sworn he heard a gasp, even though no

one made a sound. But everyone stilled, Moiran drawing in a breath and holding it. Her gaze danced back and forth between Aeren and Eraeth, neither of the two looking toward the other, Eraeth holding himself stiffly. His stance looked uncomfortable.

Only Fedaureon dared to speak. "But you're my father's Protector."

"That does not mean that he needs to be near me at all times, Fedaureon. He has left my side before." Aeren shifted in his chair, twisting to look at Eraeth. "If this is what you wish, I will not forbid it."

Aeren's voice was carefully controlled. Colin could not read anything from it, could not tell whether Aeren approved or disapproved, was angry or elated or even surprised.

The silence held, everyone waiting for Eraeth's response. He finally looked at Aeren. "It is the best solution to the current problem. One that satisfies everyone, I believe."

He looked at Colin questioningly, as if asking whether or not Colin trusted him. But there was no question. Eraeth had carried Colin from the battlefield at the Escarpment, had taught him Alvritshai, had done countless other things since. He trusted Eraeth as much, if not more, than Aeren himself.

But he had not thought Eraeth would separate himself from Aeren's side. He had before, on Aeren's order, but never like this. Not for an extended period of time. And not at his own suggestion.

Moiran glared in protest, although she did not speak, obviously restraining herself.

Aeren finally nodded. "Then so be it."

~

Colin left the warmth of his rooms in the Rhyssal House manse and moved through the darkened halls toward the secluded gardens on the promontory of rock overlooking the lake. He paused outside the great room that was also Aeren's study, heard the low murmur of voices, recognized Aeren's and Moiran's, their tones intense and fraught with worry and tension, so he moved on, past the kitchens where a few servants saw him but did not approach, and then through the outer doors.

The night air was biting, but he did not turn back. He breathed it in deeply, let it scour his lungs clean, then closed the doors behind him and made his way into the gardens. They were designed for relaxation, the pathways curling in and out among rock and bush and tree, nearly all of the plants dead and denuded of leaves by winter. A few conifers, carefully sculpted into windswept layers by the gardeners under Moiran's supervision, appeared black in the moonlight. He passed through them, over stone or wooden bridges with ponds frozen beneath, through a few drifts of snow that had piled up from the winds during the day, until he stood on the wide wooden terrace that had been built over the edge of the stone promontory. Resting his hands on the railing, the breeze gusting into his face, reddening his skin, he stared out over the black water, flecked with reflected light from the moon above.

He tried to think of nothing. But all he could see in the black surface below was the movement of the Lifeblood underground, the pull of the current as whatever Walter had done—and he knew in his gut it had been Walter— drew it eastward.

In the back of his mind, he heard the Wraith that had attacked them at the Well whisper, *We are already moving, our armies already in motion. This is merely the removal of an . . . annoyance.*

He snorted at the insult, but frowned. What armies had the Wraith meant? Were the Shadows on the move? And what of the other Wraiths? They had never established exactly how many there were, and if Walter had found another source of the Lifeblood besides the Wells that Colin had warded, he could be creating even more.

His hands tightened on the polished wooden railing as the old, bitter hatred filled the back of his throat with the taste of bile. It seethed inside him, as the Lifeblood did, roiling to the surface like the black marks beneath his skin.

They had had decades without any interference from Walter or the Wraiths, but that was coming to an end. What frustrated him the most was that he couldn't see *how* it was ending. He couldn't see what Walter intended to do.

He had sunk so far into his hatred and frustration that he did not hear the footfalls until the figure was at his back. He reacted instantly, instinctively, seizing time and slowing it nearly to a halt even as he spun. The absence of his staff made him growl in his throat—his hands were already swinging it around even though they were empty—as he slid smoothly into a low crouch, knees bent, shoulders forward, balanced on the balls of his feet.

He let out his pent-up breath in a sigh as he saw who stood behind him, his face frozen in the first indications of surprise, eyes beginning to widen, his upper body beginning to jerk back. Fedaureon hadn't realized his approach had gone unnoticed.

As Colin relaxed, he fought back his own surprise. He would have expected Eraeth or Moiran to join him, perhaps even Aeren.

He would never have foreseen Fedaureon seeking him out.

Standing up straight and positioning himself off to one side, a step or two away so that he wouldn't appear threatening, Colin allowed time to resume.

Fedaureon lurched backward, a gasp escaping him even as his hand reached for the cattan strapped to his side. The blade was out before he'd found his balance, his gaze shooting frantically to either side before he caught sight of Colin standing at the railing.

It took him another few deep, shuddering breaths before the tension bled from the Rhyssal heir's shoulders and he stood, resheathing his blade.

He bowed formally toward Colin. "I apologize. I didn't intend to startle you."

Colin considered lying, then smiled. "I should have been aware of your approach long before you got here. It was my fault." He turned away. "I must admit that I'm surprised to find you out here. Did you seek me out on purpose?"

Fedaureon hesitated. Colin glanced toward him from the side, noted the angularity of his face, the eyes that came from Moiran, yet all so young. There was only a vague hint of maturity about him, something subtle in the youth's stance.

He wondered if the Trials had continued whether or not the signs of adulthood would have been ground deeper by this point. It had seemed so for Aeren, and Fedaureon would have returned from his own Trial by now.

"Yes and no," Fedaureon finally answered. "I came to see if you would ask Eraeth to remain. My father has always had his Protector there, not just for protection, but for advice. But I know what you will say."

"That your father is capable of making his own decisions? That he does not need Eraeth there to help him?"

Fedaureon's mouth twisted with irony. "Exactly."

"You came for reassurance." When Fedaureon didn't answer, shifting uncomfortably where he stood, still not looking toward Colin but out over the water instead, Colin added, "Your father is capable of facing Lotaern and the Evant by himself, without Eraeth at his side, Fedaureon. You forget that he will have you near at hand. He will rely on you instead of Eraeth for his strength."

"You mean he will rely on my mother."

Colin's eyes widened at the thread of bitterness in his tone. "He didn't speak to your mother at all at dinner tonight. He received the report from you."

"He will speak to her about it later, I'm certain." Fedaureon said the words tightly, but Colin heard the doubt that had crept into the bitterness.

"I doubt they are arguing about you at the moment."

Fedaureon turned toward him and Colin's heart lurched at the vulnerability in the youth's gaze. He'd never seen such an expression on Aeren's face and he had to remind himself that this was *not* Aeren.

He faced the youth, straightening. "Fedaureon, do you think that I would allow Eraeth to leave your father's side if it weren't important? This is bigger than the Rhyssal House, bigger than the Evant and Lotaern, bigger than even the Alvritshai. You have never had to deal with Walter and the Wraiths and Shadows, never seen what they can do. We halted them before, but not until after they'd awakened the Wells and allowed their sphere of influence to expand to the entire known continent. And now they are beginning to act again . . . have already begun, if what the Wraith told us at the Well in the White Wastes is true and not a bluff. If I do not find out what is happening, then the Alvritshai, the dwarren, and the Provinces will be caught unaware. I need Eraeth's help, no matter how much I protested having help at first. I need it more than Aeren does at the moment. Your father understands that, even if he does not like it. That's why he agreed to let Eraeth go."

Fedaureon considered the information in silence for a long moment, head bowed. When he finally looked up, something had settled in his gaze. His eyes had hardened and his shoulders had squared. "Thank you."

Colin reached out and gripped Fedaureon's shoulder, even though he knew such familiarity was not common among the Alvritshai. He was glad to see Fedaureon did not stiffen at the touch. "Relax, Fedaureon. In the morning, Eraeth and I will leave with Siobhaen for dwarren lands, and you and your father will handle whatever it is that Lotaern is planning here. We'll halt whatever is happening, as we did before."

Fedaureon nodded at the reassuring words.

But Colin heard the falseness in his own voice, felt the roil of uneasiness in his own stomach and in his skin, in the black taint of the Well there. He knew how close the Alvritshai had come to being destroyed at the Escarpment. And he knew how brutal and vicious Walter and the Wraiths could be.

And he knew that on the plains, with the dwarren, he wouldn't be able to protect Aeren, Fedaureon, or Moiran from whatever Lotaern or the Wraiths were planning.

10

T OMSON SWORE AS HIS PLOW clanged against yet another stone, and with a yank of the traces he brought the plowhorse to a halt. The horse stamped her foot on the hard-packed earth, covered over with a thick layer of soggy grass that had been crushed to the plains by the winter snows and had only been exposed to the sunlight two days before. It was still wet with snowmelt, which made for good plowing. The earth was as soft as it was going to get.

But it was riddled with stones.

Wiping the sweat off of his brow with a handkerchief, Tomson shifted the plow to one side and exposed the rock, uttering a silent curse at its size. He knelt down and reached a hand around one edge, pulling it out of the ground. Rich black earth fell away as it came free and he gasped at a twinge in his back as he lifted it up. Carrying it with arms extended straight down, he hobbled toward the edge of the field—only a few rows away—and dropped it where a dozen other stones already littered the ground, then brushed the dirt from his hands and turned.

The rolling hills at the far eastern edge of Temeritt Province filled the horizon, dotted with random copses of trees near streams and the occasional exposed plinth of granite.

Farther to the northeast, he could see where the hills fell away to what the dwarren called the Flats—a vast expanse of dusty earth that stretched to the horizon. The sheer flatness of it sent a shudder through Tomson's shoulders as his eyes scanned south and west. He could barely make out the beginnings of the cliffs called the Escarpment, the natural boundary between human and dwarren lands. Somewhere to the south would be the Serpent River, what most considered the edge of Temeritt lands, but it was lost among the hills. No one had settled beyond the Serpent, which was why Tomson was here. Most claimed that going beyond the Serpent placed settlers beyond the boundary of the Autumn Tree and within the reach of the Shadows.

Tomson had rolled his eyes at the old men in the tavern at the warning three months before, scoffed and walked away with his drink to the far corner of the room. The Shadows. An old wives' tale, used to keep children from sneaking out into the night and getting into trouble. And the Autumn Tree was nothing but a legend as well. GreatLord Kobel used it to keep those in his Province within his grasp, to keep men like Tomson from claiming what was rightfully theirs. The threat of the Shadows was empty, nothing but a ruse to keep settlers away from the fertile plains between the Serpent and the Flats, land that GreatLord Kobel claimed belonged to the dwarren.

Tomson had been out here for two months already and he'd seen no dwarren. Nor any Shadows. Only wide open land, ready to be taken.

His horse snorted and tossed her head, breaking him from his contemplation of the southlands. He frowned at the animal's fear-whitened eyes and flared nostrils. When he moved suddenly toward the bucket of water and his satchel, his horse flinched and shied away from him, drawn up short by the attached plow.

"Steady," he said soothingly. "Steady there, girl."

He knelt down and dug through his satchel, bringing out a sheathed knife and pulling the blade free. He scanned the field, searching for what had unsettled his horse, but saw nothing.

Rising slowly, he turned full circle as he made his way to her side. The muscles beneath her smooth brown coat twitched when he touched her and she snorted again. Her legs were rigid with tension, her body trembling.

"Hush." He stroked her neck, but she didn't gentle.

His frown deepened, his gaze shooting left and right. But the plains were quiet. No breeze stirred. The sky was an empty pale blue overhead.

And then, from the corner of his eye, Tomson caught movement.

He spun, startling the horse forward a pace before his hand closed down on the bridle to hold her. But there was nothing there, nothing visible—

Yet something had changed. Twenty paces away, a section of the unplowed grasses had caved in, as if a giant had poked his finger into the ground.

He straightened, patting the horse's neck again as he shifted forward. His grip tightened on the handle of the knife. Sweat dripped from his forehead into his eyes and he scrubbed it away hastily. More sweat slicked his shirt to his back. The mild spring day suddenly seemed too warm.

He halted a step away from the hole. Earth fell from its edge, dangling by strands of grass a moment before breaking free. He hesitated, then knelt, leaning forward, knife held before him protectively.

The hole had no bottom. It descended into darkness, sunlight flaring down one side, exposed roots jutting from the sides of earth like worms. He breathed in deeply, smelled loam and damp grass, and underneath that a heady scent, like that of a wet muskrat.

Movement. Deep down in the earth.

He leaned farther forward, eyes narrowing—

And then his horse shrieked.

He lurched backward, heart thudding in his chest so hard he gasped and clutched at his shirt with the hand holding the knife. Falling to the ground on his side, he shoved hard with his feet, scrambling backward even as he felt the dirt at the edge of the hole give way. He fell onto his back and rolled, his horse shrieking the entire time. She reared, still tethered to the plow, feet kicking as she shook herself in fear. When she landed, her legs sank into the ground as if it were made of mud, all the way up to her knees.

She shrieked again, began kicking and thrashing, the plow jerking behind her as she tried to back up. Mud churned; through the flying grass and dirt Tomson saw blood streaking the animal's forelegs, splattering high enough to hit her belly. Bile rose to the back of his throat, but terror clamped down hard on his chest. He watched in horror as his horse shrieked a third time, the sound so like a woman's scream that he cringed as it grated across his shoulders and down his spine. The horse redoubled her effort to free herself from the loose soil, but she merely sank deeper, her legs caught beneath the ground, until her belly rested against the earth.

And then Tomson screamed. From the churned earth on either side of the animal, claws reached up and raked across the horse's sides, flesh parting and blood spilling into the already softened soil. His horse screamed again, but the sound held no strength, her head already sagging forward as the ground continued to surge around her body. Tomson's voice shattered the stillness of the rolling plains as completely as his horse's had a moment before. Beneath his own ragged scream, beneath the low rumble of moving earth, he heard another sound, a soft sound, like the dry scratching of leaves. If he could only stop screaming, he thought he might be able to make out words.

But he didn't stop. When his horse's head fell to the

ground and the dry hiss of near conversation escalated, he rolled onto his stomach and lurched to his feet. He staggered three steps, intent on reaching the hollowed-out knoll that he'd made his home, but on the fourth step his leg sank into the soil.

The sudden loss of stability cut his screams short as he collapsed to his hands. He clutched at the sodden grass, gasped once—

Then felt claws sink into his calf muscles and tug sharply down.

He hadn't thought he could scream any louder than before, but he did.

Jerking his leg free, hearing a frustrated hiss from beneath the ground, he scrambled forward on hands and knees, panting, tears streaking his face, sobs escaping in the hitched breath between screams. But twenty paces later the ground gave way completely and he plunged beneath the earth.

His screams lasted another ten minutes, until they were drowned out by the soft hiss of dried leaves. Five minutes later even that faded.

Silence descended on the plains, where the handles of a plow jutted into freshly churned, bloody earth.

~

"Why are we waiting here?"

Colin didn't turn toward Siobhaen, although he caught movement out of the corner of his eye and realized that Eraeth had. He didn't need to look to know there would be a scowl on Eraeth's face. The two had squabbled with each other their entire journey from Artillien, across the Rhyssal, Baene, and Ionaen House lands, and onto the edge of the dwarren territory simply called the Lands. No actual confrontations. But plenty of heated glares, half-muttered comments, and the occasional barb.

Colin had considered abandoning them both on multiple occasions, simply slowing time and escaping. The constant bitterness and suspicion was draining.

"We are waiting here on the edge of Alvritshai lands because of the Accord the Alvritshai and humans made with the dwarren," he said patiently, reaching forward to stroke the neck of his mount. "The Alvritshai agreed to respect the Lands, the Tamaell himself performing the rituals at the Escarpment and offering a formal apology to the dwarren and their gods. The Accord stipulates that no one, human or Alvritshai, may enter the Lands without an accompanying dwarren escort or the express permission of the Cochen."

He turned to face Siobhaen, the young member of the Flame staring out across the dwarren plains, half standing in her saddle, her face scrunched up with doubt. He suddenly realized that Siobhaen's journey to the White Wastes had likely been as far from Caercaern and her own House lands as she'd ever been. But this was different.

They were wandering into occupied territory now.

"You are too impatient," he said. "We haven't been waiting long."

"But what are we waiting for?"

"The dwarren."

Her eyes widened. "But it could take days for them to see us! We aren't even on a road!"

"There are no roads in the Lands. At least, not what you think of as roads. The dwarren believe permanent roads are destructive to the Lands. And the dwarren have already seen us. An escort is on its way."

Siobhaen glared out at the plains in clear disbelief. "I see no one."

But even as she spoke, a group of Riders crested a far ridge and swept down its near side. The group—no more than five in strength—vanished beneath another obstructing fold in the land.

Siobhaen gaped.

"The dwarren have watchers everywhere," Colin explained. "Even though you may not see them."

They waited, Siobhaen's tension rising as the dwarren drew nearer, her mount picking up on her uneasiness, huffing and skittering where it stood. She reached down distractedly to calm it. When the five Riders drew close enough that they could hear the gaezels' hooves, her hand twitched toward her cattan, but she jerked it back with a tight frown.

The dwarren drew up twenty paces distant. Each rode one of the tawny gaezels, the lithe animals smaller than a horse but with wicked looking horns reaching back from their heads. Their sides were streaked with patches of white-and-yellow coloring. The dwarren sat astride saddles, copied from those introduced by the settlers from Andover, who brought the first horses to Wrath Suvane with them, but they didn't use reins; they controlled the gaezels using their horns.

The leader of the dwarren glared at them all, then focused his gaze on Colin. A look of uncertainty crossed his face. All five were dressed in the leather armor of a Rider, their long beards threaded with beads and gold trinkets. Gold chains ran from earrings to their pierced noses, the leader with three chains, the others with only one. One of them bore the markings of a shaman.

The leader also wore a gold armband around his right forearm.

"Why do you wish to enter the lands of the Thousand Springs Clan? What business do you and the Alvritshai have with the dwarren?" he demanded in his own guttural language.

Colin nudged his horse forward a step, the dwarren tensing. "My name is Colin Patris Harten, known as Shaeveran. I've come, with an escort, to speak to the Cochen."

The dwarren stirred at his name, the four behind the

leader shooting glances toward one another as their mounts pawed the ground. No one spoke, but two of them edged away from the group. Only the leader appeared unruffled, his eyes narrowing.

"Prove it."

Colin hesitated. He'd never been asked by the dwarren to prove his identity. He wondered what had happened in the past ten years to change that. But he reached down and pulled up the sleeve of his shirt, exposing his forearm to the bright midmorning sunlight. The swirling patches of darkness beneath his skin were clear enough that the dwarren gasped, murmurs hushed by the leader with a sharp look.

"That proves only that you are one of the elloktu."

"Would one of the Lost be able to stand here on the Lands, this close to the Summer Tree?" Colin couldn't keep a hint of annoyance out of his voice.

The dwarren leader considered in silence, then gave a grudging nod of acknowledgment and respect, although Colin could still see suspicion in his eyes. "Shaeveran. We will escort you to our clan chief, Tarramic."

He spun his gaezel and issued a few curt commands, then motioned them all forward, the group breaking away and one of the dwarren ululating as the scouts spread out to either side.

"What did they say?" Siobhaen asked harshly.

"They questioned who I was, but have offered to escort us to the clan chief."

On his other side, Eraeth said shortly, "That is the first time I have ever seen the dwarren question who you were. Or been so wary of those entering their land. Something has happened."

"We already know that the balance of the Wells has been disrupted. The return of the storms would not have gone unnoticed by the dwarren. Perhaps that is all it is."

All of Eraeth's doubt was voiced in a look.

Colin kneed his mount forward, Eraeth and Siobhaen doing the same to either side. They charged down the low slope in the wake of the dwarren, their horses catching up to the gaezels after a long moment of hard riding, the two groups slowing and adjusting to a steady pace that wouldn't drain their mounts. The leader of the dwarren party ranged out ahead, the other four members dividing and slipping to either side.

~

They rode for two days, setting a fast pace, halting at odd times during the day at water sources to eat and rest, the dwarren raising small tents for sleep at night. Their route was circuitous, the dwarren leading them off the direct path in order to keep their water sources and warren entrances hidden. Twice during the first day, they sighted occumaen in the distance. Not as large as the one that had torn through the battlefields at the Escarpment, but big enough to engulf a man and his horse. Both times, the scouts brought the distortions to the dwarren leader's attention, his face hardening at each occurrence. The second day, storm clouds pounded the plains with a deluge of rain and blue-purple lightning to the north. The entire group paused on a low rise to watch, sunlight shaded with raised hands. Colin felt a tingle of remembered hatred, the cold hands of the dead against his skin. Karen and his parents—along with the rest of the doomed wagon train—had survived such a storm, only to succumb to the Shadows afterward.

For a moment, despair washed over him. What had he achieved since then? Nothing had changed. The world was still plagued by the Wraiths and Shadows, the unnatural storms and the Drifters still riddled the plains. What had been accomplished during all of that time?

"Nothing," he said out loud. Eraeth gave him a sidelong look, but he ignored it.

But something within him hardened. His jaw clenched and he straightened, his hands trying to grasp the handle of the staff Vaeren had taken from him. He would need to ask for a replacement, wasn't certain that the Ostraell would grant it. And he needed to convince the dwarren that the time for complacency was gone. He wasn't certain how he would do that, not with the protection of the Seasonal Trees in place. For the first time since he'd created them, he wished he hadn't. They were defensive, and they were powerful enough to allow the three races to settle back and cower behind that defense under the guise that nothing was wrong. The fact that Walter and the Wraiths hadn't been able to break the defense, that they had vanished from Wrath Suvane as if they had never existed, hadn't helped. Too much time had passed, and the races had grown complacent and lazy.

But no more, he vowed.

He turned toward the leader of their escort. "How much farther to the Thousand Springs cavern?" He knew, but he did not want the dwarren to lose their sense of isolation and security.

The leader tore his gaze from the storm to the north. "Two days, at most."

"No. Not how long if we continue to travel the way we have been traveling. How long if we head directly there?"

The leader scowled, shot a glance toward the dwarren who had the markings of a shaman. When the shaman shrugged, the scowl faded and he caught Colin's gaze. "We can be there by the end of today."

"I need to speak to your clan chief immediately. It concerns the storm and the occumaen and the renewal of the Turning."

The dwarren's eyes widened, and the shaman suddenly stared intently at Colin.

"We will take you to him now."

It was the shaman who spoke, nodding to the leader curtly in an unspoken order.

The leader glared at the three of them as if they'd somehow shamed him on purpose, then pulled on his gaezel's horns to bring the beast about. He said nothing, merely kicking the mount forward with a wordless guttural cry.

All formality fell away as the Riders tore across the plains, the horses struggling to keep up. Colin found himself leaning forward over his horse's neck, urging it onward with soft words. To the side, Eraeth and Siobhaen did the same, although he thought he heard Eraeth cursing. The land fell away, yellow-green grass blurring as the storm to the north edged farther southward, dogging them. The group flowed over the low hills and sped across open flats, heading almost directly south. By the time the horizon began to flare with orange along its length as the sun set, still shimmering with the day's heat haze, Colin felt every muscle in his body burning with the exertion and shudder of the horse's muscles beneath him. He thought they were going to have to ride into the night.

But then they crested another rise, no different than the scores they had already crossed, except that this time, the plains opened up to reveal one of the dwarren tent cities.

Colin had seen them before, but not for twenty years. Thousand Springs had grown since then.

A huge central pole thrust up out of the plains, as thick as the boles of the cedars near the Well in the Ostraell, shorn of limb and with the bark peeled back. Colin had been to the center of the tent city before, had touched that central spire and knew its strength. Blue cloth had been fastened and wound around it, flaring outward at seemingly odd intervals, creating the main enclosure beneath, composed of a hundred rooms, the material twisted, draped, and wrapped around a thousand additional lines, poles, and stakes. The result was a reversed whirlpool, the swirls of cloth winding upward and drawing the eye to the darkening sky above, where the first stars were beginning to appear. In the twilight, the blue of the cloth appeared violet.

The rest of the city had been constructed around this central tent, never reaching as high, but crafted in such a way as to mimic the central flow so that when the winds blew across it, the rippling of the cloth echoed the currents of a river. From this distance, the entrance to the underground warren and the true home of the Thousand Springs Clan couldn't be seen. A hundred years before, the tents would have been erected only when the dwarren were preparing to fight one of their own clans, or the invading Alvritshai or human forces. Now, it appeared more permanent. Lanterns were being lit, and through the silhouettes of tents and the figures of dwarren going about their nightly business, he spotted the wooden fence of a corral alongside a rounded water tower with sluices that led to troughs. Some of the land had been plowed recently, and a few granary huts stood to one side. There were no defenses of any kind; no walls or watchtowers. The dwarren's greatest defense was to retreat beneath the plains, to their interconnected strongholds underground.

The escort of dwarren tore down the side of the ridge without pause, Colin taking in the differences in the tent city as his horse's gait jarred his bones. To the side, he caught Siobhaen gaping at the sight. Within moments, they were moving between the outermost tents, dwarren scrambling out of their way as they began to slow. But the leader of the escort didn't halt. He raced through curved thoroughfares between the tents, moving steadily inward toward the entrance to the caverns beneath. Dwarren shouted at them as they passed, Colin catching shocked faces as the men and women saw the Alvritshai and human in their midst.

By the time they made the last turn, the dwarren who guarded the entrance were waiting for them. There were enough to block the entrance, and the escort was brought up short. The leader and the shaman cantered their gaezels forward to speak to the guards. As they did so, Colin scanned the group, frowning at what he saw.

"What is it?" Eraeth asked immediately.

"There's more than one clan represented in the Riders guarding the entrance. I see Thousand Springs warriors, but also Silver Grass and Shadow Moon Clans here as well."

"What does it mean?"

"If it were merely one other clan, I'd say nothing, but two...." Colin shook his head. He took a closer look at their armor. "They aren't dressed for a formal visit either. They're dressed for war."

The shaman and their leader broke into heated argument, the Riders they spoke to eyeing Colin skeptically. Whatever the shaman said, though, the guard finally relented.

"Stay close," Colin said. "Tensions are bound to be high with three clans present."

Three additional Riders joined their escort, one from each of the three clans, and then the shaman led the group down into the black entrance to the dwarren tunnels. The three horses balked at passing underground, but relented after some coaxing.

The main entrance opened up into a large room, then narrowed to a doorway, giant doors pulled back to the side beneath a massive mantle of carved stonework. For the first long leg, the grade of the slope was smooth, the corridor shored up and lined with cut stone of various colors from across the plains, massive support columns at regular intervals. Each support column had a central keystone in place at its height, which Colin knew could be knocked out, allowing the arch and a good portion of the tunnel roof to collapse. If the main doors couldn't be held, then the dwarren were prepared to seal the entrance completely. Each section between keystones was lit with metal sconces of oil to either side.

Once they passed beyond this initial defense, the corridor narrowed and branched, the cut stone giving way to a type of granite that was too smooth to be natural, with no obvious seams to indicate how it had been constructed. It appeared to be made of solid rock, yet with carved murals at various points along its length. The number of sconces dropped, so that they passed from one pool of light to the next, the space between growing dark, but close enough to the next sconce that it wasn't completely black. More and more dwarren appeared, carrying baskets or satchels, some pulling carts or pushing wagons loaded with stone or grain or unidentified barrels. Interspersed among them all were dwarren Riders, usually in groups of two or three, an occasional messenger trotting alone, a carved wooden cylinder clutched in one hand like a baton.

Then the corridor changed, sloping downward sharply enough that the escort Riders were forced to slow. The number of dwarren increased as well, the corridor now thronged with them—women and children appearing with greater frequency, nearly all of them carrying baskets or satchels of food. More joined them from side corridors in steady streams. At Siobhaen's questioning look, Colin said, "They're returning from the surface. They must be harvesting early spring crops."

The corridor ended suddenly, opening up into a massive cavern filled with the roar of thousands of dwarren and the thunderous crash of water. As they descended a ramp to the wide flat plaza that made up the center of the cavern, Colin heard Siobhaen gasp. Even Eraeth drew back in shock.

Water streamed down the entire far wall of the cavern, its source coming from at least three major tunnels and two smaller ones, the streams crashing together in midair before plummeting in a single column to a massive pool below. The air was filled with mist, lit by hundreds of sconces scattered around the plaza and shining from the openings that covered the remaining walls of the rest of the chamber. This was the dwarren's true city, rooms carved out of the walls all the way to the ceiling that towered overhead. Stairs and ledges zigzagged from door to door in a maze that nevertheless appeared to follow an intricate pattern, one that Colin thought he would be able to make out if he could spare the time. It was a hive of activity, bustling with dwarren as they moved from one level to another. Near the base of the walls, larger doorways led to storerooms, and nearer to the waterfall lay the chambers set aside for the clan chief, the head shaman, and the keeva—the room reserved for ritual contemplation and the heavy decisions made by both.

The escort surrounded them and led them toward the keeva after a word with a group of dwarren standing guard near the entrance to the cavern. As they approached, Colin picked out the heavy scent of yetope smoke beneath the thick layer of dampness and the heavy musk of earth and dwarren living in enclosed quarters for centuries on end. The doors to the keeva were shut, but he could see light shining in the cracks between it and the frame. A faint wisp of smoke curled from the edge near the top.

When the dwarren escort halted outside the chamber, Colin dismounted. Without waiting for the group to speak to the shaman guards who stood outside the door, he strode forward, leaving Eraeth and Siobhaen in mid-dismount.

The two shamans tensed instantly, reaching to block his path with the two scepters they carried, the snakes' rattles and strings of beads clicking together with a sharp crack.

Colin seized time, stepped between them and beneath the supposed barrier, coming up before the keeva's door. He reached for the door handle, releasing time a moment before he touched it and shoved the door open, ducking down through the low lintel designed more for the dwarren than humans. He straightened as much as he could inside, hand still on the door, heard gasps and shouts of consternation behind him, but he ignored it all, knowing that Eraeth and Siobhaen could defend themselves if necessary. He focused his attention on the six dwarren who sat in a rough circle around the central hollow of the fire pit, obscured by the thick haze of yetope smoke.

"If you're discussing the Turning," he said, "then I have information for you."

The shouts from behind had changed to anger. He slid to one side, the six dwarren clan chiefs and shamans glaring at his hunched form, one of them sucking on the end of a pipe even though the yetope was thrown in the central fire for such meetings. One of the shaman guards burst into the room, anger twisting his face into a tight knot. He gave Colin a vicious look, then turned to the clan chiefs and head shamans in the room.

Brandishing his scepter, he bowed his head and said roughly, "Apologies, Old Ones. This *human*—" he spat the word "—passed between us before we could halt him. He is one of the elloktu!"

The eyebrows of the shaman sucking on the pipe rose. He took two more draws, then removed the pipe and blew smoke into the miasma already beginning to thin from the draft coming from the open door.

"The elloktu cannot survive here," he said in a cold, deep voice cracked with age. "Or have you forgotten the gift of the Summer Tree?" He turned his wizened eyes on Colin again. "Shadowed One. We have not met, but I know of you. Your legend has been passed down to our generation, even though it is not yet an old legend."

Colin nodded. "I am thankful to hear that."

A silence followed, the shaman who'd spoken not taking his eyes off Colin. The rest of those gathered shared glances, until one of the clan chiefs stirred.

"Leave," he said, motioning the guard out. "You are disturbing the smoke."

The guard straightened, cast a questioning look at the head shamans in the group, but got no support from them. With a last scathing look at Colin, he departed, shutting the door behind him.

The tableau held for a moment, then one of the clan chiefs motioned toward a space before the fire, a natural shelf of rock that acted as a bench. Colin settled himself, his position still awkward, then leaned back against the rock wall. The entire chamber had been hollowed out by water ages past so that the contours were smooth, not carved or chipped. With the door closed, the heat in the room doubled, sweat breaking out on Colin's back, chest, and armpits. He breathed in deeply, taking in the sweet, cloying yetope smoke, even as one of the clan chiefs tossed more of the dried plant onto the coals in the pit. Flames flared as it was consumed, smoke drifting up, until it was so thick Colin could barely make out the other dwarren in the reddish light.

When he exhaled, slowly, so as not to break into a fit of coughing, the shaman with the pipe spoke. "Welcome to our council, Shadowed One. I am called Quotl, head shaman of Thousand Springs, and this is Oaxatta of Shadow Moon, and Attanna of Silver Grass."

"And I am Tarramic, clan chief of Thousand Springs." The dwarren who'd ordered the shaman guard to leave motioned toward the other two clan chiefs. "Iktamman of Silver Grass, and Ummaka of Shadow Moon."

"May Ilacqua bless this meeting and bring us wisdom in our decisions," Quotl intoned, motioning with his pipe as if it were a scepter. The words were reverent, but a smile turned one corner of his mouth a moment before he drew again on the pipe. In the dimness, Colin thought his eyes flared with amusement.

Tarramic shifted where he sat. "What do you know of the Turning, Shadowed One?" His tone suggested he doubted Colin would know anything of importance.

"The balance of the Wells has been disrupted."

Iktamman snorted. "The storms have plagued the plains for months, and now the Eyes of Septimic have returned."

"The gods are angry," Oaxatta agreed. "It is a sign. The Turning is upon us."

Quotl's eyebrows rose again. "The Turning began generations ago. It has simply begun to speed up."

Most of the dwarren fell silent at this, a few making rumbling sounds of agreement in their chests.

"It is more than that," Colin said, already beginning to feel the effects of the smoke and heat. His arms and legs tingled, both taking on additional weight. At the same time, the heaviness was countered by a lightness in his mind, as if he were lifting free of his body. The dual sensation brought with it a sense of clarity. "The Wraiths and the Shadows—the urannen—have found a deeper, richer source of the Lifeblood to the east. They've opened up a conduit between it and the Wells here in the west."

All six of the dwarren eyed him warily, then traded a glance. Something passed between them, and then Quotl gave Tarramic a curt nod. The head shaman no longer seemed amused.

"We called this meeting because of what we have seen on the plains. The storms and the distortions have grown too numerous and too dangerous for us to ignore them any longer. We have also heard from the other clans that there are disturbances to the east, an increase in the activity of the urannen and a resurgence of the kell. The clans have always sent war parties out beyond the reach of the Summer Tree to hunt them, kill them where we can, but their numbers have increased and they have begun banding together. The war parties, the trettarus, can now be overwhelmed. There are also disturbing sightings beyond the borders of dwarren lands, beyond the plains, in the depths of the Thalloran Wasteland. The trettarus report bands of figures—Alvritshai or men—walking the sands. No one has dared enter the Wastelands to confirm this.

"We gathered to discuss whether or not a Gathering of all of the clans should be called. We have been discussing it for three days now."

Colin's heart sank. He thought again of the Wraith's words at the Well in the White Wastes. Even the lassitude brought on by the yetope could not still the sudden urgency that gripped him.

"What have you decided?" he asked.

Before the clan chiefs and head shamans could respond, the dull boom of drums resounded through the room, damped by the walls of stone that surrounded them. Colin glanced toward the closed door, even as the six dwarren stirred from their seats. Only Quotl seemed unfazed by the interruption.

When Colin turned toward him, he smiled.

"The decision has been made for us. We Gather. All clans, all Riders. We Gather at the Sacred Waters, beneath Ilacqua's gaze. We Gather for war."

11

"**W**HAT'S GOING ON?" Siobhaen asked the moment Colin stepped out of the keeva, the rest of the clan chiefs and head shamans already out in the cavern. The sound of the drums, at least three times louder in the chamber than inside the small room where the meeting had been held, had driven the dwarren into a frenzy of activity. He could hear the clan chiefs shouting orders, Riders scrambling to obey, the rest of the dwarren sprinting to get out of the way. The sudden activity and the harsh boom of the drums had set the horses and gaezels on edge.

"The dwarren have been called to a Gathering."

"And what does that mean?" she asked in frustration. A group of dwarren jostled past her and she frowned down at them in annoyance, one hand gripping her horse's bridle as she stepped back.

"It's like calling the Evant," Eraeth said. "The dwarren only call a Gathering for something of extreme importance, something affecting the dwarren as a whole. Otherwise, the clan chiefs deal with it individually."

"The presence of three clan chiefs in one territory was significant enough, but this will bring them all together."

"Where? And over what?" Eraeth asked.

Colin paused and listened to the deep bass throat of the drums. "The call is coming from the Painted Sands Clan, the easternmost dwarren territory. But they're meeting at the Sacred Waters. They're headed toward the Confluence."

As he said it, the heavy boom of the drums faded. The dwarren paused for a moment, then resumed their frantic activity at a growled shout from Quotl. At the same time, a smaller drum within the chamber picked up a different rhythm, the sound echoing through the hall and up the long corridor toward the surface.

"I still don't understand," Siobhaen muttered.

Colin ignored her, stepping forward into the edge of the confusion. The two Alvritshai, Colin, and the horses had been left by the keeva, practically unattended. He searched for Clan Chief Tarramic, found him arguing with two of the head shamans, all three of them gesturing toward the mouth of the corridor where the summons had originated.

Behind, he heard Eraeth speaking to Siobhaen in a soft voice.

"The Confluence is the religious center of the dwarren. It's the heart of their culture. No Alvritshai has ever been there. It was the goal of the Trials that those in the ruling Houses made before the Accord put an end to it. The sons and daughters of the ascendant lords were sent into the plains in search of the ruanavriell, the Blood of Aielan. Most found tunnels on the plains that led to streams or pools of water suffused with the healing water's runoff, but no one ever found the source."

Colin thought of the vial of pink-tinged water that Aeren had gifted to his father, the result of Aeren's own Trial, and felt a tug of bitterness, the emotion too used and worn to remain long. Whatever his father had used it for had been for naught once they reached the Ostraell.

Siobhaen considered what Eraeth had said, then stepped up to Colin's side. "But it doesn't make sense. The dwarren aren't reacting to what we know has happened to the sare-navriell. They can't be. The drums came before you emerged from the room with the clan chiefs."

"You're right. This is something else." He hesitated, then added, "I think it has to do with the activity to the east."

"What activity?" Eraeth demanded.

"Activity with the Shadows. Sightings of another creature they call the kell in larger and larger groups. And bands of Alvritshai or perhaps humans deeper in the Thalloran Wasteland."

"Alvritshai in the Wastelands?" Siobhaen scoffed. "Impossible. We come from the north. We would never survive in the desert."

"Are you so certain? You've adapted to the southern reaches of the mountains rather well."

"Regardless," Eraeth interjected before Siobhaen could respond, "we should send word back to the Evant. The Tamaell should be aware of the dwarren movements, especially on such a large scale."

"Lotaern should be forewarned as well."

Eraeth shot her a piercing look and Colin nearly sighed. Siobhaen would have to bring up Lotaern now, after the two of them had been grudgingly civil to each other for the past few days. But surprisingly, Eraeth said nothing.

"We aren't going to get the chance to send word."

Both Eraeth and Siobhaen reacted at the same time. "Why not?"

Colin let the rumble of thousands of hoofed feet pounding into stone answer for him. Both of the Alvritshai guards turned toward the sound as it filled the cavern with its echo, the drums that had called to the surface falling silent. The dwarren who filled the giant plaza suddenly parted, surging to either side and clearing the space before the main corridor opposite the waterfall. As they did so, the three clan chiefs stepped forward, the head shamans a few paces behind.

A moment later, the leading edge of Riders emerged from the corridor, standing five abreast. Row upon row of the gaezels appeared, the leading group swinging around in a wide circle to make room for those coming behind in a pattern that Colin had first seen on the plains above decades ago. As the wide plaza filled, the number of Riders growing large enough that Colin's heart skipped a beat in his chest, he noted that not all of the gaezels bore dwarren. The group had brought down the mounts of those already below.

Tarramic raised a hand when the last of the Riders appeared, his other stroking the beads and feathers interlaced in his beard. Those milling about in the central plaza stilled, the cessation of sound spreading like a ripple on water from Tarramic's position, although it was impossible for the hall to fall totally silent with the waterfall raging in the background.

As he began to speak, his rumbling voice filling the cavern, Siobhaen grasped Colin's arm in irritation, forced him to look at her. "What is he saying?"

"He's telling the clans—all of the clans present—to prepare to leave for the Sacred Waters. We'll depart at dawn."

"We can send word back to Caercaern then," Eraeth said succinctly.

Colin shook his head. "No. We can't."

"Why not!" Siobhaen's grip tightened.

He turned a somber gaze on her. "Because we won't be traveling on the surface. We'll be traveling underground."

~

Aeren Goadri Rhyssal stood on the balcony of his House holdings in Caercaearn and stared out across the tiered city as it came to life. Lanterns were doused by patrols as the sun dawned on the horizon, gray light filtering through the peaks of the Hauttaeren Mountains where they dipped southward east of the city, purple with distance. The Sanctuary chimes rang utiern.

Aeren's thoughts turned toward Lotaern and the Order of Aielan. He frowned, one hand rising to grip the pendant he wore beneath his shirt, a symbol of all that he had achieved while an acolyte within the Order, before his father and brother died on the battlefields of the plains and forced him to return to ascend as Lord of the Rhyssal House. If he had remained in the Order, would he support Lotaern now, in whatever power play he was making?

He didn't know. It would have been a question he posed to Eraeth, a musing that the man who had practically raised him would have discussed with him in the early hours of dawn before the day began, but his Protector was not here. He felt the loss as a pang in his chest, a hollowness that he had not realized he would experience when he had given the Phalanx guardsman permission to accompany Colin.

Eraeth had been more of an integral part of his life than he had known.

A bitter, ironic smile turned his lips. He should have known. He could not remember a time when Eraeth had *not* been there, except for his years spent in the Sanctuary as an acolyte. His earliest childhood memory was of reaching for his father's sword—the Rhyssal House sword—and having his Protector slap his hand away. He'd glared at the young guard who'd been hovering over him, even as he rubbed the ache from his hand, and vowed revenge. Days later, he'd lined the guard's ceremonial helmet with black ink. It hadn't quite dried yet when Eraeth had donned it for the Licaeta House's arrival that afternoon.

It had taken two more years before he'd outgrown the pranks and come to a grudging acceptance of Eraeth's presence at his side at all times. He'd experienced pain when he'd left the Protector at the doors of the Sanctuary to begin his studies there, but nothing like the loss he felt now.

That pain had lasted a day, perhaps two, before he'd set it aside to focus on the Scripts and his lessons.

This pain was worse. Much worse. Eraeth had departed Artillien with Colin and Siobhaen over a month before and he still found himself turning to ask Eraeth a question at odd moments. He could feel the emptiness of the balcony and the room behind him even now.

He let his hand drop from the pendant and turned, stepping into the inner room where a servant had left a tray of fruit and a plate of scrambled eggs—a commoner's dish he'd grown fond of while trading up and down the Provincial coast. The smell turned his stomach this morning, but he splashed a hot sauce imported from Andover over the eggs and forced himself to eat.

He had a meeting with Tamaell Thaedoren.

"Wait here. The Tamaell will be with you shortly."

Aeren nodded and the servant who'd escorted him to the audience chamber departed, leaving the door open. Two of the White Phalanx, the Tamaell's personal guard, were at the door, along with Aeren's own escort. Hiroun stood with his back against the far wall of the corridor looking in. As the sole surviving Rhyssal guardsman from the journey to the White Wastes—aside from Eraeth, of course—Aeren had added him to his personal escort. He'd found the House Phalanx member to be competent at handling the nuisances of a lord's schedule, as well as its abrupt changes.

At Hiroun's questioning look, he smiled and shook his head, turning away to scan the audience chamber, noting the changes Thaedoren had made since he'd ascended the throne. His father, Fedorem, had kept the Tamaell's chambers in Caercaern sparsely furnished, with chairs, tables, and side tables surrounded by a few urns, tapestries, and pedestals holding statuettes or other artwork. Most of the art had been chosen by Moiran, he'd learned. Those touches permeated the Rhyssal House manse in Artillien now.

Here in the highest tier of Caercaern, all traces of Moiran's or Fedorem's touch were gone. A wide oak table stained a dark color was surrounded by eight similarly stained chairs; a brass platter containing fronds of ferns and an arrangement of flowers filled its center. Similar arrangements lined the two side tables, interspersed with gold candleholders and assorted gold objects. Dried greenery hung from the walls, evergreen boughs tied at their base and fanned out to frame dangling pine cones or seed pods from the fall. The scent of cedar filled the room.

It did not feel like Thaedoren; the Tamaell had little patience for such things. Aeren sensed the new Tamaea's hand in this. Reanne came from Licaeta, had been raised in the forested hills below the mountains, and from what Aeren had heard had not wanted to leave her own House lands. But a marriage into the ruling House of Resue would not have been something she could deny; nor could the Tamaea reside anywhere but Caercaern. It appeared that Reanne had made every effort to bring her homeland to Caercaern with her after the official bonding last summer.

"She has taken over everything here in Caercaern during the winter."

Aeren turned to find Tamaell Thaedoren standing in the doorway, flanked by two White Phalanx.

The youth that had ridden hard with Aeren to meet with the dwarren and convince them that the Alvritshai intended peace those long years ago was gone. Aeren had thought the Tamaell Presumptive back then irresponsible, arrogant, and unable to set aside his bitterness over his relationship with his father to act in the best interests of the Alvritshai. He had been wrong.

Thaedoren had brought the dwarren to the battlefield against his father's wishes, then worked with them to form the Accord after his father's death. He had been instrumental in forging the alliance that had held for over a hundred years, and during those years had managed the Evant and the Alvritshai lords with a firm hand. Aeren had not agreed with every decision the Tamaell had made during that time, had been vehemently opposed to some on the Evant floor, but that did not lessen the respect he'd come to hold for him. The years, and the trials, had left their mark. The proud youth he'd first seen had been tempered, face scarred with the political and physical battles he'd waged since then. Weariness edged his eyes, lined his cheekbones, dulled his black hair. He smiled and motioned Aeren to take one of the chairs around the table.

"You've come to Caercaern early," Thaedoren said, taking the opposite seat while his escort moved deeper into the room. "The Lords of the Evant are not expected back here for another three weeks."

"There are a few issues that I felt needed to be brought to your attention immediately, before their arrival."

Thaedoren's smile faltered and he leaned back. "I thought it unlikely you came simply for a family visit."

"I would have brought your mother and half brother if so. I left them in Artillien." He met Thaedoren's gaze. "For their own safety."

Thaedoren tensed, the change nearly imperceptible. The smile was gone.

His gaze flicked toward the open door and the hall outside, then the two White Phalanx standing inside the room, before returning to Aeren. "Where is your Protector?"

Aeren grimaced. "He is with Shaeveran."

Thaedoren hesitated, then motioned to one of the Phalanx. The guard strode to the door to the audience chamber and said something soft to those outside, then made to close the door. Before he could, Hiroun stepped forward into the room. The White Phalanx guardsman glanced toward Thaedoren, but at the Tamaell's nod allowed the Rhyssal House guard to remain.

When the door had been closed, Thaedoren leaned forward. "What word do you bring? Why would my mother need to be kept safe in Artillien?" His tone was that of the Tamaell, demanding an answer.

Aeren drew in a deep breath to gather his thoughts, then said bluntly, "There are two threats—Lotaern and the Wraiths."

Thaedoren didn't react. "Go on."

"Lotaern has always been a threat. He craves power, political power rather than strictly that which he wields as the Chosen of the Order of Aielan."

Thaedoren waved a hand dismissively. "This is not new. He has gained much since the rule of my father, although I have tried to curb him where I could, with the help of you and our allies. Some would say that your attempts to block him come from a personal grudge against him, that it has nothing to do with the interests of the Alvritshai or the Evant. You defied him openly when Shaeveran brought us the Winter Tree, when he planted it in the marketplace without the consent of the Evant."

The hint of warning in his voice could not be missed and Aeren bowed his head. "That was not planned."

"So you have said before. And I'm certain my mother would back your claim. Regardless, it still gives credence to the accusations that you have your own agenda, your own purpose. And part of that purpose is to oppose Lotaern."

Aeren's head snapped up. "I oppose Lotaern because he strives to gain power that does not belong to him. The Order has no place within the Evant, and yet he wishes to be treated as a lord, as if he ruled his own House. He gained hold of his own Phalanx in the battlefields at the Escarpment with his Order of the Flame, and since then he has reached for more. He is now asked to attend all of the meetings of the Evant, has his own voice in those proceedings. He is a lord in every respect except title. That is what I oppose. There should be a division between the secular and the spiritual, between politics and religion."

Thaedoren waited a moment, allowing Aeren to regain control. "I do not disagree, although there is little I can do about it. He gained this power by using the lords' and the people's fear of the Wraiths and the sukrael. But you already know this. What has he done now? How does he seek to grab more power?"

Aeren hesitated, suddenly realizing that Thaedoren hadn't meant to goad him, but to warn him. If he presented his claim before the Lords of the Evant, he would receive the exact same argument in return.

He closed his eyes and forced his anger back. He wasn't even certain where the anger had come from, except that he had not expected Thaedoren to argue with him. He'd come in search of an ally, one he felt he desperately needed. He had assumed Thaedoren would support him without question.

Perhaps Eraeth's absence had affected him even more than he'd thought.

But when he opened his eyes the first thing he saw was the spray of greenery above Thaedoren's head and his breath caught in his chest.

Reanne.

His gaze fell and he found Thaedoren watching him. Except now he noticed a difference, realized that this wasn't the Thaedoren he'd known since his bonding with Moiran so many years before. Since then, they had been allies in nearly everything in the Evant, strategized together on some of the most important political issues brought before the lords. But he wasn't dealing with Thaedoren alone anymore. He was dealing with Thaedoren *and Reanne*.

He'd known that the power within the Evant would shift

with Thaedoren's bonding, with the linkage between House Resue and Licaeta. He hadn't realized Reanne would have begun wielding her influence over Thaedoren so fast. Licaeta had always supported Lotaern and the Order, had been one of the forces adamant about including the Chosen in the Evant's proceedings.

"I believe Lotaern intends to use the Alvritshai people against us," he said, his voice calm and matter-of-fact, even though tension thrummed through his body. He suddenly didn't know what to expect from Thaedoren, didn't know what side he would take. His approach to the Tamaell shifted subtly, even as he continued. "Are you aware that he has sent members of the Order of the Flame, with escorts, into the individual Houses? They have been traveling from town to town, village to village, stopping at the temples of Aielan and performing the rituals along with—or sometimes in place of—the local acolytes. He is reminding the people of their ties to Aielan and to the Sanctuary. To him."

Thaedoren made to protest, but Aeren halted him with a raised hand. "Let me finish.

"This by itself would make me uneasy, but there is something else. Lotaern and Shaeveran have been working on a blade that will kill the sukrael and the Wraiths, a weapon that will give its wielder an advantage over them. Shaeveran thought he had finally created such a blade and revealed the knife to Lotaern. The Chosen did not react as he expected, so Shaeveran kept the knife himself. However, since then, Lotaern has managed to gain possession of it."

He told Thaedoren of the trek to the sarenavriell in the White Wastes, of the discovery of the Well and the Wraith and sukrael that waited for them there. He told him of the Flame's betrayal during the attack, and the subsequent theft of the knife by Vaeren and the others.

"I assume the knife has already been returned to Lotaern, although as far as I know he does not realize that it does not work as Shaeveran had hoped. Siobhaen knows this, but the rest of the Flame departed before the Wraith recovered and vanished. Shaeveran felt that the revelation of whatever has happened in the east was more important than retrieving the knife, and so he, Eraeth, and Siobhaen have gone to the dwarren to see what they know of the awakening of the Lifeblood there. He sent me here to forewarn you of Lotaern and the renewed threat from the Wraiths and sukrael. He doesn't know what that threat is specifically, but the Wraiths have begun to act again."

"Have they found a way around the Seasonal Trees? Will they be able to attack Alvritshai lands?" Thaedoren had straightened in his seat as Aeren spoke. But only when Aeren began speaking of the Wraiths and sukrael; he didn't appear concerned over Lotaern's theft of the knife.

"Shaeveran checked with the Winter Tree before coming to Artillien with the Order of the Flame and said that the protection from the Trees was still in effect. I don't think we are under any immediate threat of attack."

"But an attack could come?"

"He doesn't see how. But the Wraith that attacked us in the White Wastes was clear: the Wraith's armies are already moving."

"What 'armies?' Did he mean the sukrael?"

Aeren shrugged. "I don't know. Neither does Shaeveran. But he believes that it is more than simply the sukrael. He says that the dwarren have been warning us all for decades that there are more creatures involved in what they call the Turning than the sukrael."

Thaedoren fell silent, his face pinched in thought. After a moment, he stood and began pacing along the length of the table, head bowed.

He halted at the far end of the room, his gaze locked on one of Reanne's cedar wall hangings. "What does Shaeveran expect us to do about the Wraiths and this army?"

A flash of nausea and irritation passed through Aeren, making him grateful that Thaedoren was not watching. Thaedoren appeared to have dismissed Lotaern entirely. "He's left that for us to decide. But I do not feel that we have enough information to make any decisions. We need to know what he discovers from the dwarren first, and what he finds to the east."

"But if what the Wraith said is true, we may not have time to wait."

"The Winter Tree will protect us." He swallowed back the bitterness in this throat and tried one more time, watching Thaedoren carefully. "Lotaern is a more immediate threat, one that we can deal with now. We should concern ourselves with him."

Thaedoren turned to face him, not bothering to hide his own irritation. "And what do you propose to do about him? Sending the Order of the Flame out to the temples is within his rights as Chosen of the Order. You cannot confront him over that."

Despair slid into Aeren's chest. "His action has made many of the lords uneasy," he said. "I think that fact, coupled with the knife he stole from Shaeveran, may be enough to bring the Evant against him."

Thaedoren looked doubtful. "How do you intend to do that?"

"I will meet with each of the Lords of the Evant individually, explain to them about the knife and the Order's betrayal of Shaeveran at the sarenavriell, see how they react.

"And then I will confront Lotaern in the Hall of the Evant."

It was his only option now. He couldn't count on Thaedoren's support any longer, not unequivocally. The Tamaell's bonding with Reanne, with House Licaeta, would change everything.

He would have to warn Moiran. He wasn't certain she'd
believe him.

~

Thaedoren remained standing after Lord Aeren and his escort had departed, staring out into the corridor even though
they had long since moved beyond sight.

One of his own escort shifted toward him in concern.
"Tamaell?"

He raised a hand to cut him off. "Give me a moment,
Naraen. I need to think."

The White Phalanx guard took a step back but did not
withdraw.

Thaedoren bowed his head. What Aeren had said regarding Lotaern was disturbing, but he thought the lord's
concern was misplaced and doubted his attempts to sway
the lords would work. Lotaern had always been a thorn in
their sides, from the moment Thaedoren's father had given
his tacit permission for the Chosen of the Order to maintain
the Order of the Flame. Lotaern had taken that as implicit
approval to expand the group, even before Fedorem's death
at the Escarpment.

But what Thaedoren had done had sealed the Flame's
position in the Order. He'd acknowledged the need for the
Flame on the battlefield, had used them. After that, there
had been no chance of demanding that the unit be dis-
banded. For better or worse, the Order of the Flame had
become a permanent addition to the Order of Aielan, subject to the orders of the Chosen.

And Thaedoren had not regretted that decision. In the
years that followed, with the resurgence of the sukrael under the direction of the Wraiths, the Order of the Flame had
been invaluable. None of the other House Phalanx, nor the
White Phalanx, had a hope of standing up to the sukrael.

Only the powers wielded by the Flame had been able to keep the sukrael at bay, and even then....

He shuddered at the memories. Those first forty years of his rule as Tamaell had been devastating, the sukrael's attacks on the southern and eastern borders vicious and maddening in their randomness. There had been no method to their destruction, no way to prepare or to plan a defense. All of his training within the Phalanx and his years of service as caitan along the border fighting the dwarren with his brother had been useless. Their only effective tactic, the only useful strategy, had come from the Order of the Flame.

From Lotaern.

The fact that the Chosen now had a weapon that could be used against the sukrael and the Wraiths, no matter how he had come into possession of that weapon, could only make the Flame more effective.

And with word that the armies of the Wraiths were in motion, they would need the Flame—and Lotaern—even more. He would not relive those years of frustration fighting a force that attacked from the shadows and withdrew before the defenses could be rallied and the powers of the Flame brought to bear. Too many Alvritshai had been lost.

Naraen stirred and Thaedoren glanced up to find Reanne standing in the doorway, a startled look on her face, a large tallow candle wrapped in cloth clutched in her hands.

"Oh, I thought the meeting had ended," she said. "I can return later." But she did not move.

Thaedoren stood and smiled. "No need, Reanne. The meeting has ended. I was simply thinking."

She hesitated, the almond-colored eyes he loved flaring with concern, then entered, moving toward one of the side tables. "You look troubled," she said, as she unwrapped the candle and began adjusting the arrangement there. "Nothing serious, I hope."

Thaedoren shifted to her side, but did not touch her,

aware of Naraen at the door. "Lord Aeren was expressing concern over the Chosen."

Reanne grimaced. "Again? I do not understand his hatred of the Chosen. He was an acolyte once, was he not? How can he turn his back on everything he was taught then?"

"He hasn't. But he has to think of the needs of his House now as well."

"He can do both. Look at my brother, Orraen. He runs Licaeta and remains faithful to Aielan."

"Aeren *is* faithful to Aielan."

"If he were faithful," Reanne said, an edge to her voice, "he would support the Chosen in all that he does. Lotaern has done nothing but aid the lords in their defense against the sukrael." She fussed with the candle and the cedar boughs, then sighed, head bowed. "But I know he is family." She faced him with a wry smile. "Besides, the enmity between Aeren and Lotaern is not enough to trouble you this much, not when it is so old and worn. What other news did Lord Aeren bring?"

Thaedoren hesitated, but only because his bonding with Reanne was so new. They were still feeling each other out, even after a full winter together here in Caercaern, and the two years of courting that had come before that. But he wanted what his mother and Aeren shared, knew that they consulted each other on everything, including what occurred in the Evant.

"He brought me a warning from Shaeveran about the Wraiths."

Reanne stilled. "What warning?" Fear tinged her voice.

"That they are moving. They've been manipulating the sarenavriell again. He didn't have anything more substantial to tell us than that. Shaeveran has gone to investigate."

"And the Winter Tree?"

"It still protects us."

Reanne relaxed slightly. She turned back to the candle, fussed with the placement of the greenery again. "It makes Aeren's disrespect of Lotaern even more suspicious, though. If the Wraiths are acting again, shouldn't he be supporting the Chosen? We may need Lotaern. We may need the Flame, as we did before the protection of the Winter Tree."

Thaedoren quelled a shudder at the reminder. But Reanne was right. The Alvritshai might need the Order and the Flame sometime soon, depending on what Shaeveran found. He needed to find out what Lotaern intended, regarding the knife and the news of the Wraiths' movements. As Tamaell, he needed to protect the Alvritshai lands first and foremost. Perhaps it was time to deal with the tensions between Lotaern and Aeren once and for all. And time to prepare for whatever the Wraiths had planned for them next. He knew that Lotaern sought power, but that power might be better curbed by the Evant and the other lords if they saw Lotaern as a rival, as Aeren did.

"Naraen," he said, glancing toward the guardsman even as he straightened. "Have word sent to the Chosen of the Order of Aielan that I wish to speak with him."

"Immediately, Tamaell."

"And summon my brother. Tell him the White Fox is needed once again in Caercaern."

Lotaern stood beneath the massive branches of the Winter Tree, sunlight filtering down through the silvered leaves in dappled patches all around him. Stone paths converged here, meeting at a low circular table inscribed with quotes from the Scripts before winding away to other parts of the garden. Halfway between the entrance and the bole of the great tree, secluded and isolated by the city and the Sanctuary by the massive stone wall, it was one of Lotaern's favorite places for contemplation.

And a simple place for a meeting away from prying eyes.

He moved to the edge of the heavy stone table, his gaze glancing at the inscriptions without reading them. One hand drifted toward the package in the left pocket of his robes, its weight more than physical, but he caught the motion and forced his hands to clasp before him. Breathing in deeply, he closed his eyes and murmured a soft chant, quieting his heart and the nervous trembling of his arms.

The prayer did little to still his troubled conscience.

"It belongs with the Order," he muttered to himself. "He had no right to claim it for himself."

"Talking to yourself, Chosen? Is that not one of the signs of corruption according to Aielan?"

Lotaern's heart juddered in his chest at the familiar voice and he grimaced. He did not open his eyes and turn until it had calmed and he'd smoothed the lines of his face.

"Some of the most revered acolytes within the Order over the ages talked to themselves," he said to the cloaked and hooded lord who stood at his back. "Even Cortaemall was said to rage within his own chambers."

"So it is said." Lord Orraen hesitated, then added, "What is it you wish to speak of?"

"We are waiting for another."

Orraen shifted stances, tense now, wary, hand drifting toward the cattan Lotaern assumed was hidden beneath the cloak. His hood turned to one side, as if he were scanning the distance. "Who? I thought this meeting private. We should not be seen together. It is too soon to be revealed."

Lotaern frowned. "You are too paranoid. The other will come cloaked and hooded, as you are. In fact, he has already arrived."

Orraen turned as another figure appeared farther down one of the twisted paths, joining them, his boots crunching in the crushed stone of the walkway. He halted on the far side of the circular stone table, hood shifting back and forth between Lotaern and Orraen. Perhaps a hand taller than Lotaern, he carried himself with utter confidence, and when he spoke, his voice growled with age and unquestioned authority.

Lotaern wondered briefly if Orraen would recognize Lord Peloroun's voice. He should. He'd heard it used often enough on the floor of the Hall of the Evant.

"You have news? Something worth risking our presence in Caercaern so early?"

"I do."

"Did you know that Lord Aeren has also arrived early? If he discovers us here, weeks before our scheduled arrival, it will raise his suspicions. We have managed to keep our alliance secret thus far. I would hate to have it compromised for something trivial."

Lotaern did not acknowledge the threat in the deep voice, nor the lacing of contempt. "This is not trivial. I believe we may finally have something to use against the Wraiths."

He reached into his left pocket and pulled out the small leather pouch. Releasing the drawstrings, he removed the fine metal mesh wrapping the object inside and set it on the stone table. Unfolding the mesh, he revealed the wooden-bladed knife.

Both lords leaned forward for a closer look.

"What is it?" the younger Lord Orraen asked.

"A knife forged of heartwood, soaked in the ruanavriell, and tempered in the fires of Aielan. It was created with the sole intent to kill the sukrael and the Wraiths."

"Does it work?"

Lotaern tried not to react to the doubt in Peloroun's voice. "It was forged by Shaeveran, and it has killed. I can provide witnesses to attest to this fact, members of the Order of the Flame."

"And Shaeveran gave this to you willingly? We all know where his loyalties lie."

"Its sole purpose is to fight the sukrael and the Wraiths," Lotaern said harshly, "and that battle falls to the Chosen, not Lord Aeren."

Peloroun leaned back from the knife, his gaze falling on Lotaern. The Chosen could feel it, even though the lord's face was hidden. He wondered if the lord could read the guilt inside him, if he could see how Lotaern had started at the slightest sound for days after Vaeren returned with the knife in hand. He'd expected Shaeveran to arrive, unannounced, at every waking moment since then, the human's figure blurring into existence before him, demanding the return of the blade. He'd been so afraid that Shaeveran would take it that he'd kept it on his person ever since, even sleeping with it, starting awake at odd hours of the night, his heart pounding in his chest, terrified, until his hands closed on the fine mesh beneath his pillow.

But Shaeveran hadn't come. Not yet. He'd begun to believe that the sukrael-tainted human wouldn't come, that he'd finally seen the logic behind allowing the Order control of it.

Lotaern simply didn't believe it completely.

"With this," he said, swallowing back his doubts, "and with the Order of the Flame, we can bring the Wraiths to heel. Once they realize that they are not invulnerable, that they can die at our hands, we can control them. They will not be able to threaten Alvritshai lands again."

"But we need them," Orraen protested. "We can't gain power in the Evant without them."

"Agreed," Peloroun said. "But what the Chosen is offering us is a way to limit their power once they have helped us achieve our goals. That has always been what has stopped us before. We've needed their strength, to break the Evant and drive the Alvritshai to us, but that strength has never had a leash.

"The knife, along with what the Chosen has promised his

Order of the Flame can accomplish, may be that leash. A thin leash, granted, but a leash."

"We need only trick the Wraiths into donning the collar," Lotaern said.

"Leave that to me," Peloroun said, his voice soft.

·{ 12 }·

J AYSON FREEHOLT SPAT a curse when he heard
the fifty-pound bag of barley grain slung across his
shoulder begin to rip. He spun and swung the bulk
toward the wall of the mill, but the burlap tore even as he
moved. The weight of the half of the sack pressed against
his back suddenly lifted as grain sloughed to the wooden
floor with a hideous hiss and scattered, the small seeds skittering into cracks and crevices and pattering against his legs.

He stood stock-still for a long moment, listening to a last
few escaping grains as they fell and bounced across the
floor, then his shoulders slumped, the weight of the front
half of the barley still heavy against his chest.

It had been one of those days.

"Corim!" he bellowed, letting anger tinge his voice.
"Corim, where in Diermani's bloody Hands are you?"

"I'm on the meal floor!" The shout was muted by the
grinding of the stones of the grist mill on the floor that separated them. "I'm tying off th—"

The rest of the young boy's sentence was lost, but Jayson
didn't care. "Leave it and get the hells up here! And stop the
bloody mill on your way up. We're done for the day!"

Spitting another curse, he carefully shifted the remaining
weight of the bag clutched to his chest, wincing as more

grain escaped. The barley crunched beneath his feet as he hauled the half sack to the wall, grabbed a length of twine from a hook, and tied it off for tomorrow. As he snatched up a broom and wide metal pan from the back wall of tools and bent to sweep up the grain, he heard the steady drone of the two stones fade and grunted to himself. Corim must have lifted the stone nut that halted the milling.

A moment later, Jayson heard Corim's feet pounding up the stairs from the stone floor to the sack floor. He poured the first pan full of grain into the bin of the hopper when Corim appeared.

"Why are we stopping?" Corim asked, then halted, mouth a wide O, eyes even wider as he saw Jayson standing in the middle of the scattered grain.

"Because I've had enough." Jayson tried not to smile at the look on Corim's face. His apprentice was barely twelve years old, but was already as tall as Jayson, all gangly legs and arms. Jayson expected the boy would outgrow him in the next year or two. But Corim still had the face of someone younger and the look of shock was too comical.

"But we haven't even gotten Harlson's order ground yet—"

"I don't care. We had problems with the sluice gate this morning, Harlson delivered his sacks of grain late, *someone*—" he shot a glare toward Corim, who winced, "—dropped an acorn into the hopper that took forever to fish out, and now this. Holy Diermani has cursed this day and I've had enough. Besides, by the time we get this cleaned up it'll be dark, so grab a broom."

Corim scurried off to find a second broom, and Jayson wiped the gritty sweat from his brow with the back of his arm. The motion became a long stretch, his lower back tight. With the grist mill stopped, the groan of the giant water wheel and the rush of the water from the sluice and the stream filled the building; he'd always found those sounds soothing.

Sighing, he began sweeping the loose grain into a single heap near the center of the room, trying to keep the grains from falling through the cracks to the floor below. Corim returned a moment later to help.

By the time they finished, night had fallen completely and they were working by the soft glow of two lanterns. Jayson's back ached from bending over and he had a mild headache. But the sack room floor was as clean as he'd ever seen it since the mill had been built.

He squeezed Corim's shoulder once, then pushed him gently toward the stairs. "Come on, let's get you home."

They went through the mill, Jayson closing the sluice gate to shut off the wheel, Corim gathering their things into satchels and readying the mill for their arrival tomorrow morning. They both grabbed a lantern and exited through the wide wooden doors at the back of the mill, away from the stream. Corim held Jayson's lantern as he pulled the door closed behind them with a grunt.

When Jayson turned around to take his lantern back, Corim stood rigid, muscles tensed, one of the lanterns held out before him. The boy's gaze was locked on the edge of the forest beside the narrow dirt lane that led to the village.

"What is it?"

Corim jumped at his voice, turned frightened eyes toward him. "I thought I saw something on the lane."

Jayson shot a glance toward the empty roadway. The trees were dark to either side, the lanterns' glow illuminating only a small grassy area around the mill, the ground rutted from wagon wheels and carts delivering grain. Overhead, the sky was clear, stars like pinpricks, the moon hidden behind the trees and the surrounding hills.

Jayson frowned into the darkness. "What did you see?"

Corim shook his head. "Something ran across the road, at the edge of the light. Low to the ground. But—"

"But what?"

Corim swallowed. "It had eyes. Yellow eyes, like cat's eyes. But it didn't move like a cat. I think it saw me. And ... I think it hissed at me."

Jayson's frown deepened. He hadn't heard anything, but he'd been struggling with the door. "It probably was a cat," he said, straightening. He tried to shrug his sudden unease aside as he took his lantern, but he found the back of his shoulders prickling and itching as he moved toward the lane, Corim a step behind. One hand slid into the satchel slung across his chest, rooted around at the contents inside until he found the handle of his sheathed knife. Without taking his eyes off the lane, he unhooked the clasp and drew the blade free, keeping it close to his side. The village wasn't far—a short stretch along the lane to the main road, and then a half mile to the center square. The mill would have been in the center of the village if the founders hadn't built near where the river widened and the current was sluggish. He needed the swifter currents upriver to work the grist stones.

They entered the lane, trees to either side, low underbrush coming up to the road's edge. Branches arched overhead, leaves rustling in a light breeze. Otherwise, the forest was silent, with none of its usual sounds—the hoot of an owl or the rustle of something passing through the underbrush. Jayson shivered.

They'd made it halfway to the main road that led to Gray's Kill when Jayson heard the hiss, low and scratchy and nothing like a cat. It crawled up beneath his skin and set the hairs on the back of his arms and neck on end.

He halted. Corim bounced into his side from behind as he scanned the shadows thrown by their lanterns.

Then Corim cried out, pointed, and even as Jayson turned, knife raised defensively, he saw the eyes—pale luminescent yellow, wider than a cat's, set in a malformed, black face, above a mouth opened wide and riddled with teeth.

The creature leaped from the underbrush, straight at

Jayson. He barked out a yell of horrified surprise, tripped over a rut in the road, and stumbled as the thing latched onto the forearm of his knife hand, teeth sinking in deep. He screamed, landed hard on his back, air whooshing from his lungs, the light from the lantern dancing wildly. He flung his arm to the side, trying to shake the creature off, and felt its growl shuddering through his arm. Claws shredded the sleeves of his shirt, scored his flesh, and he slammed it into the ground, once, twice, then dropped his lantern, switched his knife to his free hand and swung at the thing wildly. The blade struck the creature across the back and it released him with a piercing shriek, falling away. Jayson kicked back, scraping along the dirt as the creature scrambled to right itself, moving unlike anything he'd seen before, all leathery muscle and sinew and tendon. It glared at him, the malevolence in its eyes, in its stance, palpable. It hissed again, tensed itself to leap toward him—

And then Corim appeared from the forest, a large branch in one hand. He raised it overhead and with a panicked cry brought it down on the thing's back so hard the branch cracked and split.

The creature yelped like a beaten dog and scuttled away from them both, but turned with another hiss before dodging into the underbrush of the forest.

Jayson gasped into the night's silence, Corim shifting closer to him.

"What was that thing?" Corim asked. His voice was raw and cracked, shaking.

Jayson sat up, winced as he tried to use his mangled arm, then brought it closer to the lantern light. "I don't know. I've never seen anything like it before."

Blood stained his sleeve, seeping sluggishly from several ragged cuts and the jagged curve of the bite mark, but none of the cuts were dangerous. They stung when he moved his arm, but he'd recover.

Something darker stained one side of his shirt though. He frowned down at it, touched it with one finger and felt his skin burn at the touch.

"What is it?"

"Blood," Jayson said, wiping it off on the bottom of his shirt. "From that thing. I must have cut it when I swung at it with the knife."

The undergrowth rustled and they both lurched upright, Corim brandishing his branch, Jayson the knife. But the noise receded. Jayson scrambled to his feet as something skittered across the lane just outside the light of the lanterns, followed by two more on the other side.

"Holy Diermani preserve us," Jayson muttered, eyes wide, his gut clenching so tight he thought he'd piss his pants. "There's more of them."

"And they're headed toward the village."

Jayson stared at Corim in shocked silence, then whispered. "Lianne."

He snatched up the lantern and began to run. Corim's harsh breath followed him. Jayson's feet pounded into the earth, his own breath tight and constricted in his chest as the forest of the lane flashed past, shadows and trees juddering wildly in the swinging light. A chittering sound surrounded them, punctuated by harsh hisses, a few shapes darting in and out of the light through the underbrush, as if tracking them, but Jayson didn't pause. He burst from the lane onto the hard-packed, flatter roadway, tripped, and fell to the ground with a curse. Corim caught up to him as he regained his feet.

Then a gust of wind brought the thick stench of smoke and he stilled.

Ahead, lurid against the black silhouette of the trees, a fire raged. A horse's scream pierced the air and abruptly cut off, but in the stillness that followed he picked out different sounds: faint shouts, the harsh baying of a dog, the clash of weapons, and as a backdrop to it all, the low, rushing sound of flames roaring into the night.

The wind shifted again, blowing black smoke across the road. He choked on it, on the oily soot and hot ash that stung the skin of his face. Coughing, he hunched forward, his wounded arm coming up in a vain attempt to shield himself.

Beside him, he heard Corim suck in a ragged breath. "Ma!" he cried out.

The youth leaped forward, but Jayson snagged him by the arm and jerked him back. Corim nearly slipped from his grasp, but Jayson tightened his grip, hard enough to bruise. "Corim!" he growled, and shook the boy. "Corim, stop! Look!"

Corim turned on him, the look of panic and horror sending a dagger into Jayson's heart. The same sick nausea roiled in his own stomach as he thought of Lianne, of her silver-shot brown hair, hazel eyes, and smooth cheeks that dimpled when she laughed. But he swallowed the taste of bile at the back of his throat and forced Corim to meet his eyes.

"Look," he repeated, and nodded toward the road in the direction of the fires.

Corim twisted in Jayson's grip to look back over his shoulder.

At the horse's scream—Holy Diermani, Jayson prayed it had been a horse—the chittering in the forest had fallen silent. But the creatures hadn't left. In the shadows beneath the trees, made pitch-black by the red-orange blaze where Gray's Kill burned, pale yellow eyes glowed in the reflected light of their lanterns. He counted half a dozen pairs between them and the village. But even as he watched, more shifted to the edge of the road.

A pack. They *had* been tracking them, and calling in the rest of their group.

In his grip, Corim tensed and a small whimper escaped

the boy. Jayson's gaze flicked toward the burning village, his mouth suddenly dry with fear, but he couldn't risk Corim. The boy had been entrusted to him by the youth's parents.

A dozen of the creatures now gathered at the edge of the road, and they were moving closer. Jayson didn't know what held them back—the light from their lantern or if they were waiting for greater numbers—but he didn't want to linger to find out.

"The barge," he murmured, backing up, drawing Corim with him. The boy resisted a moment, straining toward Gray's Kill, toward his home, as Jayson's heart yearned to seek out Lianne, but then the boy relented. Jayson nearly choked with relief. Voice thick, he said, "We're going to run for it, straight to the river, no stopping, no matter what. Understand?"

Without taking his eyes off the creatures in the forest, Corim nodded. Another shift in the wind and a hot blast of smoke skated across the road, obscuring the creatures from sight.

"Go!" Jayson barked, dragging Corim around and thrusting him in the opposite direction, away from the raging inferno of Gray's Kill. The youth cried out, stumbled but caught himself, and then they were both tearing down the darkened road, Jayson holding his lantern high, his other hand clutching desperately at the knife. His satchel slammed against his side, his legs already burning, but he pushed himself harder. Behind, he heard a sharp hiss and the sudden crackle of underbrush and swore beneath his breath, but he didn't turn to look. When Corim slowed and tried to glance back, Jayson gasped, "Run!" and gestured with his knife hand.

Whatever Corim saw made his eyes flare wide and then he raced ahead, outpacing Jayson. He caught one of the creatures out of the corner of his eye, lithe and black in the swaying lantern light, racing him along the edge of the road. It bared its needlelike fangs and dodged toward him.

Jayson cried out and flailed with his knife, hitting the creature and knocking it to one side, but not before its claws dug into his calf, shredding his breeches and drawing three slashes down his leg as it fell away. Pain lanced up into Jayson's gut, even as two more of the creatures raced out before him on the other side. Corim was already twenty paces ahead, and Jayson shouted, "Get on the barge and untie it! Don't wait for me!"

Corim didn't acknowledge him, merely gained another five paces as Jayson lagged, blood flowing freely down his calf. His breath tore at his lungs. His heart shuddered in his chest. Every fiber of his body trembled with exhaustion, tingling with spent adrenaline.

Corim rounded the last bend in the road, the creatures shrieking as they bounded in to cut him off. But they hadn't gained enough on the boy. Jayson heard Corim's feet thundering on the wooden planks of the dock, then rounded the curve, the sound of the river suddenly loud, breaking through the pounding of Jayson's heart in his ears and his heaving breath. He caught Corim frantically untying the barge, the guiding rope tied to the small dock arching down and out into the darkness, the river glinting with lantern light.

The two creatures were charging the dock.

With a roar, Jayson flung himself forward, dropping his lantern as he reached for them, swinging with his knife. His blade sank into the flesh of one, its scream shattering the rush of the water, the creature scrambling away to one side. His hand closed about the leg of the other even as his body slammed into the ground.

He rolled, his roar cut off with the impact, grappling with the creature as it twisted in his grip and snapped at his face. The dirt from the road gave way to the wood planking of the dock as he brought his knife around, slicing down the creature's back. It hissed as black blood splattered onto

Jayson's face, burning, but Jayson slashed again and again, striking the creature with each blow. It shrieked and then fell to the dock beside him, struggling weakly. He kicked it hard, watched it roll off the wood to splash into the river, leaving a trail of blood behind it, and then Jayson staggered to his feet.

The other creature he'd stabbed as he fell writhed on the sloped bank, a harsh keening filling the night. Others had emerged from the forest and were milling about just outside of the spill of the dropped lantern. Jayson counted at least ten, their eyes glaring in the darkness as they leaped forward and hissed before retreating. He could feel the creatures watching him, his skin prickling beneath their gazes, beneath their hatred. They seemed wary of the flames.

Or the water.

Someone snagged at his shirt. He lurched to one side before realizing it must be Corim.

"It's untied," the youth said, voice shaking. "Let's go!"

Jayson nodded and pushed him toward the barge, keeping his eyes on the creatures. They screamed and grew frenzied as the two climbed into the bottom of the barge, Corim already pulling on the rope to draw them away from the dock and out into the river's current.

Then, suddenly, all of the creatures on the bank stilled, heads turning toward the left side of the road. A few traded glances, their large, luminous eyes narrowed—

As abruptly as they'd appeared, they vanished, slinking back into the shadows beyond the light of the torch.

"Wait," Jayson said, creeping forward in the barge. "Don't pull us any farther out."

"But—" Corim protested, the single word fraught with fear.

"They're leaving."

Jayson felt the barge rock as Corim shifted forward, his

hand still on the guiding rope. The youth crouched down beside him. Exhaustion shuddered through him, and Jayson's calf throbbed with pain, but he still reached out a reassuring hand and gripped Corim's shoulder.

They watched the end of the dock and the roadway beyond, the light from the abandoned lantern flickering and threatening to go out. Far distant, over the tops of the trees, the glare of another fire pulsed against a thick column of billowing smoke.

Jayson's heart had just begun to calm, the sweat on his skin cooling in the night air, when a branch cracked in the forest to the left. His muscles twinged as he started. Corim gasped.

He raised the knife before him, blade out.

Five figures emerged onto the roadway into the edge of the fading light from Jayson's lantern and it took a moment before Jayson recognized them as dwarren. Half the height of either Jayson or Corim, they plowed through the underbrush, chopping at it with axes and short blades. Their beards were woven and braided with beads and feathers and pendants, their arms covered in metal bands, bodies with thick leather armor scored with patterns and whorls. Two of them carried long spears, the shafts etched with carvings, the tips shaped metal, like a rounded leaf.

The dwarren halted in the roadway, the leader of the group staring hard at the lantern, the body of the creature that now lay still, and Jayson, ignoring Corim completely. The pure hatred in the dwarren's eyes, the sheer intensity of the emotion and the determination that bled from the dwarren's body, left Jayson speechless.

The leader waved to the rest of the band, the gesture dismissive. The other four plowed into the forest on the far side of the road, the leader hanging back a moment, keeping his eye on Jayson. Then he vanished as well with a rustle of undergrowth and the dry snapping of branches.

Jayson didn't move until Corim touched his arm.

"Those were dwarren," the boy said.

"I know." Jayson forced himself to relax, to lower his knife. He turned and grabbed the rope, the flat boat rocking at his movements, their only remaining lantern guttering in protest.

"They were headed toward the village."

"I know!" Jayson spat. Without another word he hauled on the rope that connected this side of the river to the other. The rope sang as it pulled through the metal rings attached to each end of the barge, the wooden slats creaking as they moved farther away from the dock and into the river's current. But the rope held. The current wasn't strong enough here to make the crossing difficult, especially when the barge wasn't laden down with supplies or horses.

"What do you think they were—?"

"I don't know!"

Corim fell silent, his eyes wide.

When Jayson judged they were halfway across, he stopped. Shifting to the center of the barge, near the lantern, he squatted down, rubbed his hands together briskly, and blew on them for warmth. The night had turned chill. Corim joined him a moment later. They couldn't see either side of the river; the lantern Jayson had dropped had burned out. The rope arched out into darkness on either side, the surface of the river glinting in ripples all around. The moon—barely more than a sliver—had risen above the surrounding hills, but it cast little light. The air was thick with the scent of water and smoke, and both Corim and Jayson reeked of fear sweat. Jayson could taste ash in his mouth.

A long, silent moment later, Corim asked tentatively, "What are we going to do?"

Jayson said nothing, breathing in steadily, slowly, to calm himself, thinking about the creatures, of Lianne and the dwarren. He thought of the fire—at least three of the main

buildings in Gray's Kill were burning, probably more—and
the sounds of fighting. The village had been attacked. He
didn't know why, or by whom, didn't know what those creatures were, but the dwarren were here. He'd seen them,
clear as day.

Cobble Kill lay a day's ride distant, and it housed a barracks of the Legion.

But Lianne. And Corim's parents. . . .

He was Corim's guardian now, until they knew what had
happened to the boy's parents.

Reluctantly, he said, "We have to go to Cobble Kill.
GreatLord Kobel needs to know what has happened here."

"I never realized the dwarren tunnels were so . . . extensive."

Colin glanced up from removing the satchels and saddle
packs from his horse to where Eraeth stood, staring out
over the wide cavern the dwarren had chosen as a resting
area. Unlike the chambers where the dwarren lived, this
cavern was long and wide, the ceiling low, perhaps twice as
high as Eraeth was tall. The river surged through the chamber in a deep channel to the right of where they'd entered,
glinting with torchlight as the army of dwarren warriors began unpacking their camp. At the front of the combined
army, one of the dwarren had removed a drum and beat out
a steady rhythm into the mouth of the next tunnel, announcing their position, the information being passed down
the way stations between them and the Confluence.

Two days before, they'd been joined by another large
group of dwarren, the size of the army nearly doubling. At
first, Colin had thought they came from one of the other
clans, but as the new warriors dispersed, he realized they
had merely been reinforcements for the three clans that
were already part of the group.

It unsettled him. He wondered how many dwarren were being called to this Gathering, and to what purpose.

He shoved his speculations aside. He'd done nothing but ponder the possibilities during the ride so far and had come to no solid conclusions. He didn't have enough information, and he wouldn't get that information until they reached the Confluence. None of the clan chiefs or the head shamans knew anything beyond what they'd told him in the keeva, or they were unwilling to share their information if they had it. The fact that he knew nothing had nearly driven him to abandon the dwarren and Eraeth and Siobhaen altogether and use his powers to reach the Confluence ahead of them, but he'd resisted.

Besides, there was something he needed to do here.

"The dwarren tunnels run beneath the entire length of the plains," he said in answer to Eraeth's unasked question. "From the Escarpment all the way to the edges of the Thalloran Wasteland, from the mountains to the north to the Flats in the south. They have controlled them for generations, so long that they've lost count."

Eraeth turned aside from his perusal of the dwarren as they methodically settled in to rest, the smells of a hundred cook fires beginning to fill the room. Colin's stomach growled, but he ignored it.

"Did the dwarren build them?"

"No," Colin said with a smile. "According to their legends, they were given the network of chambers and corridors by their gods, so that they could oversee the preservation of the Lands above and so they could protect the Sacred Waters. As far as I can surmise based on their histories, they have done so for well over two thousand years, but it's hard to judge."

"So they believe their gods built it for them?" Siobhaen said with a touch of derision.

"Of course," Colin said. He frowned down at the contents of the satchel in his hands. He didn't think he'd need much for his excursion, knew that most of what he had brought would be useless. He shrugged and cinched the satchel tightly, throwing it over one shoulder.

Eraeth was suddenly at his side. "Where are you going?"

He met the Protector's frown. "I need to speak to the Faelehgre . . . and to the forest."

"And were you going to tell us you were leaving?"

Colin turned in surprise as Siobhaen stepped up behind Eraeth. Both of them gave him a nearly identical look of anger. They barely spoke to each other on good days, but in this they were united? He shook his head. "I'll be back before the dwarren rouse themselves and continue on."

"That's not the point," Eraeth said.

"One of us should be with you," Siobhaen added.

Eraeth nodded. "That was the whole point in having us accompany you."

Colin glanced back and forth between them, eyes narrowed in sudden suspicion. But no, there was still a tension between the two, an unspoken distrust. They simply both agreed, grudgingly, that he shouldn't be traveling alone.

He sighed, focusing on Eraeth. "You can't come with me. I don't want to leave the dwarren army, and I have to travel too far to take either of you with me." He let his voice harden. "I'm going to Terra'nor and the Well, that's all. I'll be gone at most a few hours."

Siobhaen frowned in confusion. "You know where we are? How? I lost any sense of direction the moment we were taken underground."

"I can sense the Well," Colin said, not looking away from Eraeth. The Protector's eyes searched his own. "We're beneath the Ostraell, have been for the past day or so. We're in the domain of the Faelehgre and within the bounds of the Seasonal Trees—the Summer Tree actually. I'll be protected."

Eraeth considered a long moment, then nodded once. "Very well."

Siobhaen scowled, arms crossed over her chest.

"Don't be too hard on him, Siobhaen," Colin said. "He knows neither one of you could stop me."

Then he slowed time and stepped to the side, catching the beginning of Siobhaen's surprise before turning away and leaving them behind.

He Traveled, slid among all of the gathered dwarren in the midst of setting up camp, through pockets of the warriors circled around campfires, eating and drinking, all of their actions caught in mid-motion. He stalked past others herding the gaezels they rode to the far left, grain thrown out onto the floor to lure them away from the rest of the underground encampment. The dwarren were leading them in small groups to the river's edge to drink. As he passed the head of the army, he noted the clan chiefs and head shamans were seated around a brazier, the sharp scent of ye-tope heavy on the air, even with time slowed.

And then he moved beyond the army, entering the wide mouth of the tunnel beyond.

He picked up the pace as soon as he passed into the darkness, reaching into his saddle to withdraw a wooden box. From inside, he took out a clear stone prism about as long as his hand, like quartz, but polished smooth on its faces. A tendril of white fire lay trapped inside the prism, whisking back and forth along its length, tongues of smaller flames flicking outward from the main tendril to trace along the edges of the crystal.

Siobhaen would be shocked to her core if she ever found the stone. As a member of the Order of the Flame, she'd recognize that the flame Colin had captured inside the crystal was part of Aielan's Light, taken from the pool of fire that burned beneath the mountains of Caercaern. He had not asked for permission to capture the flame, not from Lotaern or the Order. He knew what the Chosen would have said, that the Fire was not a tool, but a manifestation of Aielan, that it should not be abused in such a manner.

Colin understood the significance of the Fire to the Alvritshai and, in particular, to the Order. He understood the need for faith. His mother had raised him beneath the Hand of Holy Diermani; he had read from the Codex, had attended church with his mother at his side, had prayed beneath the Tilted Cross, and had planned on taking his vows with Karen with the blessings of one of Diermani's priests.

That would never happen now.

But he thought Lotaern and the Order were blinded by their faith. Aielan's Fire could be used for other things, like the crystal he now held up to illuminate the passage before him. They had begun to explore such possibilities; the Alvritshai had witnessed the use of the Fire at the battlefield at the Escarpment, when Lotaern and that first battalion of the Flame had called it forth from the earth to disrupt the attack by the Legion. And Lotaern had used the Fire to help him in their first attempts at forging a weapon to use against the Wraiths.

Lotaern would never have considered removing part of the Fire itself from its natural cauldron, though.

Colin had no such compunctions ... although he *had* merged with the Fire beneath Caercaern and asked Aielan for permission before he'd done so.

When he'd emerged from the Fire, the white flame had already inhabited the crystal.

The white light glowed on the smooth surface of the tunnel as he moved, broken only at intervals by support arches. At the first junction of the tunnel the dwarren army followed and another tunnel running crosswise to it, he turned left. He could feel the Well's power through the walls of earth on either side, pulsing subtly. He followed the new, narrower corridor, passed a few open arches that led to empty rooms, both large and small, then paused at another junction. He stared at the three remaining openings, prism held aloft, then stepped into the entrance to each one, released time, and breathed in deeply.

The central corridor that ran straight ahead appeared to lead in the direction of the Well, but the tunnel to the left brought with it the faint scent of forest, of cedars and loam.

He headed to the left, slowing time again as he went. The corridor stretched on and on, seemingly endless, but then the support arches began to appear more frequently and within moments the corridor ended in a set of stone stairs, rising in sharp turns. He began to ascend, moving faster now.

Near the top, the scent of the forest strong enough to permeate his surroundings, he discovered that the original opening had collapsed. Earth riddled with roots and stone filled the stairwell, appearing black in the harsh light.

He held the prism higher and scanned the collapse in frustration. The profusion of roots suggested he was close to the surface, even if the collapse had happened decades before.

And he'd smelled cedar, not just loam.

He let go of time and caught the faint breath of a breeze. It touched his face and pushed at his hair, damp with a recent rain.

Craning his neck, he found he could barely see past the fall of dirt at the turn in the stairs. It didn't appear to block the entire stairwell.

Keeping the crystal firmly in one hand, he shoved his satchel around to his back and began climbing the fallen debris. His free hand sank into the dirt and sent it cascading down behind him, but he struggled on, catching at the thicker roots the higher he rose to help pull himself upward. He lost his footing twice before he grasped desperately for the corner of stone that marked the stairwell's turn, then hauled himself up around the corner with both hands, the edges of the prism biting hard into the flesh of his palm.

Propping himself against the corner, he raised the light and saw where the earth had caved in under the weight of centuries of debris. A narrow hole opened up through the earth. Beyond it, he could see cedar branches stirring and the pinpricks of stars.

The hole wasn't large enough for him to fit through.

Cursing, he tucked the prism back into the box, replacing it in his satchel. The stairwell was sheathed in darkness, broken only by the faintest of light from the opening above. Drawing his shoulders up with a deep breath to steady himself, he let out the pent-up air with a sharp exhale and scrambled up the remaining slope to the hole.

His arm reached through to the fresh air and night sky above, then clawed at the ground as he shoved his head into the narrow opening. Dirt dislodged in his struggles rained down around his body trapped below, some falling beneath his shirt and skittering down his back and chest. He gasped and kicked with his feet, but he was too big.

He ceased struggling and found that his other arm, the one still below ground, was now lodged against his side.

He bit off another curse and forced himself to relax, to think. Dirt had caught near his mouth and he spit it out.

Growling, he tried to retreat. His free arm flailed, but he was lodged tightly in the hole now, head, arm, and left shoulder above ground. Spitting curses—at Diermani, Aielan, even Ilacqua, the dwarren god—he writhed in the hole, shoved hard against the needle-strewn earth, and finally collapsed backward as much as he could, spent.

His body was simply too damn big.

Then, staring up at the night sky, he started laughing.

Shaking his head, he focused.

The years sloughed off, his body growing younger and younger. The skin and wrinkles of the sixty-year-old man firmed and hardened into that of a thirty year old, then a twenty year old, before softening again as he drew himself back to the body of the twelve-year-old boy who had first drunk from the Well nearly two hundred years before.

A boy whose body was much leaner than the sixty-year-old form Colin normally wore.

He pulled himself from the hole easily, with only the satchel getting snagged on a root to impede the process. At last, he lay back on the dead needles shed from the trees, panting with the effort, then chuckled to himself again.

He hadn't transformed his body to such a young age in decades, perhaps not since the Accord between the three races had been signed.

Climbing to his feet, he brushed off the dirt and debris from the forest floor, his clothes hanging on his thin frame. He thought about keeping the youthful form, but without proper clothes. . . .

He settled on a man in his mid-thirties, the clothes only slightly loose, then began winding his way through the trees toward Terra'nor.

When he reached the edges of the city, he found Osserin waiting. The piercing white light of the Faelehgre hovered beneath a large stone archway that still stood over one of the main roads, the towers, fountains, and lower buildings interspersed with the huge boles of trees receding into the distance behind him. Like most of the buildings of Terra'nor, the arch showed signs of its age. One corner had cracked and crumbled away, another crack running down the center of the arch, but it still stood.

Welcome home, Shaeveran, Osserin murmured, pulsing once. *Have you come because of the Wells? Of their new awakening?*

"Yes, and to ask the heart of the forest for another gift."

We thought so. You are not the only one.

Colin shot the Faelehgre a startled glance. "What do you

mean? Who else has been here? How did they get past the Faelehgre and my wardings?"

The Faelehgre began leading Colin through the city, the white towers with empty windows and shattered balconies looming on either side. Osserin turned down a central street lined with standing columns, most toppled. When Colin had been here before, nearly all of them had been standing.

No one has been to the Well. But the dwarren shamans have been to the heart of the forest.

"Why? What have they come for?"

Like you, they come asking for gifts, for shards of heartwood that their hunting parties—the trettarus—can use against the Shadows and the Wraiths. And the other fell creatures of the Turning.

Colin continued walking in silence, his body thrumming with shock. When the pair reached the height of the amphitheater's stair that cupped the edge of one side of the Well, he halted. "I had not realized the dwarren knew of the heart of the forest."

Osserin didn't halt, drifting down the stairs toward the wide pool of flat water that spread out beneath them, the forest itself picking up where the city and the amphitheater ended. Below, the Well pulsed with blue-tinged light like the Well in the northern wastes, illuminating the surrounding trees and buildings with a harsh glare. More of the Faelehgre's lights hovered over the water.

Their shamans knew of it ages ago, would come to the Heart to speak to the forest, to commune with the Lands. Until the Shadows found them. The dwarren did not come again after that, the cost too high, until they realized that the Summer Tree had freed them from the Shadows' threat.

But come. There are more important things to discuss. The Faelehgre have been awaiting your arrival.

Colin wanted to ask more—he found the news that the dwarren communed with the heart of the forest unsettling and heartening; perhaps he was not as alone in his struggles as he had thought—but as he began descending the stairs, moving toward the Well and the intoxicating scent of the Lifeblood it contained, he realized Osserin spoke the truth. The Faelehgre around the Well were agitated, flashing and spinning over its waters. As he drew closer, he caught the edges of their conversation, the air humming with its pulse.

Osserin never got the chance to announce him. When he reached the stone lip of the Well—made from rounded river stone, not the stone used to build the city—the nearest of the Faelehgre noticed him and shot toward him.

Is this your doing? Have you awakened the Well to the east?

The air throbbed with the light's anger, prickling along Colin's skin. He glared at the Faelehgre.

"Of course not. Do you think I would be so stupid as to upset the balance it took me nearly thirty years to achieve?"

Then who was it? Who has awakened the Source?

And what do you intend to do about it?

More of the Faelehgre had darted toward him, so that he was now surrounded by at least ten, a few others remaining at a distance. All of them were pulsing with anger or concern, a strange echo of the light from the Well beneath them. Colin's gaze shot from one to the other where they hovered.

"If I didn't awaken this . . . this Source, then it must have been one of the Wraiths," he said, trying to keep his voice level, reasonable. He hadn't expected to be attacked by the Faelehgre when he arrived.

Walter.

Not necessarily, Ulyssa, Osserin replied.

He's the one who started all of this! He's the one who broke the Shadows free!

"But we know he has used the other Wraiths to awaken

other Wells. Even so, I still believe that Walter is behind this new awakening." A wave of satisfaction flooded the air, followed by disgruntlement.

Colin brushed it aside. "I've come from the northern wastes, where I felt the new Well through the Lifeblood. I know that it lies to the east, beyond the dwarren plains in the Thalloran Wastelands, but that is all. The currents flowing from these Wells to it were too strong for me to discover more than that. What can you tell me about this new Well? Why do you call it the Source?"

Because it is so powerful, one of the Faelehgre moaned from behind the front ranks.

At least three of the Faelehgre flared in annoyance, Osserin darting to the front of the group directly before Colin.

When the Well was first awakened, the pulse from the Lifeblood shook the entire city. Towers collapsed, columns cracked, and streets buckled. It was the strongest pulse any of us have ever witnessed. Its magnitude indicates that the Well that was awakened is large, much greater than any other Well since Walter began the process.

We sent Faelehgre to the nearest Wells to confirm what we found here: all of the Wells are connected, and all of them are now part of this larger source of Lifeblood to the east. Somehow, the two systems were separated in the past, our system blocked from the other. But that blockage has been removed. We're now all part of the same system, feeding off of the mingled Lifeblood. But the removal of the blockage has thrown the two systems off-balance.

"I know all this," Colin cut in, frustrated. "I sensed it all through the Well in the north. I've seen the effects in the storms on the plains and the resurgence of the Drifters. What I need to know is what needs to be done to stop it, to restore the balance."

All of the Faelehgre hovered in uncertain silence for a long moment.

Until the one Osserin had called Ulyssa drifted forward.

There are only two options we can see, he said. *Either the blockage that was removed needs to be restored. . . .*

Or someone must go to the Source and restore the balance from there.

· 13 ·

"'S OMEONE' NEEDS TO GO to the Source and restore the balance," Colin muttered as he stalked away from Terra'nor and the Well and into the forest beyond, time slowed once again. "Guess who that's going to be?"

He'd been on his way to the east already, to find out whatever he could about the sea of Lifeblood he'd sensed beneath the earth and how it had unbalanced what he'd so carefully wrought with the Wells in the west. The Faelehgre had simply given him more information about what to expect when he arrived: another Well, perhaps, one much larger than the one in Terra'nor. How he was to find the Well was a different matter. They didn't know precisely where it was, only that it was beyond dwarren lands, in the wastelands farther east, and that he should be able to follow the flow of the Lifeblood deep within the earth to find it.

But that was what galled him: the assumption by the Faelehgre that he would do it. There had been no question; they simply expected it of him. They'd said "someone," but they, and he, knew there was no one else who could. And they both knew he would have to face the Wraiths and the Shadows once there, perhaps even Walter himself. There would have to be a confrontation. The Wraiths would not awaken the Well and then simply let him repair the damage. They needed the Well for something. The Faelehgre could now travel to the east—the awakening of the Well expanded their sphere of influence—and they could deal with the Shadows, but they could not handle the Wraiths. The Alvritshai, dwarren, and humans could not manipulate the Well to achieve any kind of balance.

It had to be him.

He slowed and bowed his head, the weight of the responsibility suddenly too heavy. There was too much to do, too much to handle: the new Well, whatever was forcing the dwarren to Gather, the ambiguous threat he'd been given by the Wraith in the north, and whatever Lotaern had planned for the Alvritshai and the knife Colin had forged. The world had felt steady and stable for decades. He hadn't been idle; he'd been working, traveling, studying, looking for a way to destroy Walter and the other Wraiths.

He thought he'd have more time.

A few days ago, he'd accused the races of being complacent, but he'd behaved in exactly the same way. The Seasonal Trees had only bought them time. He'd known that the moment he'd planted them, known that they would not keep Walter and the others at bay forever. Even so, he'd allowed himself to relax, expecting them to last for hundreds of years.

And now the Wraiths were active again. He was being forced to catch up, to *wake* up.

Everything was happening so fast.

He shook himself and tried to shove aside the weight that pressed against him, but he could feel it draped across his shoulders, like the bar of a penance lock.

He shuddered at the old memory, then struck out grimly again into the forest. The dark boles of the cedars closed in around him, the red-tinged bark scenting the air, their roots making the unmarked path treacherous. They grew larger as he neared the heart. He passed close to one, rested his hand against its bark for support, and felt the deep thrum of the wood beneath his hand, the life-force that pulsed through the tree even with time slowed. He unconsciously drew strength from it, and the melancholy mood brought on by the Faelehgre's expectations lifted slightly. He pushed away from the comfort and continued.

Moments later, he slipped around another trunk, letting his hand brush its essence as he did so, and found himself at the lip of a small, empty hollow.

Cedars lined the space, the ground dipping down and leveling out, littered with fallen needles, small cones, and twigs. Faint moonlight sifted down through the branches overhead, everything in various shades of gray and black. The ridge that surrounded the hollow was natural, although startlingly circular, composed mostly of exposed cedar roots. Colin stood at its edge, letting the soothing light surround him, then stepped down to its center.

As he moved, he saw the first signs of the dwarren's return. When he'd come here before, the hollow had been empty save for the trees and their leavings. Now, he spotted a dwarren spear thrust into the ground at the lip of the hollow, ceremonial feathers tied to its end. Other offerings were scattered on the ground among the cones and twigs—a carved scepter, a tangle of leather strands woven into a band, a latticework of beads and bone. He paused over a small mound of earth, like an anthill, that had been heaped up, a depression made in its center. Something dark had been poured into the depression, an offering of water or blood.

There were no dead embers or charred brands anywhere. Fire was not something used to appeal to a forest.

The fact that the dwarren had rediscovered their connection to the forest gave him some small hope that perhaps he wasn't fighting the Wraiths and the Shadows alone. Aside from the spiritual connection to the Lands that the hollow provided, there was only one reason to come here.

The same reason Colin had come.

He found the center of the hollow, where the ground had been tread upon so often it had been swept clear of all debris and packed solid. He stared up into the patch of night sky above, then let time resume. The branches of the cedars swayed in a gentle breeze that did not penetrate to the hollow. The cloying scent of cedar—heavy with time slowed—became almost overpowering with its intensity. He breathed it in deeply, allowing his lungs to adjust to it, and felt it affecting his body, similar to the smoke of the dwarren yetope. His gaze dropped to the surrounding trees, the trunks that lined the edge of the hollow suddenly sharp and distinct in the darkness, as if they'd been lit with a soft, hazy yellow light. He circled once, twice, and then settled to the ground, legs crossed before him. He let his arms drop into his lap and hung his head forward, back hunched.

And he breathed. Slow, deep breaths, drawing the scent of the forest inside him, letting it permeate him. His arms began to prickle after ten such breaths, the ground to grow warm beneath him as his body relaxed, his heart calming. He felt himself drawn deeper into that earth, centering downward, to where the roots of the forest twined among the stone and the flow of the Lifeblood. The essence of the forest he had only brushed when touching the boles of the trees grew thick and viscous, like sap. It smothered him as he submerged himself in it, surrounding him with its luminescence. And then he opened his mind, to allow it to see his need.

Unlike the Lifeblood, more like Aielan's Light, the essence of the forest was animate and aware, but in a way that Colin could not comprehend. He'd learned long ago not to try, to simply allow the forest to feel him, to taste him. He sensed its presence, filtering through him like the growth of roots through soil, searching.

Distantly, he heard a sigh, as of wind through branches, and the creak and groan of wood shifting. Something brushed his shoulders, his hunched back, tickled the base of his neck. He shuddered at the touch. Then the sensation retreated, the essence of the forest withdrawing from his mind. The earth pushed him up out of its warmth.

He gasped and opened his eyes, straightening where he sat, his lower back screaming with tension. He rotated his aching neck, green needles falling from his shoulders to patter onto the ground around him. Something sticky on his neck caught at his shirt and he reached back to touch it, his fingers coming back tacky with sap. As he twisted the pain out of his shoulders, he noticed what had been left on the ground before him.

A new staff, its length riddled with twisting lines, like those found beneath the bark of a branch after it had been peeled away. He reached out to take it automatically—it was what he had come for, a staff to replace the one stolen by Vaeren in the northern wastes—then paused.

The forest had left another gift. A scattering of arrows, made of the same wood as his staff. He counted at least four dozen, along with two longbows like those the Alvritshai carried.

For Eraeth and Siobhaen.

He glanced out into the surrounding forest with a frown. He had not asked for the bows, nor the arrows. Yet the forest felt he needed them.

The sentience behind such a gift sent a shiver down his spine. He had thought he'd come here often enough to understand the forest, had thought that it was aware, but only enough to know what he asked for and why.

It had never anticipated a need he had not anticipated himself.

Leaning forward, still uneasy, he closed his hand around the staff and felt the recognition of the life-force within it pulse. He drew that life-force around him, the contact easing a tension he hadn't realized he'd felt. The presence of the staff completed him in some way. He had held one nearly all of his life, since drinking from the Well and becoming part of Terra'nor, part of the forest. He took a moment to run his free hand up and down its length, smiling.

Then he gathered up the two bows—without string, he noticed—and the arrows, the shafts made of a single piece of wood, the points sharp, but with no fletching. He bound the arrows in groups of twelve using twine, six dozen in all, and shoved the bulky bundles awkwardly into his satchel. He worked quickly. It had taken longer to commune with the forest than he had expected. He needed to find his way back to the dwarren war party, before Eraeth and Siobhaen panicked at his absence.

Everything packed, he took the staff up in one hand, the two bows in the other, and turned to scan the circle of cedars one more time. He bowed his head and murmured, "Thank you, for all the gifts you have given me before, and for those you have given me tonight."

Lotaern nodded to the White Phalanx guardsman who'd escorted him through the Tamaell's personal chambers on the highest tier in Caercaern to the rooftop gardens. As Chosen of the Order, he had been to these gardens on several occasions, usually for small, casual gatherings of Lords of the Evant and other Alvritshai of power in the city, hosted by either Thaedoren himself or, more recently, Tamaea Reanne.

He had never been summoned here to meet with the Tamaell alone.

Thaedoren stood on the far side of the garden, his hands

on the wide stone abutment. He gazed out over the city of Caercaern, the Hauttaeren rising off to one side, water cascading down the rocky mountain face in thin sprays that reflected the afternoon sunlight. Some of those falls were caught above the tier and funneled into a stream that wound through the garden, the water escaping in another waterfall down the side of the highest level before winding its way down to the city below.

Lotaern frowned at the Tamaell's back, his stomach clenching. The summons had arrived that morning, while he'd been meeting with Peloroun and Orraen beneath the Winter Tree. The timing made him wonder if the Tamaell knew of his dealings with the two lords, of what they had planned. It would be the end of Thaedoren's rule of the Evant and the Alvritshai as Tamaell, and the rise of Lotaern and the Order in its place. Did he suspect anything? He could not imagine how the Tamaell would have found out.

And yet, Thaedoren had asked to see him. . . .

Straightening his shoulders, Lotaern stepped forward, his features carefully neutral. He did not know what the Tamaell knew, so would assume nothing. The summons could concern anything, from the Evant to Aielan and the Scripts.

His hands clenched at his sides before he forced them to relax.

"Tamaell," he said as he approached, smiling. "You wished to see me?"

Thaedoren turned from his perusal of the city, but did not smile. "Chosen."

Neither of them nodded or bowed to the other.

Thaedoren considered him a long moment, then stepped away from the edge and motioned Lotaern to accompany him as he began strolling through the various pathways of the garden. "I called you here to address a few concerns that have come to my attention regarding the Order."

Lotaern's heart stuttered in his chest, but he managed to keep his voice mild. "I see. Who brought these concerns to your attention?"

"A few of the Lords of the Evant."

Lotaern's eyes narrowed. He thought he could name at least one of those lords. "What has the Order done that concerns the Evant?"

Thaedoren shot him a sideways glance, his voice taking on a hard edge. "Everything the Order does concerns the Evant, Chosen. Especially now that you have become a part of the Evant."

"Of course, Tamaell. I meant, what is of concern to these particular lords?"

Thaedoren continued on for a few more slow steps. "They are concerned about the members of the Order of the Flame who are circulating among the temples in their House lands. Some feel that it is a show of force, a subtle threat. After careful consideration, I have to agree."

Lotaern bridled, although his fear that Thaedoren knew of his alliance with Peloroun and Orraen relaxed. "Having the Flame move among the temples is certainly within my rights as Chosen of the Order and it has nothing to do with the Evant."

"Having acolytes traveling on pilgrimages from temple to temple has nothing to do with the Evant. However, you cannot argue that the members of the Flame are simply acolytes. They are not. They are warriors, trained in the art of battle, with the power of Aielan's Light behind them, as you have proven on the battlefield at the Escarpment and in the attacks of the sukrael and the Wraiths in the years since. As warriors—as members of the Order of Aielan's Phalanx—they fall under my direction as Tamaell of the Evant, just as all of the House Phalanx are under my command when necessary. Are you saying that the Flame should not be treated as a military unit?"

"They are acolytes of the Order, learned in the Scripts, with Aielan's Light behind them."

Thaedoren shook his head. "You cannot have it both ways, Chosen. The Order of the Flame is either a Phalanx under the direction of the Evant, or they are acolytes of the Order and nothing more."

Lotaern sensed the threat behind the words. The Flame gave the Order the aspect of a House. If the members of the Flame became mere acolytes, then the Order of Aielan and Lotaern himself would lose his standing within the Evant. He couldn't afford to lose that now.

But if he agreed that the Flame acted as the Order's Phalanx, Thaedoren would have the power to seize control of it in times of need.

Thaedoren had halted and was watching him. He suddenly realized he hadn't answered quickly enough, that his response should have been instant.

He smiled, knew it was forced. "The members of the Order of the Flame are warriors, of course. Warriors who are ultimately under the direction of Aielan."

Thaedoren's expression did not change. It was an ambiguous response, but Lotaern could not read how the Tamaell had taken it. His only words were, "Very well. Keep that in mind during the opening of the Evant."

Was there a hint of warning in his voice?

"Was there anything else, Tamaell?"

"No. You may leave."

Lotaern had made it to the entrance to the garden when Thaedoren called after him. He halted in his tracks, his hands clenched at his sides.

"I have heard of other concerns from the Lords of the Evant regarding the Order, and the Chosen. Be careful of what you attempt to gain, Lotaern. Do not attempt to extend your influence too far."

Lotaern didn't answer, couldn't answer through the sudden

fear that seized him. Instead, he turned and bowed his head in acknowledgment before stalking through the door and into the uppermost tier of the palace. Two White Phalanx fell into step to either side behind him, but he barely noticed, his mind racing.

What did Thaedoren know? What could he possibly have learned from the other lords? Had Peloroun or Orraen revealed their plans? But that did not make sense. Both lords had been concerned over revealing themselves, and both of them had too much to gain by allying themselves with him. Peloroun had lost power with his support of the ill-fated traitor, Lord Khalaek. And Orraen was too impatient to await a rise in the Evant after replacing his father, even with his sister now bonded to the Tamaell as Tamaea.

No, neither Peloroun nor Orraen had betrayed him.

He forced his heart to calm, the constriction in his chest easing. Taking a few deep breaths, he reconsidered the Tamaell's last words, turned them over in his head, searching for what had not been said. The longer he thought about them, the more relaxed he became. The accusation had been vague, without specifics. If Thaedoren had known something specific, especially something as volatile as what he had planned, the Tamaell would not have resorted to veiled threats. No, Thaedoren knew nothing.

But he was suspicious.

Lotaern and his escort had reached the corridor that separated the Tamaell's private chambers from the rest of the palace, the two White Phalanx taking up positions to either side of the entrance as he passed through. Lotaern ignored them, searching the round room for Vaeren, his sandaled feet clopping against the massive marble floor. The caitan of the Flame, along with Petraen, were waiting against the far wall, watching the servants, Phalanx, and other clerks pass by with studied disinterest. Both straightened as soon as they saw the Chosen.

Vaeren picked up on his uneasiness instantly. "What did the Tamaell want, Chosen?"

Lotaern scowled. "He wanted to discuss the finer points of law regarding the Order of the Flame. I fear he intends to use it somehow at the opening of the Evant. But he hinted at knowing something more. He warned the Order against overstepping its bounds."

"He has always been cautious with the Order, unwilling to allow us power, but more than willing to use the Flame for his own ends."

"That will change," Lotaern muttered. "If the Alvritshai hope to survive the Wraiths and the sukrael, it will have to change. Only the Order and Aielan's Light can lead us out from under their shadow. Thaedoren, and the other Lords of the Evant, will understand that shortly."

Peloroun sat behind his desk within his personal chambers in Caercaern, staring across it toward the Ionaen House Phalanx guardsman who stared back. Few knew that he had already arrived for the opening of the Evant. Most of the lords of the Houses would be arriving in the next week.

Some were already here.

The muscles of his face hardened as he thought of Lord Aeren, then relaxed. He had dealt with Aeren since before the Escarpment, although since then the lord had gained much influence in the Evant. His exposure of Khalaek as a traitor had been the impetus behind much of that.

But Aeren's time would come.

Peloroun smiled. The nervous guardsman across from him winced.

"You're probably wondering why I called you here, Iroen."

The guardsman swallowed, but straightened in his seat. He did not seem comfortable being seated in his lord's presence. His hands shifted from the arms of the polished oak chair to his legs and back again before settling there. "No, Lord Peloroun. I am Ionaen Phalanx. I serve you without question."

"I see."

Iroen's words were more sincere than he knew, although he and Courranen had made certain that Iroen and his two fellow guardsmen would not remember why.

Peloroun regarded the guardsman for a moment, then abruptly stood. As he moved around his desk, he picked up the small blade he used to open missives, only half the length of his finger, its handle made of bone. It was not especially sharp—it was not meant to be—but it was sufficient for his purposes.

Iroen watched him as he circled the desk. The guardsman did not miss the retrieval of the knife, which made Peloroun wonder if perhaps he should use one of the other two guardsmen instead. He hated to waste a promising guard.

But no, Iroen was here now. It would take time to summon the others.

"I have a problem, Iroen. One that you can help me with. I need to speak with someone, but he is too far away to summon, so far, in fact, that it would take weeks to find him simply to deliver the summons."

Iroen frowned. Peloroun saw it as he passed behind him, the guard's head dipping forward in confusion. "I don't understand. How can I help you with this, my lord?"

Peloroun leaned back against his desk on Iroen's far side, near enough he could have killed him with the letter opener before the guard could react if he'd wanted to.

"Do you recall the survey of the Provinces that we endured nearly twenty years ago, when I and three other Lords of the Evant traveled from Rendell in the north, along the coastal lands controlled by the humans, and then eastward from Portstown across the southern Provinces, through Temeritt, Borangst, and Yhnar?" When Iroen nodded, he continued. "You won't remember, but while we were traveling from Temeritt to Yhnar, you and I and two other Ionaen House Phalanx left the main group, ostensibly to take a closer look at the Flats that separate the human lands from the Thalloran Wasteland. We met a friend there, on the Flats—the person I need to speak to actually. During that meeting, he left each of you with a . . . gift."

Peloroun's smile didn't change, but the guard shifted uneasily. He held Peloroun's gaze. "I don't remember any of this."

"I said you wouldn't. But if you draw back the sleeve of your shirt, you will see what he left you."

Iroen glanced toward the arm that Peloroun pointed to, resting on the edge of his seat. At Peloroun's prodding, he slid the sleeve back to his elbow and turned his arm palm up, exposing the pale underside riddled with veins. Near the wrist, a small black mole stood out against the pale skin.

Except it wasn't a mole.

Peloroun shifted away from the desk, his motion casual, although Iroen looked up at him, his confusion growing.

"I don't understand—" he began.

Peloroun clamped his hand down on the guardsman's forearm to hold it steady and jabbed the small knife into the black mark, felt it pierce skin and dig into the tendons of the wrist beneath. Iroen cried out in shock, jerked back, fury infusing his face, but Peloroun had already released his arm and stepped back. He moved around the desk, tossed the knife aside, a few drops of blood speckling the papers there, and seated himself carefully.

Iroen clutched his wounded wrist in one hand, anger twisting his features into a hard grimace that he fought to control, his breath coming in heaves. Through clenched teeth, he spat, "What did you do that for, my lord?"

Peloroun raised his eyebrows in feigned shock. "I thought you served without question, Iroen?"

The guardsman huffed a short breath, his glare his only answer.

Movement caught Peloroun's eye and his gaze dropped to Iroen's arm, the sleeve still pulled back to the elbow. A thin line of blood had escaped from beneath the guardsman's hand where he tried to staunch the flow, but that wasn't what riveted Peloroun to his seat. The Ionaen lord felt the blood drain from his face, his features going slack. Iroen noticed and followed the direction of his gaze.

From beneath the guard's hand, black liquid, like ink, streamed down the length of his arm. But unlike the trail of blood, it spread beneath the skin.

Iroen gasped and jerked back, letting go of his wrist as he flung his arm away from his body, as if he could dislodge the black fluid by shaking it off. His own blood spattered the desk, a drop hitting Peloroun's cheek, causing him to flinch. But the lord didn't move, didn't raise a hand to brush the blood away. He couldn't move, transfixed by what was happening to Iroen. The guard flailed his arm again, a cry escaping him, but the black fluid had already reached his elbow, had begun to work its way into his upper arm, snaking beneath the cover of the shirt.

Iroen shot a panicked look at his lord, then gripped and ripped the sleeve of his shirt free. By the time the fabric gave, the blackness had seethed upward to his shoulder and appeared to be growing. Iroen lurched up from his chair, cried out again as Peloroun watched the ink spread across the guard's chest, so dark it was visible beneath the white shirt. Iroen's right hand pounded the area above his heart as he gasped, his breaths painful now, his face contorted with a struggle that Peloroun could not comprehend. His fingers seized the flesh over his heart, as if trying to dig into the cavity beneath where the blackness had pooled. Cords stood out on the guard's neck as he arched backward, mouth open in a rictus of pain—

Then Iroen stilled. He emitted a choked sound, his features going slack. . . .

And he collapsed back into the chair beneath him. His head lolled, as if his neck had been broken. His arms fell into his lap. Blood stained his shirt from the cut in his wrist. Peloroun would have thought he was dead except that he could still see him breathing.

The lord remained in his seat, frowning at his guardsman. He wasn't certain he should move—wasn't certain he could. Courranen had not told him what to expect when he released the piece of Shadow implanted in each of the guards, only that if there was a need for contact, to cut the black mark so that the darkness could reach the victim's bloodstream.

And from there, the heart.

Peloroun eyed the black stain that he could see under the guard's shirt. He shifted forward, wincing when his chair creaked, and realized his hands had gripped the arms of his own chair so hard they'd cramped. He forced them free, shook them out, his forearms aching from the strain.

Then he stood.

As he did so, Iroen's body spasmed.

Peloroun choked on his own breath, leaned forward onto his desk to regain his composure. As he drew in air, he noticed the black stain over Iroen's heart had begun to move. Tendrils snaked out toward the guard's arms and legs, a thicker tendril working its way up his neck. It split and curled around his mouth and nose beneath the skin, then each converged on the guard's eyes.

Peloroun saw the black liquid spill into the whites of Iroen's eyes as if it were, indeed, ink. The guard's body jerked again as the oil filled the whites completely.

Iroen blinked once, twice . . . and sat up straight in his

seat. He regarded Peloroun across the desk with eyes as black as night, traceries of the darkness beneath his skin like tattoos across his face, arms, chest, and legs.

"You wished to speak with me?"

The voice was not Iroen's.

It was Khalaek's.

Peloroun's legs lost their strength, and he dropped heavily back into his seat. The same shock he had felt decades ago when he had gone to the Flats, uncertain of who would meet him, and finding Khalaek waiting shivered through his body again. It had been the only time he had seen the fallen lord since. Khalaek had looked the same as when he had been carried out into the churned-up plains at the edge of the Escarpment and given over to the human King Stephan, after being banished and exiled by Thaedoren and the Evant . . . except that his pale skin had been mottled with the same shadowy oil that had suffused Iroen. Khalaek had been accompanied by another of the sukrael-touched, another Alvritshai named Courranen, but Courranen deferred to Khalaek, standing a step behind the Lord of House Duvoraen.

Peloroun had fallen to his knees when he'd seen him, the winds that blew incessantly and tasted of salt burning his face and parched lips. The fine-grained sand of the Flats had cut into his knees as he bowed his head and muttered, "Lord Khalaek."

Khalaek had frowned down at him, even as Peloroun's escort of three guardsmen knelt in guarded consternation behind him. "Not Khalaek," he'd said, his voice hard. "The Evant has banished me, have they not? I am no longer Lord of House Duvoraen. I am Khalaek-khai now."

Hearing Khalaek's voice—the inflections, the tone— coming from Iroen's mouth brought that meeting back so intensely Peloroun could taste the salt and feel the heat of the sun-baked earth beneath his knees. He licked his lips and tried to speak, but couldn't.

A look of annoyance crossed Iroen's face, then the black eyes glanced around the room, coming back to rest on Peloroun. "Say what you have to say, Lord Peloroun. I have no time to waste. Events are escalating, and this connection will not last long."

The thought that perhaps he had made a mistake flashed through Peloroun's mind, but he leaned forward. His first words cracked and broke, as if something had been lodged in his throat, but as he spoke, his voice steadied. "All of the arrangements have been made here in Caercaern and throughout Alvritshai lands. The Chosen has begun his campaign to bring the people to our cause, and we have gathered together allies within the Evant. But there is a problem."

Creases appeared in Iroen's forehead as Khalaek narrowed his eyes. "What problem?"

Peloroun stood and growled, "Lord Aeren." When Khalaek's frown merely deepened, he continued. "The Lord of Rhyssal House has taken it upon himself to oppose Lotaern and his use of the Order of the Flame. He has been visiting each lord as they arrive in the city in person, in private, to argue against the Chosen and the Order. I believe that he is gaining support. Most of the lords have already expressed unease at having members of the Flame walking through their lands, although so far only Lord Aeren has vocalized those concerns publicly. I do not know what he has said to bring the lords to his side, but I fear that his politicking will interfere with our plans."

"And what do you propose I do about it?"

"We," Peloroun said, emphasizing the word, "were hoping that the timing of events could be shifted forward. We thought perhaps you or one of the other Wraiths could

arrive sooner than planned, along with your armies, preferably before Lord Aeren has the chance to dismantle everything we have worked to achieve."

Khalaek stared at him over the desk, and for a moment
Peloroun wondered if he knew of their real intent in bringing one of the Wraiths within Lotaern's grasp. Fresh sweat
broke out along his skin. He didn't know what the Wraiths
were capable of. Could Khalaek reach out through Iroen's
body and kill him where he stood if he suspected their
treachery? Or would it be simpler to use Iroen's own cattan
to kill him?

Could Peloroun harm Khalaek if he fought back, or
would it only destroy Iroen's body?

"Impossible," Khalaek finally said, the single word riddled with finality, his next words with derision. "The Winter
Tree is still a factor. The Wraiths and the majority of our
armies cannot attack Alvritshai lands until the Tree has
been destroyed. That is the reason we are even discussing
an alliance with you and the Chosen. Without the Tree, we
could seize all of the Alvritshai's lands without your help."

Anger sparked inside Peloroun, prickling along his
shoulders and down his arms. "Then how can we destroy
the Tree?"

Iroen's lips twisted into a smile. "You cannot. Nor can
the Chosen. But we have already begun. The Trees are
weakening, their power lessening." The smile vanished.
"But it will take time. That is what you and the Chosen are
intended to do: provide us with that time. You know this.
Soon there will be calls to war. The Accord that all three
races signed a generation ago will be tested. That is when
you will be needed. You must keep the Alvritshai distracted
while I and the rest of the Wraiths bring down the Seasonal
Trees and begin our march on Wrath Suvane. That is your
goal. Or have you forgotten?"

Peloroun's hand closed into a fist at the flat derision in

Khalaek's voice, but he bowed his head. "I have not forgotten."

"Deal with Lord Aeren on your own. Do whatever it takes to stop him."

"Of course, Khalaek-khai."

Iroen's black eyes bored into him, the guard's features shifting subtly, taking on more of Khalaek's aspects than Iroen's. "You failed me once in the past, Peloroun, there at the Escarpment. Do not fail me again."

Before Peloroun could respond, the darkness left Iroen's eyes and the guard's body slumped forward, forehead thudding onto the desk. He glared at the body, tried to control his breathing, then shook himself. He shoved Iroen's body back, noted the too pale skin, the black marks like tattoos no longer swirling like ink, no longer mobile.

He knew before he pressed his hand to Iroen's neck that the guardsman was dead.

~

"You must watch the lords and their retainers as closely as possible while I speak," Aeren said to Hiroun for the tenth time as all around them the proceedings of the Evant continued. He did not look at the guardsman as he spoke, his gaze flicking from one lord to another, to the Chosen and the Tamaell, and then back to the rest of the room. "I will be too focused on presenting my argument to see everything. I'm counting on you to catch what I miss."

"Yes, Lord Aeren. I'll watch them carefully."

Aeren kept the frown from his face at the hint of irritation that had crept into Hiroun's voice and kept his eyes on the Hall of the Evant's activity. He knew he'd repeated himself too much, that the repetition came across as a lack of faith in Hiroun, but he couldn't help himself. He'd felt Eraeth's absence too much in the last few weeks as he arranged meetings with each of the individual lords as they arrived in

Caercaern. All of his requests had been granted, even by Lord Peloroun, who had opposed him since before the Accord. The arrangements for the meetings and the preparation required had been taxing. Without Eraeth there to share the burden, he'd been forced to handle everything himself. He'd taken to talking out loud to his empty rooms, as if Eraeth were there listening.

Of the six lords he'd met with after speaking to Thaedoren, only one supported him outright. Lord Terroec, still young in his claim to his House after his father's death, had been the most disturbed by the presence of the members of the Flame in his lands. Aeren hadn't even informed him of Lotaern's theft of Shaeveran's knife before he was agreeing to back him if he brought the matter of the Order to the Evant floor. Peloroun, the oldest lord next to Aeren, had listened attentively, eyebrows raised at Lotaern's treachery, but had been evasive and ambiguous regarding his support. Aeren had expected nothing less, yet had left the lord's apartments in Caercaern faintly troubled. There had been something about Peloroun's household that hadn't felt quite right. It had taken him two days before it struck him why—the guardsmen and servants had been too settled, too fixed into a routine. Peloroun had told him he and his entourage had arrived only the day before, and yet Aeren hadn't seen any unpacked chests or wagons being unloaded. Servants were not hastily scrubbing floors or dusting shelves, clearing away the effects of leaving the rooms and corridors vacant for the long winter months. Everything had already been cleaned; even the smell of the scented water used for such efforts had faded.

He suspected that Peloroun had been in Caercaern longer than he admitted publicly. Eraeth would have noticed the discrepancy immediately. It annoyed Aeren that it had taken him two days to figure it out on his own. But what reason would Peloroun have to arrive early? He didn't know.

He scanned the remaining four lords. Orraen and Houdyll were both relatively new to their positions, although Orraen carried himself as if he had already risen to the highest ranks of the Evant, if not the Tamaell's position itself. Houdyll was different. Watching the young lord's nervousness on the floor and during their private meeting only made Aeren believe that Jydell, Houdyll's father, would be disappointed. Jydell had been a strong leader, careful to make alliances that only aided his House, aligning himself with no one permanently and maintaining alliances only when they were still beneficial to him. Houdyll attempted to please everyone. He had nodded agreement with everything Aeren said during their meeting, leaving Aeren completely uncertain about where he would stand when it came time for a vote in the Evant.

Saetor and Daesor were more experienced and, like Peloroun, hedged their responses. Both had expressed concern over the Flame, and surprise over Lotaern's actions regarding the knife. Saetor, with his military background as part of Khalaek's Phalanx, had nearly admitted that he agreed with Lotaern, that the knife should be in the hands of the Order, where it could be used most effectively. Daesor was more taciturn about his thoughts.

It was not the reaction Aeren had expected. When Daesor had seen his frustration, he'd merely said, "Perhaps the reason you feel so strongly about this is because the affront was so personal. Lotaern's Flame practically stole the knife from beneath your own hand."

Aeren had had nothing to say to that. Daesor had been the last lord he'd spoken to before the Evant was convened.

Now, Lord Daesor stood in the middle of the oval chamber, reporting on his activities over the winter months,

including travel to Andover across the Arduon Ocean, os-
tensibly to solidify trade agreements with the Northern
Fleet Trading Company and the Taranto and Avezzano
Families of the Court.

"—have signed agreements with the Northern Fleet
based on these accessions on their part. I believe the compromise will increase our trade with the Court in Andover
and help solidify our political ties with the Doms of each of
the northern Families. I hope that this will allow the estab-
lishment of a presence of Alvritshai goods on the Andover
markets unprecedented in our history with that nation."

Daesor nodded to Tamaell Thaedoren as he finished. The
murmur of conversation increased as he made his way to
his seat, flourishing the maroon-and-gold colors of his
House. A page leaned forward to hand him a note, which he
frowned at as he read it. More pages were making their way
back and forth across the room, Aeren keeping a close eye
on those who arrived and departed from Lotaern's seat.

On the raised platform that held the Tamaell's seat, the
Tamaea's and Tamaell Presumptive's thrones empty, Thaedoren allowed the conversation to continue for a time. As
soon as the pages' activity began to abate, he caught Aeren's
gaze and nodded toward him, then rose.

"Lord Aeren has expressed a desire to speak to the Evant
regarding some of the recent activity of our own Chosen,
Lotaern, of the Order of Aielan. I yield the floor to him."

Thaedoren's voice was perfectly inflected; Aeren could
tell nothing of which way the Tamaell intended to throw his
support. But Aeren remembered the meeting in his chambers too clearly, recalled Reanne's presence, so strong and
self-evident once he'd noticed it. The Tamaea was not in
attendance at this meeting of the Evant, but he could feel
her nonetheless.

He rose, cast Hiroun one last look, the young guardsman
nodding in acknowledgment, his face set. Aeren felt heart-

ened as he watched the guardsman begin to scan the rest of the chamber as he himself made his way to the center of the floor.

He smiled and surveyed all of the lords before settling his gaze on Lotaern. He bowed his head. "I beg the Chosen's forgiveness for bringing this to the Hall of the Evant, but it is something that I felt needed to be addressed by the assemblage as a whole."

Lotaern had stiffened where he sat, a dark frown touching his eyes and turning the corners of his mouth, but he did not respond. Aeren realized he already knew what he intended to say, and he felt a flicker of annoyance.

One of the lords must have informed him before the gathering of the Evant.

He shrugged his sudden unease and despair aside and turned to the rest of the Evant. He could not escape the feeling that the decision regarding his complaint had already been reached, but he forged onward.

"I have already spoken to all of you separately and in private about my concern, so here let me remind you that I was once an acolyte with the Order of Aielan myself. I have lived within the Sanctuary, trained beneath the Chosen's hand, studied the Scripts myself, and even immersed myself in Aielan's Light before I was called back to my House to become its lord after my father's and brother's deaths. I pledged myself to Aielan, to upholding the principles set out in the Scripts and established by all of those Chosen for the Order from times past. In my role as Lord of Rhyssal House, I have striven to maintain those principles and incorporate them into the policies of the House, even though by taking up that leadership I was forced to forsake the vows I took as an acolyte.

"At first, I found integrating the two—the principles of Aielan and the responsibilities of a lord—to be difficult. But I persevered, and over the years have surmounted the challenge. The two can coexist. I believe the Accord that was established between the three races was the culmination of that coexistence, at least for me.

"But recently, some of the actions of the Order of Aielan, and in particular, the Chosen, Lotaern, have caused me concern. I have found it more and more difficult to accept these changes made within the Order. I know that many of you are now thinking that my own reservations are born out of a personal conflict with Lotaern, a grudge or feud with him that I have harbored since I left the Order, perhaps rooted in my own dissatisfaction at being forced to leave. I tell you now, this is not so. When I left the Order, it was with the greatest respect for Lotaern and for the Order itself. It is only recent events that have troubled me. I know they have troubled some of the rest of you as well."

He paused, looking around the room, taking in the expressions of every one of the lords where they sat behind the tables lined with cloth of their House colors. Most of their faces were carefully blank, their postures reserved. Lord Terraec's gaze was locked on Lotaern, who sat behind his own table draped in folds of white, his hands hidden. Aeren turned to the Chosen as well as he continued.

"I have spoken to all of the lords regarding the members of the Order of the Flame, what is in essence the Order's Phalanx, that have been actively invading our individual House lands under the auspices of being acolytes. They have been performing the rituals of the Order in the temples, acting as acolytes, and in most cases the acolytes who have been sent to care for the local populations at each temple have deferred to them. As a Lord of one of the Houses of the Evant, I would not condone the use of one of my fellow lords' Phalanxes in my own lands without that lord first seeking permission from me and my fellow caitans. I would humbly request that the Chosen order the current members of the Order of the Flame who inhabit my lands back to the Sanctuary here in Caercaern, until such time as the Chosen seeks and gains permission to have the Flame enter my lands. I strongly suggest that the rest of the Lords of the Evant do the same.

"I would ask that the Evant reprimand the Chosen for his actions, for this blatant invasion of House lands. He has overstepped the bounds of the Order."

A silence thrumming with anger followed his words. Aeren felt that anger trembling in his arms, the hands behind his back clasped so hard he knew the knuckles were white. The strength of the emotion surprised him. But what he had said in his speech was true: he had left the Order with the greatest respect for Lotaern and what the Chosen had taught him while he was an acolyte. The emergence of the Order of the Flame and the actions Lotaern had taken since then had been difficult to accept. Lotaern was not the mentor he remembered so fondly from his studies anymore. He had changed.

But the anger in the room did not come solely from him. He could feel it radiating from Lotaern as well. Somehow, over the course of years, the two had grown apart, grown distant.

A part of him regretted that distance and hated the enmity between them now. But he could not let Lotaern's actions stand unchallenged.

Behind him, he heard the Tamaell stand and step forward, his tread unmistakable, but he did not turn to face him.

"As Tamaell of the Alvritshai," Thaedoren said, his voice filling the chamber, smooth and dark with import, "I find that some of Lord Aeren's concerns have merit. There are issues regarding the Order of the Flame that we have not yet addressed, one of which is how the Flame is to be treated. Should the Order be considered a House and the Flame its Phalanx? Lord Aeren has stated that is how he feels, and as such the Flame should not be allowed to arbitrarily enter a fellow lord's House lands. The alternative is to agree that the Flame is not a military force at all, but merely a group of specialized acolytes, in which case the Order would not be considered equivalent to a House in its own right.

"I pose the question to Lotaern, the Chosen of the Order of Aielan, first. Does the Order wish to be considered the equivalent to a House, with the Order of the Flame as its Phalanx, subject to all of the expectations and restrictions of a member of the Evant?"

Aeren felt his heart lurch as the words sank in. This was not what he had intended when he brought his concern to the Evant. He had simply wanted the lords to force Lotaern to remove the members of the Flame from House lands. He had not wanted to bring the Order's place among the Evant into question. What Thaedoren had brought to the floor would solidify the powers that Lotaern wielded within the Evant. It would answer the question that had hounded them all since the Order of the Flame had been revealed. If the lords agreed, Lotaern would become the equivalent of a lord. Instead of merely having a say in the Evant, his opinion easily dismissed since he had no true power, he would gain political weight.

Aeren turned to regard the Tamaell in horror, but Thaedoren was not looking at him. His focus was on Lotaern. Aeren spun back to the Chosen of the Order, his heart now beating too fast in his chest. For he knew how Lotaern would answer.

Standing slowly, the Chosen of the Order addressed the room as a whole, not once looking toward Aeren. He kept his face impassive, although Aeren noted a hint of smugness in the thrust of his chin.

He doubted any of the other lords knew him well enough to see it.

"As you know, I have long sought to have a say within the Evant. It is my belief that the voice of Aielan should be considered when matters that affect all of the Alvritshai are being decided. Because of this, I would claim that the Order has always been the spiritual House of the Alvritshai. This would simply be recognition of that fact by the Lords of the Evant."

Thaedoren had frowned, but after a moment he turned to the rest of the Lords of the Evant. "Then I demand an accounting. All those in favor of recognizing the Order of Aielan as a House of the Evant, and the Order of the Flame as its Phalanx, with Lotaern, the Chosen of the Order, as its current lord, please stand."

Aeren spun as first Orraen, then Daesor, Saetor, Houdyll, and finally Peloroun stood. Only Terroec remained seated. Fury hardened him, forced his shoulders back as Thaedoren turned to face him, even though despair left him empty inside.

He had not come here to validate Lotaern's and the Order's position in the Evant. But he could see no way to stop it.

"What say you, Lord Aeren?"

Aeren gritted his teeth and blew a short breath out through his nose, eyes lowered, then answered, looking up toward Thaedoren. "I am *not* in favor of the proposal, Tamaell."

Thaedoren nodded. "So I expected. However, it is long past time for this to be addressed. The proposal is passed. The Order of Aielan has been granted the same responsibilities, duties, and expectations of a House of the Evant. Do you accept these responsibilities, duties, and expectations, Chosen?"

Lotaern nodded humbly. "I do."

"Then so shall it be recorded."

A loud murmur spread through the entire Hall as Lotaern took his seat, a brief, triumphant smile touching his face. Before it could settle there permanently, Thaedoren halted it with a level glare.

"As the equivalent of a Lord of the Evant, with the Flame as your Phalanx, I am forced to agree with Lord Aeren regarding his grievance of members of the Flame entering his House lands without first seeking permission. As Tamaell, commander of all of the House Phalanx, I command you to order their return to the Sanctuary immediately. Not only from Rhyssal House lands, but from all of the lands of the Houses."

At Lotaern's grudging nod, Thaedoren turned his gaze on Aeren again. Aeren could see the message there clearly: his concern regarding the Flame had been addressed, but it had come at a cost. One that Aeren wasn't certain he would have been willing to pay had he known of it beforehand.

"Was there some other grievance that you wished to address regarding the Order of Aielan?" the Tamaell asked.

Aeren hesitated. Thaedoren was giving him the opportunity to bring up the theft of the knife from Shaeveran, giving him a chance to retaliate. He had told all of the lords of Lotaern's actions during their private meetings, knew that they were watching him now.

But he knew he couldn't make an accusation before the Evant. Not without Shaeveran at his side. Not without more evidence. It would be seen as a personal attack on the Chosen himself, as Thaedoren had pointed out earlier. It would be hearsay, nothing more.

Aeren had not survived this long within the Evant, risen to the heights he had, by being politically naïve, no matter how much he wished to bring Lotaern down. It was time for a strategic retreat.

Jaw clenched, he shot a glance toward the Chosen, head raised . . . then bowed his head.

"No, Tamaell, I have nothing further to bring to the floor."

14

JAYSON AND CORIM STUMBLED into Cobble Kill with the sunset, the sheet of thin clouds overhead blazing with a deep burnt orange. Jayson halted at the end of the stone bridge over the stream that gave the town its name, leaning heavily against a stone pillar with a lantern already lit at its top. Corim slumped down on the stone abutment of the bridge.

"We're almost there, Corim."

He tried to keep the words light and encouraging, but it had been a long walk and neither one of them had slept much since the night of the attack. It had taken them three days to reach Cobble Kill, which would normally take a day on horseback. They had seen no one on the road the first two days, but that afternoon, while taking a break near a small creek, they had heard a horse-drawn cart trundle past on the dirt road. Corim had shot Jayson a terrified glance, his body rigid with fear. Jayson had shushed him with a hand gesture, motioned him to stay still. He'd been facing the road and had caught glimpses of the cart through the heavy undergrowth.

He hadn't thought it was a threat, but he wouldn't take the chance. Not with Corim at his side.

"Let's find the Legion's garrison," he said, staring down

toward the town square. He pushed himself away from the stone pillar and urged Corim up from his seat. The boy groaned, but came along. Jayson kept one hand on his shoulder, in case he collapsed.

Cobble Kill claimed three taverns and an inn, a stable, two smithies, and three mercantiles, one from each of the three major trading companies. All of its streets were paved with cobblestone and converged on a main square lined with two-story buildings, a few with balconies overlooking the square. Nearly all of the buildings were made of river stone. Shutters were drawn and windows glowed with candle or lantern light. More of the stone pillars topped with lanterns lined the road into the square and Jayson and Corim followed them as the day faded and night fell. A burst of laughter and noise spilled from one of the tavern doors as it was opened and someone staggered into the street. Both Jayson and Corim stiffened, Corim drawing a step closer. But the man didn't see them, moving off toward the west.

Jayson scanned the street, noted the horses and two carts that marked the taverns and inn and the low fence that surrounded the stable yard. Wind sighed through the trees, new spring leaves rustling. He didn't see anything that looked like a Legion garrison. He'd been to Cobble Kill a few times before, delivering ground grain to the mercantiles, but he'd never had need of the garrison before.

Without any idea of where to go, he moved toward the nearest tavern. Corim hesitated at the door, but glanced out into the settling darkness with a shudder and followed Jayson inside.

There were at least a dozen men and women seated at rough wooden tables arranged around a central hearth, the fire low, a pot on an iron hook set over the flames. Lanterns hung from the exposed wooden beams of the ceiling, a set of stairs angling up to the rooms above to one side, opposite the hearth. A pair of doors led to the kitchen in the back.

As he halted inside the door, the raucous laughter trailed off, everyone taking notice of them. Most were simply curious, trading questioning glances and receiving shrugs in return. One or two expressions were hostile for no apparent reason.

Before the silence could become awkward, the doors to the kitchen opened and a woman stepped through, hair held back with a folded scarf, an apron tied around her broad waist. "Got yer venison right here, Carl, no need to—oh!"

She halted as she saw them, a platter with steaming meat held aloft in one hand, a mug of ale in the other. But only for a moment. A smile broke across her initial surprise, then she set the platter and ale down in front of Carl. She wiped her hands on her apron and stepped forward, her gaze dropping to Corim, then back to Jayson, settling on the bloodstained sleeve of his arm and the torn cloth he'd used to bandage the wound.

"You two look famished. Need a room for the night? Some food?"

Jayson's stomach growled, but he shook his head. "We're looking for the Legion's garrison. We're from Gray's Kill."

She frowned. "Not much of a garrison here, more like an outpost now, although it used to be larger."

"Where is it?"

"Left, down the main road about a half mile."

Jayson gripped Corim's shoulder harder as the boy began to list. He reached down to support him with his other hand and said, "Thank you," but before he could move them toward the door Corim sagged into him.

He caught him as the woman cried out, reaching forward to catch the boy's other arm.

"Here, now, he's so exhausted he can't stand! And so are you," she added reprovingly. She dragged Corim toward the nearest empty chair and sat him down, Jayson forced to follow. When she stood, she pointed to a second seat and said with a glare, "Sit."

Her glare darkened when Jayson made to protest, so he swallowed his words and slid wearily into the proffered chair. The woman nodded and swept off. He leaned forward onto the table and his own exhaustion swept over him, shaking his shoulders and trembling in his arms and legs. He knew the rest of the tavern's patrons were watching them both, but he didn't care enough to glance up.

He heard the door to the kitchen kicked open and a moment later two bowls of stew clattered to the table before him and Corim. He shoved back from the table, but before he could mention that they had no coin to pay for it, the woman said, "Eat. You both need the strength."

There was no questioning the command in her voice. And when he breathed in the rich scent of the stew, he found his body wouldn't let him protest. He pulled it toward him, noticed that the smell had roused Corim as well, the boy shifting forward, snatching up the spoon, and shoveling the stew in as fast as he could. They'd had only not-quite-ripe berries and whatever tubers and leeks Jayson could scavenge for the past three days.

"Thank you," Jayson managed, before diving into his own bowl. Corim muttered something that may have been thanks around a mouthful, and the woman nodded.

"I'll be back with some bread. Don't eat it all before then. And Carl—" she said, spinning toward the man, who froze, a forkful of venison half raised toward his mouth, "—get yer lazy ass out of that chair and hike it down to the garrison. Bring back one of the Legionnaires. This man needs to speak to him."

Carl grumbled something under his breath, then shoved the forkful into his mouth, chewing as he rose and wiped his hands on his breeches. He eyed the two from Gray's Kill, then shook his head and stalked out into the night, the door slamming shut behind him.

"Jayson." The woman turned as he spoke. "My name's Jayson Freeholt, and this is my apprentice Corim."

"Pleased to meet you, Jayson and Corim." Corim flinched at his name and the woman frowned, casting a sharp eye at Jayson. "My name's Ara and this is my tavern." She held out her hand and Jayson shook it. Her grip was strong, which shouldn't have been a surprise. She was built solidly, broad shoulders and body, ample breasts, round face. Not fat, but stout, her carriage no-nonsense. "What brings you to Cobble Kill?"

The stew in Jayson's mouth turned tasteless. He swallowed with difficulty and set his spoon back in the bowl. "Someone attacked Gray's Kill," he said, his voice hoarse.

The words unlocked something in his chest he'd held onto tightly since the night of the attack, all of the images—the smoke, the reflected fire, the hissing of the creatures that had struck from the darkness, and the chill of sleeping on the barge in the middle of the river—all of it flooding back in a sudden wave. He choked on it, his heart seizing, tears burning at the corners of his eyes, but before they could spill over, he heard Corim sob.

He reached out without thinking and drew the boy close to him, the youth burying his head in Jayson's chest, snuffling loudly. The murmurs that had started up as soon as Ara returned with the stew stilled again, and Jayson looked up to find that Ara herself had drawn back a step in horror, one hand raised to her mouth.

"Who?" she asked. Then, with more force, "Who attacked Gray's Kill?"

Jayson shook his head. "I don't know. We never made it back to the village. We were attacked by creatures on the road, and then the dwarren came—"

At mention of the dwarren the people in the tavern gasped and broke into excited conversation, the sound cutting Jayson off. An elderly man spat to one side and muttered, "I never did trust those earth-diggers. Bunch of sneaky bastards, they are." A round of general agreement passed through the room, Ara looking on in disapproval, hands now on hips.

The anger that had been stirred might have escalated if the door hadn't opened and one of the Legionnaires stepped into the tavern, followed by Carl.

Dressed in armor, he blocked the door, although he wasn't a bulky man. His gray eyes swept the room, taking in everything with one glance, his gaze settling on Jayson and Corim with a frown. He held himself with a stiff, military bearing, head high, shoulders back, feet placed firmly. Yet when he took the few steps from the door to their table, removing his helmet, his motions were smooth. One hand fell casually to the pommel of the sword strapped to his side as he cradled the helmet with the other. He couldn't have been more than a few years older than Jayson.

"You wished to speak to the Legion?" he asked gruffly. His eyes measured both Jayson and Corim. "If it is about enlisting, there's a general call held every—"

"It's not about enlisting, Gregson," Ara cut in sharply. "He says Gray's Kill has been attacked."

Jayson wouldn't have thought it possible, but Gregson straightened where he stood.

"Attacked," he said, the word sharp but hesitant. "By whom?"

Jayson opened his mouth, but Ara beat him to it. "He doesn't know. Creatures, he said, and the dwarren!"

Gregson's frown deepened. "Is this true?"

"Yes."

The Legionnaire glanced around the room, at the avid faces of the other patrons, then sighed. He set his helmet on the table. "May as well question you here," he muttered, "rather than risk rumors running rampant after we leave." He pulled the chair up opposite Jayson and Corim and seated himself, his armor making his position awkward. "Now, explain what happened."

Jayson drew in a deep breath to steady himself, then launched into the story, relating everything that had happened from the moment they stepped out of the mill to arriving in Cobble Kill. Corim added a few comments when asked directly by Gregson but otherwise remained quiet. The rest of the patrons were silent except for an occasional snort or gasp. Ara listened attentively, but kept everyone's mugs of ale full, even bringing Gregson a cup, which he did not drink.

Gregson said nothing at first when Jayson finished. He leaned back in his chair and regarded both Jayson and Corim intently. Then: "Let me see your arm."

Jayson shifted forward and began unwinding the hasty bandage he'd placed on the wound. The recitation of the attack had numbed him, his motions slow, even though the stew had restored some of his strength. He grimaced when the last few lengths of torn cloth pulled at the cuts.

The claw marks were reddened, swollen, and crusted with scabs. A few fresh dots of blood welled up where the removal of the bandage had reopened the wound.

He held his arm out for Gregson, who grunted as he leaned forward to examine it, taking Jayson's arm and twisting it this way and that in the lantern light. Ara craned over his shoulder, then tsked and disappeared into the back room again. She returned before Gregson had finished, fresh bandages hung over one arm and a squat jar of unguent in one hand.

"Those are some serious wounds," Gregson said as he finished. "Not from any animal I've ever seen."

"One of them caught my leg as well."

Gregson's eyes dropped to his leg. The skeptical note had faded from his voice.

Ara had already begun attending to his arm. He hissed as she slathered the first layer of unguent across the cuts, the thick paste stinging, but he held still as she began tying fresh bandages across it.

Gregson appeared to reach a decision, standing and taking up his helmet. "We'll need to see Gray's Kill before I send someone to Hartleton or Temeritt. Rest up here, if Ara's got the rooms to spare—"

"Of course I do," she said succinctly, looking to Jayson and then Corim with a smile.

"—and I'll gather together some of the Legion. I'd like you to accompany us, if you would, Jayson."

Jayson frowned as Ara tied off the last bandage and patted his arm, even as relief flooded through him, the burden of responsibility lifting from his shoulders. He had intended to return once he passed on the warning. He needed to find out what had happened to Lianne.

"I'm coming, too."

Both Jayson and Gregson turned at Corim's quiet declaration. The youth had said little on the trek to Cobble Kill, sunk into a state of shock. But now something had sparked in his eyes. He sat up straight in his chair, his face haggard and exhausted, but lined with determination.

At Gregson's frown of disapproval, the apprentice turned toward Jayson. "I can't stay here. I need to find my parents." His voice broke slightly, but he crossed his arms over his chest stubbornly.

Jayson grimaced and turned to Gregson.

The Legionnaire settled his helmet into place. "He's twelve, of age. He can come if he wishes."

~

Gregson appeared early the next morning with three other members of the Legion and two additional horses. Ara stood beside both Jayson and Corim outside the tavern as they rode up from the eastern road. The youngest appeared to be no more than eighteen.

"Gregson is a good man," Ara said, "and a better Legionnaire than he believes himself to be. You'll be safe with him." She patted Corim on the shoulder, then stepped back as the group of Legion approached.

Gregson motioned to the three men who accompanied him. "This is Terson, my second, and Curtis and Ricks." Terson gave them a curt nod; both Curtis and Ricks smiled. "I've brought you mounts."

Jayson glanced at the two animals skeptically, but stepped forward. He'd ridden before, of course, but not for long distances and never on horses as fine as these. He helped Corim into the saddle first, the youth tense with fear and excitement, petting his mount's neck after situating himself in the saddle, then Jayson swung himself onto his own horse.

Gregson kicked his mount into motion and the rest followed with little prompting.

They rode out of Cobble Kill, a rock promontory that Jayson had not seen in the fading light the night before jutting out of the forest over the town to the north. Trees closed in immediately after they crossed the stone bridge, sunlight dappling the road beneath as the leaves rustled in a faint breeze. Dust danced beneath the foliage above the undergrowth to either side, passing from shadow to light, but Jayson found himself paying more attention to remaining on his horse than the scenery. The pace was swift.

They rode throughout the day, pausing often to rest the horses and once to eat. As they drew closer to Gray's Kill, Gregson slowed, to Jayson's relief. After taking the northern fork when the road split, he dropped the pace even further.

As they rode toward the break that would lead toward the barge, Jayson found himself scanning the edge of the road, watching the shadows beneath the forest. His gaze darted from side to side, toward the shivering bush as a squirrel shot away with an annoyed chatter or the flutter of a bird startled from its branch. Sweat broke out across his shoulders and his breath quickened.

He nearly jumped out of his saddle when Ricks sidled closer and said in an undertone, "Relax."

Jayson turned toward him, caught the confident grin on the younger man's face. A wave of shame slicked through the apprehension in his gut and he straightened slightly.

"I don't know what we're going to find in Gray's Kill," he said.

Ricks frowned at the tone of his voice, pulling back slightly, but before Jayson could explain Gregson slowed to a halt and motioned Jayson forward. Corim remained behind, his horse skittish, picking up on the apprentice's unease. He saw the youth's eyes flick toward the shadows beneath the trees.

Gregson nodded toward the road ahead. As soon as they left the main road, it had begun winding through the cuts and gorges of the area, stone outcroppings and sharp slopes visible through the trees. "How much farther until we reach the barge?"

"Another hour at most," Jayson answered. "It's hard to tell. I've never traveled the road on horseback before. I've always had a cart laden with sacks slowing me down."

"I see." The Legionnaire looked toward the sun, already low on the horizon. "We should have enough time to reach the village before sunset then. But I want to proceed with caution in case whatever attacked is still around."

"We didn't see anyone on the road to Cobble Kill when we fled."

Gregson turned toward him with a raised eyebrow. "Perhaps because they stayed in Gray's Kill."

Jayson's stomach tightened and he felt sick.

Without a word, they moved down the road toward the river, the four soldiers forming up around Jayson and Corim, their swords loosened in their sheaths, their eyes scanning the trees as they moved. The apprehension that had seized Jayson on the road returned and his mouth went dry.

An hour later, they reached the barge. It appeared to be in the same place he and Corim had left it, unused since that night.

Jayson felt his heart shudder, grief welling up inside. But he forced it down.

Gregson and Terson slid from their horses and led them onto the barge. Jayson dropped down to the ground, but then froze. His breath had quickened, a sense of light-headedness enfolding him, but he swallowed and climbed onto the barge before anyone could comment, Curtis giving him an odd look. Corim followed him, Curtis and Ricks bringing up the rear, and then they were moving across the river, the Legion pulling on the rope to draw them across.

Gregson stepped off of the barge and onto the dock before it had come to a rest, Terson behind, both leading their horses. He contemplated the forest, the sun slanting through the trees at a sharp angle now, then turned to Jayson.

"Show us Gray's Kill."

Jayson moved to the front of the group with Gregson, the rest of the Legion drawing their swords. As he struck out down the main road, he glanced to either side, scanning the area where the dwarren had appeared and then vanished. But of course there was no sign of them.

They reached the lane.

"My mill is down there," he called back.

Gregson nodded and sent Curtis and Ricks down the lane, their horses left behind with Terson, but motioned Jayson forward.

Swallowing, Jayson continued. He saw nothing in the undergrowth, nothing in the trees, no movement at all, and the
silence was unnatural. He'd lived in Gray's Kill for nearly
fifteen years, since moving there to run the new mill. They
were close enough now there should have been sounds
from the village—someone chopping wood, dogs barking,
the clang of hammer and metal from the smithy, perhaps
even a few shouts from children. But there were no signs of
life, not even the smell of woodsmoke.

Then he rounded the last bend and halted in the middle
of the road. Gregson, Terson, and Corim drew up behind him.

Terson swore.

The village was gone. The smithy, the tavern, the mercan-
tile, and church were nothing but husks of blackened wood
and stone. Only one wall of the church remained standing,
the stone of the other three blocking the road to one side in
a low heap. The fire pit of the smithy sat in the middle of a
few charred timbers. And among all of the ruin, among all
that remained of the village, lay bodies.

Tears burned his eyes and threatened to choke Jayson as
the horror of that night returned. He smelled the thick
smoke as he half dragged Corim away from the backwash
of fire he knew had come from the center of town, felt the
heat searing his face and tasted the ash as the smoke blew
over the road.

He'd known this was what they would find, but he hadn't
been able to accept it. Not until now.

Gray's Kill was dead.

Someone shifted past him, brushing his arm, and he
started, raised a hand to scrub away the tears fiercely as he
watched Gregson move to one of the bodies near what had
been the entrance to the tavern. Terson was tying the horses
off near the trees at the side of the road.

"Who was this?" the Legionnaire asked, kneeling down
to stare at the man's face.

Jayson could barely bring himself to look. What if it were Lianne? But he knew it wasn't. He could tell by the shredded and bloodstained clothing it was a man.

"Tobin," he said, voice rough. "He was the blacksmith."

All four of them turned as Curtis and Ricks returned, their boots crunching in the gravel of the road. Their eyes were wide with shock as they entered the village.

"Nothing but the mill down the lane," Curtis reported. "It's still standing, untouched."

Gregson stood and the rest of the Legion began moving through the village, looking at the bodies, nudging them with their feet or the tips of their swords or scanning the forest to either side.

"The animals have gotten to them," Terson said.

"That's to be expected. They've been left out in the open for over three days." Gregson shaded his eyes from the sun as he looked up. "I'm surprised there aren't any crows here now, though."

"It wasn't animals that got them," Jayson muttered under his breath, thinking of the creature that had ripped into his arm and clawed his leg.

From his right, Curtis cast him a sidelong look. He hadn't realized he'd spoken loud enough for anyone close to hear.

"Fan out!" Gregson ordered.

Jayson frowned. "What are you looking for?" he asked Curtis.

The soldier shrugged. "A sign of whoever did this."

Jayson felt anger spark deep inside him, deeper than the grief. "But I already told you who did this. It was those . . . those things! Those creatures! The demons with the lantern eyes!"

Curtis shifted uncomfortably. "The GreatLord will need proof—"

"The Diermani-cursed things attacked me!" Jayson growled and shoved back the sleeve of his shirt to expose

the bandage from the still-healing claw marks on his forearm. He'd drawn breath to argue further, Curtis' face skeptical, when Terson shouted.

Everyone turned, Gregson and Ricks already moving
toward the second, who stood over one of the bodies near
the edge of the stone church. Curtis trotted forward as well;
Jayson and Corim trailed behind. Jayson didn't need to see
any more bodies.

But when everyone tensed and drew back, hands tightening on their swords, Gregson grunting, he stepped forward.

It wasn't one of the villagers. It was one of the dwarren,
the body lying on its back, the pale face staring upward. The
hands were arranged together across the chest, over the
braided and bead-woven beard, a small ax clutched in their
grip. The legs were laid out straight.

It didn't look like the dwarren had died in battle. There
were no wounds, and the body had obviously been arranged, almost ritualistically.

"So," Gregson said, voice tight, as the Legion's faces on
all sides turned grim, "the dwarren *were* here. There hasn't
been a dwarren attack on Province lands in over a hundred
years. GreatLord Kobel needs to be informed immediately."

The angry silence was broken a moment later by Corim.
He clutched at Jayson's arm, his eyes too wide, his face too
open. No one should ever see such vulnerability in another
person's soul. "My parents," he whispered.

Lianne, Jayson thought, but he fought the urge to abandon Corim and the others and race to his cottage. He wasn't
sure he could face what he'd find there yet. He glanced
around at all of the bodies scattered around the small village center and swallowed against the stone lodged in his
throat. "Let's look," he said to Corim.

They began searching, Corim dashing from body to

body, his actions growing more and more frantic even as tears gathered and then trailed down his face. His breath caught in his chest, coming in hitching gasps, and he continuously wiped snot from his upper lip. Jayson watched in silence, strangely numbed, as he followed in Corim's wake. He found Paul, the tavern keeper, and his wife Amy, both with weapons in hand, their bodies charred by the flames as the tavern burned down around them. The stableboy, Ander, had been torn to pieces in the back, his body left close enough to the fire it had been roasted. Huddled near the church, half-buried beneath the rubble of a collapsed wall, he found the healer Reannon, her body lying protectively across her two children, Tara and Ian. But none of the bodies belonged to Corim's parents. Or Lianne.

When there were no more bodies to check within the village center, Corim turned to him and said, "Home. They must be at home!"

He tore off down the road.

"No, Corim, wait!" Panic seized Jayson's chest and he charged after the boy. He heard Gregson curse and shout an order, followed by boots running after him, but he ignored it all. His heart thudded in his chest as he ran, and for the first time he felt the grief he'd shoved down hard before this shuddering up from his gut, hot and choking. His eyes burned with it and he scrubbed at them futilely as he ran. Ahead, he saw Corim dodge down a secondary path, the one that led to his parent's cottage, heard the crack of a door flung open—

And then a young boy's hoarse cry shattered the unnatural stillness of the air.

Jayson's heart wrenched in his chest as he stumbled down the last of the path and caught himself on the casement of the cottage's door. He leaned there, gasping, and then reeled back from what he saw inside.

The room was covered in blood, the stench of it rolling

out of the door in waves. Splashes of it streaked the walls, the table, the stone of the chimney and hearth. Corim knelt in the center of it all, a fallen chair to one side, his mother's body lying across his knees. He hugged her tight to his chest, sobbing over her, even though she was covered in her own dried blood. Jayson gagged when he saw chunks of her flesh had been ripped free, her left foot entirely missing, most of her fingers gone, gnawed down to nubs of bone.

Behind Corim, in the doorway to the back bedroom, he could see a leg clad in a workboot sitting in a wide pool of blood.

"Corim," he said, but his voice cracked, barely above a whisper. "Corim, come here. You can't help them now."

Corim didn't respond. From behind, he heard two of the Legionnaires—Curtis and Ricks—pounding up the path, halting beside him. They looked in over his shoulder and Curtis sucked in a breath of horror. Ricks stumbled to one side and vomited into the small herb garden beneath the cottage's window.

Corim's wail had died down to a hitching moan. Gathering himself, Jayson stepped into the cottage and to Corim's side. He reached down to grip Corim's shoulder, the boy rocking back and forth where he knelt. He didn't react to Jayson's touch, so Jayson barked, "Corim!"

The boy flinched and looked up at him, his expression lost. "They're dead," he whispered.

"I know." He squeezed Corim's shoulder. "We can't do anything for them now. We need to leave." And he needed to find Lianne, although he wasn't certain he wanted to find her now. Grief pressed hard against him, nearly swallowed him.

He sucked in a steadying breath and choked on the stench that permeated the house. "Come on. Let's go."

Corim didn't move, so he reached down and hauled him to his feet, the boy's mother's body sliding to the floor. Mercifully, she landed facedown. After seeing what had been done to her hands, Jayson could only imagine what had been done to her face.

As soon as he'd regained his feet, Corim latched onto Jayson, arms encircling his chest and drawing him in close. Curtis appeared in the doorway to the bedroom, caught his gaze and shook his head, although Jayson had already known Corim's father was dead as well.

He half-carried, half-led Corim outside into the fading sunlight.

"We should head back to the village center," Curtis said. Ricks had recovered, stepping up to them from one side as he wiped his mouth with one hand. He still shook and his face was pale.

"No," Jayson said. "Not yet. I need to find Lianne."

Ricks nodded and Jayson realized that the Legionnaire had been offering him a way out. But he couldn't leave without knowing for certain.

Pushing Corim away gently but forcefully, he handed the youth off to Curtis and then headed down the path to the road.

His own cottage and lands were not far. He walked to them without speaking, the others trailing behind. He saw the cottage through the last of the trees, then passed through the small gate and garden to the front door. There he hesitated, thinking of the blood and stench in Corim's home.

But he had to know.

He opened the door.

An invisible hand closed around his throat, choked off his breath, his voice. All of the strength drained from his legs and he slid down into a crouch. He held one hand out before him, as if he could ward off what he saw within, as if he could block it out.

Lianne sat slumped over the small table near the hearth, her head on its side, her blank hazel eyes staring toward the door, as if she'd been watching for him. One hand lay on the table beside her head in a pool of spilled stew, the bowl upside down by her fingertips. The other lay in her lap. The rancid smell of broth and potatoes and onion filled the room, the stew pot still hanging over the long-dead fire.

Corim's hand fell onto his shoulder and Jayson dragged in a wheezing breath, his throat too tight and raw. He brought his hand down, then heaved himself upright and staggered to the table, knocking against it hard enough it scraped across the wooden floor, the bowls and utensils jouncing. Lianne's hand slid through the congealed stew, the weight of her arm dragging it off the table. It swung, gelled chunks dropping from the fingers.

A noise he'd never heard himself make escaped him and he reached forward to brush Lianne's hair, to touch her cheek. Her skin felt unnaturally cold and soft, as pale and lifeless as that of the dwarren's body in the village center. Unlike Corim's parents, there wasn't a mark on her. No blood had been splattered through the house. It was as if she'd died while sitting down to eat.

He knelt down beside her, rested his head against her side and reached his arm around her shoulder. The constriction in his throat shifted down to his chest, so tight it felt as if he'd torn something deep inside his lungs, but he held it in, swallowed it down, his eyes squeezed shut with the effort. His body hitched as he sucked in a deep breath, trying to control himself—

"Lianne," he murmured.

"She's—" Corim began, but cut himself off.

Dead, Jayson finished for him. *Lianne's dead.*

The constriction that bound his chest tightened, but he found himself getting up, releasing her as he rocked back and stood.

"Let's go," he said. His voice was unnaturally hard. "There's nothing we can do here anymore."

·{ 15 }·

"WE'LL REACH THE CONFLUENCE today," Colin said.

Both Eraeth and Siobhaen looked up from where they sat around the fire, Eraeth holding a pan over the flames, the scent of frying eggs drifting up to mingle with the smoke and smells of the hundred fires already burning as the dwarren roused themselves from sleep. With a casual gesture, he flipped the eggs.

"And what will happen once we get there?" Siobhaen asked. Exasperation tinged her voice.

Colin shrugged. "There will be a Gathering."

"And what does that mean?" Siobhaen snarled. "I'm tired of traveling without knowing what's going on. We came to the dwarren to find out what they know, but they haven't told us anything. You've dragged us along with this war party without any explanation of why, gone wandering off on your own to visit the sarenavriell, and brought us these weapons that you claim are a gift from the heart of the forest, and yet you haven't told us anything about what you found out or what they're to be used for!"

Colin stared at her a long moment, at a loss for words. He glanced toward Eraeth, the Protector meeting his gaze with a shrug.

"She's right," he agreed. "It's frustrating."

"It's frustrating for me as well," Colin said, letting anger touch his voice. "I know as much as you."

"No," Siobhaen said, cutting him off. "You know more than you've told us. You've met with the shamans on more than one occasion since we left the Thousand Springs cavern. I refuse to believe that they've told you nothing, and I refuse to believe you haven't kept something from us."

Colin considered her intense gaze for a long moment, then said stiffly, "I haven't told you everything—"

"Ha!"

"—but that does not mean that telling you will make anything clearer."

"It might help," Eraeth murmured, removing the eggs from the fire and separating them onto three plates. "We've been on edge for the entire underground excursion, not knowing whether we can trust the dwarren, not knowing where we are headed or what we will find when we get there." He caught Colin's gaze and lifted an eyebrow in rebuke. "It's difficult to protect you when I don't know what I'm to protect you from."

Colin shifted uncomfortably as he accepted the plate of eggs. He was willing to brush off Siobhaen's complaints as an effort to gain information for the Order of Aielan, but if Eraeth also felt compromised. . . .

He sighed. "If I knew for certain, I would have informed you. This is all I know:

"Perhaps eight months ago, something—I assume Walter and the Wraiths—awakened a Well to the east. This Well has a reservoir of Lifeblood greater than any of the Wells we know of, so vast that the Faelehgre believe that it is the source of all of the Lifeblood across the continent."

"Why?" Siobhaen asked. "Why would they awaken this Well?"

"It will expand the territory that the Shadows can hunt extensively, perhaps as far south as Yhnar, or further."

"But that doesn't make sense. There aren't many humans down that far, and no one has traveled or settled in the Flats or the Thalloran Wasteland. There must be another reason to awaken the Well."

"Such as?" Colin wondered if Siobhaen would answer, wondered if she knew something she'd learned from Lotaern or the Order, perhaps unwittingly.

"I don't know. I don't know what the Wraiths and the sukrael want."

Both Colin and Eraeth shared a glance. She'd answered too quickly to be lying. "The Shadows want freedom," Colin said, rubbing his eyes. He'd just rested, but he already felt tired. "They were trapped near the Well and Terra'nor for so long their only goal is to escape it so they can feed. You saw their hunger in the years after the Wells were awakened."

"No, I didn't," Siobhaen said. "I was not born until after the Winter Tree was planted. But that is what the sukrael want. What of the Wraiths? What of this Walter who leads them?"

Colin frowned. *Walter wants to kill me,* he nearly said, but stopped himself. It had to be more than that. But what did Walter want? He knew what the bully who had beat him in Portstown had wanted: the attentions of his father, Sartori, as well as his respect. That boy had gone on the expedition that had ultimately claimed the lives of everyone Colin cared about, so that Walter could prove himself to his father.

But Walter's father was dead. He would never find the acceptance he'd craved as a boy, would never be the Proprietor of Portstown, the predecessor of what was now a GreatLord. Was that what Walter strove for now? Power? Did he want to rule as his father had?

Or did Walter's wishes no longer matter? Had he been

tainted by the Lifeblood to such an extent that the Shadows and their goals were all that mattered now?

Colin shuddered at the thought and unconsciously clutched at his own arm and the marked skin beneath his shirt, an empty pit opening in his stomach.

"The Seasonal Trees," Eraeth said suddenly, dragging Colin away from his thoughts. The Protector glanced between both of them. "You asked what the sukrael and the Wraiths want. You say they want freedom to roam the land and feed. The only things stopping them now are the Seasonal Trees. They want to eliminate them."

"Can they do that with a new Well?" Siobhaen asked.

Colin bowed his head, staring into the fire, brow creased in thought. "I'm not certain. The Lifeblood and the Trees have never appeared to interact with one another in any way." Except that was a lie. In order to create the Trees, he had used the Lifeblood to give their seeds strength, in order to augment their powers so that it would spread across the lands of the three races to protect them, and to make certain the Trees would last for hundreds of years. The Lifeblood was an inherent part of the Trees' power.

He looked up. "But it's possible. The Trees appeared unaffected when I checked with the Winter Tree in Caercaern, but I will look again once we reach the Confluence."

"How?" Siobhaen asked.

"I'll use the Summer Tree."

At the front of the dwarren encampment, drums sounded and the dwarren began to stir, tents collapsing as they began packing, fires doused with water from the river cutting down the center of the round cavern they'd chosen as a rest area. Colin glanced down at his eggs. He hadn't had a chance to eat. Both Siobhaen and Eraeth were nearly done.

Siobhaen caught his arm. "What else? What did you learn from the shamans?"

"The Faelehgre told me to find the Well and do whatever

was necessary to find balance again. None of the head shamans know anything of the Source. They only know the Wraiths and the rest of the creatures of the Turning have been gathering in the Thalloran Wasteland, creating an army, one to rival all of the races—dwarren, Alvritshai, and human—combined. They think that the awakening of the Well is a sign that their armies are ready to begin seizing control of all of Wrath Suvane. But it's all speculation."

"What do you think?"

Colin paused, then said quietly, "I think the dwarren are correct. They have prepared for the Turning their entire lives."

All around them, the dwarren were smoothly and efficiently breaking camp. None of the fires remained, all of the tents were down, and the gaezels were already being spread throughout the group.

"Eat," Eraeth said, nudging Colin's plate of eggs. "We'll get the horses and pack our tents."

Without waiting for a response, he poured a bucket of water onto the fire, smoke and steam rushing upward. Colin began shoveling the eggs into his mouth as Siobhaen headed for the horses. They'd learned from experience that when the dwarren were ready to depart, they wouldn't stop to wait for the human or the Alvritshai to catch up.

The two Alvritshai had their gear ready by the time Colin finished his breakfast; Eraeth washed the plate clean in the river and stuffed it into one of the saddlebags. The pounding rhythm that signaled the dwarren to move out came a moment before Colin swung himself up into the saddle.

Then they were riding, the dwarren leading them through one of three possible branches from the room, none of them markedly different from the others. As soon as they entered the tunnel, Colin turned his attention to what Eraeth had suggested, that the Wraiths were using this new Well to affect the Seasonal Trees. He had sensed nothing when he checked the Winter Tree in Caercaern, but he didn't think the Well had been awakened long before that. And from what he had discovered using the Well in the White Wastes, the newly awakened Well in the east was still drawing Lifeblood from the reservoir beneath it. It was still gaining in power and strength. The Wraiths may not have attempted to use it to affect the Trees yet.

But the more he thought about whether it could affect the Trees, the more uneasy he felt.

He needed to see the Summer Tree, needed to touch it as he'd done with the Winter Tree in Caercaern.

They heard the Confluence before they saw it, a slow roar beginning to build beneath the sound of the gaezels' hooves against the stone of the tunnel. The roar grew, until it thundered through the tunnel, shuddering against Colin's skin and shivering deeper in his bones. When the noise had reached an unbearable pitch, the tunnel suddenly ended.

Colin had been to the Confluence before, but the immense cavern still took his breath away as the dwarren army spilled out of the corridor and down the short ramp to the main floor. To the north, cascades of water fell from the heights of the rock wall, over a hundred streams and rivers converging on this one location, spilling down from the rock watershed in a torrent. Mist rose from the falls, glowing with the pale green luminescence of the moss and algae that coated the damp, exposed rock around them and from the soft red light coming from the center of the chamber. There, the immense stone floor fell away in two short circular tiers to a red-tinged lake—the Sacred Waters of the dwarren. The roar of the churning water was deafening, but as the column of dwarren raced across the vast open area, a trick of the architecture of the cavern deadened it to a bearable level.

Colin felt dwarfed by the immensity of the room—if it

could be called a room. Massive arches, thicker than the
boles of the most ancient trees he'd seen in the heart of the
Ostraell, curved up from the sides of the cavern, terminat-
ing in a huge circle of stone that formed the apex of the
dome. Chunks of that stone had crumbled and fallen away
over time, the gaps in the flowing architecture glaring, but
the structure had withstood the ages well.

To the right of the massive falls, the dwarren had carved
out rooms between the pillars and arches. Hundreds of
dwarren were gathered along the massive wall and the tiers
that led up to its base, yet beneath them, on the floor that
surrounded the lake, there were thousands more. Tents riddled the area, dwarren in the armor of Riders milling about,
their gaezels corralled off to one side. Others wove among
the groups, dressed in the everyday garb of the dwarren,
distributing food and blankets. It appeared that another
group had arrived shortly before them, their gaezels only
now being taken to the main stabling area. The leaders of
that group were greeting the Cochen and the Archon, the
head shaman easy to pick out of the crowd due to his massive feather headdress.

Colin scanned the bed of activity, taking it all in as the
column of dwarren headed directly toward the Cochen and
Archon, drums announcing their arrival, but his attention
shifted almost immediately to the right of the falls, toward
the Summer Tree. It had been planted in the middle of the
tiers, the shaft of the seedling he'd brought slammed down
into the stone of the cavern's floor much as he had done
with the Winter Tree's seed in the marketplace in Caercaern. Its roots had cracked the stone as they burrowed and
climbed down the tiers, the bole of the tree shooting skyward, although there was no sky for it to find. It had
branched almost immediately, spreading outward rather
than into the heights, more rounded than the Winter Tree,
like a sycamore or oak. Its leaves were the darkened green

of summer, as wide and flat as those of the Winter Tree, but not rounded. These leaves came in groups of three and like the oak were serrated. They rippled in a breeze generated by the falls, revealing the silvered undersides in flashes, like reflected sunlight on water.

Colin searched for signs that the Tree was failing, but saw nothing. Beneath the branches, nestled within the giant root system that trailed all the way down to the Confluence, he could see where the dwarren had set lanterns in stone bowls. The light was reflected from the walls of the cavern, providing more illumination than could have been generated solely by the lanterns. A few of the dwarren shamans sat among the roots, kneeling in contemplation or prayer, or tending to the Tree's needs.

A shout tore Colin's attention back to the Riders. The column slowed as the three clan chiefs and the three head shamans pulled away to meet with the Cochen and Archon. Colin searched the dwarren already encamped on the tiers, seeking out clan symbols, trying to gauge how many of the clans had already arrived.

He was shocked at how many dwarren had gathered.

"There are approximately ten thousand dwarren in the encampment," Eraeth said.

"And there are two clans not represented," Colin added. "I see no groups of Riders from Painted Sands or Broken Waters."

"Which means what?" Siobhaen asked. The awe of seeing the Confluence for the first time had not yet faded from her face.

"It means that there will be more dwarren joining us shortly. And that I may have time to check the Summer Tree before the true Gathering begins." He glanced back toward the Tree, distracted.

"Quotl is attempting to catch your attention," Eraeth said.

Colin swung around to find the elder head shaman frowning in his direction. He nodded toward Colin.

Colin sighed. He wanted to know what had caused the dwarren to call such a large Gathering, but the need to verify that the Summer Tree still held was more pressing. "Follow me."

He nudged his horse forward, the ranks of dwarren parting for him and the two Alvritshai. As they reached the front of the column, a drum sounded and the entire group broke, scattering toward an empty section of the encampment, bags and pouches already being removed from their gaezels. Dwarren rushed forward to seize the animals' reins and lead them off to be scrubbed down, combed, and fed.

The Cochen and Archon quieted as Colin and the Alvritshai drew close and dismounted, all of the dwarren considering them with narrowed eyes and taut faces. The Cochen had scars down one side of his face, emphasized by the angle of the chains that draped from the ring in his nose to his ear. Glancing at the intricate beading of his beard, Colin could tell it came from surviving a lion attack when he was younger. The scars made him appear more dangerous and brutal than the other dwarren clan chiefs, which was likely why he'd been chosen as the Cochen.

The Archon appeared older than Quotl, thin and frail in comparison to the Cochen's brusque stature, although Colin could sense the power the Archon commanded. He carried the scepter of the shamans, resting his weight upon it like a walking stick. He inclined his head toward Colin, but cast a glare at Eraeth and Siobhaen.

"Clan Chief Oraju of the Red Sea, Cochen of this Gathering, and Archon Kimannen of Claw Lake," Quotl said as introduction. "I present the Shadowed One, and his two Alvritshai companions."

"You have come to warn us," the Archon said, "but you are too late. It has already begun."

Oraju glanced toward the rest of the clan chiefs and shamans, but answered as if the Archon had not spoken. "We
are honored to have you here for this Gathering, Shadowed
One. I hope that you will help us decide the right course of
action."

The Archon snorted. "Our actions have already been
decided, by Ilacqua and the actions of the elloktu! We must
act now, before it is too late!"

The clan chiefs shifted awkwardly, not daring to look at
the Archon, but Quotl met Colin's gaze. "The Archon
speaks truly. Ilacqua will guide us through this Turning, as
he has through all of the Turnings before." He turned to the
Cochen. "Are we ready to call the Gathering?"

Oraju shook his head. "We wait for Clan Chief Asazi, of
Broken Waters."

"What of Painted Sands?" Colin interrupted. "I don't see
their Riders here."

Oraju made a sound deep in his chest. "Clan Chief Cor-
ranu cannot attend the Gathering. It is news from Painted
Sands that has caused the Gathering in the first place. But
that should be discussed once we have all gathered beneath
the eye of Ilacqua. Clan Chief Asazi and the rest of the
Broken Waters Riders should be arriving shortly. We will
Gather tonight." He turned toward the Archon. "Archon
Kimannen, prepare the keeva."

The Archon nodded and the cluster of clan chiefs and
shamans scattered, the Cochen heading off toward the cliff
dwellings, Tarramic and the rest of the clan chiefs toward
the encampments to one side. The shamans trailed after
Kimannen.

Quotl remained behind, turning to Colin as soon as the
others had moved beyond hearing. "The Cochen did not tell
us everything—he'll explain why the Gathering was called
tonight—but he did say that there is a force gathering in the
Thalloran Wastelands near the edge of Painted Sands land.

Corranu has sent word of what he has seen, and he has gathered his Riders to meet this army."

"Which army?" Eraeth said. "No one lives in the wasteland to the east."

Quotl shook his head, lips a thin line. "The Cochen did not say."

"And what of the occumaen—the Eyes of Septimic? Did he mention those or the unnatural storms caused by the unbalancing of the Wells?"

"He mentioned neither."

"I have news on both, but I need to touch the Summer Tree to verify why the Wells were unbalanced."

Quotl pursed his lips in consternation and flicked a glance toward the retreating Archon. "Matters regarding the Summer Tree are sent to the Archon, and he has no respect for you or what you have done for us. I doubt he will let you near the Tree."

Colin felt a moment of annoyance, followed by defiance. The Archon could not stop him from seeking out the Tree. He was Shaeveran, the Shadowed One.

But then Quotl turned back, a hint of a wicked smile in his aged eyes. "However, I think the Archon will be busy at the keeva. Come. I will escort you to the Tree."

"Won't you be needed to prepare the keeva?" Eraeth asked.

Quotl chuckled. "The Archon and I have never seen eye to eye. He will not miss my presence."

The head shaman motioned for a few of the dwarren to take the horses, the lucky few approaching the animals with trepidation. As they led the animals away, three dwarren to each horse, Quotl headed around the edge of the Sacred Waters toward the Summer Tree. All three non-dwarren traded glances, then scrambled to keep up.

"He moves fast," Eraeth grumbled, "for one of the dwarren."

They skirted the lake, crossing over numerous bridges where the water was being channeled and siphoned off to form smaller pools for dwarren use. At one such bridge, its arch higher than many of the others, Siobhaen gasped and pointed down toward the center of the lake, moving to the railing at the edge.

"There's something in the Blood of Aielan," she said, "something in the water's depths."

Eraeth shot Colin a questioning gaze, but when he didn't answer, the Protector moved to the railing beside Siobhaen. They both stared at the depths for a long moment. Colin moved up behind them.

"It looks like some kind of reddish light," Siobhaen said. "As if there were a fire under the water."

"No." Eraeth shook his head. "There are multiple rings of fire, all of them swinging around a central sphere, some faster than others. The sphere in the center is what's glowing."

"There is another in Andover," Colin said. "They call it the Rose. Its discovery was what caused the Feud that drove my family and the rest of the Andovan refugees across the Arduon here, to Wrath Suvane. The power struggle there for the Rose ripped the Andovan Court apart, and nearly destroyed all of its Families. It also allowed the Proprietors of the settlements on the coast—towns like Portstown—the chance to break free from Andover and form the Provinces. If it hadn't been for the Rose, and the Accord with the Alvritshai and dwarren, the Proprietors would never have been able to keep Andover at bay. Their attentions would have been split.

"This Rose has been the heart of the dwarren religion for as long as the dwarren can remember. It is what gives the waters of the Confluence their reddish tinge, and imbues it with the healing powers that it is known for."

Eraeth crossed his arms over his chest. "This is what the

sons and daughters of the Alvritshai lords used to search for during their Trials, what Aeren was searching for when he first met you and your wagon train crossing the plains: the Blood of Aielan."

"Yes."

"You two are the first Alvritshai to be allowed to see the Sacred Waters," Quotl said from behind them. "You should feel honored."

Eraeth bowed his head. "It is an honor."

Quotl nodded in acknowledgment. "We should hurry if you wish to touch the Summer Tree before the Gathering," he said to Colin, then moved on.

Colin stepped up to the railing and looked down through the depths at the Rose, the rings of fire rotating beneath the churning surface, broken and indistinct through the waves.

"It's beautiful," Siobhaen murmured, "almost as beautiful as Aielan's Light beneath Caercaern."

Colin said nothing, thinking of his family, the memories dredged up by his thoughts of Andover and the Provinces. He had kept himself distant from his own kind, but with what was happening now—with the Seasonal Trees and the Wells—he was beginning to think that his isolation from them had been a mistake. They might need the Provinces' help before this was done; they might need Andover's, even though the relationship between the Provinces and Andover was still strained.

Troubled, he turned away to follow Quotl.

They rounded the edge of the lake quickly, halted only once more when a sudden flurry of drums sounded from the far side of the dome. Quotl listened attentively, but merely shook his head when questioned by Colin. As they drew nearer to the Tree, some of the shamans Colin had seen meditating beneath its branches noticed them, stirring from their positions to come out to meet them. Their stances were hostile and protective until they recognized Quotl.

Even then, a few of the younger shamans glared at the Alvritshai and Colin, clearly ready to protest.

Quotl conferred with a slightly older dwarren who stepped to the fore of the group, the leader's gaze flickering toward Colin and the others as they spoke. Then the dwarren stepped forward and bowed slightly toward Colin.

"Shadowed One," he murmured, head still lowered. "It is an honor to meet you. I am one of the Keepers, as are those gathered behind me."

A sudden flurry of gasps and whispers spread through the shamans on all sides. A few of them bowed their heads as well, all of the hostility suddenly gone.

"I need to touch the Summer Tree, Keeper. I fear that what is causing the dwarren to Gather has something to do with the Seasonal Trees."

The leader lifted his head. "We have not noticed anything in our ministrations to the Tree. If there is something that we have done wrong—"

"I don't believe the dwarren have had anything to do with it, Keeper, if there is even anything amiss. But I will not be certain until I have spoken to the Tree."

The Keeper's eyebrows rose, although he was clearly still worried. "What can we do to aid you?"

"Nothing. Except make certain that I am not disturbed."

"That we can arrange."

Colin turned toward Eraeth and Siobhaen. "Stay here. I won't be long."

"You intend to go on alone?" Siobhaen asked, frowning around at the younger Keepers. "They weren't all that friendly when we approached. You should have one of us with you."

"I'll stay within sight. I only need to touch the Tree."

"But you will be vulnerable while you speak to it," Siobhaen muttered. "You forget that I was there when you touched the Winter Tree in Caercaern."

Colin frowned as he glanced back over the Keepers. They had begun to spread out around the Summer Tree, forming a rough perimeter, others stepping up through the tangled roots and broken stone to those who were still meditating, gently touching shoulders and drawing them down away from the bole of the Tree.

"We need to trust them," Colin said, "especially if what I believe I will find is true. We're going to need them."

Her jaw clenched in disagreement, but she said nothing as he turned away and stared up at the tangle of roots and the Tree overhead. Gathering himself, he sighed once and then struck out, passing the dwarren Keepers, their eyes following him as he climbed the massive root system as he'd done in Caercaern for the Winter Tree. Unlike the Alvritshai Warders though, the dwarren had built paths through the roots, stairs and bridges of stone and wood winding among them, lanterns on tall poles at irregular intervals.

When one of the paths veered near enough to the base of the Tree that he could reach out and touch its bark, he halted. He planted his hand against its side and closed his eyes.

The Tree sensed him instantly and drew him into its heart, the pulse of its sap enfolding him. Like that of the heart of the forest in the Ostraell, he felt the Tree welcome him, recognize him as a part of its creation, but the Tree was more sentient than the forest. As soon as he'd accustomed himself to its soft summer taste and smell—like honey and sweet corn—he felt the shuddering discord at its edges.

Something was definitely wrong.

He surged out along the Tree's roots, down toward the Rose, where it drew strength from the healing waters deep below, and then he spread outward over the Tree's field of influence, as he'd done in Caercaern with the Winter Tree so many months before, searching for damage, for the source of the malignancy that he could feel at the heart of the Tree.

The farther from the Confluence he moved, the weaker the Tree became, but that was normal. Nothing appeared to be wrong—

Until he hit an obstruction to the east and south.

He shifted his focus, drew himself back from the north and west and concentrated his attentions eastward. Something hindered the protection of the Summer Tree there. Something had pushed that protection back, was eating away at the boundaries of the Tree that should have extended all the way to the edges of the Thalloran Wastelands. Instead, the Tree's protective barrier had been shoved onto the plains, the force weakening that protection on all sides. The grasslands that formed the largest portion of Painted Sands lands were now exposed, no longer under the influence of the Summer Tree. And the degradation of the barrier grew worse the farther south Colin traveled. He felt his heart shudder at the extent of the damage already done as he skirted the barrier and tested its edge, traveling farther and farther southward. But even as he did so, he could taste that source—like snow and loam and leaves.

The Lifeblood. The force pushing against the protection of the Trees, the force slowly breaking that protection down, was the Lifeblood.

Eraeth had been right. The Wraiths and Shadows were using the newly awakened Well to compromise the Seasonal Trees.

He hesitated, his essence hovering along the invisible boundary between the Source and the Tree. He could feel the two forces battling against each other, a subtle ebb and flow as the barrier shifted and gave. The power behind the conflict was immense, the friction sending waves of residual energy across the plains in all directions. He could feel those stresses building, knew that they would find release in the unnatural storms that battered the grasses and the occumaen that riddled the lands to the west. Even now, purplish lightning flared to the far north along the barrier's edge. As he watched it etch a jagged line across the sky, black storm clouds building at an impossible rate, the truth of what he was seeing struck him.

The Seasonal Trees were failing.

A wave of despair and hopelessness washed over Colin, stultifying in its depth. He staggered back from the barrier, began retreating back toward the Confluence and his own body, but then forced himself to stop, to draw deep breaths to control his stampeding heart, to steady the trembling that coursed through his body even though it was hundreds of miles distant.

The Trees were failing, but he'd known they would not hold forever. He'd simply assumed they would last longer than this, hundreds of years longer. He had not anticipated that Walter or the Wraiths would find a way to circumvent or destroy them. Not so soon.

But they had. And now he and the rest of the three races would have to deal with it.

Pulling himself together, he glanced toward the gathering storm, more lightning seething across the skies in a spider's web of raw energy, then turned his attention southward. He needed to know how badly the Trees had been compromised. He had felt nothing wrong when he touched the Winter Tree in Caercaern, but the Wraiths had had months since then to wreak havoc here in the east. The Summer Tree was under attack, but what of the Autumn Tree in Temeritt? He needed to check both it and the Winter Tree again.

He sped southward, blazing along the barrier between the Summer Tree and the Well to the east, feeling the fluctuations, taking note of how far the Summer Tree's influence had decayed. As he came to where the Andagua River broke apart, the massive system of tunnels and ancient buildings that the dwarren used here shattered by a cataclysm in ages past, he slowed. The dwarren called the region Broken Waters, the river collapsing into thousands of smaller streams and cascades that spread through the chunks of stone and seeped out onto the plains and the region beyond called the Flats, but this was also where the Summer Tree's influence ended and the Autumn Tree's began.

Except he couldn't sense the Autumn Tree at all.

Nausea rolled through his stomach. Where the Autumn Tree and the Summer Tree were supposed to merge, he sensed only the intruding presence of the Source. It cut into the area where the two Trees had mingled.

Colin followed the edge south and west, shuddered with relief when he finally sensed the Autumn Tree merging with the Summer Tree. The two had not been separated and torn apart completely. Walter and the Wraiths had merely used the Source to drive a wedge between the two.

But what he sensed from the Autumn Tree, even weakened by the distance from the Confluence, left the taste of ash in his mouth.

He lingered long enough to verify that what he'd felt was true, and then he turned to speed toward the Confluence and the Gathering of the dwarren. He thought he knew now why they had Gathered.

And he needed to warn them of what they faced.

"Is the Tree safe?" the leader of the Keepers asked anxiously as soon as he came within twenty paces. They had all watched him as he descended from the bole of the Tree, had already seen the serious cast to his face, the numerous shamans collecting near their leader, surrounding Eraeth, Siobhaen, and Quotl.

"The Tree has been compromised," Colin said, turning his attention to Quotl as the rest of the Keepers gasped.

"The Wraiths are using their newfound power to attack the protection that the Tree offers. There is nothing that the Keepers can do here to salvage the situation, except to bolster and support the Tree as much as they can. They may be able to hold off the destruction for a time, but they cannot hold it off forever unless someone seizes control of the newly awakened Well.

"And there's more—"

Before he could continue, a sudden flurry of drums resounded throughout the chamber, all of the dwarren turning.

"The Broken Waters Clan is arriving," Quotl murmured.

Even as he spoke, a column of dwarren emerged from one of the widest tunnels leading to the southeast. Colin estimated at least two thousand Riders poured forth, spilling across the stone floor, spreading out as they emerged into the massive chamber. A roar rose among the dwarren, voices raised and weapons clattering against stone and chests.

Quotl turned to Colin. "The Gathering will be called immediately. We must return."

"What can we do for the Summer Tree?" the Keeper asked. His eyes were still wide with shock.

"Lend it your strength," Colin said, glancing around at all of the dwarren shamans. "The Summer Tree still holds, and the longer it holds, the greater the chance that we can find a way to defeat the Wraiths."

"Shadowed One!" Quotl called. The head shaman of Thousand Springs had already climbed down from the edge of the Summer Tree's roots. He motioned toward the milling group of dwarren who had just entered the chamber. "Come!"

Colin nodded toward the Keepers, then urged Eraeth and Siobhaen after Quotl.

"You said there is more?" Eraeth said as they moved

around the Confluence, the background roar of the turbulent water to one side.

"It's far worse than I thought possible in such a short amount of time," Colin said in answer. "But I'll explain it all at the Gathering."

They reached the chaos created by the arrival of the Broken Waters Clan and forced their way through the group to the forefront, where Oraju and Kimannen were greeting the clan chief. The Archon shot Colin and Quotl a dark look but said nothing.

"—unusual activity to the south," Clan Chief Asazi was growling as they approached, "on the Flats. I sent out scouts to determine who and what it was, but they did not return. We only have the word of one of our trettarus, and they say that the group was headed southward, not toward dwarren lands."

Oraju raised a hand to forestall him. "Save the report for the Gathering. Is the keeva prepared, Archon?"

Kimannen nodded. "All is ready. The fires have been lit and the yetope prepared. The blessings have all been spoken. Ilacqua has been called to give us counsel."

"Then we will begin immediately. Summon the rest of the clan chiefs and the head shamans."

"And the Shadowed One?" the Archon asked with a glare.

"Ilacqua has seen fit to bring him to us at this time. He must attend as well."

The Archon grunted, but Colin ignored him. "My two Alvritshai companions should be part of the Gathering as well," he said. "As we will see, there is more at stake here than dwarren lands and dwarren interests."

The Cochen frowned, eyes raking the two Alvritshai before he nodded in reluctant agreement. "Bring them."

The entire group turned and followed the Archon up into the myriad stairs and walkways of the cliff dwellings carved into the side of the chamber. As they ascended, Era-eth tugged on Colin's sleeve.

"Why did you want us as part of the Gathering?"

"Because what I said is true. You will both be there to represent the Alvritshai's interests. You will represent the Lords of the Evant, and Siobhaen the Order of Aielan."

"But we have no standing in the Evant," Siobhaen pointed out. "And I have little in the Order. Besides, I don't understand dwarren!"

"That does not matter. The Alvritshai need to be seen here, or they will be forgotten."

They reached a wide opening, rounded like an egg, where three of the head shamans of the clans waited, chanting quietly. They bowed to the Cochen and Archon, the chants never ceasing, and motioned with their scepters, the snakes' tails tied to them rattling as they shook them. The Archon bowed in return and ushered the Cochen into the chamber, the rest following. Inside, embers pulsed red in a pit dug out in the center of the floor, yetope smoke already rising from the dried weeds tossed on it. Like the keeva at the Thousand Springs Clan, natural worn seats surrounded the central pit. The Archon and Cochen took up positions against the far wall, the rest spreading out around both sides. As Colin settled down, Eraeth and Siobhaen to his right, he glanced toward the rest of the clan chiefs and their shamans. Tarramic and Quotl were seated across from him, Quotl removing his pipe and packing dried leaves into its bowl. He placed the end of a stick into the coals of the fire pit and lit his pipe with a few puffs of smoke, a contented smile entering his eyes.

Then the doors to the keeva were closed.

The heat was instant, sweat breaking out on Colin's face as he tried to find a more comfortable position. The smoke from the fire pit began to fill the chamber.

Siobhaen began to cough, but Eraeth leaned over and said, "Breathe it in deeply and let it out slowly."

After a moment of struggle, her breathing steadied.

When the smoke had grown dense enough that Colin could barely see Quotl across the fire pit, the Cochen stirred.

"We Gather for war," he said bluntly. None of those within the keeva acted surprised. "This is what is known, sent to us by Clan Chief Corranu: A force of many thousands has gathered in the Thalloran Wastelands to the east. We have seen signs of this gathering for many months. Corranu and Asazi reported bands of men along the desert and in the Flats to the south, although never more than a hundred at one time. In addition, the creatures of the Turning have increased in number. War parties were sent, and the trettarus have noticed that the creatures are no longer acting singly. They are acting in groups, attacking as one more and more frequently.

"Corranu believes that the small bands have come together and, at last report, were moving toward Painted Sands lands."

"There is more," Asazi said, speaking before anyone could react. "As the Broken Waters Riders were preparing to leave, we received reports that a second army of creatures of the Turning had crossed the Flats, heading south."

"So you are saying there are two armies prepared to enter dwarren lands?" one of the other clan chiefs growled.

Asazi nodded.

"But how is this possible?" the Archon said sharply. He shot a glance toward Colin. "The Summer Tree protects us from the creatures of the Turning. How could these armies threaten dwarren lands?"

A murmur of agreement rose from nearly all of the dwarren gathered, although it wasn't as hostile as the Archon's words.

Colin sighed. "Because the Summer Tree is failing."

A few of the dwarren cried out, one of them leaping to his feet, his figure vague in the thick smoke. Colin saw Clan Chief Asazi nodding, his eyes dour. Broken Waters had already been affected by the failure; he had likely suspected it before he had arrived.

"What do you mean the Summer Tree is failing?" the Cochen asked, a tremor behind the grave words.

"The Seasonal Trees were created to hold the urannen and the other creatures of the Turning at bay, a barrier they could not cross, but they were not intended to last forever, only long enough for us to find a defense against them. And they were not intended to withstand an assault."

The head shamans suddenly leaned forward as the words sank in.

"What kind of assault?" Quotl asked, drawing on his pipe.

"One that I believe has been organized by the Wraiths." He glanced around the dim, smoky keeva. "You have all witnessed the abrupt return of the unnatural storms on the plains and the resurgence of the occumaen."

At a few confused looks, Quotl said, "The Eyes of Septimic."

"The reason these have returned is because the Wraiths have reawakened a massive Well somewhere in the east, somewhere in the Thalloran Wastelands from what I can determine. They are using the power of this Well to assault the barrier provided by the Seasonal Trees. I touched the Summer Tree before the Gathering and I have learned that their assault has pushed the barrier within the boundaries of the dwarren plains."

"How far into the plains?" the Cochen demanded.

"Far enough that if Corranu sends the dwarren to meet this army coming from the Thalloran Wastelands, he will not be protected by the Summer Tree. But there is more.

The assault is not on the Summer Tree alone. The Wraiths have also targeted the Autumn Tree and the human Provinces to the south. They are driving a wedge between the two Trees, separating them at their weakest point, where the two merge. This threat is not strictly a dwarren threat. It encompasses all three races—dwarren, human, and Alvritshai. In fact, I believe that one of the two armies is headed toward the human Province of Temeritt, even as the other heads here."

Arguments broke out on all sides in the rough, guttural language of the dwarren as the consequences of the Summer Tree's failure began to take hold. As Colin settled back, Eraeth leaned closer and said forcefully, "We must get word of this to the Evant."

"And the Order," added Siobhaen from across Eraeth's body. Eraeth had been translating as much as he could of the discussion. "The Chosen must know, so that he can prepare the Order if the Winter Tree fails!"

Colin nodded. "I know. I'm hoping that the dwarren will see the significance of this and abide by the Accord and send word themselves. Otherwise, I'm not certain how we will let them know." He caught their gazes. "Unless one of you is willing to return on your own to warn them."

Eraeth and Siobhaen cast each other heated glares. Colin knew that Eraeth would not leave him alone with Siobhaen; he still did not trust her. And he knew Eraeth would not trust Siobhaen to deliver the message. He didn't know what kept Siobhaen at his side—a sense of duty to Lotaern, or a sense of guilt over what had happened in the White Wastes—but he doubted she would leave him now after traveling this far.

"What about you?" Eraeth said abruptly. "You could travel to Caercaern and forewarn the Evant and then return in far less time than it would take one of us to reach them ourselves."

"I could, but it would still require days of travel and I would return exhausted. I don't think the dwarren or the human Provinces have such time to spare. You heard Asazi. The Wraiths are moving now. If the dwarren or the humans are to have any chance of stopping them, we need to act now. And there is something that only I can do to help them."

Before Eraeth could ask what, the Cochen stood and bellowed, "Enough!" cutting all of the arguments off. He glared around at those gathered, the scars on his face highlighted by the pulsing reddish light of the fire pit as he spoke. He focused his attention on Colin.

"You say that the Summer Tree is failing, Shadowed One." His voice throbbed with the weight of the Cochen. "What, then, can we do to fight these armies?"

Colin stood, barely able to fit within the keeva without hunching forward. He scanned all of the dwarren gathered. "You must fight them on the grasses of the plains. You must take your Riders and meet them head on, before the Summer Tree weakens so much that they are upon your doorstep, within your warrens or even here, at the Sacred Waters. You must battle them with ax and sword and spear, with the blood of your Riders and their gaezels, protecting the Lands that you were sworn to protect ages past. And you must honor the Accord that you signed with the Alvritshai and humans. You must call them to action to aid you against this threat, as the treaty proclaims."

The entire group began to murmur among themselves, but the Cochen's gaze did not waver. "And what of you? What will you do to face this threat?"

Colin smiled, his eyes flashing grimly. "I will find this Well the Wraiths have awakened and halt the attacks on the Seasonal Trees."

16

COLIN BLINKED AND RAISED a hand to shield his eyes from the glaring sunlight as he, Eraeth, and Siobhaen emerged from the tunnel opening onto the eastern plains of dwarren territory. He pulled his horse to a halt, Eraeth and Siobhaen doing the same behind him, the animal tossing its head and prancing. He released the reins to allow it to crop at the mid-spring grasses. To the east, the grassland was broken by variegated red layers of stone outcroppings and mesas, the distinguishing feature of Painted Sands land. The reddish stone would increase in frequency, until the grassland gave way to a harsh landscape of stone, scrub, and sand of every color imaginable, finally falling into the wastelands beyond.

"Aielan's Light," Siobhaen gasped, throwing her head and arms back to soak in the sunlight. "I never thought I'd see the sun again. How long were we traveling underground?"

Colin smiled. "Nearly a month."

Siobhaen reached back to loosen her long black hair from the cord that tied it away from her face. She shook her head with a scowl. "I don't understand how they can live that way."

"The Alvritshai used to live within the mountains beneath Caercaern and along the Hauttaeren."

Siobhaen snorted. "Because we were driven there by the glaciers and the harsh winters in the north. We didn't live there by choice, and we didn't live there all year. Look at all of this land they aren't using!"

Colin glanced around, then dismounted. "This land is what they were sworn to protect. They do use some of it—for farming and such—and they have set aside portions of it for trade, but no, they don't use the rest of it. It's sacred to them."

Siobhaen shook her head. "I still don't understand."

"You weren't raised with the dwarren beliefs," Eraeth said, following Colin's lead and dismounting, allowing his horse to graze. "Should we rest here before continuing?"

Colin grinned. "A moment to enjoy the sun would do us all good, I think."

Eraeth pulled some dried meat from his packs and passed it around, Siobhaen lying down in the grass to soak up the sun, eyes closed. Colin took his staff and moved off to one side, scanning the southern horizon. The black clouds of a storm could be seen there, too distant to be threatening, moving away from them.

"Do you think the Cochen will send a warning to the Alvritshai and the Provinces as he said he would?" Eraeth asked as he halted next to Colin and handed him a strip of the meat.

"Yes. The dwarren take their vows seriously. Look at how long they've protected the Lands they were given. When they signed the Accord, they were the only ones who truly meant to keep its word to the letter. I suspect that a group of dwarren has already been dispatched to Caercaern and Corsair, sent before the gathered army headed toward the east." He motioned toward the storm, a flare of lightning brightening the clouds for a moment. "That is what truly concerns me."

"We've dealt with those storms before."

Colin shook his head. "No, not the storm. What it portends.

The Wraiths are using the Source to target both the Summer Tree and the Autumn Tree, and the Autumn Tree is in Temeritt, far from Corsair."

"Then the dwarren should send a warning to Temeritt and whatever GreatLord rules there."

Colin nodded. "I urged Cochen Oraju to do that, and he said he would. But I'm afraid the warning may come too late."

"Should we try to warn them ourselves?"

"We don't have time. The dwarren and the Provinces will have to fend for themselves."

"What about the Winter Tree?" Siobhaen asked. When Colin turned, he found her propped up on her elbows, her dark eyes concerned. "Have they attacked the Winter Tree? Is Caercaern in trouble as well?"

"The Wraiths haven't targeted the Winter Tree yet. At least, not that I could sense through the Summer Tree. The Source doesn't border on the Winter Tree's influence."

"And what about the Spring Tree?" Eraeth said, one eyebrow raised, his tone casual.

Colin shot him a hard warning look, but the Protector didn't back down. "What makes you think there is a Spring Tree?" he asked bluntly.

"Common sense."

Colin snorted, then noticed Siobhaen had sat up completely, her attention focused on Colin far too intently.

"Very few have asked about the Spring Tree," Colin said guardedly. "I gave one Tree to each race, so that there would be no squabbling, no preferential treatment or sense of entitlement from anyone. But the fourth Tree. . . ."

"Where is it?" Siobhaen asked.

Colin settled a dark glare on her, frowning, then said curtly, "I have told no one where it is hidden, and there is no need for anyone to know. All you need to know is that it is safe and that it is well protected."

When Siobhaen drew breath to press him further, he moved toward his horse and pulled himself up into the saddle, his staff set across his lap. He glowered down at both of them, noted Eraeth's unequivocal acceptance of his assertion and Siobhaen's blatant doubt and interest.

"We need to keep moving if we're going to stay ahead of the dwarren army underground," he said.

Then he kneed his horse into motion and headed out onto the empty plains, not waiting for either of them.

Moiran sat in her personal chambers in the Rhyssal House manse in Artillien, papers scattered across the small, low table before the settee where she reclined. Incense burned in a brazier of dwarren fashion on a pedestal in one corner, the fragrance sharp and spicy. The wood-paneled walls glowed in the light of a dozen candles strewn around the room on other tables of various sizes and shapes. A few held potted plants, vines hanging down to the floor, while others sported glass art from artisans across Wrath Suvane. Three additional chairs surrounded the main table at Moiran's right, used when the ladies of the other Houses of the Evant visited, even though such occurrences were rare. The Ilvaeren—the equivalent of the Evant but run by the women, dealing with the trade agreements between the Houses—only met for a bonding of a lord, when a new lady would be introduced to the Ilvaeren, or upon the death of one of their own. There was simply no need otherwise. They could handle all of the necessary transactions through sealed letter and courier.

Moiran currently considered one such letter, tilting the parchment toward the sunlight coming in from the window and frowning. Lady Yssabo's handwriting was elegant, her use of the quill superb, but the perfection of her letters could not blunt the refusal behind her words. She had no remaining grain to trade with Rhyssal House, she said. Vivaen, the Lady of House Licaeta, had asked for a larger than usual supply of barley and flax nearly two weeks before and she had seen no reason to refuse at the time. She sent her regrets.

Moiran lowered the letter, lips pursed, brow furrowed.

"If Father were here, and could see your face, he would apologize profusely for whatever he had done wrong."

Moiran turned to find Fedaureon standing in the open doorway, a tight smile on his lips, a missive clutched in one hand, the paper crumpled. Daevon hovered behind him, unobstrusive. Even though Fedaureon's words had been joking, they were tense.

Like his shoulders.

She arched an eyebrow at him. "And would he be wrong to apologize?"

Fedaureon shook his head with a small laugh. "Probably not."

Her gaze dropped to the paper in his hand. "Is that from Aeren?"

Fedaureon stepped into the room, taking a seat across from her as she set the letter from Lady Yssabo on top of the pages on the table before her. Daevon took up a station to one side of the door. "It is. He sends word on the opening of the Evant. It isn't good."

He handed her the missive, ignoring her sharp glance. She smoothed the wrinkled parchment across her knee, Aeren's smooth print soothing in its familiarity. He had departed for Caercaern with his escort of Phalanx and a covey of servants over three weeks before. He would already have spoken to many of the lords as they arrived, before the Evant was called into session. The Evant would have convened only three days ago.

As the realization struck, she looked up, eyes widening.

"How can this be about the opening of the Evant? There hasn't been enough time for a courier to arrive. Unless . . ."

"Two horses were ridden to death to bring this to us as fast as possible."

When Fedaureon didn't continue, she turned her attention to the letter. She read it fast, her breath quickening as the implications began to dawn on her, even as she murmured, "This isn't possible. How could Thaedoren have allowed this? The Order of Aielan has always been separate from the Evant. Always. And now it is the equivalent of one of the Houses?"

"So it appears." Fedaureon's tone was serious, but Moiran couldn't help but hear the youth in it. She didn't think he understood what this would mean to the Evant, what it would mean to the stability of the Alvritshai.

How could he understand? He had only just begun to learn what it took to become a Lord of a House of the Evant. She had handed all of the basics of running the House to him when Aeren left for his foolhardy excursion to the White Wastes, had in effect allowed him to be the Lord of House Rhyssal, but that was nothing compared to the lord's duties in the Evant and Caercaern.

"You don't understand," she snapped, more harshly than she'd intended. She tossed the parchment to the table as she stood. "The entire balance of the Evant will be disrupted. The power structure of Caercaern will shift. The Order has always had influence on the Evant, the faith of each lord affecting his decisions for that House, but this . . . this allows that same faith a position on the floor. The Chosen will be able to coerce the lords directly now. He'll be able to introduce his own proposals, will wield the name of Aielan to sway those lords to his side, and with their votes—and his own—he will be able to push his policies through unopposed!" She began to pace, thinking aloud, Fedaureon watching her silently. She could feel his eyes on her as she moved. "Too many of the lords put their faith before their own interests. It's too much power in the hands of one man. Why would Thaedoren allow it?"

"According to Father's letter, the Tamaell did more than simply allow it," Fedaureon said, retrieving the letter from the table. "He says that it was Thaedoren's suggestion."

"Your half brother would never do such a thing," Moiran muttered dangerously.

"He must have had his reasons. The letter mentions Lady Reanne. Father says he can feel her influence in Caercaern already."

Moiran shot Fedaureon a glare. She knew Fedaureon had never gotten along with Thaedoren and Daedalan, even though they were half siblings. There were too many years between them, Fedorem's sons already full grown before Fedaureon's birth, Thaedoren already the Tamaell of the Alvritshai. There had been little interaction between them, except on a political level.

That still did not excuse the bland condescension in Fedaureon's tone.

"Tamaell Thaedoren is of your blood. You will not speak of him with that tone. Nor of Lady Reanne."

Fedaureon held her gaze for an angry moment, before a measure of shame flickered through his eyes and he lowered his head slightly. Moiran straightened where she stood, then motioned toward the letter in his hands.

"What else does your father say? What does he suggest we do?"

Fedaureon scanned the parchment, although Moiran doubted he needed to reread the words. "He says that the Evant has ruled against the presence of the Order of the Flame in House lands unless they have the express permission of the lords to enter, but he doesn't say anything about what we should do regarding the Order becoming a House itself."

"He's leaving that up to us, then." She paused, then added, "Up to you." When Fedaureon looked up, she said, "You are the Lord of Rhyssal House in his absence, not me. So what do you suggest?"

She watched as he considered, his brow furrowed in thought.

"There isn't an overt threat yet, although both you and Father seem to think so. We should warn the Phalanx in our House lands, especially those who are patrolling the borders."

"Anything else?"

Fedaureon considered, glanced toward Daevon, who merely raised one unhelpful eyebrow. "Increase the Phalanx guard here in Artillien."

"Nothing more?"

He frowned. "No. The creation of a new House within the Evant isn't enough to warrant anything more, not until the Order of Aielan has done something more blatant."

"What about the members of the Order of the Flame that are already within Rhyssal House lands?"

Her son glanced down at the letter in his lap. "Father says that they have been ordered to return to Caercaern, unless given permission to remain by the lord of that House. He wants those within Rhyssal to leave, but we have to give them a reasonable amount of time before we can act. I don't think we can do anything about them at the moment."

He looked up, seeking her approval. But he was old enough and wise enough not to need it. She didn't need to validate his decisions any longer. She couldn't. He needed to begin standing on his own.

Instead, she said, "Very well, Lord Presumptive of Rhyssal House. You should make your wishes known to the Phalanx and the rest of the House."

Fedaureon stood uncertainly, then departed, Daevon bowing formally and falling in behind him. She heard her son issuing orders before he'd reached the end of the hall, his voice sharp with confidence, all of the uncertainty gone. She nodded to herself, pleased, then moved to the table to pick up parchment and quill, dipping the nub into the bottle of ink to one side.

Fedaureon may not be able to do more without some further sign of aggression from Lotaern and the Order, but the Ilvaeren had no such political bounds.

She began to draft a letter to the ladies of those Houses allied most closely with Rhyssal. Halceon Nuant and Sovaeren Baene needed to be apprised of the situation as soon as possible. Perhaps they would be able to help. She wasn't certain how, just yet, but as Tamaea, she'd learned long ago to keep her options open.

~

"We have to get word to GreatLord Kobel immediately," Gregson said as soon as they entered the town of Cobble Kill. "Terson, begin drafting a missive as soon as you get back to the garrison. Curtis, Ricks, send out the alarm and begin gathering the rest of the Legion in the commons, along with anyone in town with a sword or who knows how to fight. And someone fetch the councilman."

Terson nodded sharply and took off ahead of them, Curtis and Ricks following a horse-length behind, cutting past the few people who lined the street and the commons. Jayson watched them for a moment, then turned to find Gregson looking at him.

"What do you and the boy intend to do?" the lieutenant asked.

The question sent a jolt through Jayson's body, prickling along his spine and shoulders. He involuntarily straightened in the saddle and sucked in a sharp breath. The numbness he'd felt since seeing Lianne's body shuddered through him, and he glanced quickly toward Corim. He hadn't permitted himself to think since they'd left Gray's Kill, Gregson not even allowing them time to burn or bury the bodies. As soon as they'd verified that Lianne and Corim's parents were dead, he'd ordered them back on horseback and herded them toward Cobble Kill. Jayson hadn't protested and it never crossed his mind to stay behind. There was nothing left of Gray's Kill, even though his mill remained standing. There were no farmers now, no one to bring grain to be milled.

But he hadn't considered what he would do in Cobble Kill either.

"I don't know," he said and caught Corim's eye. "I . . . I haven't had time to think."

Gregson nodded. "For now, I want you to stay here," he said, and Jayson realized they'd stopped before Ara's tavern. "Ara will put you up at the GreatLord's expense. I'll need to speak with the councilman of Cobble Kill. He may want to speak with you himself. And perhaps some of the other dignitaries in the town. After that . . . well, we'll see. I may have to send you and the boy to Temeritt to give them your own accounting of what happened."

"Temeritt?" Jayson swallowed. "I've never been farther than Jenkin's Peak."

Gregson's eyebrows rose.

He jumped when a bell suddenly clanged, shattering the afternoon stillness. All heads in the commons turned toward the noise, including Gregson, who hadn't even flinched.

"That's the call to arms," the lieutenant said.

On the stone plaza, men and women traded quick glances, women herding children back toward their homes, their errands forgotten. The men's faces turned grim, hustling off in the direction Terson and the others had taken.

The doors to one of the main houses that looked out onto the square abruptly flung open and an elderly man stepped out onto the street, glaring toward the sound. Two other men appeared in the doorway. The man spat on the ground to one side, then noticed Gregson astride his mount before the tavern. His expression twisted into a grimace and he headed straight toward them.

Gregson sighed, but straightened in his saddle. "Councilman Darren."

"What is the meaning of this?" the councilman growled as he approached, motioning toward the clamor from the garrison. "Why are you summoning the Legion? I have visitors, merchants of significance to two trading houses, including one Signal. This interruption to our business is intolerable!"

Jayson's gaze shot toward the two men who had sidled out onto the front steps of the stone manse, looking after the councilman curiously. They were dressed in the vests of the trading companies, although the dark blue of the man on the right was obviously of finer quality, even from this distance. He must be the Signal.

Gregson's eyes darkened. "Your business dealings are of no concern to me, Councilman. The safety of this town is."

Darren spluttered. "I fail to see how the safety of the town is threatened at the moment."

"Have you not heard?" Gregson said stiffly. "The village of Gray's Kill has been razed to the ground, nearly all of the villagers slaughtered."

The councilman stared at the lieutenant, eyes wide, mouth open.

Doubt had just begun to filter through the initial shock in the man's eyes, changing almost instantly into disbelief and rage, when Jayson heard a hiss followed by a thunk as something struck the councilman in the chest.

Jayson's heart lurched even as the councilman staggered, gaze dropping to the black arrow that protruded at a sharp angle just below his heart. Blood already stained his shirt, seeping downward. One hand rose to clutch at the shaft of the arrow, tugging at it weakly.

The councilman turned a confused look toward Gregson. "What—" he began, his voice no more than a whisper.

Then his legs gave out and he thumped down to his knees.

Jayson gaped, frozen, unable to process what had happened. The arrow didn't make any sense; it had come from nowhere.

Then Gregson kicked his horse forward, his narrowed gaze shooting toward the rock promontory that overlooked the town.

Jayson looked just in time to see a figure stand and draw, the bow black against the blue sky, tufts of clouds scudding along behind him. Then he gasped, jerked forward, encumbered by his seat in the saddle, but managed to grab Gregson's arm and haul him backward.

The arrow shot past Gregson's shoulder and sank into the flank of his horse.

The animal screamed and reared, wrenching Gregson from Jayson's grip and throwing him from the saddle, before charging across the commons, trampling the councilman as it passed.

"Diermani's balls!" Gregson spat as he scrambled to his feet. On the promontory above, ten more archers had appeared. "Those aren't dwarren," he whispered. "They're Alvritshai."

Arrows lanced down into the commons, breaking the tableau as women shrieked and men dodged toward cover. Gregson's horse had vanished down the southern road. The two tradesmen stared in shock at the councilman's body, the attackers hidden from their sight by the councilman's manse. Jayson couldn't think, his breath coming in short huffs, his entire body humming. Reaching for Gregson had been pure instinct, nothing more.

Gregson suddenly spun. "Warn Terson," he barked, then slapped Jayson's horse on the rump. The animal lurched forward, nearly throwing Jayson from the saddle. He cried out, hissing as the muscles in his legs spasmed, but caught himself. He heard Corim's frantic shout from behind him, twisted in the saddle in time to see Gregson hauling the apprentice down from his horse moments before two arrows sank into the animal's neck. It reared, screaming shrilly, feet kicking, but Gregson and Corim were already sprinting toward the protection of the tavern's corner, the Legionnaire roaring warnings at the men and women caught in the open square. Jayson's heart seized as three men and one woman fell to the cobbles, and then something skimmed across his own back, tracing a line of fire from shoulder to side, tugging at his clothing. He spun in his seat, grabbed at the reins and leaned forward over the horse's neck as it careened through the fleeing people of Cobble Kill. More arrows rained down, shattering on the stone of the roadway. He heard a roar of rage, saw a man spin as an arrow took him in the throat, saw a woman dragging her daughter's body into the cover of the stable yard, blood glistening bright on the stone beneath her—

And then the erupting chaos of the commons was left behind as his horse galloped down the southern road. Jayson gasped at the sudden calm that descended, although he could still hear the screams from the town behind. His heart thundered in his ears, the horse's body thudding into his chest beneath him. His thoughts flickered from Corim to Terson to Gregson, torn between responsibilities, and he choked with indecision.

"Gregson has Corim," he whispered to himself, voice ragged. He swallowed against the sudden sourness in his mouth and throat.

And then the garrison appeared ahead. Men were already gathered in the roadway, some of them pointing back toward the town with their swords, bellowing questions. Three of them surrounded Gregson's horse, holding it steady as Terson jerked the arrow from its flank. It whinnied and shied away from him, but the Legionnaire ignored it, frowning down at the bloodied shaft in his hand.

At a shout from one of the men, Terson glanced up, caught sight of Jayson's horse charging toward them, and stepped directly into the animal's path.

Jayson's bit back a curse and pulled hard on the horse's reins to bring its frantic bolt to a halt. As it dug into the road, he rose in the saddle and roared, "The town is under attack!"

"From where? By whom?" The cries came from all directions, but Terson caught Jayson as he fell from the saddle, others stepping forward to calm his horse.

"Archers," Jayson gasped, his body trembling with adrenaline. "Archers are on the promontory overlooking the town. They're firing down into the commons. And they aren't dwarren. They're Alvritshai."

Terson shot him a strange look, then bellowed, "To arms! Every man who's here, grab your swords and form up! Curtis, sound the alarm. This isn't a call to assemble any longer; it's a call to war. Now move! Move, move, move!"

The entire group of men broke and scrambled, some charging toward the garrison that wasn't much more than a wooden outpost on the side of the road with a stable in the back. The steady clang of the bell suddenly changed, another joining it, the combined sound now frantic. Ricks barreled out of the garrison, still fully armored from the ride to Gray's Kill.

"What's happening?" he asked.

"Get the men armed and organized here on the roadway as quickly as possible, then we'll head toward Cobble Kill."

The young soldier dashed off toward the stables, shouting orders as he went.

"Tell me what you saw," Terson ordered, turning on Jayson.

"I only saw archers on the rock bluff overlooking the town. They nearly got Gregson before he ordered me to warn you and sent me here." He tried not to think about Corim, about the others caught in the square.

"Are these the same men who attacked Gray's Kill?"

"I didn't see any Alvritshai or archers that night. I only saw the creatures and the dwarren."

Terson swore. Behind him, men were struggling into armor, additional horses being herded from the stable to the road by a group of stableboys, saddles hastily being cinched tight. "Cobble Kill isn't designed to withstand an attack," Terson growled as he watched. He suddenly motioned toward Ricks. "Get me a spare sword. Now!"

When the soldier returned, he handed the weapon to Jayson. "Have you ever used one before?"

Jayson took the sheathed blade in both hands as he shook his head, surprised at how heavy it felt. He swallowed once, his heart already quickening. He couldn't seem to clear the sourness in his throat. "No."

Terson grunted and slapped him on the back. "Do the best you can."

He shoved Jayson toward his horse and turned to the rest of the men, most of them ready and waiting. Jayson hastily began belting the sword around his waist.

"I want Curtis to take you four and try to circle up to Grant's Overlook and deal with those archers. The rest of us are going straight into Cobble Kill. Got it?"

The entire group broke out with a "Yes, sir!" Curtis motioned his selected men to one side. Someone brought Terson his horse and he mounted, Jayson drawing his horse to the side of the road and swinging up into the saddle. The sword felt awkward and cumbersome at his side, but he held onto its pommel with a death grip. He could hear his pulse pounding in his head, sweat causing his shirt to stick to his back. His upper shoulder stung and he reached back with his free hand. He felt nothing except a rent in his shirt, but his fingers came back with traces of blood.

He suddenly recalled the lancing pain he'd felt as he'd raced from Cobble Kill. He must have been grazed by an arrow.

The thought sent a shudder through his muscles, but he didn't have time to think about it. Terson suddenly ordered the group forward. Heels dug into his horse's flanks and he charged down the road toward the town at the back of the group of soldiers. After Curtis' band broke away, heading into the forest to one side, he counted no more than thirty men remaining, only twenty of them Legionnaires, the rest commoners.

He had a moment for his stomach to roll in apprehension, to notice that the others had already drawn their swords—

And then they were passing the outskirts of the town, cottages and buildings appearing along the sides of the road amongst the trees a moment before the forest gave way completely and they broke into the wide commons.

The flagstones were littered with bodies, but otherwise empty.

Arrows shot into the group instantly, the man next to Jayson crying out as one took him in the shoulder. He spat curses as he wrenched the shaft free without slowing. Through the clamor of the horses' hooves on the stone, he heard Gregson bellow, "Over here!" and saw a flash of movement from the direction of the stable yard.

Terson swung toward the lieutenant, the rest of the men following in a tight, disordered group. Gregson stood at the door to the stable's barn, two other men holding the doors wide open. They charged through into the straw-scented shadows within, the barn barely holding all of them. Jayson twisted in the saddle as men drew the doors of the barn closed behind them, scanning the people within, searching for Corim. He saw the two merchant men from the trading companies, a woman with two children clutched close to her side, Ara from the tavern, and an assortment of other men and women, maybe seventy townsfolk in all. Someone close was muttering, "This can't be happening, this can't be happening," the litany repeating over and over. Jayson tried to turn his horse but the quarters were too cramped. In frustration, he yelled out, "Corim! Are you here?"

"I'm here!"

Corim thrust through a huddle of women and elderly men to one side, fighting his way to Jayson's side.

A heaviness around Jayson's heart eased. "Thank Diermani," he muttered.

"Report," Gregson ordered as soon as the barn doors closed.

Terson shoved his way to the front of the barn. Nearly everyone quieted, hushed and panicked voices falling silent to listen.

"I've sent Curtis and a small group up to the promontory to deal with the archers. The rest of those who'd managed to gather at the summons are here."

"You didn't see any other Alvritshai? No other attackers besides the archers?"

"None."

Gregson frowned. "There must be another group somewhere nearby. They wouldn't have archers watching the town otherwise."

"Perhaps we spooked them by ringing the bell," Ricks said to one side.

Gregson glanced around at the townsfolk huddled in the stalls and loft of the barn. "If that's the case, then we'd better get everyone out of here as soon as possible, before the main force arrives."

This brought frightened murmurs from everyone, the unease of those still on their mounts transferring to the animals as they jostled against each other.

Ara pushed to the front of the group. She carried a scythe in her hand, and Jayson noticed that many of the others had makeshift weapons gathered from the barn. "What about those who sought shelter in the taverns or the other shops? And where do you think we'll be going? This is our home. I'll not be leaving without a fight."

A few of the men grumbled agreement.

"Cobble Kill wasn't designed to be defended," Gregson barked, before the murmurs had grown too loud. "Our only real advantage is that no one can approach it easily through the forest. They'll likely come by the roads, but we can't hold those with the hundred people here, only twenty of those trained Legion, the rest with scythes and pitchforks! We couldn't hold them even with the entire town gathered— men, women, and children!" The grumbling quieted.

"We have to flee," Gregson continued. "There's no other choice. Terson, we'll use those mounted to protect the rest of the townsfolk as we leave. I want everyone to gather in the center of the barn, the horses to either side. When we open the doors, the Legion will go out first and then the rest will follow. Take the southern road. Did everyone hear? Take the southern road once we're out and keep on going! Don't stop for anything—food, clothing, nothing! Our only chance is to reach Patron's Merge. Their town is walled and is protected by the rivers."

At the fear-sickened murmurs that followed and the sudden shifting of bodies as everyone tried to follow directions, punctuated by curses and low sobs, Gregson nodded, then drew Terson, Ricks, and a few of the other Legion to one side. Jayson had been jostled close enough to overhear.

"We need to forewarn the surrounding towns," the lieutenant muttered. "As soon as we get free of Cobble Kill and hit the crossroads, I want Tirks and Vanson to break off and head toward Ulm's Kill and Farriver. Warn them and order them to continue spreading the word."

"What do we tell them?" a blond-haired man said. He couldn't have been more than twenty.

Gregson frowned at that. "Tell them Gray's Kill was razed by an unknown group, and that Cobble Kill has been attacked. Tell them dwarren and Alvritshai have been sighted, along with some other creature that we've never seen before. Tell them whatever you Diermani-well please, Tirks, but get them to arm themselves! I don't know if these are bandits or raiders or something worse, but they need to be prepared."

Tirks didn't react to Gregson's gruff tone. Gregson scanned the fidgeting group of townsfolk behind the restless horses, then caught Jayson's gaze. Jayson's heart suddenly quieted. Gregson appeared calm and controlled, and he felt some of that calmness seep into him. Even though the Legionnaire's expression was grim, it was still confident.

Jayson drew in a steadying breath, let it out slowly. He was still trembling, his body tingling and on edge, but he'd regained some of his composure.

He turned to catch Corim's attention, leaning down over the saddle when his apprentice moved closer. "Stay with the Legion, no matter what happens."

Corim nodded, his face serious but lined and anxious. Jayson noted he carried a knife, but said nothing.

Everything was changing, moving too fast. A strange energy filled the confines of the barn, the too-sweet scent of straw now overlaid with a stench of fear and the warmth of too many bodies. Jayson wiped sweat from his forehead.

"Ready?" Gregson bellowed.

Jayson spun back to the barn door. The Legion had dispersed, remounted, and were now spread across the front of the group. Four of the townsmen had taken hold of the doors, ready to swing them open. Someone had given up his horse to Gregson. Everyone who had swords had drawn them. Jayson reached around and pulled his free with a grating snick and held it awkwardly as his horse shifted beneath him, snorting and stamping its hoof. He swallowed against the lump that had risen in his throat, tasted the straw dust in the air, the scent of fodder and horseshit.

Then Gregson nodded toward the men at the doors and they shoved them open wide.

Blinding sunlight streamed into the front of the barn, but Jayson kicked his horse forward as the Legion burst through into the yard beyond, fanning out with practiced movements, allowing room for the townsfolk to pass between them. Gregson roared, "Move it! Come on, run, Diermani curse you!" and the people surged forward, one of the children shrieking, another sobbing with his head buried in his mother's shoulder where she carried him on her hip. All of the men on horseback shouted and urged them forward into the sunlight. Jayson found himself shunted to one side just outside the barn doors, waving his sword high, pointing toward the main street, shouting nonsense to keep everyone moving. He saw Corim pass, the boy's eyes wide—

And then the arrows started. Shafts spat into the group, four of the townsfolk and three of the riders felled in the space of a heartbeat. Jayson's heart faltered, his throat locking, as one of the women screamed.

The entire group lurched forward in a wave of panic. He saw someone fall, get trampled underfoot, heard the Legion roaring orders and cursing at the same time as more arrows snicked down from the heights.

Suddenly, Gregson was beside him yelling, "Go, go! There's no one left in the barn!"

Jayson kneed his horse after the townsfolk, saw them break through the yard onto the street, spreading out on the road, nearly all of them turning sharply to the south, toward the garrison, arrows flying down like black rain. Three men broke away and headed north toward the bridge, one of the men on horseback screaming for them to come back. Two arrows took the rider in the back; he slumped over, his mount panicking and charging forward. One of the three men fell, a shaft jutting up from his leg. His scream sliced through Jayson's gut like a knife.

"Leave them!" Gregson roared as two of the Legion turned to help them. "Let them go! They made their choice!"

Jayson spun his horse, clenching his jaw as he heeded Gregson's orders and abandoned the men, urging his mount after the rest of the fleeing townsfolk. An arrow shot through the space between his face and his horse's neck, sent a shivering jolt of fear through his legs, but he pushed on, herding everyone toward the main road south, shouting, his sword held out uselessly before him. Gregson was charging back and forth along the rear of the group, still bellowing orders. Two more of the townsfolk fell to the deadly shafts and then a cry rose up on the promontory.

Jayson turned in time to see one of the archers fall from the rock face, the hail of arrows ending as Curtis and the rest of the Legion appeared on the outcropping, the archers turning to fight them. Most of the townsfolk slowed, those on horseback cantering in place as two more archers fell, a cheer rising from the group. Hope flared in Jayson's chest, burning so hot he tasted it in the back of his throat. He roared, thinking of Lianne, of all of the men and women of Gray's Kill who had never had a chance. As Curtis and the other four men took out the last of the archers, throwing their bodies over the edge to the forest below, all of the grief and despair that had throttled him since that first night was subsumed by a chaotic, fierce joy strangely mixed with vicious anger. It swelled inside his heart, tasting of bitter revenge and relief.

The relief was short-lived.

Even as the cheer died down and the townsfolk's fear began to dissipate with shaky laughs, Gregson shouted, "Keep moving! This isn't over. That was only a scouting party—"

Whatever he would have said next was cut off by a thunderous growl that shuddered across the commons and reverberated off the promontory of rock. Everyone turned in the direction of the northern road, where the two men had fled earlier, along with the horse with its dead rider. The man who had been shot in the leg had crawled to one side of the road and sat hunched near Ara's tavern door.

"What in Diermani's name was that?" Ara said from the middle of the townsfolk. Her hand rested on Corim's shoulder protectively.

Before anyone could answer, the animalistic roar split the silence again, followed by the sharp crack and shush of a tree falling. A few of the people cried out and stepped back. The horses snorted and shied away as more branches snapped, something large moving through the forest along the northern road. Gregson trotted his horse across Jayson's field of vision, pacing before everyone gathered in the roadway, his brow creased in a tight frown.

Beyond him, the tops of the trees began to sway with movement, even though there was no breeze. Insanely, Jayson heard Gregson's voice from earlier in the barn saying, *Our only real advantage is that no one can easily approach through the forest.*

Another splintering crack followed and one of the swaying trees fell, everyone moving back another pace, even those on horseback.

Then, through the crackle of trodden branches and breaking limbs, Jayson heard a soft chittering noise and a chill tingled through his arms and legs, prickling in his fingers.

"It's them," he whispered, his mouth suddenly dry. "It's the creatures."

Gregson shot him a sharp look.

Behind him, the massive trees over the stream suddenly shuddered and parted, a monstrous gray shape trailing broken branches and bracken appearing. Its body was huge, twice the size of a man, two gigantic arms hanging at its sides. It paused at the edge of the creek, yellowed eyes scanning the town, its stony head swiveling on a thick neck. The creature snuffled the air, the nostrils in its craggy face crinkling, and then its eyes latched onto Gregson and the group of petrified townsfolk.

It sucked in a huge breath and bellowed, the sound splintering the shocked silence. More than one person screamed, the sounds melding into a strange war cry, and as the thunderous sounds broke, the catlike creatures with the pallid, empty eyes Jayson had fought while fleeing Gray's Kill spilled from the undergrowth around the monster's feet and scampered across the bridge. Even as Jayson choked on his own breath, men on horseback appeared on the roadway, the riders dressed in black-and-silver armor, dozens of them emerging from the shadows of the trees around the twist in the road.

Not men, Jayson thought, ice-cold fear settling in the pit of his stomach as the mounted riders drew closer. *Alvritshai.*

Even as one of the Alvritshai at the forefront of the attackers raised a black horn to his lips and blew, a single, clear note piercing the town, the smaller creatures surged forward, the still spring air filled with their hissing. They fell on the man cringing against the tavern in an instant, his screams jarring Jayson from his paralysis. He spun, eyes seeking out Corim automatically. Pointing to the southern road with his sword, he yelled, "Run! Go, now!" the words so loud and forceful something in his throat tore.

Corim moved before anyone else, turning to sprint toward the southern road, clutching at Ara and dragging the tavern woman along with him. The tableau broke, people screaming, pointing, lurching forward as the smaller creatures streamed toward them from the far side of the commons, moving faster than Jayson remembered from that night, bodies sleek, like liquid in motion, brown-black in the sunlight, ears flattened against their knobby skulls. Gregson managed to bellow, "Legion, to me! Protect the flanks!" before the first leaped to latch onto his leg. He cried out, his horse rearing and screaming, his sword swinging as three more joined the first, the things crawling up the horse's side. The Legion members charged forward with fierce cries, and Jayson saw blades flash in the sunlight, blood flying as they cut into the creatures. The massive stone giant, at least twice as tall as Jayson, roared again and thrust itself from the tangle of the trees, its entire body a solid mass of hairless gray-brown flesh. It staggered across the stream, water sparkling in the light, a branch the size of Jayson's thigh in one hand. It swung it like a club as it reached the first Legion riders, knocking one clear of his mount and flinging him across the commons.

Jayson hesitated behind the first line of Legion, along with a few of the other non-Legionnaires on horseback, none of them trained to fight, but all of them carrying swords. Jayson's heart thundered in his chest, his gaze shifting left and right, the sights and sounds of the battle overwhelming. He didn't know where to look, didn't know how to react, blades cutting down into the sleek hairless cats, three men dodging the larger creature's blows, while the Alvritshai riders came inexorably closer, the column now at the beginning of the bridge. More kept appearing behind them, hundreds in sight already, without any sign that the column was going to end.

That realization twisted something deep inside of Jayson,

the frigid, queasy fear that seized him roiling and hardening into something solid, into anger and hate.

"This isn't a group of bandits," he heard himself whisper, the man who wavered beside him shooting him a confused look. "These aren't raiders." His voice hardened along with the realization, along with his heart. His eyes narrowed. His shoulders squared and his back straightened. He spun his mount to catch the attention of those who'd hung back from the main fighting. "This isn't a raiding party!" he shouted. "Look at them! Look at how many of them there are! They aren't here to sack your homes and then go, they're here to seize everything and slaughter us all!"

Not waiting to see their reaction, he dug in his heels and felt the skittish horse beneath him answer, charging toward the back of the fray. He plowed into the creatures swarming over Gregson, at least ten in all, swinging his sword wildly, his horse kicking and trampling the hissing monstrosities underfoot. His blade connected with one, the contact jarring up into his arm, but he swung the blade to one side and flung the body free, black blood splattering in an arc. Heat seared up from his gut, the heat of rage, and as his blade flashed and spun, as his body jolted with each impact against flesh and each stamping of his horse's hooves, he saw images of Gray's Kill across his vision. The gnawed-off nubs of Corim's mother's fingers, the blood-splattered table, the bodies littering the streets before Diermani's church, and Lianne's hand lying pale and lifeless in rancid stew. All of the grief and anger that had remained beneath the surface suffused him, shuddering through every strike, every flailing blow. One of the creatures bit into his leg, claws and teeth sinking deep, and he hissed and swung, hitting it with the flat of the blade with enough force to rip it free, but cutting himself with his own sword in the process. He cried out at the white-hot pain in his calf, felt the warmth of blood soaking his breeches, but ignored it to cut savagely into another creature scrambling up his saddle. The creature shrieked, its own blood spattering Jayson's face and chest as it fell back.

Something grabbed his sword arm, spun him around. He lashed out with the sword, but steel met steel, blocking the blow, and he found himself face-to-face with Gregson, the Legionnaire's face tortured into a grimace, bloody with cuts.

"Fall back," he shouted, shoving Jayson toward the empty southern road. All of the townsfolk had fled. "Fall back now! There's no way we can hold off the Alvritshai. Retreat and protect the townsfolk!"

The lieutenant gave Jayson one last push toward the road and then slid past him, shouting the same orders to all of the others. The Alvrithsai riders had crossed the bridge and were filling the far side of the wide commons, watching the battle coldly, their pale faces hard and implacable. Jayson had never seen an Alvritshai before, but there was no mistaking their sharp features, the angular cheekbones, and dark hair of the hearthfire tales. He shuddered at their arrogance, at their calmness. They did not seem concerned about the twenty-odd horsemen who fought their catlike creatures and the rugged giant who'd killed five men and three horses. Instead, the leader—the Alvritshai at the forefront—merely raised a hand to halt their progress and then gestured.

"Retreat!" Gregson roared again, the edge of command in his voice. "Now!"

Jayson spun his horse and kicked it hard toward the southern road, nearly every one of the Legion and the others like him breaking away from the fight and doing the same. He glanced over his shoulder and saw at least twenty archers raise bows from among the Alvritshai ranks. He swore, his back feeling like a giant target, and hunched himself forward over his mount's neck.

He heard the snap of the bowstrings and the outcry of at

least two men as the arrows struck. One of the men who'd
pulled ahead of him slumped and fell from his saddle, his
body hitting the road with a sickening thud, but Jayson
didn't slow. The man's horse continued on, unencumbered
now, mane and tail thrashing with the wind of its passage.
The two-story buildings and the cottages fell behind, Jayson's breath ragged, burning in his lungs.

A moment later, the garrison appeared. They passed it
without pause.

"Keep going," Gregson yelled from somewhere off to
one side and behind, his words almost lost. "Don't stop until we catch up to the townsfolk."

Jayson didn't intend to stop even after that. Cobble Kill
was lost.

There was nothing to do now but make for Patron's
Merge.

17

COLIN GLANCED UP as a sudden gust of wind blew sand into his face and tugged at his shirt. His horse whickered, tension rippling through the muscles of its neck and shoulders. He stared out across the grassland, minor plinths of striated rock piercing up through the soil on all sides. The sky was a vivid blue, no clouds in sight.

But the air shuddered around him. For a moment, he could see it, like heat waves shimmering above the earth, distorting the panoramic view on all sides. It was hot, sweat a faint sheen against his skin, but not hot enough for heat waves.

He twisted in his saddle and whistled to catch Eraeth's and Siobhaen's attention. "We need to find shelter!"

"Why?" Eraeth shouted, already heading toward him. Siobhaen followed, scanning the horizon with a look of confusion.

"We've reached the edge of the Summer Tree's influence," Colin said. "There's going to be a storm."

Siobhaen shot a glance upward. "But the sky's clear—"

The air around them suddenly crackled, all of the hair on Colin's arms standing on end, his skin prickling. A sharp metallic scent struck them. Siobhaen gasped, nose wrinkling from the stench even as she shuddered, but Eraeth shrugged the sensations aside and pointed.

"Over there," he shouted over another gust of wind, all three hunching down in their saddles. The wind was bitterly cold and stank of rain. "That rock formation!"

Colin merely nodded and spun his horse about, kicking it hard toward the column of rock Eraeth had indicated. As he neared, he saw why. Chunks of stone had fallen ages past, forming a rough arch against its side. It looked like it would be large enough to shelter all of them and the horses.

When he was still a hundred yards away, the land beginning to slope down before rising toward the rock column again, a shadow descended over the plains.

Colin's gaze shot upward as Siobhaen cried out from behind. Massive black clouds had begun to build, shooting skyward in roiling plumes along a clear-cut front that undulated high overhead, running north to south. The cloud cover spilled westward from the sharp demarcation, like a flood of black water rushing across an unseen surface. Colin slowed, his horse gnawing at the bit, but waved Eraeth and Siobhaen toward the shelter. He could feel the energies building now, pressing against his skin. Wind blew more sand and grit into his face, but he squinted and raised a hand to shield his eyes. He wanted to see how the storm built, how it was created.

But then jagged purplish lightning sizzled across the clouds, so close the hair stirred on his scalp and his horse jolted forward with a panicked scream. As he cursed and seized the reins, bringing it back under control, he felt the first drops of rain patter against his skin. He nudged the horse toward the shelter, where Eraeth stood staring out after him, his face hard with disapproval, Siobhaen behind him holding both of their skittish mounts.

A moment later, Eraeth and Siobhaen vanished behind

a deluge of rain, sheets of it blocking Colin's view. He spluttered, digging in his heels, felt the horse begin the climb up
the slope toward the stone plinth. A moment later, soaked
to the bone, he and his mount passed beneath the over-
hanging ledge of rock. Eraeth grabbed hold of his mount's
bridle and drew him deeper under the enclosure.

"Why did you slow down?" Eraeth demanded as Colin
slid from the saddle, reaching to pull his packs down as well.
Colin shivered, water runneling off him in streams.

"I wanted to see how it formed," he said through chattering teeth. He caught Eraeth's gaze and muttered, "It's
cold."

Eraeth shook his head.

"Where did the storm come from?" Siobhaen asked, taking Colin's lead and removing packs from the other two
horses. "The skies were clear. It came out of nowhere. Literally."

"It's the boundary between the Summer Tree and the
Source the Wraiths are using to attack it. The friction between the two powers creates energy, and that energy has
to be expended somehow. That's how the storms are
formed, and something similar creates the occumaen, although I've never seen the occumaen's formation in person."

"But you said the Source was only recently awakened.
The storms began long before that."

"The storms are created when two magical forces are at
odds with each other. The storms from before came from
friction between the unbalanced Wells. The balance had not
been thrown that far off, so the storms weren't as common,
the occumaen not as strong. But when Walter and the
Wraiths began waking the dormant Wells. . . ."

He didn't finish; another bolt of lightning sizzled outside
their shelter, the crack of thunder so loud he felt it lancing
through his bones. It sounded as if stone had shattered. He

gritted his teeth against it and stared out at the suddenly blackened day, rain sheeting off the stone shelf above them so fast it formed a waterfall over the shelter's entrance. Somewhere in the rock plinth behind them, the water had found a niche or crack and ran in a slower trickle down one side of their alcove.

"How long will this last?" Siobhaen asked, her back pressed against the crumbling stone wall farthest from the entrance. Her eyes were wider than normal, her shoulders hunched. When she saw both of them watching her, she stiffened and glared. "I don't like lightning." Her voice dared them to laugh.

Colin shrugged. "It's hard to tell. I'd settle in, though. I don't feel any lessening of the energies that are creating the storm at the moment."

Siobhaen nodded and began rooting through her satchel, pulling out a package of smoked meat and a skin of water, both provided by the dwarren. Colin remained near the opening, faint spray from the rain dampening his face. He shivered again at the chill, although the worst of it had passed. His clothes clung to his skin.

Eraeth shifted beside him.

"You realize what this means, don't you?" Colin said softly.

Eraeth nodded. "Once the storm passes, we'll be outside the protection of the Summer Tree."

"We'll have to keep sharper watch. The Shadows and the other creatures of the Wraith's armies will be able to attack us."

He felt Siobhaen still behind them, staring at their backs. Then Eraeth turned away from the driving rain.

The storm lasted for nearly six hours, the lightning and thunder fading to the west, the trickle of water that had become a small stream lessening as the rains abated. Eraeth and Siobhaen had begun sniping at each other after the first hour, glowering and glaring in the small, confined shelter. Colin had ignored them and their bickering, finding a shelf of rock that acted as a bench. He'd settled in and closed his eyes, trying to sense the energies of the storm as they were created, but he found himself limited. He couldn't connect to the Summer Tree here, could only feel its presence through its interaction with the Source, and then only barely. The play of the two powers overhead was obscured by the chaos of the storm. Only the effects could be seen, not the cause.

He'd finally given up and made himself comfortable, allowing himself to nod off to the sounds of the rain and the scent of dampened stone.

He startled awake to a low growl of thunder, looked through bleary eyes to see both Eraeth and Siobhaen stretched out on the stone floor, satchels used as pillows. The horses whickered when he rose, nostrils flaring as they fidgeted where they stood. He moved to calm them, then stood in the entrance and watched the storm retreat across the plains to the west. They'd lost the entire afternoon, the sun setting, burnished light glinting off of the rain-washed red stone plinths that dotted the landscape. He couldn't see the sun itself, but he watched the shadow of the column of stone that had sheltered them elongate as it sank toward the horizon. In the last of the fading light, he heard a hawk shriek and saw it dive toward the freshly washed grasses, struggling back up into the sky with a hapless prairie dog or rabbit clutched in its talons.

For a moment, the sharp memory of hunting prairie dog with his sling cut painfully into him.

When the sunlight had reached its most vivid, the reddish-orange stone all around glowing with its vibrance, he heard Eraeth stir, then rise and join him at the entrance to the shelter.

"We've lost the daylight," Colin said.

"You should have woken us," Eraeth said, the reprimand sharp in his voice.

"I only woke myself a short time ago. The storm has only just receded."

"Then we should travel at night to make up the lost time."

Colin shifted restlessly. "I don't think that would be wise. The Wraiths and Shadows hunt much more effectively at night."

Eraeth nodded. "Then we should rest while we can."

"Go. I'll take the first watch."

Eraeth returned to his makeshift pallet.

In the morning, Eraeth shook him awake. They fed and watered the horses, then mounted and rode hard to the east, watching the horizon intently for any sign of the Wraiths, the Shadows, or the purported army they had gathered. They saw nothing that day or the following day. The landscape shifted around them, the grasses giving way to hard-packed earth and stone and sand, the fingers of rock growing in size and complexity and color.

"I never knew rock came in so many colors," Siobhaen muttered at one break, staring out across the wide horizon, eyes shaded. "It's mostly gray and white and blue in the Hauttaeren."

Two more of the strange storms developed over the course of the next few days, but always to their west, marking the edge of dwarren and Wraith lands, the black clouds moving away from them. To the east, the sky was almost preternaturally blue, only a few faint white clouds scudding across it, heading southeast.

On the fourth day, Siobhaen cried out and pointed into the sky. "What is that?" she shouted, keeping it in sight as she urged her horse closer to Colin and Eraeth. "Do you see it? There, above that mesa with the arc of stone jutting off to one side."

Eraeth squinted into the distance, began to shake his head—

But then both he and Colin caught its movement. Something black and winged hovered in the sky over the massive table of rock. It glided over the mesa for a moment, then banked sharply and vanished behind the upthrust stone.

Eraeth and Colin traded troubled looks.

"It wasn't a hawk or a vulture," the Protector said.

"It was too big," Colin agreed. "And there was something odd about its wings and feathering."

"Do you think it saw us?" Siobhaen asked.

"We have to assume it did, and that it may be part of the Wraiths' army."

Eraeth swore.

Colin twisted the reins in his hands, bringing his horse about. "Let's move. Put some distance between us and the mesa. We may be far enough away from the army that they won't be able to track us once their scouts get here."

"What if that thing *was* their scout?"

"Then we fight."

They rode the horses hard for a short time but saw no one pursuing them, and no second sighting of the winged black creature. But unease crawled across Colin's shoulders and he startled at every sound. They paused at a pool of water hidden beneath an overhang of umber rock, the water a vivid blue-green. Siobhaen refilled their waterskins as Colin scanned the skies, shrugging his shoulders in an attempt to relax the tension there. But the sensation wouldn't pass.

He'd lived too long to ignore the warning. He didn't know what was causing it, but he'd listen.

"Something's wrong. I think we should halt here for the day, even though there's at least an hour of daylight left. Siobhaen, see if you can find something besides the dried meat to eat, but don't wander far. Eraeth—"

"I'll come with you."

That wasn't what Colin had intended, but he saw the stubborn set of the Protector's jaw and let it go.

"Of course I'm the hunter," Siobhaen muttered under her breath, but loudly enough to make certain they both heard. She pulled some lengths of leather gut from her pouch and with a few quick twists knotted them into snares. She halted before Eraeth, face-to-face, a little too close, but Eraeth didn't draw back. "Next time, I accompany Shaeveran."

Then she stormed out from beneath the overhang.

Eraeth didn't comment, raising an eyebrow toward Colin. "Lead the way."

Colin gathered his staff and satchel, slinging it over one shoulder, then motioned toward the north.

They followed the edge of the mesa at their backs, the stone rising vertically to their right, the ground sloping away to the left. Rocks cascaded down the slope as they moved, catching in the dried sagebrush, sword grass, and scree. The loose soil and pebbles made keeping their balance difficult, Colin's staff nearly worthless. He grunted, catching himself against the crumbling wall of the mesa as his left foot slid out from under him. They rounded one edge of the mesa and found a wall of stone protruding from the far side, an irregularly shaped hole piercing through it, its edges smoothed as if by water. Stones perched precariously on top of the jagged arm of rock, as if set there by a child-god's hand. Colin made for the hole and the patch of blue sky through it.

"What are we looking for?" Eraeth said when they were halfway there.

"I'm not certain. But something isn't right. I can feel it."

Eraeth grunted. Colin caught him loosening the clasp on his cattan as they reached the base of the wall of stone, the loose rubble giving way to layered shelves of sandstone and basalt. They began climbing the layers like steps, moving diagonally toward the hole in the wall. To the west, the sun had dipped nearly to a horizon dotted with more rock formations. Colin passed into the shadow cast by the wall, the ridge of rock striking almost due west. He paused to wipe sweat from his brow in the cooler shade, then pulled himself up into the lip of the hole.

Then he froze and ducked back down behind the stone, even though he stood in shadow.

"What is it?" Eraeth hissed, scrambling up the last leg and settling down beside him.

"The Wraith army," Colin whispered, his voice grim.

He waved a hand toward the wide stretch of sand and stone spread out before them, even though Eraeth had already pulled himself up high enough that he could see. The Wraith army stretched from beneath the mesa across the plateau, a black stain on the reddish sand and stone. It was too distant to pick out many details, but it had obviously halted for the night, fires already blazing across its breadth, smoke trailing into the sky. It appeared to eddy and flow as groups moved back and forth, punctuated by gray as tents were raised and horses and gaezels were herded and penned for the night. A line of supply wagons trailed behind the main force, and Colin could see others trundling across the scrubland to the east, coming to join them. At least a score of the strange black birds they had sighted earlier circled above, wheeling through the layers of smoke. A few shrieks pierced the dusk's quiet, along with an occasional bellow or cry. The army was too distant for general sounds to carry.

"What do you see?" Colin asked after giving Eraeth a long moment to look.

Eraeth's jaw clenched and he didn't answer immediately. Then: "You aren't going to like this," he muttered, but didn't wait for Colin to press him. "The army appears to be split into groups. I see at least three, although those in the middle seem to be mixed. I can't tell who's in the far group—they're too far away—but the middle group has creatures I've never seen before in it. The group closest to us," he hesitated and caught Colin's gaze, "is Alvritshai."

Colin felt the shock course through him, then harden into anger. "How is that possible? What House do they come from? Who sent them?"

"I can't tell from here. But they can't be from any of the Houses of the Evant. How would they have gotten here? A betrayal of the Evant of this magnitude would not have gone unnoticed over the winter months!"

"What about the Houses to the east? Licaeta and Uslaen? They border the Ostraell and the eastern Hauttaeren. They could have sent their Phalanx to the east along the mountains over the winter."

"Across the northern dwarren lands as well? Without them noticing?" Eraeth shook his head. "The dwarren would not have missed an Alvritshai army of that size, and they would have sent a protest to Caercaern immediately."

Colin drew breath to argue, but realized that Eraeth was right. An army, even a small group of Alvritshai, would never have gotten past the dwarren's attention. They patrolled their lands too well. And no one could have gotten that far east by passing north of the Hauttaeren; the glacial plateau butted up against the mountains in that area. He couldn't imagine the Alvritshai army marching across the ice, then crossing the mountains east of dwarren lands.

He stared down at the Flat, the sun sinking fast, shadows filling the dips and depressions in the land as more fires were lit in the encampment.

"How many do you think there are down there?" he asked, thinking of the dwarren that were coming to meet them.

"At least seven thousand altogether. Somewhere between one and two thousand are Alvritshai."

"The dwarren outnumber them."

"The dwarren have to," Eraeth said, no derision in his voice. "They are shorter. Their strength lies in their numbers and their ferocity. Based on their size, I'd guess these . . ." he waved a hand toward the army that was fading from view as night fell ". . . *things* rely more on brute force. And then there are the sukrael and the Wraiths, which the dwarren have no defense against. I'd say that the two forces are evenly matched."

"The dwarren have more of a defense than you think. Remember, they have sought out the heart of the Ostraell and received the forest's gifts."

Eraeth frowned, and Colin saw his hand clench, as if he'd realized he'd left the bow he'd been given back at the pool.

Colin shifted away from the Flat as the last of the sun's rays faded to the west. There was nothing to see now except a black landscape dotted with hundreds of campfires. The night was already turning chill, stars overhead, moonlight faint, barely enough to help him pick his way down from the wall of rock. He heard Eraeth descending from their vantage a moment later, small rocks and pebbles clattering down the slope ahead of him.

He reached the edge where stone gave way to sand and scrub, Eraeth a step behind him. He'd just drawn breath to tell him he was going to check out the encampment when something reared up out of the shadows before him with a hideous hiss, stone and sand scattering from the figure. Colin caught a scent of bitter spice, saw moonlight touch a curved blade as it rose above his head—

And then Eraeth shoved him aside, cattan out, slicing up under the figure's guard and into his side. He heard Eraeth grunt with effort, dodging back as the figure's blade fell, then the Protector darted forward again, cattan striking and penetrating the figure's chest. He caught the man as he fell, settling the body to the ground before Colin had even thought to exhale.

Stones rattled in the darkness beyond. "There are two more of them," Eraeth barked.

Colin reacted without thought, his surprised paralysis broken. Reaching for the knife tucked into his belt, he slowed time, moving toward the area where he'd heard the stones rattle. When the figure emerged from the darkness, shrouded in a cloak, he loosened time enough to plunge his knife into the figure's back—once, twice, feeling something odd through the knife, the skin unnaturally tough—then slowed time again before the figure had begun to fall, before he could even gasp, spinning toward the second cascade of rocks. The second man was crouched low, his sword curved in an S shape, thicker at the end than near the pommel, held out to the side for balance as he skidded down the slope. Caught in mid-move, Colin slid up behind him, opposite the strange blade, and stabbed him in the throat at the same time as he released time once more. He reached around and grabbed the man's chest over one shoulder to hold him steady as blood gushed over his fingers, the momentum of the man's skid dragging Colin along with him. He cursed as he lost his footing and the two slid down the small incline. To one side, he heard a hissing gasp from the first figure he'd killed, caught sight of the figure slumping forward face-first to the ground and rolling once before coming to a rest.

Heart pounding, breath coming hard and fast, his chest aching, Colin jerked his knife free of the man's throat. Adrenaline made his arms shake as he backed away from the body. He'd killed in the past, forced to by the Wraiths and their actions, but he had almost always killed the Shadows, rarely anyone else.

The stickiness of the blood on his hands sent a shudder through his body.

Footsteps crunched as Eraeth darted toward the first slumped figure, then the second, checking for a pulse.

"Both men should be dead," Colin said, swallowing. His voice was rough and shaky.

Eraeth looked up from the last body. "They are. But they aren't human."

Colin's breath caught in his throat. Then he jerked forward, coming to Eraeth's side next to the figure. "What do you mean they aren't human? Are they Alvritshai? They aren't tall enough to be Alvritshai."

"They aren't either," Eraeth said roughly. "Look."

He flicked the hood of the cloak aside.

Colin recoiled instinctively at the face beneath. The skin was scaled like a snake, with mottled colorations whose true colors were impossible to determine under the washed-out light of the moon. He reached forward and touched it, smoother than he'd expected. But the skin was the least of the strangeness. The features were snakelike as well, the neck—thicker than a human's—emerging from the shirt and cloak and widening into the rounded head and snout of a snake, the nostrils slits along each side, the mouth open slightly, fleshy fangs barely visible. The eyes were large, yellow-orange with black pupils, set on either side of the head beneath bony ridges. Blood seeped out of the cut Colin had made in its neck and from the corner of its mouth.

After his initial shock, Colin leaned forward with interest, turning the head to either side as the bitter spice scent struck him again. Folds of skin were drawn inward on either side of the neck, but he couldn't see the creature's tongue. Not without putting his hand inside its mouth to pry it open. He didn't trust the liquid glistening on the exposed fangs enough to try.

He turned his attention to the rest of the creature's body. Eraeth sat back silently as he exposed the hands, scaled like the rest of the body, although with only four fingers, some webbing between them near their base. Each finger ended in a small, pointed talon. Colin pried the strange sword from the creature and handed it off to Eraeth.

"What are they?" Eraeth asked, taking the blade and hefting it, feeling its weight. He swung it sharply a few times, nodding to himself.

"The Scripts refer to them as the Haessari," Colin said, sitting back. "The oldest Scripts. The dwarren call them the orannian, the Snake People. I didn't realize that they still existed. They haven't been seen by the Alvritshai or the dwarren in generations."

"These Haessari must be the third force in the Wraith army, the one I couldn't identify." Eraeth pointed toward the creature with the blade. "This would explain how the Wraiths managed to create an army. They had the help of the Haessari, along with whoever these Alvritshai are, plus those other creatures like the sukrael."

Colin frowned and met Eraeth's eyes. "I need to see the army up close. We need to know who has betrayed the Evant, and I need to see exactly what creatures the Wraiths have managed to bring to their side."

Something flickered in Eraeth's gaze, but he finally nodded. "Be careful. There are likely Wraiths and sukrael down there."

Colin heard what Eraeth truly meant. Even with time slowed, the Wraiths and the Shadows could find and attack him if they sensed him near. Their presence on the plateau may have been what had made him uneasy earlier.

He stood and stepped away, the world going still around him as he headed toward the army encampment. As he moved, he thought about all of the creatures the Scripts had described, all of those that the dwarren had insisted were part of the Turning, that would make their presence known in the world again. The orannian, kell, urannen, terren, others—all at one point were part of the dwarren Turnings in the past. He already knew the urannen—the Shadows—were part of the army, and now they had the orannian. How many of the others had the Wraiths found? How many of the others still existed?

And where were they coming from?

Except he already knew. The three races had only explored part of the continent they called Wrath Suvane. The humans were still exploring the lands to the south, had barely settled Borangst and Yhnar at their farthest edges. And the Thalloran Wastelands had impeded settlement to the east. Common sense told him that the Haessari likely came from the desert, with their snakelike skin. And what lay beyond the Wastelands? Men had risked the desert to find out; none had returned.

With the planting of the Seasonal Trees, the Wraiths and Shadows had been forced into the desert and the northern and southern reaches. They'd been driven there. And they'd had over a hundred years to find and coerce or force the creatures they found to their own ends.

All except for the Alvritshai. How had they come to be part of the Wraith army?

Colin's intense frown darkened as he reached the flat and neared the outskirts of the encampment. He halted as a figure appeared among the scrub of the rocky flat, huddled down to make a smaller target, cloak and hood drawn up over his shape to give the impression of a boulder. Moving closer, he realized it was another of the Haessari, its beady eyes staring out into the nightscape. Colin suddenly wondered if they'd been chosen as guards because they could see in the dark. He didn't recall reading anything in the Scripts about that ability. He shrugged, unwilling to test the theory, and pushed on. Within a hundred paces, he came upon the edge of the Alvritshai camp. He moved swiftly among the men and women, noting their clothing, their tents, the armbands that a few of them wore and the emblems on necklaces and bracelets, trying to determine their House affiliation. He saw numerous pendants of white gold in the shape of flames and other images of Aielan. Many of the armbands had an eagle's talon etched into the metal, more such markings on tent flaps and the few banners he saw. But none of the current Houses of the Evant used the talon—

He halted abruptly in the vivid orange light of a fire, surrounded by ten of the Alvritshai.

None of the *current* Houses.

He scanned those seated around the fire, caught in midmotion as they gambled, most laughing, one scowling at the outcome of the dice he'd just rolled, another clapping him on his back in commiseration. They all wore black and gold, the colors of House Duvoraen.

Khalaek's House.

It was as if someone had plunged a knife down deep inside Colin's chest. He staggered beneath the blow, felt his grip on time slip, the crackle of the fire and the raucous laughter of the group of Alvritshai bursting through his control. Even as he seized time again, sweat breaking out on his skin, he noted one of the Alvritshai's gazes flick toward him, a frown beginning to touch his face.

At the same time, he heard Vaeren's voice from months before, beneath the Hauttaeren Mountains, before they'd climbed to the pass and Gaurraenan's halls: *I'd been part of Duvoraen for decades, had been raised to serve Lord Khalaek, been trained to protect him, to revere the black-and-gold uniform, to live under the Eagle's Talon. I couldn't shrug the Duvoraen House mantle aside so easily. I couldn't simply vow to serve Uslaen after all that I'd done, after spilling my blood for Duvoraen on the battlefield.*

Vaeren had joined the Order rather than become part of Uslaen. Others had done the same.

But not all. Vaeren had said hundreds had simply vanished, had abandoned their service to Uslaen and disappeared. No one knew where they had gone.

Until now.

Colin grimly scanned the tents that stretched into the horizon, seeing the men and women who had not been able to abandon Lord Khalaek. They had become khai-roen, had exiled themselves rather than face what Khalaek had done. They still claimed allegiance to the Duvoraen House, still bore its standard into battle.

There were more than simply a few hundred men and women here, though.

He silently cursed the Alvritshai pride and tradition that forbade them from public declaration of dishonor. How many of the Alvritshai had truly abandoned their lands? Not hundreds. At least a thousand, if Eraeth's estimate of the size of the Alvritshai contingent here was correct. Was this all of them? Were there others?

He didn't know, and there was no way he could think of to find out. Not without abandoning his search for the Source. He couldn't even contact the dwarren to warn them of the army, not even through one of their trettarus. They hadn't seen any of the small war parties they used to hunt the creatures of the Turning since they'd separated from the main dwarren army and emerged onto the plains. Most of them had been recalled once the Gathering had been summoned.

He swore.

A sense of vertigo enveloped him, the world tilting beneath him, uncontrolled. His heart quickened, hammering in his chest, blood rushing in his ears. Nausea washed through him and he sank into a crouch, one hand reaching for the ground for support, to halt the dizziness. He sucked in a sharp breath. Everything was happening too fast, too many factors in play, some of them he wasn't even aware of. He couldn't control them all, couldn't be here, be with the dwarren, be facing whatever the Wraiths were doing in the south, all at the same time, even with the powers of the Well coursing through him. He couldn't send word to King Justinian in Corsair, or to Theadoren in Caercaern—not in time to aid the dwarren against this threat.

He dug his hands into the rocky soil, ground the stones into his knees where he knelt, using the pain to push the vertigo aside and seize control again. He managed to retain his grip on time as well, holding it tight. The world steadied around him, the sense of being overwhelmed retreating.

When he felt stable again, he pushed up from his crouch and stood, glancing around at the army of exiled Alvritshai one last time before pushing on. He couldn't warn the dwarren, or even the human Provinces, couldn't summon them help. But he could determine exactly what they faced, what he might face once he reached the Source.

Then he'd return to Eraeth and Siobhaen and gather their horses and get as far from this army as possible, even if they had to travel at night. They'd have to risk it.

Because suddenly time weighed heavily on Colin's shoulders.

18

"**G**REGSON!"

Jayson jerked up out of his half-sleep in the saddle at the shout, to see two of the Legionnaires who'd been sent out slightly ahead of the column of refugees charging down the road on their horses. Gregson rode at the front, with Terson and a small entourage of Legion. Behind walked the survivors of the attack on Cobble Kill and nearly a hundred other refugees that had joined them as they fled toward Patron's Merge. Some were farmers and others who lived outside of Cobble Kill, driven out by the Alvritshai army, but others had come from outlying villages in the surrounding area, like Gray's Kill. Jayson scanned the group of ragged and weary people, shaking off his own grogginess from the last week of slow travel as he searched for Corim. He found the youth—he could no longer think of him as a boy—with Ara, both of them trudging along at the edge of the hundred and fifty men, women, and children Gregson and the Legion had taken under their wing. Two lone carts, pulled by workhorses, trailed behind, reserved for whatever food and supplies they'd managed to scavenge from isolated farms and cottages along the way. Not all of those they found joined the group, and some who had started with them had split and gone off on their own after arguing with Gregson or the Legion, or simply because they wanted to find missing family members. A few had deserted during the night. But more stayed than left, others joining them in ones and twos the farther south they traveled. Jayson had heard Gregson wondering why, speaking to his second, Terson. The Legionnaire lieutenant didn't seem to realize that they stayed because of him, because of the strength and stability he represented. Even the bandages he still wore from wounds taken at Cobble Kill were a sign of his strength.

The refugees brought with them little except stories of death and despair, each questioned intently by Gregson or Terson as they arrived, both Legionnaires desperate to find out what was happening. As far as Jayson could ascertain, nearly every village and town of any reasonable size north of the river called Patron's Kill had been attacked, and the army—composed mostly of Alvritshai warriors dressed in black and gold bearing an Eagle's Talon mark—was moving steadily southward, although at a slow enough pace their group had managed to keep ahead of it. They had creatures of every sort with them—the lantern-eyed cats that had attacked Gray's Kill, the gray-skinned giants like the one they'd encountered in Cobble Kill, leathery-winged birds, among others—all marching in a ragged line toward Temeritt, ransacking and burning everything they did not need behind them, reminiscent of the tales everyone had been told as children. Tales meant to frighten and keep those children obedient, or to entertain the adults around the hearthfire at night after the children had gone to bed.

Now those tales had come horribly to life and Jayson had begun to wonder what other stories from his childhood he should be worried about. Old superstitions suddenly weren't easy to scoff at, the fear of the black creatures that had driven them out of their homes settling over them all like a disease. Jayson could see it in the eyes of everyone who'd joined them. Faces lined with despair, haggard with desperation. The refugees had already started calling the army the Horde, a name that sent a chill through Jayson every time he heard it.

Yet something in him had changed in Cobble Kill. The despair he saw on everyone else's face hadn't affected him in the same way. They looked battered and defeated, shuffling forward toward what they hoped would be a refuge, a haven from the devastation.

Jayson knew better now. He'd fled to Cobble Kill with the same expectation, that once he arrived the Legion would take care of everything and he could go back to being a miller, could reshape his life somehow. What he'd found was that Cobble Kill was no haven and that the threat was larger than anything he could have anticipated.

The Legion—at least, the small outposts and garrisons that dotted the Province along the dwarren border and the Flats—couldn't handle the Horde. They needed help.

They needed GreatLord Kobel.

And he wasn't even certain the GreatLord knew of the attacks yet. Gregson had sent three Legionnaires ahead of them to warn Patron's Merge, but no one knew if they'd arrived safely to deliver the message. They hadn't met any of the Horde on the road so far, had managed to stay ahead of their line, or at least out of its path. In the end, they were moving blindly toward Temeritt, without any guarantee that GreatLord Kobel would be able to help them.

Ara looked up at that moment, her lined face grim, and met Jayson's gaze, startling him out of his thoughts. He straightened in his saddle. The tavern keeper glanced toward Corim at her side, then gave Jayson a questioning look. He shook his head. Reassured that Corim was safe, he checked the rest of the refugees and the men on horseback that hemmed them in on both sides of the road, then turned back toward the front of the line.

Gregson and Terson had ridden out to meet the two returning scouts. Their faces were edged with tension. One of the scouts pointed toward the distance and Jayson involuntarily glanced upward.

Something clutched at Jayson's heart—the despair that the anger and realization in Cobble Kill had shoved aside—and he swore under his breath.

"What is it?"

Jayson jumped at the voice, looked down to find Ara and Corim standing beside him now. She brushed aside some strands of hair that had come loose from the cloth she'd used to tie it back, then turned to see what had caught Jayson's attention.

The tired smile on her face went slack when she saw the black smoke that rose above the trees. Jayson felt an urge to shield Corim from the same reaction, but knew that it was pointless. He would see the smoke eventually.

And he did, his breath sucked in sharply in response. Jayson was shocked to see the despair that widened his eyes briefly flare into sudden anger, his apprentice's hands unconsciously squeezing into fists at his sides.

"Is it Patron's Merge?" Ara asked, her voice strangely lifeless.

"I don't know," Jayson said, "but I think we're going to find out."

The refugees had caught up to where Gregson and the others had conferred. The lieutenant of the Legion was still in deep conversation with the two scouts, both nodding or shaking their heads and pointing to the east and west. As the column slowed to a halt, the rest of its members began to notice the smoke as well, now darker and spread farther out. It had reached the upper winds, which meant that it was more distant than Jayson had first thought. He relaxed a little, even as the rest of the column's tension heightened. People began to murmur and point, their voices edged and brittle. The days of traveling with little food and restless sleep were beginning to take their toll.

One of the other men, a blacksmith, suddenly called out, "What are we stopping for? Is the smoke from Patron's Merge?"

Most of the refugees fell silent, waiting for Gregson's answer.

Gregson shifted uncomfortably in his saddle, shot his scouts a quick look, then sighed wearily and turned his horse to face the rest of the group. He drew himself up and said bluntly, "Patron's Merge burns."

Nearly all except the Legion gasped, clutching loved ones close, their eyes darting to the faces around them and out into the surrounding trees lining the road, faces lined with panic. Corim turned to Jayson, his jaw clenched, mouth pressed into a hard, determined line. Ara had dropped her head, shoulders rigid. He heard her muttering a prayer to Diermani under her breath, the words curt.

"What do we do now?" the blacksmith suddenly shouted. A few of the others joined him.

As if he'd been waiting for it, Gregson answered immediately. "According to the scouts, the Horde that's hit Patron's Merge has come from the east. There aren't as many towns and villages out there, and they're easier to find. They aren't nestled in the broken rocks and forest like they are here beneath the edge of the Escarpment. That means they moved faster than the line of Horde that's behind us."

"How do you know the Horde is still behind us?" someone cried out. "What if they're in front of us? What if we're walking right into them?" His voice escalated on the last question.

Gregson cut him off before he could fall into an all-out rant. "Because my scouts are watching the main roads! If the Horde is making its way south, they'd have to use those roads, especially the Alvritshai with their horses. The land is too rugged, with too many clefts and gorges and streams for them to travel quickly on any other route."

This appeared to quiet those who were on the verge of panic, although the worried grumbling and fearful glances didn't stop.

Gregson waited a moment, then drew in a deep breath to steady himself. "Since we can't find safety at Patron's Merge, we're going to head directly toward Temeritt, as swiftly as possible. There's a crossroads ahead. We'll take the western road and try to bypass Patron's Merge and the Horde that surrounds it. I need everyone to pick up the pace."

The lieutenant turned his back on the bevy of groans, but the refugees began reorganizing, mothers and fathers picking up children, some of the wounded men on horses pulling the youngsters into the saddle before them. A few shouldered their packs, those that hadn't dropped them days past when they became too heavy to bear. Two elderly women were already driving the cart that carried some of the younger children. The rest of the children were old enough to continue on foot.

Gregson whistled and the group began to move again, at about twice the pace they'd been going before, but not fast enough for the horses to break out into a trot. The two scouts galloped on ahead, vanishing around a bend in the road.

Terson cantered back along the line, pausing at each of the mounted guards to issue orders. When he reached Jayson, he said, "Keep alert. We don't know how far out the Horde has scouts. Be ready for anything." His gaze dropped meaningfully to the sword strapped awkwardly at Jayson's side, before he rode off to the next man.

Jayson's hand dropped to the sheath and he swallowed back sudden nausea. He hadn't had the sword out since Cobble Kill. He wasn't certain he wanted to ever draw it again, yet knew that he would.

"You need to learn to use it," Ara said abruptly and gave him a flat stare. "If you really want to protect us. Protect him." Her head tilted toward Corim. "I can't be patching you up every time you nick yourself in battle."

Jayson felt his face flush.

They reached the crossroads and turned west.

An hour later, through a break in the trees, they caught sight of Patron's Merge.

Built on an island formed at the junction of Patron's Kill with the Silt River, its walls soared from the water to a height of thirty feet, two stone bridges connecting the island to the main shores on either side, the middle of each bridge wooden so they could be drawn up for protection. A third bridge joined the island to the land between the two rivers to the west. Two main towers rose from the massive city huddled within those walls, the highest on the southeastern point, the second near the center of the island, part of the stone church to Holy Diermani judging by the tilted cross at the top. The city was at least twenty times the size of Cobble Kill, but from their vantage on a ridge overlooking the lands that sloped down to the river valley, Jayson couldn't see the houses and shops crammed in between the streets and walls within. The city was too distant. He couldn't imagine living in such close quarters, with neighbors within spitting distance, or perhaps sharing the same buildings.

Nearly all of it was burning. Flames reached toward the sky, black smoke billowing out from the southern quarter of the city. A portion near the highest tower appeared untouched, but Jayson could tell it was only a matter of time. The Horde swarmed across the two drawbridges, both down, an undulating mass of men and creatures made indistinct and hazy by distance and smoke. And more of the Horde waited on the flatland along the riverbanks, a black stain against the slate blue of the rivers, against the spring greenery of the trees and the trampled fields that lay on both sides of the rivers. They'd surrounded the island completely to the north and south; only the mainland between the two rivers to the west remained open. The citizens of Patron's Merge were fleeing across the third bridge: men, women, and children running for their lives. The bridge was so packed Jayson could see figures falling from its edge into the river below.

They were too distant to hear anything, the silence of the battle oddly disturbing. But in his mind Jayson could hear the flames of Gray's Kill crackling, could feel the heat of the fire and taste the ash.

"Keep moving!" Gregson barked, his steed passing before Jayson and cutting off his vision of the dying city as he charged down the line. "Keep moving! We don't want the Horde to see us!"

Jayson nudged his horse back into motion. He hadn't even realized he'd stopped.

Before the city passed out of sight, the church tower cracked diagonally upward as if sheared off with a blade, then slid to the side in a seething mass of smoke and embers, breaking in two as it fell.

Moans rose from the refugees as Gregson and the rest of the Legion urged them on. Jayson caught fervent whispered prayers, saw many crossing themselves or clutching pendants or blood vows openly or through their shirts, their faces ashen.

As the trees obscured the view and the road began descending toward the river valley below, Jayson's hand fell to the hilt of the sword secured at his side.

Ara was right. He was going to have to learn how to use it.

~

The dwarren broke out into battle cries as soon as they emerged from the warrens into the midafternoon sunlight on the plains of Painted Sands. Quotl refrained from joining in, blinking in the blinding light as the mass of gaezels and dwarren Riders from the Thousand Springs Clan spread out in a sweeping arc from the entrance, scouts blazing out ahead of the main army as it slowed. Ahead, Clan Chief Tarramic and his closest advisers halted, searching the horizon in all directions. Quotl urged his own gaezel forward, caught the attention of all of the shamans that accompanied him, including Azuka, who would take his place as head shaman when he died. With a hand gesture, he sent Azuka and the rest to the edges of the surrounding area to begin the blessing of the land with an appeal to Ilacqua and the gods of the Four Winds for protection and strength. Gripping his own scepter, he joined Tarramic and nodded as he came to a halt beside him.

"What do you see?" Tarramic said, motioning to the horizon.

Quotl searched, his expression intent even though he desperately wanted to dismount. He was nearly forty years old; his bones no longer cared for long journeys by gaezel. His back ached and his legs were practically numb. But he was the head shaman.

And sometimes the aches and pains in his joints told him more than the signs the gods left for those who could see.

The plains of Painted Sands were different than those of Thousand Springs—more rugged, stonier, the grass thinner and more brittle. He reached down from his seat and let his hands run through the stalks, grunting at their feel, already farther along than the grass of Thousand Springs would be at this time of year. He gripped the heads of three stalks and pulled the kernels of grain free, husks and all, and held them out on his wrinkled, weathered palm, studying them. A breeze grabbed many of the dislodged husks and sent them flying. He followed them with squinted eyes, watched the paths they took, then considered the seeds left behind and their arrangement. As he did so, he felt a sense of calm envelop him, as if he stood outside of the tension and turmoil of the army as it continued to emerge from the warrens behind them all, spilling out from beneath the ground and onto the plains like water from a gushing well.

"Corranu and the Painted Sands Riders are over a day's ride to the east," he said, eyeing two seeds at the base of his middle finger. His gaze shifted to a grouping of five seeds nearer the center of his palm but to the right. "Cochen Oraju, the Red Sea Clan, and the Broken Waters Clan have already emerged from the warren to our south. I do not see Shadow Moon or Silver Grass, but—" he pointed to a lone kernel of grain on the far side of his palm, "—Claw Lake has also left the tunnels."

He frowned at a grouping of seeds caught in the creases between his fingers. All of them were withered and brown, except for one tiny seed near the tip of his smallest finger, which looked new and must have come from the tip of the one of the stalks.

He shuddered at the sight of the diseased seeds, his stomach twisting. He counted seven total.

"What is it?" Tarramic asked.

Quotl glanced up, considered for a moment, still uncertain about what the single, small, unformed but healthy seed meant. Then he scattered the seeds in his palm to the ground. "The Wraith army is nearing Clan Chief Corranu's position. We will intercept them within the week."

Tarramic nodded grimly, the rest of the Riders around them shifting in their saddles as they watched their leader contemplate.

"What else do you see? Anything? Does Ilacqua not give us a sign of what is to come?"

Quotl straightened in his saddle at the uncertainty in Tarramic's voice, something so subtle he doubted that many of the other Riders could hear it. But he and Tarramic had known each other too long for the clan chief to hide it from him. They'd led Thousand Springs Clan side by side since Tarramic took over upon his father's death.

Tarramic wanted reassurance. He hadn't agreed with the Cochen's plan at the Gathering.

Quotl turned in his saddle to scan the horizon and the Riders as the last of them emerged from the tunnel. Tents were already being raised, holes driven in the ground and poles hoisted for the clan chief's main tent. They had ridden hard since the Gathering at the Sacred Waters, splitting off from the Cochen's main force after the first few days and riding on alone. They would be meeting up with the Painted Sands Clan east of here within the next two days, once their main provisions arrived.

But the storms to the northwest were what caught his attention.

Without conscious thought, he nudged his gaezel a few steps in that direction, then instantly cursed himself as Tarramic and the Riders around him tensed, one drawing a sharp breath and expelling it in a short prayer.

"Is it an omen?" Tarramic asked, voice tight.

Quotl cursed himself again and desperately wished he could take out his pipe and leaf. He found it more calming than the rattling of his scepter.

Instead, he closed his eyes and drew in a deep breath, letting it out in a slow hum, hoping to calm the Riders with the sounds while at the same time calming his own heart. He brought his scepter forward, shaking it to the north, south, and west, modulating his humming as he did so.

When he opened his eyes, he saw Azuka waiting for him a short distance away. Behind the shaman, purple lightning flared through the black clouds. The storm appeared to boil up out of thin air, roiling westward from a clearly defined line, sheets of gray rain slanting down from their base to the plains below. More lightning lit the storm's depths, the darkness highlighted in bluish whites, greens, and dirty yellows, like old bruises.

"The storm is not an omen," Quotl lied. "The gods are troubled, but it forms to the west, and moves away from us, leaving the Riders untouched."

Tammaric nodded and relaxed slightly, the others around them doing the same. Only Azuka frowned at this pronouncement, and Quotl shot him a warning glare to keep him silent.

"Then we will camp here until the supplies have arrived," the clan chief announced. "Echema, select two Riders and find Clan Chief Corranu. Tell him of our location and the rest of Oraju's plans. And warn him of Quotl's Seeing of the Wraith army's location."

Echema nodded and spun his gaezel, pointing to two others before all three charged out after the scouts who'd departed earlier.

Tammaric's gaze swept over the rest. "Set up patrols and order the Riders into training after they've had a chance to feed and care for their gaezels. I want everyone here gathered in my tent this evening, including you, Quotl."

The Riders dispersed, Tammaric retreating to where his tent had nearly been finished and ducking through the outer flap. Riders and aides were toting a few chests, pillows, and other assorted amenities in through the two side entrances. Quotl heard the clan chief barking orders, but turned away, finally allowing himself to dismount with a wince and groan as he twisted and bent, trying to release the tension in his back and shoulders.

Azuka stepped forward as one of the Riders led Quotl's mount away for grooming, Quotl's bags left in the grass beside him.

"You lied about the storm," Azuka accused, although he kept his voice low.

"He and the others needed reassurance, not discouragement. And the truth of the storm cannot be changed." When Azuka grunted, Quotl pierced him with a glare. "Do you know the truth of the storm, Azuka? Do you know what it means?"

The shaman suddenly looked uncertain. "It means the gods are angry, that the winds are troubled, and it bodes ill for the battle to come."

"Ha! It bodes ill for the battle to come because it tells us that we are no longer beneath the protection of the Summer Tree. The Wraiths and their army will be at full strength when we finally meet. And none of us can do anything about it." He shifted his glare toward the storm. "I will warn Tarramic and the others at the meeting, but for now they need to relax as they plan and prepare if we are to have any chance of stopping the Wraith army." And giving the Shadowed One the chance to find and halt the attack on the Summer Tree.

He suddenly realized what the small seed represented, and one of the many tensions in his shoulders relaxed.

The Shadowed One had made it past the Wraith army, then. Good.

"Head shaman?"

He glanced toward Azuka. "What?"

"You grunted and smiled."

Quotl waved his hand. "It was nothing. Have the shamans completed the ritual?"

"Yes."

"Have them gather in the ritual tent as soon as it is erected. I want to meet with them before the clan chief calls me into his Gathering."

~

"Clear the table," Tarramic ordered.

As the aides—all young Riders or those who were training to become Riders—moved forward to remove the platters of food, used plates, and trays, the clan chief motioned toward Quotl.

Setting aside his pipe and glaring at one of the aides who'd moved forward to remove it until the youth backed off, Quotl pulled the scepter of his office from his lap and stood, starting a chant in the ancient tongue as he began pacing the confines of the room. It was the largest chamber in the clan chief's tent, the table surrounded by eleven dwarren Riders, all of them of significant families within the clan and the structure of the Riders. Three more aides remained behind as the last of the dinner was removed. Quotl shook the scepter along the four sacred lines to signify the gods of the Four Winds and closed off the chamber by arranging a pattern of feathers, grass, and a scattering of grain at the main entrance, then lit the brazier that hung from the center of the tent, tossing a few herbs and scented leaves onto the flames as he did so to summon Ilacqua.

Then he turned to Tarramic. "The Four Winds protect us, and Ilacqua guides our words."

Tarramic nodded and motioned immediately to two of the aides as Quotl returned to his seat. "The map of Painted Sands. And the stones."

One aide pulled the roll of leather from a trunk set off to one side, while the other set a small, flat, wooden box at Tarramic's right side, removing the lid to reveal an array of compartments, each containing polished colored stone. The map was rolled out and secured using four heavy chunks of onyx at each of the rounded corners.

Everyone leaned forward to peer at the map. The lands of Painted Sands were worked into the leather, the straight line of the Andagua River cutting diagonally across the bottom left corner and stained a faint blue. Entrances to the warrens were marked with rounded impressions, the land scattered with three-lined marks that looked like tufts of grass. Unusual features of the grasslands were marked as well, including a jagged cut of land to the east called the Break that marked a sudden change in the landscape, grasses giving way to the red rock and sands that gave the clan its name. The cliffs were nothing in comparison to the Cut that bordered Thousand Springs Clan lands, not even half as high nor as long, but in terms of strategic land formations it was practically all that the dwarren had to work with. It ran for a significant distance, the eastern plains rising toward its base in a gentle curved slope that steepened until it hit the striated rock of the cliff face. Sometime in the distant past, a portion of the cliffs had given way, collapsing them into the plains beyond, creating a natural ramp to the upper plains to the west, where Tarramic and the Thousand Springs Clan now camped, although still two days distant.

Tarramic pointed toward the warren entrance west of the jagged line of the Break and the wide swath of land that interrupted it. "The Cochen has chosen this entrance as our retreat, if retreat becomes necessary. The bulk of our supplies will remain here, with only minimal supplies taken to our main encampment here." He pointed to a spot at the top of the remains of the massive landslide. He removed twelve blue-colored stones from the box at his side and set them down there, then turned to Quotl. "Where are the other clans, according to your Seeing?"

Quotl gestured for the markers. "The Seeing was done nearly five hours ago, but at that time the Cochen and his forces were approximately here, and Corranu was here, although I assume that his forces will join ours before we arrive at the Break. Claw Lake had emerged here." He set red-and-white-colored stones to signify the Cochen's forces, green for Corranu, and yellow for Claw Lake. "The others I can only assume are now where the Cochen ordered them within the warrens."

Tarramic nodded, his attention already on his eldest son. "Tumak, what did the scouts report?"

Quotl let the report fade into the background as he sucked on the end of his pipe and blew the smoke toward the brazier above, eyes on the map. Pieces shifted around as the dwarren Riders began talking strategy. The idea became obvious when seen on the map rather than the palm of his hand. The landslide, though wide, would provide the only feasible means for the Wraith army to reach the upper plains of Painted Sands, unless they were willing to add over a week to their march by traveling northward to where the Break ended and the grasslands merged with the red sands to the west. They could also travel southward, although the Break ended abruptly in a jumble of rock and stone debris, the land riddled with cracks and crevices, making the movement of such a large army nearly impossible.

And the army must be large, if his Seeing had been correct. The dwarren outnumbered them, but it was still a significant force. Larger than the armies that had clashed on the eastern plains before the Accord. Even at the Cut, the dwarren armies had numbered nearly half of what had been gathered here.

But that had been over five generations ago. The dwarren had multiplied since then. They were once again nearing what their strength had been before the arrival of the Alvritshai and the humans on the plains. The wars with those two races had been devastating.

He shook his head and frowned at himself, focusing on the map again. Tarramic had positioned the Thousand Springs and Painted Sands forces along the breadth of the base of the landslide, Claw Lake and Shadow Moon along the heights to either side. The northern edge of the Break angled mostly east-west, following the slide and providing Claw Lake with the opportunity to cover a retreat of the forces on the ground and hit the army with arrows and spears from above. Shadow Moon would do the same from the southern cliffs, but they would be at a disadvantage since the Break ran more north-south along that ridge. Instead, they would provide cover for the Cochen, Red Sea, and Broken Waters, who would come up from the south on the Wraith army's flank.

As the dwarren Riders argued about the details—minutia Quotl didn't think would matter in the final outcome—he contemplated the patterns in the shifting stones, seeking the one that would keep Ilacqua's and the Four Winds' favor. He breathed in the smoke from his pipe and the scents he'd thrown into the brazier, felt his body thrumming in response. The stones shifted yet again, Tarramic rearranging them as he barked at his son, and Quotl frowned. The positioning was close, the alignment nearly there. If he factored in the location of Silver Grass, and if he placed the shamans and the trettarus archers with the wood gifted to them by the forest here and here—

He cried out, his exclamation cutting the arguments around the table off as sharply as any sword could have. All of the dwarren Riders turned to face him and he squinted at them in return, a slight smile touching the corners of his mouth. He let the silence hold, then stuck the end of his pipe in his mouth and inhaled deeply, releasing the smoke before using the end of the pipe to point to the map.

"You are almost there," he said, letting his voice rumble. "However, I feel that the gods will favor the following more." Using the stem of his pipe, he pushed a few of the stones into new positions. "The trettarus should be positioned here and here, in small groups so they can move about more easily and select their targets with precision. We do not have many of the forest's gifts. They must be used sparingly."

The younger Riders remained silent, turning their attention to Tarramic, who concentrated on the new arrangement with a creased brow, then met Quotl's gaze through the haze of smoke.

"You say the gods favor this?"

Quotl thought about the portent of the storm, of what it truly foretold, what neither he nor Azuka had been able to voice, had only been able to skirt. But what he had said to Azuka was true: there was nothing any of them could do to challenge it.

He could only arrange matters to minimize the damage. He nodded.

Tarramic frowned down at the map. Quotl could sense that a few of the Riders did not agree with him, but their opinions did not matter. He knew Tarramic would heed his advice. He was the head shaman, and Tarramic always listened to the gods.

The clan chief finally looked up and muttered, "So be it."

~

Moiran stood on the balcony overlooking the open courtyard before the manse, her arms crossed over her chest. In the distance to the east, gray storm clouds loomed, the faint rumble of thunder echoing down through the hills to the lake, although she had yet to see any flashes of lightning. The wind tasted of rain, damp and metallic, and the leaves of the trees that surrounded the courtyard were turned up, exposing their pale undersides to the late spring sunlight.

In counterpoint to the thunder, the clash of weapons rose from the yard below, punctuated by the sharp commands of Fedaureon and Mattalaen, the caitan who had trained Fedaureon and a significant portion of the young men who'd joined the Phalanx at the same time. Daevon, her son's Protector stood to one side, watching intently.

Now, the caitan drilled them all, the group paired off on the stone cobbles below, swords flashing as they grunted and strove to break through each others' guard. Moiran kept her eyes on her son. Within a week of Aeren's warning about the ascension of the Order as a House within the

Evant, Fedaureon had the Phalanx on alert, the border patrols increased and the Phalanx here within the House
doubled. A week after that, he'd ordered an escalation of
the training, so that now the Phalanx within Artillien practiced at least twice a day. Fedaureon participated in nearly
all of them. He had always been more military-minded than
Aeren, more skilled with the blade and the bow and more
adept at military strategy. His anger had only risen the longer the members of the Order of the Flame remained
within House lands, his aggression obvious on the training
ground below.

Moiran frowned. So far, he had taken his rage out on the
practice field. Messengers from Caercaern had arrived at
the local temple ten days ago, supposedly relaying the edict
of the Evant that all members of the Flame within Rhyssal
House lands were to return to the Sanctuary. She had expected them to depart within two days. They hadn't. Fedaureon had sent a servant down to the temple to ask
whether the acolytes required any assistance. Their offer
had been flatly refused. The members of the Flame had continued to preach at the daily rituals, without any sign they
intended to depart Artillien as ordered.

The next message had been less polite, and had been
greeted with total silence, the acolytes of the Order not
even allowing the servant into the temple to deliver the
message personally to the members of the Flame present.
The acolytes had denied the servant coldly, then closed the
temple door in her face.

That had been two day ago. The acolytes and the Order
were skirting dangerously close to the edge of polite formality. Based on the ferocity of Fedaureon's attacks on his op-
ponents in the courtyard below, they'd already surpassed the
thin edge of his patience. In fact, the rest of those fighting had
fallen back to watch Fedaureon spar with a lone attacker.

But that was not what had brought Moiran to the balcony. No. She had sought out Fedaureon for an entirely different matter.

Below, Fedaureon cried out, blade cutting in sharply, his opponent parrying the attack, already worn down. Her son shoved the block aside viciously, stepped into the opening, and brought his elbow up into his opponent's face, pulling the blow. It still retained enough force to snap the Phalanx guard's head back and send him reeling to the ground. Mattalaen barked an end to the match and Fedaureon growled, sword already raised for what would have been a killing blow. For a moment, Moiran wasn't certain her son would heed his caitan, but then the fierce expression dropped from Fedaureon's face and he grinned, sword lowered as he reached down with his free hand to help his opponent up from the ground.

They dusted off, Mattalaen making some kind of comment regarding the match to each privately before nodding toward where Moiran stood watching. Her son glanced toward her, then sheathed his sword and moved toward the manse's entrance, Daevon falling in at his side.

Moiran stepped away from the balcony as Mattalaen picked two more men from the ranks and paired them off. She moved into the inner room and took a seat, waiting.

Fedaureon arrived ten minutes later, still sweaty from the fighting, but he'd paused long enough to remove his outermost armor.

"What is it?" he demanded as soon as he entered. His face was flushed and his breath shortened.

She raised an eyebrow and glanced toward Daevon.

"Fedaureon," the Protector said, his voice level but full of warning.

Her son grimaced, but then caught her demeanor and the impatience that riddled his shoulders and face vanished. He had the grace to appear abashed. "I apologize, Mother. You wished to speak to me?"

Moiran motioned toward the seat across from her. A low table stood between the two chairs, a stack of letters close to her left hand, a platter of cheese and a decanter of wine on her right. She began to pour him a glass as he settled into the chair, coughing slightly as he tried to calm his breathing. His mind was still on the practice field below, though.

"I think I have discovered who Lotaern's allies are within the Evant," she said.

Fedaureon stilled, suddenly attentive. "Who? Father has been trying to figure it out for weeks! It's all that he talks about in his letters."

"I know."

"Then how have you figured it out? We don't have access to the Evant. We can't see who's dealing with whom, we only have Father's letters to go by."

Moiran smiled, suppressing the motherly urge to say she had her ways. "I used the Ilvaeren."

Fedaureon fell silent, eyeing her with a frown. Daevon did the same from behind. She handed her son his wine and waited, attempting to still the trembling of her hands. She had never used the Ilvaeren in this way, had never even considered it until two weeks ago, when she realized that some of her routine requests with the Houses she normally traded with were being denied. The refusals had been annoying to begin with, but then she'd begun to sense a pattern.

She wasn't certain what she'd found was substantial enough to support her claims. She'd spent the last two days trying to organize it and convince herself, before finally sighing and deciding to present it to her son.

And then there was the other issue: the Ilvaeren did not interfere in the Evant. Women were not supposed to dabble in the political field at all. At least in theory.

"I don't understand," Fedaureon said, taking a sip of wine before setting the glass aside. "What do you mean you used the Ilvaeren?"

She ignored the guarded doubt that weighed down his words.

"It began over a month ago, although I didn't notice it at the time. I received this letter from Lady Yssabo of House Redlien. Every year, we purchase a supply of winter barley from Redlien. This year, Vivaen Licaeta bought out not only Redlien's barley, but their flax as well. I thought it odd at the time, but merely sought out barley from House Uslaen and Ionaen, both of which had some to spare. However, I began running into similar issues with other Houses for other commodities—cloth from Nuant, rice from Baene, even wood from Licaeta and Uslaen." She'd handed Fedaureon the letter from Yssabo as she spoke, but now she laid out additional letters across the width of the table from the other Houses. "I have never experienced this much trouble obtaining supplies from our fellow Houses in my term here as the Lady of House Rhyssal, nor as the Tamaea of Resue.

"And then I began to realize that the majority of the commodities were being bought up by only a few of the Houses, in particular Licaeta and Ionaen, although Uslaen appears to have begun buying similar supplies lately."

"Perhaps they are simply short this year, their crops not as plentiful as they had hoped."

Moiran hesitated at the interruption, one hand clenching in her lap before she forced it to relax. She nodded. "I thought so as well. So I began taking a closer look." She gathered up the letters she'd already presented and set them aside. New pages replaced the first, although these were written in Moiran's hand. "I started an accounting of all of the supplies that I was aware of through the Ilvaeren. This isn't an exact accounting, since no House has the right to request the trade books of any other House, but even so. . . . Look how much grain Licaeta has purchased in the last few months."

Fedaureon, Lady Yssabo's letter still in one hand, leaned

forward and regarded the page Moiran indicated. He stilled, then motioned Daevon forward, the Protector taking that as tacit permission to look as well. Moiran didn't protest; she knew Daevon well enough to believe that he would support her.

"That's enough grain to feed Rhyssal for over a year," Fedaureon said.

"Nearly a year and a half. Why would they need so much grain? Why does House Ionaen need so much wood? Or Uslaen so much iron from Nuant?"

Fedaureon leaned back, glanced toward Daevon.

The Protector's eyebrows rose. "It is a significant amount of resources. One House should not need so much of a single material."

Fedaureon nodded, his attention returning to Moiran. "What do you think?"

She drew a deep breath, exhaled slowly. "I think that Lord Peloroun and Lord Orraen are preparing for ... something significant. I believe they are stocking up on food and other supplies."

"'Something significant,'" Fedaureon said. "Such as what? And how does this connect to the Chosen and the Order of Aielan?"

"I don't know. But none of those Houses has ever done anything without forethought. And all of those Houses have opposed us in the past."

Fedaureon was silent for a long moment, then abruptly leaned forward, tossing Yssabo's letter onto the table. "It's not enough."

Moiran stiffened, anger sparking in her chest. "What do you mean?"

"What I mean is that it's not enough. Father can't take this before the Evant. What if Lord Peloroun and Lord Orraen have a legitimate reason for purchasing all of these supplies, a reason we are unaware of?"

"Like what?"

Fedaureon shrugged. "A trade agreement with the dwarren or the humans, perhaps? We have no idea what arrangements they've made, what the humans or dwarren might be interested in. We each have agreements with different Provinces and clans. They do not detail every individual trade made and for what commodity. They are generalized. It's possible that the Licaetan grain that could supply the House for a year and a half has already been shipped to their trade partners in Borangst, or even overseas to Andover. Lord Daesor announced a new trade deal with Andover at the opening session." He waved a hand and said again, "It's not enough. Not for the Evant."

"I wasn't intending to bring it before the Evant," Moiran said.

Fedaureon's eyes narrowed. "You want to know if I think it's solid enough to warn Father." He hesitated, then added, "Have you already sent a missive to him?"

She nearly chuckled at the suspicion in his voice. "No, Fedaureon. I wanted your opinion first. I know the evidence is thin, but my instinct warns me that this is significant."

Mollified, Fedaureon scanned the letters she'd presented, the papers containing the lists of supplies shifting hands within the Ilvaeren. Moiran met Daevon's gaze over his head and the Protector nodded, his mouth pressed into a grim line. She and Aeren had worked hard this past year to ease Fedaureon into his role as Lord Presumptive of the Rhyssal House. Since Aeren's departure, he had taken on that role more competently than Moiran had expected, and in the last few weeks had shown some independence in his decisions. He'd sent the servants to the temple without seeking out Moiran's opinion, had made adjustments to the daily routine of the Phalanx on his own. She wasn't certain how much Daevon had guided these decisions, but she wanted to encourage Fedaureon's independence as much as possible.

Fedaureon leaned back. "I think your instincts are correct. Father needs to be informed. Perhaps Lords Peloroun and Orraen do have legitimate trades established for this wood and iron, but I doubt it. If he knows where to look, maybe Father can determine what's really going on." He stood, his impatience returning. The clash of steel still rang from outside, even though the wind had picked up. "Did you want to warn him, or should I?"

"I believe you should, as Lord Presumptive of the Rhyssal House."

19

"H E'S GOT THE UPPER BODY STRENGTH," Terson said, "but he's still a miller."

Gregson frowned thoughtfully as he watched Ricks and Curtis sparring with Jayson, the miller's apprentice standing off to one side watching. "But he's learning fast."

"Because he's angry. You can see it in his thrusts. Whatever happened to him in his village, it's affected him."

"That isn't necessarily bad. A little anger during a fight or battle can be useful. And we'll be seeing many more like him, if what we've seen between Cobble Kill and here is any indication."

Terson's mouth twisted with derision. "An army of commoners."

Gregson turned slightly toward him. "Given what we saw at Patron's Merge, and the destruction we've seen throughout the countryside since . . . I'll take an army any way I can get it."

Terson's brow creased at the mild reprimand, but he said nothing.

In the makeshift practice yard, Ricks took a swing toward Jayson's side, grinning as sweat ran down his face. Jayson parried with a grunt, the swords clashing as Curtis barked from the sideline, "Now use the momentum of your opponent's swing to thrust his sword off to the side, leaving him open."

Jayson attempted to follow through, shoving Ricks' sword to one side and down, the natural movement still stiff and forced. Gregson could tell that Ricks wasn't countering the thrust as hard as he could, but Jayson had barely begun practicing. He and Curtis were simply trying to get him to adjust from swinging sacks of grain to handling the weight of the blade. The motions were obviously different, and Jayson needed to feel that difference in his arm and shoulders before he'd have any chance of putting it into practice during a real battle.

And it was looking as if a real battle was imminent.

They'd been traveling covertly since Patron's Merge, scouts sent out ahead, searching for the Horde as it ransacked its way across the Province. Parties of twenty to over a thousand had been sighted, forcing the large group of Legion and commoners to find alternate routes at least three times already. And the group had grown. Two days before, they'd run into another group with the remnants of another garrison, mostly younger soldiers, only one officer who was beneath Gregson in rank. He had been almost painfully relieved when Gregson had reluctantly taken control of the remains of his unit and the forty civilians and three wagons they'd been protecting.

He might have turned them away to fend for themselves, but they'd had food. He wasn't certain how long it would last, not with nearly three hundred refugees, but at least most of the men in the group knew how to hunt and trap. Although even that had been restricted. The closer they came to Temeritt—it could only be a few days away now—the more activity they'd seen from the Horde. They were closing in on the city, their scattered groups coming together and squeezing all of the refugees between them.

He'd become increasingly convinced that they were going to have to fight their way through to Temeritt, if they arrived in time to make the city at all.

His gaze passed over the rest of the men, and a couple of women, gathered to watch the match. He scratched at the bandage on his left arm, the bite marks beneath itching, then caught himself with a grimace.

"Pair up as many men as we can spare with the civilians. Use whatever you can find for weapons. Don't give any of the able-bodied men a choice. Tell them if they want to see Temeritt alive, they're likely going to have to fight."

Terson nodded and Gregson moved off toward their encampment. There were still a few hours of sunlight left, but he hadn't dared move on beyond the small field, the waist-high grasses now trampled down into a rough mat beneath his feet. The scouts he'd sent out ahead of them had reported the roads safe only up to this point; they hadn't heard from them since. Gregson tried not to let that fact bother him. The scouts had been late before and it meant nothing. The one time he'd pushed on regardless, they'd nearly run into a party of Alvritshai.

The five wagons were drawn up in a rough circle, a few of the women, Ara included, butchering some of the small game the hunters had brought in. He'd reluctantly agreed to allow a fire, hoping the breeze that whispered through the surrounding trees would be enough to disperse the smoke. As he entered the small circle, a group of children emerged from the closest section of forest, arms laden with branches. They screamed in delight as the two women who'd accompanied them herded them toward the fire, one tripping and falling, bursting instantly into tears. Their laughter cut strangely through the somberness that passed between the adults in the group.

"Children are the most resilient of us all," Ara said, jerking her knife through the rabbit's carcass as she separated the skin from the meat. Once free, she gutted it and impaled the body on a spit, passing it to one of the other women as she tossed the skin to one side and reached for another rabbit.

"I'm not used to dealing with ... children." He'd been about to say civilians. He still didn't understand why they were all here, why they continued to follow his orders. There was barely enough food or supplies for them all, most of the adults going without in order to feed the children. The rabbits Ara butchered had been a windfall. He was only a lieutenant, and out of the group of three hundred there were only thirty Legionnaires. Why did the others remain? Why didn't they break away to fend for themselves, or to find someone who could take care of them better than he could?

Ara eyed him critically, up and down, eyebrow quirked. "You seem to be doing just fine. We haven't lost a man ... or woman ... yet. Not since Cobble Kill."

The men and women cut down there by the Alvritshai arrows or the catlike creatures' claws flashed through his mind and he grimaced. He could still feel the claw marks on his legs, no longer bandaged, but still healing.

Before he could respond, one of the Legionnaires guarding the edge of the camp shouted. Nearly everyone jumped, fear skating through their eyes and faces as they tensed.

To the southeast, another Legionnaire emerged from the edge of the trees. He waved his free hand in desperation, the other holding up one of the scouts and helping him along. The young man was covered in blood, his legs barely supporting him.

Gregson was moving before he consciously thought about it, surprised to find Ara at his side, others heading toward the two men as they stumbled into the field. The Legionnaire who'd shouted a warning and another man reached them first, taking the wounded scout and lifting him off the ground, practically sprinting toward the carts.

"Over here," Ara shouted, and grabbed Gregson's arm to halt him before he moved beyond the wagons. She cleared a small section of grass, yelling, "Give us room, give us room," gruffly, shoving those who lingered too long aside. Then she caught an older woman's arm. "Get whatever rags you can find, and a bucket of fresh water."

The Legionnaire and the other man—a blacksmith, Gregson recalled, from the new group—set the scout down on the grass and Ara began checking him for wounds. Gregson crouched down beside them as the older woman arrived with an armload of rags, their meager medical box, and a bucket of water.

"Can you hear me?" Gregson asked, lightly slapping the scout's cheek.

Ara shot him a glare, soaking a rag and running it across the scout's face. Blood ran away in rivulets, the skin beneath shockingly pale, almost gray. Something clutched at Gregson's heart, but he forced it back. Three claw marks ran from the younger man's ear into his scalp, bleeding as fast as Ara could wipe it away. Ara huffed in exasperation and left the wounds, moving toward the rest of his body. Most of the blood that covered his chest and side could have come from the head wound, but not all of it.

Gregson reached down and caught the scout's jaw, turning his head toward him as he leaned far enough forward he could stare down into the glazed eyes. "I need you to focus." He saw a flicker of awareness and patted his cheek again until the awareness caught and held. "What happened? What did you see?"

The scout coughed, a froth of blood spattering his lips. Gregson heard Ara rip the man's shirt open and swear, but he didn't turn to look. She shouted for more water, more rags, and some godsdamned thread, her voice shaking.

"What did you see?" Gregson repeated.

The scout finally appeared to recognize him, smiling even

as he choked on blood. "War party," he wheezed. "Found me. Chased me. Had to get through. Need to tell you—"

He contorted with a seizure. Ara spat curses and ordered a Legionnaire to hold him steady; Gregson leaned his arm onto the scout's chest.

"Tell us what?" he demanded, even as the youth thrashed. He tightened his grip on his jaw, felt the muscles bunched beneath his fingers. "Focus, boy, focus. What did you need to tell us?"

The scout's gaze locked with Gregson's and he muttered, "GreatLord Kobel ... Legion ... line day distant ... watch birds ... not birds ..."

Then the intensity in his eyes faded and his body went limp. A trickle of blood trailed down one side of his face, staining the grass beneath him.

The activity beside him ceased abruptly and someone grabbed Gregson's hand. He turned to find Ara, hands bloody up to her forearms, staring at him intently. "He's dead."

Gregson drew in a breath and released his grip. He glanced down toward the scout's face and thought about not losing a man since Cobble Kill, then swallowed the tightness in his own chest and rose. He suddenly realized he hadn't even known the young man's name, that he barely knew any of the newer members of his group.

That would have to change, he vowed. He wanted no more nameless men dying during his command, under his watch.

A crowd had gathered, mostly women and children, but a few men among them, including Terson.

"Terson, you have the camp. You five, come with me." He'd selected three of the civilians—Carlson, Brent, and Orlson from Cobble Kill—and two Legionnaires, Leont and Darrall, all of them sturdy men with weapons already in hand. They must have come from the practice field.

As he moved away from the scout's body toward the edge of the forest, the silent crowd parting before him, Terson stepped up to his side. "Where are you going, sir?"

"To verify what he saw."

"What did he say?"

Gregson looked back to find the five men he'd selected a few paces behind them, the three civilians looking uncertain. All of them were listening, though, and Carlson, the carpenter, gave him a nod of encouragement.

"He said the front line was a day distant. We're near the Northward Ridge. I want to know if we can see it from there."

"Shouldn't we wait until the other scouts return?"

He met Terson's gaze squarely. "What makes you think they will?" he said softly.

Terson's eyes narrowed.

"We're obviously closer to the Horde's line than we thought. I want to know how close, and if we have a chance in hells of getting through to our own side."

"Very well."

He heard the unspoken warning to be careful. He didn't need it. He'd seen the scout's face and the jagged wounds along his torso.

He only wondered what the scout had meant when he'd whispered, "Watch birds . . . not birds."

"Ah," Gregson murmured to himself.

"Diermani's balls."

Gregson turned, a reprimand on his lips, but realized the man who'd spoken was Brent, one of the civilians. He caught the tail end of the man crossing himself, his eyes wide with fear, his breathing already shortened in panic.

"Steady," he said tightly, catching the man's gaze. "The line is too distant to be a threat."

Brent swallowed and gripped the pendant that hung hidden beneath his shirt, his breath slowing.

Gregson turned back. Reaching forward, he pulled a leafy branch out of his line of sight and stared down from the ridge toward the rolling hillsides below.

The Legion fought in ragged formation along a front that was far too wide to hold, not with the amount of Legionnaires present. Gregson estimated nearly ten thousand Legion had been gathered, the combined garrisons of Temeritt and all of the surrounding cities and towns within a hundred-mile radius of the Autumn Tree. His heart lifted with hope when he picked out the orange-and-black banners of GreatLord Kobel near the heart of the fighting. They were too distant for him to pick out the man himself, but he could tell they were fighting ferociously. His own muscles tensed, his hand itching to find the handle of his blade and join them, but even without the responsibility of the refugees waiting a short distance away there was no easy descent from the Northward Ridge.

Not close anyway.

Instead, he turned his attention toward the Horde. As at Patron's Merge, it undulated on the hillsides like a black wave, pushing against the Legion, the line of combat shifting beneath the late evening sunlight. Arrows darkened the sky; archers perched on the highest hilltops on both sides, the deadly shafts raining down in waves. Gregson was close enough he could hear the clash of blades and the screams of the dying, but it was muted, rising along the ridge face to his position like mist.

The sound made his jaw clench.

The Horde was composed mostly of Alvritshai, some on horseback, like those who'd attacked Cobble Kill, but most on foot. Mixed in with them, he could see more of the leathery-skinned giants and packs of the catlike creatures attacking in swarms. The giants were mindless, powering forward by brute force, grabbing and ripping and rending whatever they could get their hands on. The catlike creatures were just as vicious, but their attacks were more intelligent, their attention focused on the Legion on horseback.

The Alvritshai were precise and methodical, their lines coordinated. Gregson studied their formations with a coldly critical eye, his mouth pressed into a grim line, even as he fought a surge of respect. He had never fought the Alvritshai before. Temeritt's Province was separated from Alvritshai lands by the dwarren. They'd only had to deal with the dwarren, and with the Accord that had meant an uneasy alliance that neither race had seen fit to test significantly. There had been skirmishes, disputes over exactly where the boundary lay between the dwarren Lands and the Province, but nothing serious. The attacks were mostly posturing.

The Alvritshai below were not posturing. They were vicious and frighteningly direct. No hesitation and no attempt to back off or to seek quarter. They weren't here for concessions of land or for barter, and they weren't looking for the Legion to surrender.

They were here to kill and conquer.

Gregson's eyes narrowed as he began searching for a way for the refugees to get past the Horde's line and to the uncertain safety behind the Legion. The fighting raged across a flat stretch of rolling land between multiple hills, split by a road running more or less east-west. A low wall of stone ran across a few of the hills, most likely separating the property between two owners. Copses of trees grew in the valleys between the nearest hills.

The ridge had forced the Horde to separate and converge from the east and west as they bypassed it, but they now lay between Gregson, the refugees, and the Legion's forces. He leaned farther forward, trying to see the land beneath them, closer to the face of the ridge, but it was empty.

He frowned. Where were the Horde's supply wagons? Their supporting forces?

"Lieutenant!"

The warning from Darrall snapped Gregson's attention back to the fighting.

The Legion to the west had collapsed, the men fighting desperately as a roar of triumph washed up the ridge face from the Horde. Horns blew, the creatures and Alvritshai at the back of the Horde shifting toward the break. Gregson bit back his own curse, then felt a hand on his shoulder.

Brent's face was etched with terror. "Not there." He pointed toward the sky. "There."

Gregson looked up, his heart already sinking, to see a huge bird circling above their position. Even as he registered that it wasn't a bird—the wings were too long, the head too pointed and narrow—it shrieked, the sound slicing into Gregson's gut. He heaved up out of his crouch as Darrall, Leont, and Carlson drew their swords. Orlson panicked and vanished through the trees, racing back toward the refugee camp, but before Gregson could roar an order to stop, the creature that was and wasn't a bird shrieked again, louder than before, and swooped down toward them.

Leont and Carlson jumped in front of Gregson, both swords raised. Leont, a new recruit, bellowed in defiance, but the creature never broke the tops of the trees, banking left out over the edge of the ridge and down toward the army below, its shriek fading with distance.

The four remaining men were left gasping at the edge of the forest.

"Did you see its eyes?" Brent asked. His chest heaved, his face and shirt damp with sweat. He wiped at his forehead with one sleeve. "They were yellow. And that head! I've never seen anything like that, never even heard of such a thing, not even in the legends. It didn't even have feathers! And it was the size of a horse! It—"

"Quiet!" Gregson barked. Brent's voice verged on hysteria. He opened his mouth in shock, but Gregson didn't let him continue. "Whatever that thing was, it knows we're here. We have to warn the others. Move!"

After a moment of indecision, mouth still open, Brent turned and ran.

The rest of them followed, Gregson keeping his eyes on the patches of sky he could see through the leafy cover. The shadow of the creature passed by overhead before they'd made it halfway back to the camp, moving fast, and within fifteen minutes they heard it shrieking from the direction of the refugees. He swore, prayed to Diermani that the archers could take it down, but heard its cry veering off to the side.

When they broke through the edge of the clearing into the field, the camp was in chaos, with men, women, and children racing in every direction. Terson stood in the middle of it all bellowing orders left and right. He was surrounded by five men with arrows nocked and trained toward the sky, but the creature wasn't in sight. Everyone else was frantically throwing supplies into the backs of the wagons, calming skittish horses, or heaving children up into saddles.

As soon as Gregson took stock of the scene, he roared, "Leave it all! If it isn't already in the carts, leave it! We need to go now!"

His voice cracked over the chaos, nearly everyone turning toward him, their faces panicked. He caught sight of Orlson, the civilian who'd fled the ridge, and gave him a black glare before turning away.

"Terson, get them moving to the west. Our best chance is to skirt the end of the Northward Ridge and have everyone scatter into the forest there. If we aren't all gathered into a single group, the Horde will have a harder time finding us. We'll try to make the Legion's line through the cuts between the hills to escape notice. Go, go, go!"

Gregson's second in command stalked off shouting,

"Form up!" shoving people he passed, too roughly for Gregson's taste, but he couldn't take the time to curtail him.

Somewhere south, beyond the ridge, the creature screamed.

It was answered by another shriek, so close Gregson flinched from the sound, ducking instinctively. Nearly half of the refugees did the same, a few dropping into a crouch.

But not all.

Gregson heard the flap of thick cloth, spun in time to see a shadow fall over the group, a confusion of leathery wings, a thick body, reaching legs—

Then the talons of the creature raked across one of the mounted men, tumbling him from the saddle as blood flew. The distinct sound of arrows being released shot through the high-pitched scream that followed, Gregson registering mild respect that some of the archers had remained calm enough to fire, and then with a gust of wind that carried grass and grit into his face, the creature lifted away, something clutched in its talons.

Gregson stared after it in shock, his mind not willing to accept that the figure struggling in the creature's grip was a child. But the mother's screeching wouldn't stop. He turned to face her, body numbed, two men holding her back as her arms reached up and out toward the bird that was not a bird, already a receding shadow in the distance.

A smaller shadow suddenly dropped from it and fell toward the earth.

Gregson turned away, bile rising in the back of his throat, the mother's scream escalating before breaking into sobs as she collapsed back into the arms of the men holding her, her body suddenly limp. Two men hauled her upright and carried her to one of the carts, tossing her into the back as she protested, arms flailing, striking them and herself in her frenzy.

"Lieutenant!"

Gregson swallowed with a wince, then turned, saw Curtis and Jayson charging up to him.

"Everyone's moving out," Curtis gasped. "We need to go!"

Gregson surveyed the trampled grass of the field and acknowledged that Curtis was correct. The attack of the creature had lit a fire under everyone's ass. The carts had already reached the edge of the road heading westward, the one with the mother trailing slightly behind the others. The rest of the refugees were stumbling at a half-run out in front, the Legion, archers, and men on horseback urging them on, all with swords drawn. He shook his head. It was all falling apart. They weren't abandoning the supplies; they weren't preparing to separate into smaller groups. In their panic, they were doing the exact opposite, unwilling to break from those they'd bonded with over the last few days.

He couldn't shake the feeling they were running to their deaths, couldn't think of a way to stop it.

After they'd come so far, come so close to reaching Temeritt.

"Lieutenant?"

Someone touched Gregson's shoulder tentatively and he jerked away as Jayson pulled back.

He stared at the miller, then growled, "Let's move," harsher than he'd intended. Jayson merely stiffened and nodded.

They fled, Terson following the road that was nothing more than two dirt tracks cutting through the trees and grass of the few fields and clearings they encountered. Everyone kept their eyes trained on the circling birds overhead. The trees kept the creatures from attacking as they had in the field, but Gregson was more concerned with the rest of the Horde. The creatures must have warned the dark army where they were, but would they act? Would the refugees reach the base of the Northward Ridge in time for him to force the group to scatter before the Horde arrived?

As they descended the long slope to the west, then broke through the last of the heavy cover of the forest, he realized with a sickening wave of despair that it didn't matter. The Horde's supplies and their reserve forces—the forces he'd searched for on the ridge above—filled the hills between the west end of the ridge and the main battlefield.

There wouldn't be time for them to scatter. The refugees' time was up.

A hundred Alvritshai on horses were waiting. As the refugees emerged from the trees and were spotted, Gregson seized hold of their only hope of survival: chaos.

"Abandon everything!" he roared, even as the Alvritshai kicked their horses into motion. "Scatter and race for Temeritt!"

Everyone but the archers panicked at the sight of the Alvritshai bearing down on them, tossing whatever they clutched aside as they scattered toward the southwest, half trying to skirt the Horde's encampment toward the Legion beyond, the others racing back into the forest behind. The archers set arrow to string and fired, not stopping as the riders charged. Three Alvritshai fell in the first volley, two more a moment later, and then the Alvritshai drew their swords and ran the archers down where they stood. Two of the men dodged at the last moment, flinging themselves aside, but the Alvritshai ignored them, breaking formation to attack those who'd fled.

Not waiting to see what happened, Gregson began to run, drawing his sword in one smooth motion. At his side, Jayson shouted, "Corim!" as loudly as he could and began to pull out ahead of Curtis and himself. Gregson couldn't pick out the young boy through the confusion, gave up almost instantly, and focused on reaching a cut between two hills. Most of the refugees were heading there.

All but one of the wagons had been abandoned, two children left screaming in the seats. The fifth jounced across rough ground as the woman in the seat thrashed the horses with the reins, urging them onward. Gregson watched in horrified fascination as the bed of the cart jumped, supplies and food bouncing and spilling out. It landed with a crash, one of the back wheels shattering into splinters, but the cart kept moving, slowing as its bed tilted to one side. Three children clung to the woman in the seat, another two holding onto the cart's headboard. One of them screamed and pointed as a group of Alvritshai cut in ahead of Gregson, split into two groups, and closed in on either side of the cart, the nearest bringing his sword around in a sweeping arc.

The woman lurched to one side, the horses drawing the cart following suit, the cart careening to the right—

Directly into the path of the Alvritshai on that side.

An inhuman scream tore through the chaos as the cart and horses collided, Alvritshai mounts rearing, the cart tilting, throwing the woman, children, and all of the remaining supplies clear. The cart's horses tried to keep moving, but as the Alvritshai plowed into the cart, unable to stop themselves, the tongue dragged them down into a tangled mess of splintering wood, traces, horseflesh, and Alvritshai.

Gregson charged past a moment later, ignoring the screams from both animal and man coming from the wreck. More of the Alvritshai were scattered ahead, cutting down the refugees from behind, swords flashing in bloody arcs, men and women falling on all sides. The woman who'd driven the cart had fallen to the grass, body crumpled and unmoving, one of the children clinging to her and sobbing uncontrollably. Gregson scooped the girl up beneath his free arm as he reached them, saw Curtis doing the same with an even younger boy who stood alone and crying, and then he was moving again, breath burning in his lungs at the additional weight. He was shocked at how heavy the girl was, but shifted her awkward weight as he focused on the trees. If they could reach the trees, the Alvritshai would have a hard time following on horseback.

He'd forgotten about the flying creatures, until the shadow fell across the grass before him.

Heart quickening in his chest, he clutched the girl close and threw himself to the ground, rolling so that he'd hit with his shoulder. A talon scraped across his face and he hissed with pain; the creature shrieked in frustration and the winds from its wings buffeted him as it rose back into the sky. Not waiting, he lurched to his feet, felt blood slicking down his neck from the new wound on his jaw, the girl sobbing into his chest. He ran, noted that some of the refugees had reached the woods, Terson shoving them under the cover of the branches and yelling at them to keep running, the remains of the Legion doing the same. The Alvritshai on horseback veered off from their attack, circling around to catch those that were coming up from behind.

There were too many of them, enough to form a line blocking Gregson and the rest from reaching the trees. He, Curtis, Jayson, and the others weren't going to make it.

But Gregson didn't slow. Their only chance was to plow through.

He pulled the girl closer, holding her so tightly she began to struggle. A few of the men and women left on the field faltered, slowing, but the rest continued forward. Those with swords drawn raised them and roared defiantly.

Gregson locked gazes with the Alvritshai directly before him, took note of the strangely angular face, the too-pale skin, the deep-seated arrogance in the eyes. Those eyes narrowed with hatred as he nudged his horse a step forward, sword held ready. Gregson drew a breath and bellowed wordlessly, the Alvritshai's mouth twitching into a smile—

And then, from behind, a volley of arrows shot over Gregson's head and slammed into the line of Alvritshai, taking Gregson's in the eye and snapping his head back. All along the line, Alvritshai tumbled from saddles, their mounts snorting and sidestepping. Gregson swung his blade as he dodged the Alvritshai's unsettled horses, felt the sword cut into flesh, then plowed past. He sprinted the last few feet to the trees, passed beneath their branches and into the coolness on the far side before slowing. He caught sight of Terson to the left, veered toward him as his second stared grimly out over the field behind. The call of a horn split the air as he reached him and turned.

Behind, on the far side of the field, at the edge of the forest from which they'd come, at least two garrisons of Legion archers stood, arrows trained on the remains of the Alvritshai who'd attacked them as well as the encampment a short distance away. At least half of the heads of the arrows had been dipped in pitch and set afire.

Without a sound, the arrows were released, arcing up and over into the Horde's supply wagons. The rest were released into the charging Alvritshai, bodies falling, enough that the group veered off toward their own encampment and the rest of the reserve forces scrambling under the attack.

"What's happening?" Curtis asked, coming up on Gregson's left. He still held the boy in his arms. The rest of the Legion who had survived the flight across the field were gathering behind him.

"It appears that the Legion is attacking the Horde's supply wagons."

"So they weren't here to help us?"

Gregson turned to face Terson after another volley of arrows was released. "No. We were lucky."

"What do we do?" one of the civilians asked uncertainly. "Do we join them?"

Gregson shook his head. Weariness had settled onto his shoulders, the girl in his arms suddenly too heavy. He wanted to set her down, wanted to simply sit down himself, lean back against a tree and let the tensions of the past few weeks drain from him.

But they weren't done yet.

He sighed. "Gather up whoever you can find in the immediate area. We need to make it to the Legion's main line. This isn't our battle."

He needed to find one of his superiors, a lieutenant commander or a commander, perhaps even a lord. GreatLord Kobel needed to know what had happened to Cobble Kill, Patron's Merge, and the surrounding area.

If he didn't know already.

20

THAEDOREN SET THE MISSIVE Lord Aeren had delivered aside and, without looking toward the lord, stood and moved away from the table beneath the shade of the portico and out to the edge of the Tamaell's personal gardens. He had elected to have Aeren brought here instead of to an audience chamber on the spur of the moment, but now he was glad they were confined to a single room.

His first reaction upon reading the letter sent by Fedaureon—Aeren's son and his own half brother—had been a gut-wrenching denial, followed by a painful constriction in his chest. But he knew his mother, knew Aeren would not have brought this information to his attention unless there was substantial evidence that what they had discovered was true. But the implications, not only to the Evant, but to him personally....

The hollow that had carved out a niche in his stomach began to fill with anger. Orraen and Peloroun, in collusion. Peloroun was not a surprise; he had always had ambition, even during Thaedoren's father's reign, but Orraen? He had attempted to raise his House within the Evant since the death of his father, but he was young and unskilled, his manipulations of the other lords inept. Which might explain why he would seek out someone stronger, someone more subtle, such as Peloroun. But why would Peloroun deign to ally himself with Orraen?

Unless Orraen had learned subtlety. Perhaps he discounted him too easily. Or perhaps Orraen was being led by someone else. He didn't think Peloroun would spare the time, his disdain for the younger Lords of the Evant obvious, but who else . . . ?

Something twisted inside him and for a moment he couldn't breathe. Acid burned at the back of his throat, and he hunched forward, trying to control the sudden pain in his chest.

"I would not have brought this to you if—"

"No." Thaedoren's voice cracked. He cleared his throat and turned, met Lord Aeren's gaze. "No, I needed to know this. You realize the ramifications? You realize that if Orraen is involved—"

"That it brings the Tamaea under suspicion as well, yes."

Thaedoren suppressed a shudder, hid his reaction by moving back to the table. "She may have nothing to do with it," he said as he reached for the decanter of wine and poured himself a glass. The vintage did little to smother the sour taste in his mouth. It didn't matter if Reanne was involved or not, the fact that she could be involved was enough to taint his thoughts. Every time he saw her now, he would wonder; every time she spoke he would ask whether the words came from her heart, or were for her House. He was already running through all of their past conversations, breaking them apart, searching for hidden intent.

"I've been a fool," he muttered.

"Because you succumbed to her interest? You knew as Tamaell that there were those who would seek you out because of your title. And as Tamaell, you knew that your bonding would be made more for political reasons than emotions."

"I should have realized there was more to it!" he snapped. His lungs felt thick with fluid. His eyes burned.

Aeren remained silent a moment. Then: "If she is involved, then she and Orraen have planned this for years. And I refuse to believe that Reanne is so heartless that she has no feelings for you, Thaedoren. I have seen you both at parties, at rituals in the Sanctuary, at your own bonding."

Thaedoren sucked in a sharp breath, recalling the bonding ceremony, the white cloth that had filled the gardens beneath the Winter Tree, the lanterns hung from the branches above, the scent of the gaezel roasting in the fire pits and the mad swirl of music. Reanne had glowed in the folds of her white gown, like the flames of Aielan brought to life. In a rare show of public emotion, he had reached out to touch her face, there before the assembled Lords and Ladies of the Evant, before the basin of Aielan's Flame that burned before them all. He had traced her jaw and stared into her eyes, and now, thinking back, he could see nothing in her gaze but joy.

"Perhaps," he said roughly. "But that doesn't matter now, does it?"

Aeren straightened where he sat. "Of course it does, Thaedoren."

He swallowed more wine, grimaced, and set the glass aside. "What are they up to? What can we do?"

"I don't know. I don't understand why they would need these resources, and as Fedaureon and Moiran point out, having them accumulate these resources isn't in itself damning. It's merely an indicator that perhaps they are aligned in some way. And that they are preparing."

"For what?"

"I can only imagine a grab for the Evant. We know that has been Peloroun's objective for decades. Even more so since his fall after the Escarpment."

Thaedoren frowned. What Aeren said made sense, and yet

it didn't feel right. Or at least, not complete. There was something beneath what Aeren suggested, something deeper that Aeren held back, and he thought he knew what it was.

"You think they're working with Lotaern."

Aeren stilled, then said warily, "There's nothing to suggest it."

Thaedoren scowled. "But that's what you think." He paused in thought, factoring in the Chosen, then shook his head. "I should never have made the Order equivalent to a House."

Aeren's lips thinned. "Why did you?"

"I thought it might end the conflict between you and Lotaern, or at least settle it once and for all. You wanted him out of the Evant, but it was clear that many of the lords—and a significant portion of the general population— felt the Order should have its say as well, especially with the resurgence of the sukrael. By solidifying the Order's presence in the Evant, I thought you would turn your energies elsewhere, into curbing him legally if nothing else."

"Was it Reanne's idea?" Aeren asked bluntly.

The accusation stabbed into Thaedoren's gut, hard, but he shook his head. "No. It was mine." At Aeren's look of doubt, he added with emphasis, "Solely mine."

"Regardless, Lotaern took it as an implicit blessing of his actions. You've seen him in the Evant. He's become aggressive, pursuing his own interests with abandon, and using Aielan and the existence of the Wraiths as his prod. If Peloroun and Orraen are working with him, he holds three out of nine votes, and you know a few of the other lords will follow their lead."

"Orraen and Peloroun don't always side with Lotaern."

"But if they do when something of significance comes to the floor? Do you realize that he has yet to remove any of his Flame from the temples in any of the House lands? He has ignored the edict—from the Evant and from you."

Thaedoren leaned forward onto the table, head bowed. His chest still ached over Reanne, but he needed to focus on the Evant, on salvaging the situation if at all possible. "We need to curb them in the Evant. And we need to call on our own allies to back us when necessary. Who can we count on? And how are we going to find a connection between Peloroun, Orraen, and Lotaern?"

Aeren shifted forward. "Lord Saetor has shown some promise recently. . . ."

Thaedoren nodded as he pushed back from the table and listened. He knew he could count on Aeren—and Fedaureon and his mother, of course—but his thoughts turned toward his brother, Daedelan, the White Fox, who'd arrived in the city late last night. He would have to be apprised of the situation.

He did not think Daedelan would like the fall of recent events in Caercaern. Not at all.

~

"Are they moving out yet?"

Eraeth shook his head from his perch on top of a sandy red outcropping of rock overlooking the chasm beyond. "No. It doesn't look like they'll be moving any time soon."

Colin glanced toward Siobhaen, who paced in the shadow cast by the cliffs that surrounded them. She scowled toward the distance, one hand on her cattan, the other tossing a stone in a nervous gesture.

When she saw Colin watching her, she asked hopefully, "Can we kill them?"

They'd entered the Thalloran Wastelands days before, the land breaking up, earth cracked so much they'd been forced to descend into the chasms between the tan-and-red rocks in order to continue, walking in shadows for most of the day, crumbling cliff faces to either side. It became immediately apparent that the horses were slowing them down, and that finding food and water for them would be problematic. After much discussion, it had been decided to leave the horses behind. They'd set them free on the outskirts of dwarren lands in the hopes that the dwarren scouts would reclaim them. Colin suspected the Wraith army would find them first.

They'd entered the chasms of the wasteland shortly after that. Colin had found his shoulders itching at the sense of confinement, tension creeping into his muscles at the claustrophobia. He couldn't help feeling that the rock on either side would give way and bury them all. Even though the walls concealed them well from the strange birdlike creatures, he found himself seeking the more open chasms and the wider blue sky overhead.

But while they were concealed from the creatures Eraeth had begun calling taeredacs, they *were* threatened by the small groups of the Haessari that were scattered throughout the labyrinthine crevices. Progress had slowed as they found themselves cutting back when a chosen path ended in two cliff faces merging or narrowing too much for them to pass. It had slowed even further after they'd encountered the first group of Snake People. That fight had been short, and Colin believed they'd only survived because both groups had been caught off guard. If the Haessari scouts had seen them coming, they could have ambushed them, killing them all with the small poison-tipped darts they all seemed to carry, or with their strange S-shaped swords.

At least, killing Eraeth and Siobhaen. Colin would have survived, although he wasn't certain what the poison would have done to him.

They'd been more wary after that, Colin scouting ahead with time slowed to determine the best path and making certain there were no surprises from the Haessari. After the first two days, he'd begun to feel the edge of exhaustion from halting time often, and in such short bursts. It was easier to use it in longer intervals, but the Snake People changed position too often for him to scout too far ahead.

Still, they'd eluded at least ten of the groups within the crevasses.

Until now.

He met Siobhaen's gaze. "No. I don't want the Wraiths to know that we're coming. If we kill too many of the Haessari scouts, they'll know, and they'll be ready."

Siobhaen frowned, then turned back to pacing with a low growl. "We've been waiting for nearly an hour," she muttered under her breath.

From his lookout, Eraeth asked, "Are you certain there's no other way around them? That we have to go through the chasm ahead?"

Colin sighed, felt the exhaustion on his shoulders, dragging him down. "I've been through every fissure, crevice, turn, and niche for an hour's walk in every direction—with time slowed—and none of them seem to bypass the open area ahead."

Eraeth grunted, then began crawling down from his perch. He dislodged some of the loose sand and rock, stones rattling against each other, and stilled, double-checking on the Haessari beyond, then continued more carefully.

"We may have to kill them then," Eraeth said, dusting himself off. "They're settling in. I think they're preparing to start a fire. There's a circle of stones and what looks like a fire pit. And with nightfall only a few hours away—"

"—they'll need the heat."

From his seat at the relatively flat base of the crevasse, Colin reached down and dug his fingers into the soil at his side and closed his eyes, sinking into the earth far enough that he could feel the pulse of the Lifeblood deep within. Since they'd reached the edge of dwarren lands, he'd been using the flows of the Lifeblood to guide them, its currents drawing them farther east and slightly north. Within the last day or so, he'd begun to sense the Source, its pull immense. It pulsed through the ground and he shuddered and tasted the leaf, loam, and snow of the Lifeblood in the back of his throat. With effort, he withdrew, lifting his hand from the earth at his feet. It trembled.

"We're close," he said, and even his voice was shaky, sounding like gravel. He coughed and drew his hand across his mouth. "I think the Source lies just beyond, within a day's walk, perhaps less."

Eraeth's face pinched with concern, but he said nothing. "This may be a regular outpost, manned at all times. If there is no other path through for some distance, it would make sense to keep a patrol here. They might never leave."

"Then we should kill them," Siobhaen said, "instead of wasting time sitting here talking about it. What if they send out scouts?"

Eraeth nodded grudgingly. "I think Siobhaen is right. We can't risk waiting for them to leave on their own."

"Good," Siobhaen muttered, drawing her sword soundlessly, a vicious smile twisting her lips. "I don't like these Snake People. They're unnatural."

Colin recalled how singularly brutal she'd been taking some of them in that first surprise encounter and grimaced. "I would still like to keep our presence a secret."

"Not possible any longer."

He stood and met their gazes. "There is a way. I'll slow time for both of you as well as me. We can slip past them." At their skeptical looks, he added, "I've done it before, with the Tamaea on the battlefields at the Escarpment."

"You were exhausted afterward," Eraeth said. "This would be two people—"

"I'm stronger and more practiced now."

Eraeth glowered. "—and do you really want to be weakened while facing off with the Wraiths?"

"I don't think we have a choice."

Eraeth and Siobhaen remained quiet for a long moment, long enough Colin held out his hands for them to take. Neither one of them moved.

"Do you really think the Wraiths don't know of your presence?" Eraeth asked, his voice level. "You sensed the Wraith army, were concerned they would sense you when you went down to scout it out. What makes you think they don't already know that you're coming?"

"I sensed the army because it was so large. It would be nearly impossible to miss. There are only three of us."

"But they still may have sensed you."

"I can't sense the Wraiths right now. I assume they can't sense me."

"But you don't know that for certain."

Colin glared in irritation, then dropped his hands. "No. I can't guarantee that."

"Then the risk is too high. I won't allow you to exhaust yourself for something this trivial. We'll take out the patrol. If that forewarns the Wraiths, then so be it."

He turned away and motioned toward Siobhaen. Colin thought about defying him, grasping both of their arms and slowing time regardless. But he wouldn't be able to get them to move and couldn't possibly drag them both beyond the patrol. So when Eraeth turned, he let his anger and frustration tinge his voice as he said, "I'll take them out."

"No. You're already weak from the scouting. Siobhaen and I can handle it."

He shot a look toward Siobhaen for confirmation and she nodded.

"When we reach the Source, I'll need you to do what I ask without question," Colin said.

Eraeth ignored him, speaking to Siobhaen. "There are six of them, three each."

"Two each," Colin said, reaching for his staff. "I can fight without the use of the Lifeblood."

"Then two each. Siobhaen, you take the left, I'll take the right. The cleft opens up into an oval-shaped gap, but they're stationed on the far side, near the mouth of the crevice. They've set their packs and supplies to one side. Leave your packs here. We'll come back and get them when we're done."

Colin gripped the handle of his staff, massaging the wood. "Don't risk yourselves if they try to use their darts. I don't know what the poison will do to me, but I doubt it will kill me."

"I don't plan on giving them time to do anything but draw their swords," Siobhaen said. She turned to Eraeth. "Ready?"

He grinned.

Then they were running, rounding the rock outcropping Eraeth had used to spy on the group and sprinting toward the Haessari. The dry heat of the wastelands burned in Colin's throat as he tried to control his breathing. None of them made a sound, Siobhaen and Eraeth pulling out slightly ahead of him, even as he pushed and allowed himself to grow younger, faster, more lithe and nimble. He fixed his attention on the six figures ahead, the Snake People sitting around a fire pit made of stone, slabs of rock laid out on all sides for them to sun on. One of them was crouched down, setting wood into the pit, although it hadn't been lit yet. One other stood off to one side, holding what looked like a brace of rabbits. Their conversation was sibilant, full of elongated vowel sounds, although Colin found it hard to hear much over the rush of blood in his ears and the thud of his own feet juddering through his body.

The one making the fire saw them first, when they were twenty paces away. A sharp warning hiss escaped him.

The others reacted instantly. Their movements were fast and fluid, but Colin had been expecting it after that first startling confrontation. He closed the distance before the one who'd hissed had completely drawn his sword, his staff cracking into the Snake's head with enough force to jar Colin's arm and set it tingling. Blood flew, but the Haessari crumpled to the ground and Colin leaped over him, putting himself in the middle of the group. He heard the clash of weapons, punctuated by short hisses and grunts, but he didn't spare a moment to look at either Eraeth or Siobhaen. With a sharp thrust, he punched his staff into the stomach of the nearest Snake, turned as the creature folded, and tried to swing toward the one on his right. But the first had grabbed hold of the wooden shaft. He ducked as the second swung his sword, bringing his staff up to block it, twisting even as he sent a surge of power down the staff into the first's hands. The Snake gasped and let go, even as the second growled and drew back for another strike. Colin snapped the staff upward and hit the first under the snout, the Snake reeling backward, then spun and caught the second's next cut in the staff's center.

The Haessari glared at him, his strange eyes narrowing. His forked tongue flicked out to taste the air, his reptilian skin shiny beneath the sunlight, the black-and-tan patterns strangely enthralling.

With a suddenness that startled Colin, the folds of skin along both sides of the Haessari's neck flared open, the undersides a pale yellow in color. The Snake's jaws snapped wide as his head snaked forward to strike, two flesh-colored fangs protruding, glistening with poison.

Colin reacted instinctively, jamming his staff up into the gaping mouth even as the strength of the strike shoved him backward. He tripped on one of the stones laid out before the fire pit and fell, the Snake landing heavily on top of him. His breath rushed from his lungs and he struggled to draw another as the Snake tried to rear back, the staff caught behind his retractable fangs. Scaly hands grabbed the shaft of the staff and Colin realized the Haessari must have lost his sword when they fell. As the Snake tried to roll them, his weight lifting off Colin's chest, Colin tucked his leg up into the space between them and shoved hard, letting his staff go.

The Snake fell away, still grappling with the staff, and Colin reached for the knife sheathed at his side. He rolled into a crouch at the Haessari's side and shoved the dagger up under the snout, inside the flared hood. The Snake's struggling ceased.

Spinning, Colin caught sight of the last Haessari as the Snake fell beneath Siobhaen's blade from behind, the Snake too focused on defending himself from Eraeth. None of the other Haessari had flared their hoods, their bodies lying scattered around the fire pit. Breath heaving, Colin stood as both Eraeth and Siobhaen wheeled to face the next threat, only relaxing as they took stock of the situation. Neither one was breathing as hard as he was.

"Check and make certain they're dead," Colin said.

"I'll do it."

Siobhaen began moving from body to body. Eraeth cleaned his sword on one of the bodies before sheathing it. Colin turned to retrieve his staff. A few new nicks marred the surface of the wood. He wiped the Haessari's saliva off of it with a piece of cloth ripped from the body, then began searching the dead.

Twenty minutes later, he rose, a vial of what appeared to be the Snake's poison in one hand, but nothing else of interest. Siobhaen stood over the brace of rabbits and made a disgusted noise.

"What is it?" Eraeth asked.

"They're not rabbits. They're rats. The Snake People eat rats. Big rats. I hate them even more now."

Eraeth shook his head and turned to Colin. "Anything of interest?"

"No."

"They appear to be just another patrol, although a more permanent one. The fire pit isn't new, and there's plenty of wood stored in a niche in the cliff face over there."

Colin grimaced. "Then we better get moving. There may be another patrol due here shortly."

They left the bodies, retrieved their satchels, and entered the mouth of the eastern crevice, slipping into the cooler shadows between the cliffs. Siobhaen scouted ahead, motioning them forward at intervals, but there were no branching chasms, and few alcoves or niches where someone could hide.

Then, abruptly, they could see sunlight ahead and the end of the chasm. Siobhaen approached cautiously, crouching down as she neared the edge. After a long moment, she stood and motioned them forward.

When he saw what lay beyond, Colin found he couldn't breathe.

Eraeth grew still and muttered, "Aielan's Light."

It was the remains of a city, only unlike any city Colin had ever seen and on a scale larger than any city within Alvritshai, human, or dwarren lands today, even the ancient ruins he'd seen in the northern wastes. The crumbled buildings stretched from the base of the small ledge the three stood upon as far as they could see in all directions, the red cliff face they stood against curving away to the north and south. The closest buildings had decayed the most and were mere piles of broken rock with only the barest impressions of edges were walls had once stood. But as Colin's gaze traveled farther east, taking in the intricate and methodical system of roads, he noticed that more and more of the buildings had survived intact. The buildings increased in size as well, the ruins rising in height even as the land began to undulate with low hills. Farther distant, muted and washed out by a thin haze, he could see other buildings more or less intact, or with upper stories collapsed inward.

"Look," Siobhaen said, pointing with one hand. "There used to be rivers here."

Colin followed her arm to where the land sloped gradually down to a dried-out river basin cutting between the buildings. A second river joined it, just barely visible on the horizon. The buildings near the junction were the tallest, although it was obvious they had been taller once before. Towers—like those in Terra'nor and the Ostraell, built by the Faelehgre ages past—had once soared into the heavens. Most had been snapped off, their true heights lost in whatever cataclysm had destroyed the city ages past. The heat haze made them surreal, almost illusory.

"The Source is here," Colin said. He didn't need to sink into the earth to know. Whoever had built the city had created the Source. Or at least found the reservoir of Lifeblood and used it somehow. "They would have built it near their center of power, near the center of the city."

Both of the Alvritshai turned toward the shattered towers.

"It looks to be a day distant, at least," Eraeth said.

"And we'll likely have to deal with the Snake People between here and there," Siobhaen added. Her hand clenched on her cattan.

Colin glanced up toward the sky. The sun was behind the cliffs to their backs, keeping them in shadow. But there wasn't much daylight left.

Without a word, he turned to where the ledge continued to their right, a path leading down the side of the cliff to the buildings below.

~

Horns blew, the clamor rising over the jarring clash of weapons and the screams of men dying. Gregson's hand was clenched on the pommel of his sword, his gut shrieking for him to draw the weapon and charge out toward the battle lines less than a hundred feet distant. The backs of the Legion defenses surged, men trying to shove forward toward the main line lost among the mass of bodies. Wounded were being dragged from the press, covered in blood, others missing arms or legs, some obviously on the verge of death, most bellowing in agony or sobbing, hands clutched to a side or head or an arm. A few were completely limp, feet gouging trails in the already trampled and muddy ground.

Not all of the men were wearing the armor of the Legion. Some were civilians like those Gregson had guarded on the flight south.

He glanced back at the bedraggled group that followed him, perhaps only thirty left, with another twenty-five or so Legion. The group had scattered at the end of the Northward Ridge, over half retreating back the way they'd come. He didn't know how they had fared. For those that had headed toward the Legion's lines, the sprint to the cover of the hills had been costly, the Alvritshai decimating the group. It would have been worse if the Legion archers hadn't been there to attack the Horde's supply wagons and draw them away from those who hadn't reached the tree line.

He turned back to the group that led them behind the army's line—the commander of the unit that had hit the supply wagons and two of his lieutenant commanders—the rest of their unit behind the refugees, herding them along. Gregson and Terson had gathered those closest and headed south, only to have one of the unit's archers catch up to them within an hour and order them southwest, toward the main battle. They'd followed the guide until joining up with his unit. The few remaining refugees had been relieved to be under the protection of the two hundred men, even though they were being escorted to where the fighting raged.

Gregson had been relieved as well, but even that couldn't

cut through the reality of what he'd seen on the Northward Ridge, before the attack of that flying creature. The Legion was outnumbered and outclassed by the ferocity of the creatures that fought alongside the Alvritshai. If it had been only the Alvritshai, they might have had a chance, but he couldn't see how they could hold out against the catlike creatures, the fliers, and the brute strength of the rock-skinned giants.

But that wasn't his concern. It was GreatLord Kobel's.

Unconsciously, he looked toward the south, toward Temeritt, seeking a glance of the Autumn Tree for solace, although he wasn't certain how much he could rely on the Tree any longer. The legends and hearthfire tales said that the Autumn Tree would protect them from the darkness, from the creatures of the shadows and the wraiths of the night. If the catlike creatures with the luminous eyes and the giants weren't creatures of the night, he'd hate to imagine what would be worse.

He couldn't see the Autumn Tree, though. They were still too distant.

The commander of the archers suddenly halted and turned, focusing on Gregson. "Lieutenant, I want you to leave your men here with the reserve forces for now, until we know what GreatLord Kobel wishes to do with them. I want you and your second to accompany me."

Gregson nearly commented that these weren't really his men, but the sharp crack of command in the man's voice made him choke on the words and straighten, as if he were once again at the academy in Temeritt, in training for the Legion. The commander reminded him of many of his teachers from those days—stocky, broad of shoulder, a more rounded face than typical, offset by dark hair heavy with gray and a sharp gaze. He estimated the man at nearly fifty, with the scars of life to prove he'd lived hard.

"Yes, sir." He closed his hand into a fist across his chest

in formal salute, then snapped a glance toward Terson. He was suddenly aware of how dirty and shabby his dress and armor were from the weeks of hard travel.

As the commander turned away, giving out more orders to his own unit, Gregson turned to Curtis and Ricks, noting that Jayson stood behind them, listening intently. "Keep the men together. And tell Ara to make certain the civilians stay in a group as well."

"Yes, sir."

Gregson noted with a sense of pride that the regular Legion had already assumed the military precision drilled into them at the academy.

"This way," the commander ordered, and then headed off toward the east again, only one of the lieutenant commanders continuing on with them.

As they slogged through the muddy field, the intensity of the battle to the left escalated. Gregson saw one of the giants plowing into the Legionnaires, flinging men left and right before grabbing one and pulling him limb from limb. Gregson's stomach heaved, even as someone cried, "Release!" and a garrison unleashed a torrent of arrows at the creature. It roared, rearing back with an arm in one hand, as yet more arrows found its eyes and mouth. Scraping at the shafts that protruded from its skin, the giant stumbled backward, listed, and fell. The Legion swarmed over the spot where it had disappeared with yells of triumph.

"They're beasts!" the commander shouted over the tumult. "But they fall eventually!"

They halted as a group of reserve charged toward the front, then cut in behind them. Gregson suddenly realized they were headed toward a tent set up far behind the line, the burnt orange banner with the black oak in silhouette for the Temeritt Province flapping in the winds above it.

Terson shot him a wide-eyed glance. It appeared they were going to meet with GreatLord Kobel himself.

The commander ducked down through the tent flap, four Legionnaires to either side letting them pass. When Gregson straightened inside, he found a group of ten men surrounding a wide table, leaning on it as they peered down at the jagged lines and scratchings of a map. Four of the men were Lords of the Province, the rest commanders of the Legion. The commander who'd led them there motioned them toward one side of the tent, then positioned himself at GreatLord Kobel's back, off to one side.

Kobel himself was surprisingly young, not yet forty, with brown hair silvered near the temples, brown eyes, and scars down the left side of his cheek near the mouth. The scars made him look vicious, although at the moment his face was lined with strain and tension and determination.

The GreatLord caught sight of the commander of the archers out of the corner of his eye and straightened. "Commander, report."

"GreatLord, the fifty-seventh archery unit I command attacked the supply train as ordered. We caught them by surprise and inflicted heavy casualties while receiving few ourselves, although this may have been due to the fact that the reserve set to guard the Horde's supplies was distracted by a group of refugees led by Lieutenant Gregson trying to reach our own lines."

Kobel's eyebrow rose. "The Horde?"

The commander swallowed once. "That is what the refugees in the group call the Alvritshai force."

One of the lords, a robust man whose girth stretched the seams of his clothing and whose armor must have felt tight, snorted. "It's fitting. I daresay the entire Legion will be calling them the Horde by tomorrow morning."

Kobel ignored him, turning his attention to Gregson. He felt the GreatLord's eyes boring into him, weighing and judging him, and he stifled the urge to brush off the dust from his clothing and armor.

"Lieutenant, you were the leader of the refugees?"

"Yes, sir."

"What garrison are you stationed with?"

"Cobble Kill, sir."

The lords leaned over the map, one pointing to what Gregson assumed was Cobble Kill, although he didn't step forward to verify it. He hadn't been asked to.

"That's far behind the enemy lines," the robust lord murmured, not without grudging respect. "Are you saying you brought a group of refugees from Cobble Kill to here ... and they survived?"

Something gripped Gregson by the throat, something hot, fluid, and achy. He choked the sensation down and managed to say, "Not all of us made it, sir. I believe thirty survived, and twenty-five Legion, out of nearly three hundred. Others may have survived as well, sir, I'm not certain. We scattered when the Horde attacked us."

Murmurs broke out among the men, although Kobel didn't turn. He continued to stare at Gregson and the lieutenant felt sweat break out in his armpits and along his back, itching in the scratches he'd received in Cobble Kill and burning in the new wound on his cheek.

When the conversation had quieted, Kobel said, "You realize that no one has found their way past the Alvritshai's army ... past the Horde," he amended with a thin smile, "since their line formed a week ago?"

"No, sir, I had not realized."

Kobel's head lowered. "Well, no one has. We have had no word of what has happened to the towns and villages north of our current position. The ... Horde had already formed a hard line east to west before word reached us of the attacks on the Province. We barely managed to gather enough of the Legion to meet them, and certainly not enough to hold them." He motioned Gregson forward, Terson a step behind, and then pointed toward a section of the map. "Our first encounter was here, nearly a hundred miles from our current position. Some of the Legion were still gathering and on their way, but the Horde was too immense to hold there with so few soldiers. We were pushed southward, steadily, until the rest of the Legion joined us here at the Northward Ridge. We managed to stop them here, were holding them back—"

"But then their own reinforcements arrived from the northeast," the lord grumbled.

Kobel's expression turned grim, lips pressed tight. "We were hoping that some of the Legion stationed to the north would arrive to split the Horde's attention to two fronts." He looked up at Gregson, the question clear in his eyes.

Gregson shook his head. "I don't think that's going to happen. The Horde decimated our region, from north of Cobble Kill down. We found nothing but the dead in the villages and towns, gathered everyone who'd escaped into our group as we came."

"Patron's Merge?" one of the other commanders asked.

"Destroyed. We passed it as it fell. Everyone fled to the south. If the survivors haven't arrived here, then they're either dead or hiding."

The only lord who'd spoken so far swore. "We can't hold here any longer. We have no defenses."

Kobel's brow creased. "What are our options?"

Everyone except Gregson, Terson, and Kobel leaned over to study the map, discussion breaking out among the commanders, suggestions being thrown out and dismissed or cut off mid-voice, tones sharp and curt. Kobel watched a moment, then turned to face Gregson.

As he did, Terson took a step forward, but halted, as if the action had been involuntary.

Kobel's eyebrow rose. "You have a question?" he asked Gregson's second.

Terson hesitated, then stiffened, back so straight Gregson expected to hear it snap. But his voice was steady.

"I was wondering what has happened to the Autumn Tree, sir. I thought it was supposed to protect us from these creatures. That's what I was always taught, sir."

The group hovering over the map fell silent, all eyes on Kobel.

The GreatLord appeared uncertain for a moment, doubt flashing briefly in his eyes before he steadied himself. One hand touched the top of the table, as if for support.

"The Autumn Tree protects us from the Wraiths and the Shadows and the creatures of the dark. That is what I was told as well. But it does not protect us from the Alvritshai."

"But, sir, what about the catlike creatures, or the giants, or even the fliers?"

Kobel's hand closed into a loose fist and he tapped the top of the table. For a moment, Gregson thought he wouldn't respond. He was the GreatLord of Temeritt Province after all, and Terson wasn't even a lieutenant. But finally he sighed. "That is the question, isn't it? There is no mention of any of these creatures in our own legends, but according to the scholars and the priests of Diermani in Temeritt, they are spoken of in the dwarren histories. I would have thought the Tree would protect us from them as well."

"Perhaps it did."

Kobel turned. "And why do you say that, Lord Akers?"

"Because a week ago we were only attacked by the Alvritshai. None of these creatures were part of the army we met north of here. They only arrived later. Perhaps the Tree kept them away, and only recently has it begun to fail."

"I've had the priests of the Holy Church of Diermani who've looked after the Tree since its seeding outside Temeritt check it since the arrival of the Horde. They claim that it hasn't failed, that it appears healthy. There are no signs of sickness, of disease."

"Then perhaps it has merely weakened."

Kobel drew breath to protest, but held it, then let it out in a slow exhale. "You may be correct. Regardless, it does not change the fact that the Horde is here, the creatures are here. The Tree has failed."

Lord Akers bowed his head in agreement.

"You mentioned the dwarren," Gregson said, and suddenly every eye was on him again. "Have there been any dwarren in the Horde?"

"No, there have not. Why do you ask?"

"Because we found a dwarren body in the first village that was attacked near Cobble Kill. I thought at first they were behind it, but I haven't seen any dwarren since."

The reaction from the rest of the group was instantaneous, someone growling, "Could the dwarren have betrayed us as well?" another demanding, "What of the Accord? Does it mean nothing to any of them?"

But then Kobel raised his hand and all of the speculation ceased. "The Alvritshai may have betrayed us, but I refuse to believe the dwarren have done the same. I have met with their representatives, have even traveled to their lands. Everything I have learned has led me to believe they are an honorable people."

He turned back to Gregson, troubled. "Was it only a single dwarren?"

"No. One of the villagers who survived said that there were many."

"How many?"

Gregson frowned and thought back. The time he'd spent listening to Jayson's story in Ara's inn seemed like a distant memory, something that had happened years ago, not merely a month. "Five or six."

"One of the trettarus," Lord Akers said.

"So I would assume." At Gregson's confused look, he added, "A trettarus is a dwarren war party. They send out groups of their Riders, with special weapons designed to affect these creatures, and hunt them down and kill them. But the trettarus have never entered the Province. The Accord forbids it."

"They've never had to," Lord Akers said. "The Trees have always kept the creatures to the east. But if they've entered our lands, against the Accord, then the Autumn Tree must be failing. It's the only reason I can see for them to violate the Accord. They've always been more interested in their gods than in politics."

"But they've violated Province lands!" one of the commanders protested.

Kobel halted him with a glare. "We have more important things to attend to right now."

Everyone fell silent, the sounds of the battle that raged a few thousand feet from the tent washing over them.

Lord Akers broke the silence. "But what of the dwarren? Can we count on them to come to our aid?"

"I sent word to them as soon as we knew of the Horde's attack, to warn them and ask for help. It's too soon to expect a reply, and after what Lieutenant Gregson has said, I doubt that our message has been received. We must assume that no help will be coming from dwarren lands."

Lord Akers motioned toward the map, everyone's attention shifting back to the lines and formations drawn there. "Then I'm afraid we really have only one option remaining. Retreat back to Temeritt. Seek safety behind its walls."

GreatLord Kobel leaned heavily onto the table, head bowed. No one dared speak. Gregson and Terson shifted awkwardly, aware they were witness to discussions that were normally kept within the highest ranks of the Legion, with only the final decisions passed down the chain of command. But Gregson knew enough about warfare from his own studies to realize what retreat to Temeritt and its walls meant.

A siege, one that he doubted Temeritt had prepared for.

There'd been no time for preparation. The Horde's attack had come too fast, with no warning.

But they could not hope to hold them here, on the empty hills beneath Northward Ridge.

A moment later, GreatLord Kobel looked up, and Gregson could see all of his own thoughts mirrored in Kobel's eyes.

"Then we retreat to Temeritt. May Diermani send us mercy and the walls hold."

~

"Lady Moiran?"

Moiran frowned down at the pages of parchment sorted and stacked neatly into distinct heaps, one for each of the Houses she suspected of being in league with Lotaern. She had gathered more evidence against Lord Orraen and Lord Saetor, but Lord Peloroun appeared to have halted his purchases of food and supplies. Either he'd finished his preparations, or Fedaureon was correct and his actions were legitimate.

She pressed her lips into a thin line. She didn't believe that for a moment. Her frustration had reached its peak that morning, when she had finally managed to find a link between Lord Orraen and the Order. She'd written the Lady of House Licaeta to beg her to sell some of the grain purchased earlier in the year, offering an outrageous price for such a small amount, and Vivaen's response had finally arrived. The letter was frivolous, as nearly all of Vivaen's missives were. Moiran could practically hear the woman's giddy laugh as she read it, speaking of trivialities before finally arriving at the heart of the letter: an apology. She couldn't possibly send Moiran any grain, even at such a generous price, because the excess grain had already been sent to the Sanctuary. She would have to petition the Chosen.

Moiran had cried out as she read it, had summoned a

servant to find Fedaureon, then been too impatient to wait, gathering up the papers she'd collected and searching him out herself. He'd been in his father's room along with Daevon and caitan Mattalaen, studying the layout of Rhyssal House lands, a huge map spread out across the desk before them.

She'd presented Vivaen's letter in triumph. "Here is our connection to the Order of Aielan. They're providing the Chosen with the supplies that they purchase under the guise of tithes to the Sanctuary."

Fedaureon had frowned down at the letter where it had come to rest covering part of the map, then glanced up in annoyance. "The caitan and I are busy, Mother. Can you show me this later? I've already informed Father of your earlier suspicions."

And he'd turned back to the map, brushing the letter aside as he leaned forward. Mattalaen had hesitated, clearly uncomfortable, but after a moment had joined her son. Daevon had glared at her son's back, lips pursed, then cast Moiran an apologetic look.

Moiran had been mortified, her shock transforming into anger after only a few short breaths. She'd carefully picked up Vivaen's letter and returned to her rooms, moving slowly even as she seethed inside. Aeren would have taken the time to listen to her. But more than that, Fedaureon had shown blatant disrespect for her in front of one who was not part of the immediate family. She wanted him to be independent, but she had never thought he would take that so far as to embarrass her in front of another member of the House.

She had sat in her chamber staring at her evidence, trying to decide what she should do.

Now she murmured beneath her breath, "He's young, Moiran. He didn't realize what he'd done. You can reprimand him later, if Daevon hasn't done so already." Although now that she thought about it, she should have said something there, in the room, with Mattalaen present. She pinched her nose between her eyes and sighed, shaking her head.

At the door, someone coughed discreetly and she glanced up, mildly shocked. She'd heard the servant arrive, but had forgotten she was there. Berating herself, she asked brusquely, "What is it, Sylvea?"

The servant stepped into the room, her motions tentative. "A few of the servants went down to services at the temple this morning, for dociern, and—"

Moiran's eyebrow rose as the servant trailed off. "And?"

A look of resignation snapped across Sylvea's face a moment before she bowed her head. "The member of the Order of the Flame was speaking for that service," she muttered morosely, "and he was saying things about ... about the lords, about how they had faltered in their faith, about how some of them had lost their way. He didn't mention names, but it was obvious he meant Lord Aeren, and I know it's not true, but ... but he was so convincing! And I could tell that those at the service were listening to him, grumbling under their breath or nodding, and when I asked, they said the member of the Flame has been speaking like this for over a week now, and I just thought you should know."

Sylvea glanced up at the end, eyes pleading, her words rushing forth in a single breath.

Moiran didn't move, her body rigid with tension. Inside, her stomach roiled and she tasted bile at the back of her throat. She swallowed it down, the effort painful, then glanced toward the window to judge the light.

"Lady Moiran?" Sylvea's voice was barely a whisper, fraught with worry.

It snapped Moiran into action.

"It's nearly terciern," she said, standing, the papers and

Fedaureon's indiscretion forgotten. "Fetch my shawl . . . no, go to your own quarters and bring me back one of your own shawls or a cloak, preferably something with a hood so that I can conceal myself. I assume that this priest from the Order of the Flame will be giving the afternoon service?"

Sylvea nodded. "I heard one of the others say that he's been speaking at nearly every service for the past week."

"Good. Meet me at the servants' gate with the cloak. We'll have to walk down to the town to allay suspicion. Move quickly. We haven't much time."

Sylvea darted out of the room, the sound of her soft footsteps receding down the hall as she sprinted for her rooms. Moiran made her way toward the front of the manse. She contemplated telling Fedaureon where she was headed, but dismissed the idea. He was still in Aeren's rooms with Mattalaen. She could handle this herself.

Ten minutes later she was standing outside the servants' gate, the late afternoon sunlight not quite warm enough to take the chill out of the breeze. She shivered, then caught sight of Sylvea running toward her across the courtyard, a dark shawl bundled in one hand. She'd had the presence of mind to attire herself similarly. She slowed as she neared Moiran, who took the proffered shawl and draped it over her head, pulling its sides close to conceal her face.

"I hope this will work," Sylvea fretted.

"This is fine, Sylvea."

The shawl was large enough to cover her head and fall across both her shoulders, concealing the embroidery near her neck if Moiran pulled its edges in close. None of the servants would have such fine material for clothing, but she hoped the dimness of the temple would hide the quality of her dress. She could do nothing about the shoes without losing more time.

Satisfied, she opened the servants' gate and motioned Sylvea to follow.

They wound down the road and off the rock promontory overlooking the lake into the streets of Artillien, passing a group of Phalanx who didn't give Moiran a second glance. Relaxing slightly, she and Sylvea entered the marketplace, the servant taking her arm and chattering away as if they were searching for specific goods even as she wound them toward the temple. Moiran remained quiet, responding when necessary, but her attention was focused on the temple, her anger already building. They had known that the Order of the Flame presented a danger. Aeren had thought that confronting Lotaern in the Evant would be enough, that the Chosen would remove his warrior acolytes as requested and that would be the end of it. But Moiran had partnered with Fedorem as Tamaell long enough to know that once someone was ensconced in their role, they were nearly impossible to move. The members of the Order of the Flame had integrated themselves too deeply into the local temples to be simply ordered home. She hadn't expected Lotaern to follow the Evant's edict without a fight.

Sylvea fell silent as soon as they left the marketplace and arrived at the temple doors. Two acolytes stood outside, ushering the last of the supplicants through the doors as the chimes overhead began to announce terciern, the afternoon ritual. Moiran crossed the threshold into the shadowed interior, an acolyte's hands on her back to guide her. She bowed her head and tugged the shawl farther down over her face as he closed the doors behind them, then followed Sylvea into the back of the chamber, behind a number of other supplicants.

Moiran was shocked at the amount of people in the temple. She'd attended rituals before, but had never seen so many in the afternoon session, when most would be working the fields or minding their own shops. Utiern and cotiern had always been the most popular rituals during the day, never terciern. The fact that there were so many here at this hour sent a shudder of unease through Moiran's gut.

The supplicants knelt abruptly, and Moiran followed suit, sinking to her knees at the back of the room. Near the front, four acolytes were arranged around the basin that formed the main altar, a fire already burning in the oil that filled it, the flames skirling toward the ceiling, black smoke thick on the air. The oil and smoke burned Moiran's nostrils and she tried to take shallow breaths as the four acolytes were joined by the two who had stood guard at the door. A chant began. It was the typical terciern mantra, thanking Aielan for the abundance of food, for the sun and rain to grow it, casting blessings on the workers who tilled the soil and the harvest afterward. Moiran murmured the chant without thought, her eyes scanning those gathered and the acolytes near the basin. All of the supplicants were commoners in Artillien, many of whom she'd done business with. Most had family members who worked at the manse. The acolytes were men and women she'd seen at this temple since she began attending after bonding with Aeren and becoming part of the Rhyssal House by blood.

She began to think that Sylvea had overreacted, when the chanting began to die down and the six acolytes bowed down toward the flames that represented Aielan and backed away.

As they retreated, the member of the Order of the Flame appeared, rounding the side of the basin slowly, head lowered and concealed by a cowl. For a moment, it appeared as if the acolytes were bowing down to him instead of to Aielan, and Moiran pressed her lips together in disapproval, knowing that the misdirection was intentional. He wore the same robes as the acolytes, but with additional raiment over the shoulders—a length of silken purple cloth with an embroidered white flame on one side, a cattan on the other.

When he reached the front of the basin, the red-gold

flames billowing out behind him, he paused, then reached up to his cowl. With a flourish, he flung the cloth back, revealing his face.

At the same time, the fire behind him blazed up with a startling whoosh, the flames changing from red-gold to white.

Those assembled gasped and Moiran's eyes narrowed.

She didn't think it was anything more than theatrics, but she had to admit it had an impact. Even Sylvea turned to her with wide eyes, quickly ducking her head as if chastised when Moiran merely shook her head.

"Aielan welcomes you," the member of the Flame intoned. "She makes Her presence known in the flames of the altar, and in the embers of your heart. Feel Her presence and know that She is with you, always."

Those around Moiran whispered small prayers to themselves, a few grasping flame pendants that hung around their necks, the man beside her raising it to his lips and forehead. The acolytes who had backed away from the fire began to circulate among those assembled, touching bowed heads in blessing. A few pressed offerings into the acolytes' hands as they passed—coins, or small bundles of grain, or notes on parchment to be tossed into the flames of the basin.

"You come here seeking solace, seeking Aielan's blessing," the member of the Flame continued, "and for that we are grateful. But there are others in Artillien who are not as faithful as you, who have strayed from Aielan's path, who have lost sight of Aielan's flame and have been led or have wandered astray. Those Alvritshai should be pitied, for it is only under Aielan's guidance that we shall be shown the true path and the way back home. It is only with Her protection that we will reclaim the lands that we once ruled and bring ourselves out from beneath this banishment and back beneath Her benevolence.

"And is it not obvious that we have fallen from Her grace? Look at what has become of us. We have been forced to retreat from our own lands, the world becoming cold and bitter toward us. Even as we attempt to build new lives in these lands, we find ourselves plagued with disaster. We have dealt with death since we arrived, with famine as we attempted to work the earth of these new lands, with attacks from races we have never encountered before. As we strive to create peace, even more horrors are unleashed among us. We have seen the return of the sukrael to the world! Their legions attacked our lands as their presence spread, enabled by the human Wraith!"

"But what of the Winter Tree?" someone shouted from those kneeling before the basin. "What of Shaeveran?"

The member of the Flame scowled, began to pace before the basin, the white flames a vibrant backdrop. "What of him? He is shadowed himself. Has he not been touched by the sukrael? Does he not bear their mark?"

"But he brought us the Winter Tree," a woman murmured.

"Yes, he did, and I ask you, what has it gained us? A reprieve, nothing more. It is a false gift, one meant to lull us into a sense of safety, of complacency. He has brought us the Winter Tree so that we will trust him, but it is a lie, a betrayal!"

Cries of denial rose, and Moiran nodded her approval. Not all of the Alvritshai of Rhyssal House were so easily swayed.

But the member of the Flame merely paused and smiled. "Oh, it is a lie," he said. "The Chosen has discovered the truth. He has looked into the heart of the Tree and he has discovered that it is failing."

He said the words quietly, but the resultant gasp from those gathered took Moiran's breath away.

"It is failing, and at a time of great peril! The armies of the human Wraith are on the move even as we speak. They are heading toward our lands with the intention of killing us all. And I ask, is it coincidence that the Winter Tree is failing now? Is it mere happenstance that the Tree that was planted to protect us would begin to fall at the moment when we need it most? I say no! I say it was planned all along, that Shaeveran—touched by the sukrael, tainted by their shadow—*intended* for the Tree to fail. He has deceived us! He gave us the Tree to convince us that his heart was true, when his real purpose was to give the sukrael and the human Wraith time to prepare, time to build up their strength and their armies.

"And he has succeeded. He has succeeded in more ways than one. Not content to deceive the Alvritshai people as a whole, he has spread his taint among the Lords of the Evant, among the nobility, as high as the Tamaell himself. Look to your own lord here in the Rhyssal House. He once was one of the faithful, his loyalty pledged to Aielan Herself when he became an acolyte of the Order. Look how he has fallen! He has been seduced by Shaeveran himself into wandering from Aielan's path, stolen from the Order and set—unwittingly—on the sukrael's path!"

Moiran hissed through clenched teeth, nearly rose in protest. Only Sylvea's hand on her arm stilled her, kept her kneeling. Her only consolation was the fierce denial of a few of those kneeling beside her, some shaking their heads.

"You don't believe me," the member of the Flame said, and his voice was laden with pain. "Why should you? He is your lord. You are pledged to the Rhyssal House, and he has protected you since his ascension. He fought for you on the battlefields at the Escarpment. His family has shed its blood for you. I do not blame you for your loyalty, but do not pledge it blindly. Your lord has been deceived. The Winter Tree is a false protection, yes, but the Chosen has been gifted with a weapon and a power from Aielan Herself, one that will shift the balance of the coming war from the hands of the human Wraith and the sukrael, from Shaeveran and his tainted blood, into that of the Alvritshai. The Chosen holds the weapon in Caercaern even now.

"But Shaeveran knows of its existence. He has used his influence over your lord to try to gain possession of it. Lord Aeren even attempted to retrieve the weapon for Shaeveran through the Lords of the Evant, but failed. That is how far your lord has fallen."

Moiran felt nauseous as she glanced around the room, as she noted the faces of the commoners. Some were twisted with doubt, as if they could not bring themselves to believe the acolyte's words, and yet he was an acolyte, pledged to Aielan. A few were openly angry, brows furrowed.

She turned a hostile stare on the member of the Flame and rose from her kneeling position in disgust. Sylvea hastily stood beside her.

"I've heard enough," she whispered vehemently beneath her breath, turning from the assemblage toward the door.

"Can we save him?" Lotaern's warrior acolyte said from behind them. "Can we save Lord Aeren of the Rhyssal House? I do not know. I do not think so." His voice was laced with regret. Moiran had reached the outer doors, paused with her hand against the polished grain of the wood, listening, but she did not turn. Sylvea fidgeted beside her. "Do not count on your lord when the human Wraith and Shaeveran's army arrives in our lands. He may have traveled too far from Aielan's path."

Moiran snorted and shoved against the door, blinking at the blinding sunlight after the dimness of the room even as she stumbled out into the fresh air. She could not stand the scent of the oil and smoke any longer, could not breathe the stifling air or suffer the words of the warrior acolyte. Rage boiling through her, she walked down the steps of the temple and onto the road leading back toward the manse, moving too fast, Sylvea trotting to keep up.

"He should never have been allowed to remain on Rhyssal House lands," Moiran spat.

"What do you intend to do?" Sylvea gasped.

What could she do? She had no power to order the Rhyssal House Phalanx down to the temple to seize the acolytes or the Order of the Flame. Not even Fedaureon could order that. The temple was considered part of the Order, the ground itself now part of the equivalent of another House. It was an invasion of the Rhyssal House lands, and yet it had been sanctioned by the Evant. Any action against the temple would be declared an action against another House, practically a declaration of war.

But wasn't this war? Weren't the words the temple and the Order were spreading a declaration of war against Aeren and the Rhyssal House?

She grunted and shook her head. That wasn't for her to decide. That was for Aeren to decide.

"Lord Aeren must be informed," she said sharply.

And as long as she was writing Aeren to warn him of the Order's betrayal, she would tell him of the Order's connection to the shifting of supplies in the Ilvaeren as well.

21

QUOTL DREW ON HIS PIPE, savoring the taste of the smoke as he sucked it into his lungs and held it before exhaling slowly into the night. The air was chill, the sky clear, the stars brittle overhead. A sickle moon hovered over the horizon, casting little light. He sat, legs crossed, near the edge of the southern ridge of the Break, the Shadow Moon Riders' encampment behind him. Below, beyond the bottom of the landslide, the fires of the Painted Sands and his own Thousand Spring Riders were bright sparks on the blackened desert. He couldn't see the network of ditches and barricades they'd built over the last few days in preparation for the defense of the Break, but he knew they were there.

He also knew they wouldn't hold.

He frowned as he heard footsteps behind him, turning as Azuka settled down beside him a few moments later. The younger shaman did not look at him, head tilted toward the stars above and then the fires below.

Annoyance tightened Quotl's chest. "I came here to be alone."

"No," Azuka countered. "You came because the Wraith army will arrive tonight. You are not the only one who can read the signs."

Quotl scowled, then took another draw from his pipe. "Even the clan chiefs can see the signs."

"True."

After a long moment of silence, the sounds of the dwarren encampment behind them quiet and removed, Azuka motioned toward the fires below and the distant northern ridge where Claw Lake camped. "Will we be able to hold them?"

Quotl sighed. "Only Ilacqua knows the outcome, and even he seems uncertain. I have given the Cochen and the other clan chiefs what advice I could, based on the signs. I'm certain the Archon has done the same."

"But will it work?"

Quotl turned, chewing on the end of his pipe. In the darkness, even sitting a few hands apart, he could barely see Azuka. He considered telling Azuka the truth, but like Tarramic, he didn't think Azuka wanted the truth. He wanted reassurance.

Quotl settled for the middle ground. "As you said, Azuka, you can read the signs as well as I."

Azuka grimaced.

Quotl turned away, drew on the pipe again, but winced and tapped the ashes from the bowl onto the rocky ground before him. The smoke had turned bitter.

A moment later, something flew past overhead, wings flapping like the folds of a tent belling in a breeze. Both he and Azuka shot startled looks skyward, caught a shape blotting out the stars above. They watched it as it cut westward swiftly, then banked, circled back around, and vanished to the east.

"They're coming," Azuka murmured.

Quotl pointed with his pipe. "They're already here."

Far out beyond the fires of the dwarren encampment below, firelight had begun to flicker in the darkness, so faint it could only be seen when Quotl shifted his eyes slightly to one side. But as they watched, the light grew and spread north and south. Below, drums suddenly sounded, announcing the army's arrival in case those on the ridge hadn't yet seen it, but also warning the Cochen and his forces to the south. The edge of the army advanced, until Quotl tensed and thought they didn't intend to stop, that they'd attack tonight, in the darkness. Behind, the Shadow Moon Riders stirred, many of them coming to the edge of the cliff to watch, their presence felt more than seen. Conversations sifted through the night, broken by grim laughter, the sound of hands slapping backs in encouragement, but the humor was forced.

Everyone fell silent when the torches of the Wraith army finally halted, the faint cry of a horn piercing the night, echoed from the north and south. Quotl relaxed.

"There are so many," Azuka said.

Quotl grunted, stuck his pipe into its leather holder slung around his neck, then stood, placing a steadying hand on Azuka's shoulder.

"Come. We must make certain the shamans are ready. The Wraith army will not wait. They will attack tomorrow."

~

"Quotl, wake up."

Quotl grunted, one hand reaching up to grasp Azuka's shoulder unconsciously as he jerked out of sleep. Azuka's eyes were wide with fear. "What is it? What's happened?"

Azuka shook his head. "It's dawn. The army—" He swallowed. "The Riders are gathering."

"Dawn?" Quotl bolted upright, gazed blearily about the tent, rubbing at a twinge of muscle in his back. He blinked at the faint light—

Then suddenly remembered where they were, what awaited them.

He scrambled to his feet, began gathering his scepter, his

satchel, tucking his pipe bag inside. He'd slept in his clothes. "Why didn't you wake me earlier?" he demanded harshly, searching for the smaller totems tucked into pockets and braided into his beard.

"You worked late into the night, preparing," Azuka snapped back. "I thought to give you as much rest as possible."

Quotl growled, surprised he'd been able to sleep at all. "I don't need sleep. I need to be prepared! And now—"

The hollow cadence of drums interrupted him. He listened intently, then swore and shoved past Azuka and out of the tent.

Three other shamans stood outside, all looking east, toward the backs of the dwarren army and the sound of the drums. All of the dwarren within sight were looking in that direction.

"I brought you your mount," Azuka said as he emerged from the tent behind him.

Quotl spun and saw five gaezels waiting to one side. Without a word, he sprinted toward his mount, paused a moment to pat the beast's flank, then swung himself up onto its back, careful of the horns. The animal danced beneath his weight, then pawed the ground, neck straining forward.

Not waiting for the others, Quotl allowed it the lead.

It dug in and leaped, Quotl hunching down as far as its horns would allow. Shouts rang out from behind. To either side, he saw others scrambling to mount, some already sprinting toward the two gathered clans, but most of the dwarren were already on the battlefield.

Quotl cursed himself. He must have slept through the initial call of the drums.

He slowed as he reached the back of the army, the Riders parting for him and the four shamans behind him. Within moments, they were at the front of the line.

Quotl brought his mount up short.

Across a stretch of dry scrub, tufts of stubborn grass, and the hastily constructed defenses they'd dug into the red rock debris of the eastern edge of the plains, the Wraith army waited, a black line of nearly indistinguishable figures against the hazy, yellow dawn. Winged birds wheeled overhead, nearly three dozen of them, too large to be any bird that Quotl knew of. His eyes narrowed, dropping to the group at the front of the army, picking out riders on horseback and bulkier forms, more massive than the mounts. Others moved across the desert rock, but they were too small in shape to see clearly.

He scanned the nearer dwarren line, found Tarramic a hundred stretches distant, standing out in front of the line with a smaller group beside him. Quotl pulled his gaezel's attention right and nudged the animal forward, arriving at a brisk trot.

"Where have you been?" Tarramic demanded. Panic edged his tone.

"Preparing," Quotl growled back. "The shamans of Thousand Springs are ready."

Tarramic looked as if he'd argue, then shot Corranu, the clan chief of Painted Sands, and his head shaman a quick glance. He glowered at Quotl. "What of those on the heights?"

"They know what to do. What of Silver Grass?"

"They were in position and waiting at last report."

"Then we are as ready as we will ever be."

Tarramic nodded. "And Ilacqua? The gods of the Four Winds?"

"The ground has been blessed by the Archon, the appeals made to the gods last night after the Wraith army arrived."

Tarramic turned to face the silhouette of the army in the distance. The sun had begun to rise over the horizon, a heat shimmer making the army indistinct. "May Ilacqua guard us all," he murmured.

Quotl looked toward Azuka, reaching into his satchel to pull out a small knife. Peyo, the head shaman of Painted Sands, did the same, kneeing his own mount closer to Quotl's.

"I see the hulking forms of the terren from this distance, and I assume there will be kell. The two usually come as a group. We can handle the stone-skinned and the diggers. But what of the dreun?" He jerked his head toward the creatures flying overhead.

Quotl kept his eyes on the ground. "We will have to rely on our archers for those." When Peyo shifted uncomfortably, he added, "They have the arrows from the forest. They know what to do."

"And if there are urannen among the army?"

"Pray we have enough arrows."

A sudden horn call split the air from the direction of the Wraith army. Tarramic instantly motioned toward the Rider beside him, who pulled a drum into his lap and pounded out a short rhythm. Behind, a much larger drum passed the message along to the rest of the army, and Quotl felt the tension on the air triple. The apprehension pushed against his skin, shimmering in his perceptions like heat waves, fraught with fear and smelling of sweat and dust and leather.

He suddenly, desperately, wanted the reassuring feel of his pipe in his hand, the tang of willow bark burning his throat and lungs.

Then, abruptly, the Wraith army began to move.

Tarramic barked an order, the drum carrying the cadence to the army behind, and then Tarramic and Corranu— the two clan chiefs—suddenly broke away, Tarramic riding south, Quotl and the rest of the Thousand Springs entourage following an instant later, Corranu and Painted Sands heading north. As they charged across the rocky soil, Quotl heard a battle roar from the clan behind him, rising higher and higher, pushing him and the others at the forefront forward. His heart hammered in his chest and air still chill from the night seared his lungs. At his side, Azuka suddenly raised his scepter and cried out to Ilacqua, to the Four Winds, his words lost in the thundering of the gaezels as the main portion of the army caught up with its clan chief.

They swept across the desert, dust rising behind them, swinging out and around the ditches and ridges and onto the flat beyond. The Wraith army rushed forward to meet them. To the north, Quotl could see Painted Sands mirroring their maneuver, their plume of dust rising to obscure the single colonnade of natural rock that had survived the landslide and stood up like a finger from the desert floor, the cliffs of the Break behind.

As they drew nearer, the riders on horseback became visible and Quotl's heart shuddered, his eyes widening in shock.

"Alvritshai!" Tarramic roared from the front of the line. "Alvritshai ride with the Wraiths! We have been betrayed!"

The resultant roar drowned out the sound of the drums, even as Quotl noted that among the Alvritshai riders were the terren and the kell, and outdistancing them all were the gruen, the sleek feline creatures racing for the dwarren front lines.

It didn't make sense. The Alvritshai with the creatures of the Turning? They'd fought the urannen and the Wraiths after the Accord had been signed, had suffered as much or more than the dwarren when the power of the Wells had been released. The dwarren had been able to retreat to their warrens to escape; the Alvritshai had not. And why would the Alvritshai attack from the east, from the wastelands?

But there was no time. No time to think, no time to plan, no time to pray.

The gruen hit the front dwarren, leaping up from the ground and attaching themselves to the Riders, and before the first screams could cut through the thundering hooves of the gaezels and the charging horses, the Alvritshai behind slammed into the dwarren line.

Quotl found himself in a crush of bodies, gaezels attempting to leap forward through the press. Within ten feet of his position, dwarren were roaring and hacking at the Alvritshai and the gruen. The taint of blood flooded the air, but Quotl was too distant to use his knife. Dwarren blades rose and fell and the eerie, high-pitched screams of dying gaezels shivered through Quotl's skin. Steel clashed, the Alvritshai mounts in the front rearing and kicking. Close by, one of the dwarren ducked beneath the flailing hooves and gutted one of the steeds, then was crushed with his gaezel under the falling horse.

Quotl began chanting, raising his scepter, and felt the dwarren around him respond, surging forward as those shamans nearby took up the chant.

Then, two Riders away, a pack of the gruen appeared, their black, hairless bodies swarming over a Rider and his mount in the space of a breath. The dwarren roared, hacked at the gruen bodies as they raked him with their claws and latched onto his arms and armor. The Rider's gaezel shrieked and panicked, eyes rolling white. It tried to leap away, but there was no room.

With a startlingly quick move, one of the gruen seized the dwarren by the throat with its teeth and ripped it away.

Before the body had begun to sag, one of the gruen emitted a harsh chittering sound—

And then they all launched themselves deeper into the dwarren lines.

One leaped straight for Quotl.

He cut off his chant in mid-verse and swung the scepter, catching the gruen in the side. It barked in pain, slamming into the back of the Rider beside him, but twisted and jumped to Quotl's mount, going for Quotl's face.

Quotl brought his knife up. The impact with the creature jarred his hand, but he felt the blade sink deep into its chest. It hissed and reached with its claws, already dying, but Quotl thrust it to the side with disdain.

A sense of calm enveloped him, one that he experienced with his meditations and spirit journeys. Except here there was no smoke to help disassociate himself from his body so he could join the spirit world. He drew in the energy of that calm anyway, began to slash at the gruen with a cold, methodical detachment. The creatures' black blood flew, coating the blade, his fingers, making his hand slick, but he didn't stop. He tightened his grip and brought his scepter to bear, the gaezel beneath him reacting to his movements, shifting left and right as if it sensed his needs, leaping forward into gaps or rearing back and turning. It snorted and pawed the ground, ducked its head and used its horns, impaling gruen and scoring jagged cuts along the Alvritshai horses if they pressed too close. Quotl focused on the gruen, left the Alvritshai to the Riders' blades, and found himself muttering chants from the histories as he struck, lines from the oldest records, from the time of the previous Turning, the words taking on the distinct accent of the Ancients, punctuated by a slice of his knife or the impact of his scepter. And the gruen appeared to be reacting, flinching away from the words with hisses or sharp cries.

As he fought, continuing the chant, something new intruded on the calm that enveloped him. It seeped up from the ground, enfolding him in a warmth that radiated from within, that suffused him, tingling in his fingers and pulsing with his heart, tasting of silt and heat-baked rock. All of the aches and pains of the ride and of age were absorbed by the warmth. He felt alive, one with the Lands. He could hear the rock beneath him, taste the wind against his skin, smell the sun, and feel the grasses growing around him, even as he fought the gruen. The power of Ilacqua and the Four Winds flowed through him. He thought at first the sensation came from the Archon, but he could feel the head shaman's power radiating from the south, where he and the Cochen waited for their signal. This power didn't come from the Archon, it came from the Lands.

And the Wraith army was a malignancy on the Lands, a repulsive growth that needed to be excised. He could sense the individual creatures of the Turning—the gruen, scrambling across the earth around him and swarming the dwarren on all sides; the dreun, circling and diving at the army beneath, leather wings raking the air; the terren, massive rocklike bodies cracking the stone beneath their feet as they trundled forward—and rage ran hot and fluid through his blood. He began to spit the words of the Ancients, his blows more vicious, more ferocious. He urged his gaezel toward the creatures nearby, seeking them out, crushing them beneath his scepter, severing them from the Lands with his knife. He could not sense the Alvritshai as he did the others, so he blocked them out, focused on the malignancy, on the disease, destroying it before it could infect the Lands.

Then, abruptly, his gaezel stepped back and he found himself in a pocket of calm, his breath heaving, his heart thundering through his body, throbbing with power. The front line lay ahead, at least thirty dwarren between him and the nearest part of the Wraith army. All of the gruen on his part of the line were dead, their lithe bodies trampled underfoot as the line surged back and forth. A few fellow dwarren and their gaezels riddled the ground on all sides as well, blood seeping into the red soil. He glanced up at the sky, was shocked to see that hours had passed. The dwarren line had been pushed back nearly to the makeshift defenses. They'd held out longer than he'd thought.

But when Quotl faced east, he saw that a significant por-

tion of the Wraith army hadn't joined the battle. At least a
third still waited, watching from a distance. These were not
mounted like the Alvritshai, and something about their
stance was odd. Like the Alvritshai, though, they did not
reek of wrongness. He could not sense them through the
earth or the air.

"Quotl!"

He turned as Azuka rode toward him at the back of the
fighting. The young shaman was covered in blood, a gash
along his forehead bleeding down into his beard. His scepter was slick with the black blood of the gruen.

When Azuka came close enough to see him clearly,
shock registered on his face and he drew back in uncertainty. "Quotl?"

"What is it?" Quotl asked. His own voice thrummed on
the air, vibrated through his body and caused his gaezel to
shift in place.

Azuka swallowed, as if to steady himself. "Peyo doesn't
think Corranu and Painted Sands can hold much longer."

Quotl glanced toward the northern line. It had given
more ground than Thousand Springs, the Riders nearly to
the ditches and mounds of earth. "Tell them to order the
retreat. I'll inform Tarramic."

Azuka spun his mount and sprinted toward the northern
line. Quotl watched a moment, feeling the gaezel's hooves
trembling through the soil, then turned to find Tarramic.

The dwarren clan chief was engaged in the midst of a
roiling battle with the Alvritshai. Even as he watched,
Tarramic—mouth twisted in an animalistic snarl—stabbed
his sword into a mounted Alvritshai's side, his other hand
grabbing the pale-skinned rider's armor and pulling him
down from his horse. Blood splattered Tarramic's face, but
as the horse the Alvritshai had ridden was cut down, more
Alvritshai slid forward to take their fallen comrade's
place.

He would never reach the clan chief in time. Not through the chaos of the fight.

He spun and found one of the younger Riders who carried a drum. Kneeing his mount forward, he ground to a halt in the rocky soil at the Rider's side and pointed with his blood-soaked staff at the edge of the fighting. "Call the retreat!" When the Rider flinched, eyes going wide at the sight of the head shaman, he barked, "Now!"

The Rider fumbled with the drum, brought it around and pounded out an unsteady rhythm. Quotl didn't wait, racing down the length of the army's back, roaring, "Retreat! Fall behind the defenses!" his voice throbbing with power, reverberating on the air. Those at the rear of the army turned startled glances back at him, hesitating as the drumbeat steadied and began reiterating the command. All along the line, the shamans took up their head shaman's call, scepters raised, and slowly Thousand Springs began to pull back. To the north, Quotl heard the drums of Painted Sands echoing the call, saw the Riders breaking away and fleeing northward around the ditches, others heading directly toward them, leaping their depths with their fleet gaezels. Quotl found himself surrounded, his own gaezel snorting and stamping the ground as the dwarren retreated, but he did not allow his mount its head. The Wraith army had begun hounding the retreat, the Alvritshai leaping forward to seize the advantage, cutting down dwarren as they turned, the front of the line fighting hard to hold them back while seeking an opportunity to flee. To the north, the mixed creatures of the Turning roared in triumph, the terren and gruen breaking formation as Painted Sands gave up completely and ran, a few dwarren stout of heart overwhelmed in instants. In the south, the last line of dwarren in Thousand Springs held more firmly, intent on giving their fellow dwarren the greatest chance possible of reaching the defenses before the Wraith army.

Including Clan Chief Tarramic.

Cursing, Quotl kicked his mount forward, passing through the last stragglers racing for the ditches. As he drew up behind Tarramic's position, he bellowed, "Tarramic! Retreat! Pull back now!"

He saw Tarramic's attention waver, knew that he had heard. But the clan chief roared and dove forward, attacking with a vengeance.

Growling in frustration, Quotl reached for the power that suffused him, sank into the earth beneath on instinct, seized the patterns he found there, and without thought *twisted*.

The earth beneath the Alvritshai forces shattered, flinty stone shards flying upward into the Wraith forces like daggers. Horses screamed and reared, throwing their riders to the ground as they kicked the air with their hooves. The dwarren who had engaged them a moment before shied back, a few caught in the edge of the destruction, the gaezels milling in confusion.

Quotl himself felt a moment of utter shock, slicing down through the power that pulsed through his body, followed by a wave of weariness, but there was no time to evaluate it, no time to think. He raised his scepter and pointed toward the defenses behind them. "Retreat, you gods-damned fools! Now, before they have time to recover!"

A few of the Alvritshai already were, rallying around those who had been at the back of the Alvritshai forces and had not been caught in the blast. Riderless horses bolted across the plains behind them, but there weren't enough dead to shift the tide of battle.

And there were still the reinforcements waiting beyond.

As soon as Tarramic broke and tore toward the ditches, his entourage covering his withdrawal, Quotl jerked his gaezel about and sprinted toward the dwarren regrouping behind. The ditches and mounds of dirt stretched across the earth in an arch over a thousand strides long, a swath of flat land before the landslide began sloping toward the plains above. He could see the archers of Claw Lake lining the cliffs to the north, Shadow Moon to the south. Any of the Wraith army that passed the ditches would be in range of the archers. The confrontation on the plains had only been a delaying tactic; it had never been meant to hold for long. The real defense would now begin.

He focused on the ditches a moment before his gaezel tensed and leaped the first, landing with a jarring thud on the far side, sprinting for a breath, two, then leaping over another. Quotl grunted on the last leap, steering his mount toward the bulk of the army, saw Tarramic doing the same to one side. They arrived at the same time.

"What shattered the ground?" Tarramic asked, an edge of fear in his voice.

"The will of Ilacqua," Quotl answered.

Tarramic spun toward him, the rest of his leading Riders milling around behind him. The clan chief's eyes narrowed, tense, then widened in awe. "What's happened to you, Quotl? You're . . ." He groped for a word, shook his head when he failed.

Quotl recalled Azuka's reaction, knew that something about him had changed, although he didn't know what. But he could hear it in his voice, knew that he had caused the earth to shatter.

"The gods are working through me," he said, trying to stem the flood of panic in his chest. He'd said it softly, but most of those near heard, spreading the word through the ranks in a nearly visible ripple. Quotl frowned in annoyance, catching Tarramic's gaze. "The defenses," he prodded.

Tarramic snapped out of his awe, although Quotl could still feel its brittle edge as the Riders watched him out of the corners of their eyes. "Prepare to defend the ditches. And call in the archers."

Half of the Riders dismounted and scrambled over the earthworks, the other half herding the gaezels a short distance away before converging on the open area between where the ditches ended and the cliffs of the Break rose to the south. Painted Sands had already begun digging in to the north. From behind, the small group of archers from both clans who had waited in reserve trotted forward and arrayed themselves behind the lines.

"Is it the Archon?" Tarramic asked. "Is he channeling Ilacqua's power through you?"

Quotl's skin prickled at the gruff awe in Tarramic's voice, but he paused, took a moment to test this newfound strength. He could sense no connection between the power flowing through him and his sense of the Archon to the south. "No, it is not coming from the Archon. It's coming from the Lands."

Tarramic merely frowned. In the distance, the Alvritshai and the rest of the Wraith army had broken off their attack on the retreating dwarren and reassembled, the reinforcements that waited behind moving forward. As the new forces merged with the rest, close enough to see now, Quotl realized why they had appeared so strange.

"Orannian," Tarramic spat.

Quotl grunted in agreement. The dwarren histories spoke of those with the skins of lizards. They had once been like the dwarren, but they had been changed by the cataclysmic Shattering that had destroyed the world and re-shaped it. How the Shattering had come about, and how it had changed the world, was unclear, those oldest of oral histories fragmentary and obscure, but the mentions of the orannian were not.

And yet, Quotl could not sense them as he could the rest of the creatures of the Turning.

He frowned, but tore his attention away from the gathering forces. Wounded were dragged from their gaezels and led away, although there were few. Most of those grievously hurt had been left behind on the broken rock now beyond their reach, and those who'd managed to escape to the ditches weren't wounded enough to be pulled from the ranks. Some of the shamans were passing among the Riders with vials from the Sacred Waters, the pink-tinged liquid healing the least of the wounds so they could continue fighting; others were passing out food.

Quotl felt sick at heart over those left behind, but there was nothing that could be done.

Azuka appeared with water and dry flatbread, handing it out among Tarramic's entourage. The clan chief drank, handing the skin to Quotl. "It will be a small reprieve," Tarramic said, voice somber. "The Wraith army already gathers."

Warning drums sounded. The dwarren shifted where they stood, restless, eyes on the enemy. Quotl raised his head to the sky, the midday sun high overhead and shimmering down with a relentless heat he could feel against his skin. The power that suffused him had abated, but he could still feel it, thrumming in his blood.

Alvritshai horns cut across the desert. Tarramic tensed. The Wraith army marched forward, but this time the dwarren did not rush out to meet them. Drums sounded again, dwarren readying in their trenches, those to north and south scrambling to mount.

Tarramic glanced toward Quotl. "Can you do what you did before again?"

"I don't even know how I did it the first time."

"The Archon is going to be furious."

Something seized in Quotl's chest. He suddenly regretted his announcement earlier that the gods were working through him. But what other explanation was there? He had never done anything like that before, had only felt the gods' presence during spirit walks and meditations in the keevas. This had been different. This time, that presence had filled him, and he had used it to kill the gruen, to shatter the earth.

He shuddered at the ramifications, both for the Archon and for himself, then calmed himself. The Archon hadn't retained his position this long without knowing how to manipulate the clan chiefs and the head shamans. He would undoubtedly claim the power had been channeled through him. Only Quotl could gainsay him, and Quotl had no aspirations for the Archon's position. He could let the Archon claim responsibility.

Yet even as he relaxed, a pang of uneasiness threaded through him, of doubt. This power *should* have manifested itself through the Archon, not through Quotl. What did it mean that it hadn't?

On the desert, the Wraith army suddenly broke into a run, the orannian outpacing the rest. As they approached, they spread out, the Alvritshai and other creatures coming up behind.

"They're going to hit on all fronts," Tarramic said.

To their right and slightly behind, a drum suddenly thrummed and two hundred archers snapped their bows to the sky, arrows already placed. The drum thudded again and bows creaked as they were drawn. The whirring release sounded like a thousand birds taking sudden flight. Quotl watched the arrows arc over the ditches, some of the winged dreun banking out of the way with harsh shrieks. They fell in a deadly hail, another swath of arrows already launched, but it didn't slow the Wraith army down at all. They struck on all three fronts almost simultaneously.

Deep within, Quotl felt the power he held swell as his heart quickened.

~

Siobhaen cursed and Colin spun to find her stumbling down the last of the massive ridge of shattered stone that encircled the center of the city. It was like a wave caused by a rock cast into a pool of water had petrified in place. Debris avalanched down with her, disturbed by her feet. Eraeth took a step toward her as she neared the bottom, but she caught herself against a boulder twice Colin's height, what had once been part of a building based on the detailed carving etched across one face.

She straightened and muttered, "I'm fine," annoyance making her voice taut. She wiped sweat from her face with one hand.

Colin glanced toward the midday sun, felt the grit of dust mingling with the sweat on his own face, then focused on the broken towers ahead.

They'd found shelter in one of the half-collapsed buildings in the outskirts of the city when darkness fell, using the walls to conceal their fire. The night had turned chill. During his watch, Colin had ascended to the precarious height of the wall—the roof had caved in uncountable years past—and searched the wide valley that cupped the ancient city for signs of life, for evidence of the Haessari and the Wraiths and their armies. Most of the city had been lost in the darkness, the ruined buildings not even shapes in the scant moonlight. But the center of the city had glowed with a pale, bluish light, the shattered towers silhouetted in the distance. Colin had felt the power of the Source from his perch, had felt himself drawn to it. It had throbbed in the ground beneath him, and he knew he sensed the lake far beneath the surface, the reservoir that gave the Source its power.

And it was still awakening, its power growing. He shuddered at its strength.

That power had held his attention for at least an hour. He'd studied it, tested it, tasted it, trying to determine how he would manipulate it when the time came. Part of its power was already in use. He could sense the flow that attacked the Seasonal Trees. He would have to block that, but it would not be enough. The Source needed to be balanced with the other Wells. It needed equilibrium.

And it needed protection from interference by the Wraiths.

When he'd finally learned what he could from a distance, he'd turned his attention back to the city. It had been still, dark, lifeless. But to the north, fire dotted the landscape. An entire array of light, flickering against the black backdrop of the night. It had taken him ten minutes to realize that the fires weren't spread out flat over a wide plain, as he'd first assumed, but were vertical.

Like the dwarren in the subterranean warrens, the Snake People lived in the cliffs surrounding the city. He'd wondered briefly why they hadn't taken over the ruins themselves. Some of the buildings were still mostly intact, especially near the outer edges of what he'd come to think of as the city proper. The destruction where they had camped had not been as prevalent as what they'd passed through at the city's edge. But as the city emerged into dawn's light, he'd suddenly realized that he wouldn't want to live in the city either. Even now, what had to be thousands of years after its fall, he could feel ghosts in the streets, in the buildings, as if an energy had been absorbed by the stone and was still seeping out. An energy that had nothing and everything to do with the Source.

He'd been concerned that he'd react to that energy as he had within the caverns of Gaurraenan's halls, but he hadn't felt time tugging at him as it had in those frigid chambers. He wasn't certain why. Except that the energy here felt ... dry, used up, and old. The stone within the mountains to the north had been vital, thick with a visceral sense of blood.

They'd headed toward the Source at first light, Colin pointing out the direction of the Haessari's city. They'd kept as many of the intact buildings between them and the cliff faces where the Haessari lived as possible, even though they hadn't encountered any of the Snake People in the city at all.

As soon as they descended from the strange ridge of stone debris, the nature of the destruction changed. The buildings they'd passed through before had collapsed, ceilings and walls buckling inward as time clawed and ate its way through the structures.

Not so here, Colin thought as Siobhaen dusted herself off and joined him and Eraeth at the edge of the inner city.

"It's as if all of the stone here simply . . . fractured," Eraeth said, waving a hand toward the debris field that spread out before them. "As if it splintered and the pieces were thrown aside."

Siobhaen knelt and picked up a shard of rock at her feet. She hissed as she touched an edge, blood welling against her fingertip. "It's sharp as a blade."

"The entire central city is fractured," Colin said, motioning toward the stumps of the towers. "Unlike the outer city, the towers were sheared off, their tops blown off by some central source."

"The Well?"

Colin shook his head. "I don't know. Perhaps. Whatever it was, it destroyed the city completely. And the Source appears to be at the center of the destruction."

Neither Alvritshai said anything, both scanning the distance with shaded eyes. Then Eraeth strode forward, down the debris-covered street that appeared to head toward the confluence of the two rivers and the tallest of the truncated towers.

A moment later, Colin and Siobhaen followed.

They wound through the streets, the construction of the buildings changing as they passed from section to section. A dark red stone was used in one area, replaced in another by basalt, then a dirty white with flecks of quartz that glinted in the sunlight. Even shattered, they could discern different styles. In one district, the sandstone had been carved into blocks, in another, mudbricks. As they neared the dry riverbed, the buildings appeared to have been formed from living rock itself, sculpted like clay, what remained smooth and seamless.

They reached the riverbank, rock walls hemming the ancient water in and thick stone supports for docks and bridges jutting up from the cracked and brittle riverbed beneath. Eraeth pointed to where one of the bridges remained mostly intact and they skirted the dry river's edge to reach it.

"We'll be exposed," Siobhaen said as they stared across its length. Portions of it had been sliced away in the fracturing of the inner city, chunks of thick stone lying in the riverbed below, but a path still existed all the way across to the city. The width of the bridge was immense, at least eight wagon-lengths from side to side.

Eraeth shrugged. "As exposed as we'd be crawling across the bottom of the river below. I don't see any way to approach that isn't exposed."

Siobhaen frowned. "We haven't even looked—"

"We have no choice," Colin interrupted. "We need to cross. It may as well be here. I'll go first, in case the bridge isn't stable." He knew he'd survive the fall; the Alvritshai wouldn't.

But the stone of the bridge held.

On the far side, they slid from the end of the bridge into what Colin guessed had once been parks, the open areas littered with the bases of statues and what might have been standing pools of water or fountains. Everything was dry, and nothing grew in the patches of dirt and sand. They passed beneath massive arches, into the shade of the towers, taller than even Colin had imagined. Awe claimed him as they walked through the curved and winding streets, staring up. The towers must have stood higher than those at Terra'nor, higher than even the Alvritshai ruins in the northern wastelands. He approached the base of one, brushed his hand along the strangely textured surface, frowning until he recognized the patterns. It appeared to be petrified bark, and as he stepped back and stared up the length of the building, picking out the gaping shadows of windows along its side, he realized that the entire building was shaped like the bole of a tree.

Turning, he scanned the nearest buildings, Eraeth and Siobhaen standing to one side, confused.

"The buildings weren't built," Colin said abruptly. "They were grown."

When the two Alvritshai's frowns deepened, he motioned toward the building behind him, then the others. "Look at it! This one is like the trunk of a tree, the wood solidified into stone now. And that one there is made of thousands and thousands of vines, entwined to form walls, ceilings, windows, and doors. Even the balconies are formed from leaves."

"And that one is like a stalk of grass," Siobhaen murmured.

All three of them spun, searching the towers with new eyes, but eventually Colin felt the pull of the Source again, now so close he could feel the tug of its current drawing him closer and closer to its center. Not strong enough yet that he couldn't resist it, but insistent. A sense of urgency pulled at him as well, and he wondered how the dwarren fared with the Wraith army in the west, how the Seasonal Trees fared against the onslaught of the Wraiths and the Source. He tried to shrug the concerns aside, as he'd done since they'd reached the Confluence and he'd found that the Trees were under attack, but he couldn't. He suddenly wished he had a way to communicate with the dwarren and the humans in the southern Provinces, even with the Alvritshai and

Aeren. But he couldn't. He was isolated, alone, and he had no way of knowing whether the Trees had already fallen or there was still hope.

In the end it didn't matter.

He turned from his scrutiny of the towers and focused on a break in their soaringing heights. He could feel the emptiness that lay there, an emptiness that was slowly being filled.

He needed to stop it, at whatever cost.

Shrugging the awe of the city to one side, he descended the wide circular steps that led to the entrance of the tower and headed toward that emptiness, toward the pull of the Source, letting it draw him to its center. Behind, he sensed Eraeth and Siobhaen following. They drew their cattans, the bows gifted them by the forest slung across their backs. Colin gripped his staff tighter, but he saw nothing moving, nothing waiting in the gaping windows above or the mouths of the doors below.

They reached the center of the towers and halted. They stood on the lip of an oval depression, the ground sunken, wide stairs leading down to a low, roofless building of the same shape. The inside of the building was swallowed in darkness and the slanted shadows of the towers. Its white stone sides were cracked like an egg. Chunks of shattered crystal lay across the entire depression. A faint bluish glow emanated from the top.

"The Source is inside," Colin murmured.

"How do you know?"

"Because I can feel it." He could hear it in the edge of his voice as well. It sounded heavier, huskier, the pull of the Lifeblood strong. He hadn't felt so close to losing control since he'd first left the Well nearly two hundred years before. Like then, his body trembled—with power, with urgency, with need. He could taste the Source, the mixture of loam and snow thick on his tongue. His hand tightened and flexed against the wood of his staff and he tried not to shudder.

Beside him, Siobhaen said, "It's strong. Even I can feel it. I sensed the Well in the northern wastes. But this . . . this I can *feel*, throbbing in my gut."

Eraeth frowned.

Below, Colin thought he caught a flicker of movement in one of the shadows. He stepped forward, taking the first step down toward one of the entrances, but Eraeth's hand on his shoulder halted him.

The Protector shook his head. "I'll go first, Siobhaen behind, you in the middle. We don't know what we'll find down there."

Colin shot a glance toward Siobhaen, her expression hard and unforgiving, angry that Eraeth had taken the lead, but in total agreement. Both of them had set aside the awe and immensity of the city as he had earlier. They were House Phalanx members now, guarding their lord.

Colin nodded grudgingly. "Very well."

They moved swiftly down the stairs, noted other entrances at regular intervals around the building as they did so. Eraeth kept ten paces ahead of Colin, motioning him back if he came too close. Within moments they were at the edge of the building. If there had been doors, they were nothing more than dust now. The entrance yawned open, darkness lay beyond. Eraeth signaled to Siobhaen, who nodded, sweeping their surroundings as Eraeth ducked into the building. Colin held his breath, listening intently, breathing in the dusty rock scent of the dead city, tasting the Source. He pushed down his sense of unease and urgency. His heart thudded. Sweat dripped down his face.

He gasped when Eraeth reappeared. The Protector motioned them inside.

Colin slid into the shadows, the air within much cooler. They passed through an empty corridor, small chunks of rock littering the ground where it had fallen from the cracks riddling the ceiling. They passed through dimly lit rooms, Eraeth moving silently ahead before waving them forward. The walls were mostly blank, the rooms empty, except for an occasional vivid flash of color from painted murals or the remnants of a shattered pedestal or column. Doorways were rectangular, walls smooth, ceilings arched and high.

Then Eraeth halted at a doorway wider than the others. After a long moment, he pulled Colin closer, both crouching down low.

The room beyond was vast, open to the sky, wide tiers like round steps leading down to a huge Well, at least twice the size of the one in Terra'nor. The bluish glow emanated from the Well, but the level of the water within was too low to be seen.

Colin scanned the far side of the Source. Entrances similar to the one they crouched near circled the Well. Huge chunks of crystal littered the floor; remnants of what Colin now realized must have been a crystal dome over the Well. Alcoves dotted the walls, whatever they had once held now gone. He saw no one within the space—no Wraiths, no Shadows, nothing.

The Source pulled at him, called to him.

"I need to see the Lifeblood," he whispered, more to himself than to Eraeth, and then he stood.

Eraeth grabbed his shirt and shoved him toward Siobhaen, who reached to hold him. Without thought, Colin seized time, felt the heady rush of the Lifeblood as he did so, felt its power surging through him, ready to slip from the two Alvritshai guardians to reach the Source, but with an effort that left him heaving he fought off the reaction. He knew by Siobhaen's widened eyes that he must have blurred, that his intent had been obvious, but he ignored her betrayed look and waved Eraeth out into the open chamber, gesture curt. He leaned against the wall as Eraeth turned, tried to control his breathing, his heart, and focused on the Protector.

Eraeth stepped toward the Well cautiously, sword ready, eyes searching constantly. He spun as he moved, checking all directions, slipping between the crystal shards and stone debris as he neared the lip of the Well. Colin's unease grew, along with the urgency, prickling along his skin. The Source hadn't been completely awakened, but it was close. He could sense it nearing its peak. The currents he had followed to reach it had begun to slacken. He needed to stop it now before the Source filled completely.

He needed to seal it away.

He pushed away from the wall, Siobhaen hissing disapproval as he stepped through the doorway, Eraeth already at the lip, a sheer drop to whatever lay below, no ridge of stone like at Terra'nor. The Protector had relaxed, brow creased in confusion as his sword lowered.

"I see no one," he said, "which makes no sense. The Wraiths should be here."

The unease crawling across Colin's shoulders intensified as he stepped out from the shelter of the doorway and wound his way toward Eraeth, an unease he suddenly recognized. He'd felt this way once before, recently, in the northern wastes.

He heard Siobhaen scrambling to keep up behind him.

"They are here," Colin said. "They would never leave the Source undefended. They know in order to affect the Lifeblood I need to be here, at the Source, to touch it. This is a trap. They've known we were coming for days." Nearing Eraeth, he suddenly raised his voice, shouting into the depths of the collapsed dome. "Haven't you, Walter?"

Both Eraeth and Siobhaen shifted into guarded stances, all three of them scanning the vastness of the space. His shout died, no sound replacing it except a hollow gust of wind blowing through vacant windows.

Broken a moment later by a low laugh.

Walter abruptly blurred into existence near the top of the steps, his gray-brown cloak settling around him as he halted. He regarded them silently, smiling, darkness swirling beneath the skin of his face.

"Yes, Colin, I have been waiting," he finally said. "We've all been waiting."

And then, along the entire breadth of the steps surrounding them, Shadows emerged into the faded sunlight.

22

"SEND WHATEVER CIVILIANS are still here back to the city," GreatLord Kobel ordered as soon as he and the rest of the lords and commanders stepped from the tent. Gregson came behind, ducking under the opening as the sounds of the battle slammed into him, Terson following. "We'll hold the line as long as we can to give them a chance to reach Temeritt safely."

"What about our own forces? I don't think the Horde is going to let us retreat peacefully."

Kobel didn't turn to face Lord Akers. "We'll send as many of the Legion back as we can while the rest hold the Horde."

Akers looked skeptical.

"It's the best we can do," Kobel said, then reached for a helm held by a waiting recruit.

A short distance away, a covey of horses waited for the GreatLord and his entourage. The rest of the commanders and lords began preparing for battle, tugging on armor, mailed gloves, helmets. Gregson and Terson were forgotten, until Lord Akers noticed them waiting.

He sidled his horse close and leaned down. "Find your men and head for Temeritt!"

Gregson saluted, clenched fist across his chest, then began searching the confusion at the back of the army. "We need to find our group," he said to Terson, his second motioning toward the western edge. As they cut through the Legion's rear forces, horns blared all along the line, signaling the retreat. Everyone hesitated, and then chaos erupted, Gregson and Terson forced to dodge men as they began breaking away from the front line.

Gregson caught sight of Curtis and the rest of the Legion who had made it off the Northward Ridge with them, all surrounding the thirty civilians, including the miller Jayson, Corim, and Ara. They were huddled together, staring at the army as it heaved around them.

Additional horns sounded, more desperate than before. Gregson jogged up to Curtis and the others. "They're calling a retreat. We need to get everyone moving toward Temeritt. We don't have much time."

Another horn, this one faltering mid-blast, then cutting short.

"That wasn't a call for retreat," Terson said grimly.

"Part of the line's collapsing." Gregson spun on his own Legion, on the civilians that were rising far too slowly at the soldiers' urging. Suddenly, his patience snapped; he wasn't going to lose control as he had on the ridge. "Terson, get those damn civilians moving now! The rest of you, everyone with weapons, form up! Protect the retreat!"

Gregson shoved them into position, the men moving too slowly. He could feel the tension of the battle at his back, could feel it escalating as the Horde picked up on the Legion's intent. Terson bellowed orders and with Ara's help the few civilians remaining began staggering toward the south, additional groups of Legion breaking away from the lines and streaming toward the direction of Temeritt on every side. Supply wagons were being turned, horses fidgeting and protesting the sudden frantic activity. Curtis shouted,

"Gregson," and the lieutenant turned to see his twenty-odd Legionnaires trotting after the civilian group. He broke away from the rear of the front lines, shouting, "Keep moving!" as he motioned with one hand.

They had made the crest of the first hill, had passed beneath the limbs of the first copse of trees, half a day's ride from Temeritt, when panicked horn cries shattered the evening light.

Gregson spun, gaze sweeping across the battlefield behind, the thin line of Legion left to hold the Horde back faltering.

"It's collapsing," Gregson whispered.

He watched in horror as the minimal defense buckled in three places, the line between wavering, men roaring, horns crying, horses screaming, the air humming with rage, with defiance, with desperation—

And then the line gave.

Like a dam breaking, the Horde rolled up and over the Legion, spilling from the broken line in a black flood. Across the breadth of the battlefield, the beginnings of the orderly retreat collapsed. The Horde fell on the stragglers and the slower wagons and carts of supplies. Gregson's stomach clenched as the screams rose. The eastern flank of the Legion held, but gave ground. The western flank was shoved up against the Northward Ridge and quickly surrounded. Gregson's hand fell to his sword even as he took a step in their direction, but he ground to a halt, forcing himself to turn away from the sickening sight as the trapped Legionnaires were cut down. Swallowing against the bile in the back of his throat, the skin at the corners of his eyes tight, he found his own small group watching him intently.

"We can't help them," he said, voice rough, like gravel. "We'd only die trying. We have to get as many people as we can to Temeritt while the Horde's distracted."

He hated himself for saying it, saw a few of the men

staring starkly toward the ridge, hands tensed on sword hilts. He didn't wait for them to protest, stepping forward, hardening his voice, his expression. "Go! Move, move, move!" He grabbed Leont's shoulder and pushed him toward the south, heard Terson growl, "You heard the lieutenant!" Jayson did the same with the remaining refugees, he and Ara urging the rest onward, deeper into the trees.

Convinced they were moving again, Gregson glanced back to see the Horde scattering on the battlefield behind, the center line of resistance completely gone. A significant portion had turned to focus on the two remaining flanks, but the rest were charging up the hillside after those fleeing toward Temeritt, no order or organization to their attack. The retreat had become a rout.

He couldn't see GreatLord Kobel's banner anywhere.

Fighting back a wave of despair, he turned and ran after his own men.

They fled, ducking through trees and sprinting across fields. The evening light began to fade and from the falling darkness they could hear ragged screams and the sounds of men and creatures crashing through the forest to either side. At one point, three riderless horses charged past, their saddles streaked with blood, the animals' eyes wide with terror. When Terson and a few of the men tried to cut them off, to capture them, they veered away and vanished into the harsh silver moonlight. Moments later, they burst into a clearing where a small group of six Legionnaires were being harried by a pack of the catlike creatures. Drawing his sword, Gregson fell on the creatures with a vengeance, all of the fear and desperation he had experienced over the last few weeks coming to the fore. Sweat stung in his eyes as he lunged, growling without words, his sword sinking into flesh. His own Legion joined him, rallying to his side and killing the last of the hissing monstrosities in moments. Gregson staggered back from the slaughter, ran a hand across his forehead, felt stinging dark blood against his face, but Terson was already herding the group onward. Curtis threw one of the rescued Legionnaire's arms over his shoulder, the man covered with slashes across his face, arms, and legs. The other Legionnaires were in better condition. One of them was one of the Legion's horn bearers.

Isolated battles raged on all sides, some half-seen in the darkness, others only heard. Firelight flared in the distance. A cottage burned, its flames harsh, strange silhouettes circling the conflagration. They swerved wide around the building, saw other fires raging farther away, dotting the hillsides like orange stars. A half hour later, they encountered a group of civilians guarded by a dozen young Legionnaires barely keeping their own terror under control. They handed over their charges to Gregson in relief, following his snapped orders as if they were on the practice field, not in the midst of a rout.

The pace slowed, the civilians weary, the wounded dragging them down. Gregson mentally cursed, searching for signs of Temeritt ahead. They couldn't last much longer, but they couldn't rest either. There were too many unknown forces in the hills. He and the Legion drove the refugees on relentlessly, pausing only once at the edge of a creek, men and the few women coughing and groaning as they collapsed or sank to their knees to drink. Even though he was exhausted, Gregson kept himself moving, walking among the group, men giving him weary smiles as he passed. He knew if he stopped he might never start moving again.

Thirty minutes later they were dragging everyone back to their feet and pushing onward.

They reached the rise north of Temeritt at dawn, the burgeoning light shocking Gregson to his bones. He could not believe they had survived the night, could not believe that their group had nearly doubled in size—Legion outnumbering the civilians now—could not believe that the Horde had not caught up to them. The only explanation that made sense was that the Horde was razing the lands as they came, slowing them down.

As the sun peeked above the horizon to the east, the wide grassland below came into relief.

Surrounded by four sets of thick stone walls, Temeritt stood on the heights of a giant upsurge of ground in the middle of the grassland, the palace at the top of its steepest slope, the inner walls surrounding it, the barracks, a massive stone church, and the original defensive towers. They soared over the rest of the city, the largest that Gregson had ever seen. Three more walls encircled the city in massive tiers, buildings crammed into the different levels so tight they appeared stacked one atop the other. In the golden sunlight, it appeared radiant, the city consuming the entire hill and spilling down onto the plains below like a giant ink-stain, the majority of it to the southwest of the palace and its walls. Steeples and minor towers filled the tiers as well, smoke from fires lying in a thick layer above the city, tinted orange by the sun.

Relief flooded Gregson, so visceral he could taste it, like honey coating his throat, but what caught and held his attention was the Autumn Tree. It rose from the plains north and west of the city, its massive trunk outside of the outermost city walls, its branches casting a dark shadow on the grassland beneath. Its flame-red leaves were burnished gold in the dawn, and even from this distance he could see them rustling in a breeze, the Tree appearing to be aflame.

He shuddered at the image, his gaze falling from the Tree to the plains and roadways leading to the city beneath. People were fleeing to the gates, groups of them on the road, others heading straight for the walls across open ground. Some appeared to be sections of the Legion like them, fleeing the broken defensive line. Others were clearly refugees and civilians, carts laden with possessions dragging behind them.

He watched them as his own group struggled past. Then the flap of banners caught his attention and he straightened in his saddle, squinting into the distance.

GreatLord Kobel's banners. They'd emerged from the tree line to the east and were charging across the fields toward Temeritt's gates, not that far from Gregson's position. The GreatLord led a sizable force, perhaps three hundred Legionnaires.

Hope surged in Gregson's chest.

It turned immediately to horror.

From the forest behind the GreatLord, a contingent of the Horde emerged, Alvritshai in front, riding hard, bearing down on the smaller force of Legion protecting the Great-Lord's flank. Part of the troops paused and spun, arrows arching up and into the Horde on their heels, but it didn't do much good. They were outnumbered at least two to one. The Horde would be on them in moments.

Panic threatening to claw through his chest, Gregson spun and shouted, "Legion, form up! The GreatLord is under attack! Jayson, keep the rest moving toward Temeritt. Don't stop until you reach the gates. Terson, get these soldiers moving!"

Even as his second began issuing orders, the exhausted Legion—barely fifty men—falling into lines, Gregson turned back to the field. Behind him, Curtis said quietly, "There are only fifty of us. That's not enough men to make a difference."

A flash of anger seered through Gregson and he spat, "I will not stand by and watch GreatLord Kobel cut down within sight of Temeritt. Not when I could have helped." But he knew Curtis was right. Fifty men would not be enough.

He suddenly recalled the horn bearer they'd picked up during the night.

His eyes darted across the expanse of the land before

Temeritt, taking in all of the scattered groups that were headed toward the city's safety. Most hadn't seen their GreatLord emerge from the trees, hadn't seen the Horde hounding them, too intent on reaching the safety they could now see, knew they could reach.

A significant portion of those were Legionnaires.

"But you're right." He turned back to his own small group, heartened to see that they were all in line, that Jayson and the refugees were already two hundred paces distant. He picked out the bearded horn bearer in an instant. "Horn bearer! Step forward! I want you to sound the horn and keep sounding it until every member of the Legion on these fields hears it. Understood?"

The man nodded grimly, hand falling to the curved instrument at his side and unstrapping it from its case. Gregson didn't wait, drawing his sword and pointing it toward the field, the men before him straightening, snapping out of their weary despondency or shock. He felt the exhaustion of the night fading, saw the sudden anger in their eyes, the hardening of clenched jaws.

Reaching deep within him, summoning strength from his chest, he roared, "For the GreatLord! For Temeritt!"

Then he spun and charged.

He heard the cry taken up behind him, nearly lost in the wind in his ears, in the sudden piercing cry of the horn as the horn bearer sent the call, but he didn't turn to look. Ahead, the GreatLord's force had halted and turned to face the Horde bearing down on them. Flight after flight of arrows arched into the Alvritshai and the few giants trundling up from behind. Gregson watched, sick to his stomach, as the two armies hit.

He urged his legs to move faster, feet pounding into the grassland, sweat already streaking down his sides, his chest heaving. A thousand paces away, he saw one of the GreatLord's banners fall, the cloth crumpling into the morass of

clashing swords and dying men. Out of the corner of his eye,
he caught movement and realized some of the Legionnaires
who'd been making for Temeritt were turning, those on
horseback charging toward the battle. At a hundred paces,
he caught sight of GreatLord Kobel himself, his face slicked
in sweat and spattered with blood, twisted into a determined grimace.

Then Gregson struck the Horde's flank, slowing and
pulling his sword back over his shoulder two-handed, the
outermost Alvritshai turning to meet him. With a battle
roar, he swung the blade with all of his strength into an
Alvrishai's mount.

The horse shrieked and reared, the sound shuddering in
Gregson's arms and torso as he jerked his sword free and
stumbled back. The Alvritshai who rode it spat something
in his own tongue as he fought to control the steed. A
breath later, the rest of the Gregson's Legion fell on the
Alvritshai to either side. Their battle cry broke through the
clash of swords, the Alvritshai fighting fiercely but falling
back under the initial impact. Gregson lunged forward,
sweat stinging his eyes, and sank his blade into another
horse's side as the Alvritshai turned it to strike from above.
Blood poured down from the cut, splattering Gregson's
chest, the animal lurching back and throwing the Alvritshai's swing off. Rage boiled up inside Gregson and with vicious cuts and horrendous strength he began battering at
the Alvritshai before him. The pale-skinned demon grimaced and parried desperately, tried to jerk his horse away,
but the Alvritshai's own forces kept him from drawing back.
In such close quarters, it was all he could do to keep Gregson's sword from his gut and his mount under control.

When the horse slid in what had once been a field of
grain, Gregson seized his opening and thrust his blade up
under the Alvritshai's flailing guard, between the split in his
armor at his armpit. It sank in a handspan, slid free in the

space of a breath. The Alvritshai's eyes widened in shock, twisted in pain, and then slackened as he sagged forward, his blade falling from a lax grip.

Gregson tried to turn, to shift to attack one of the Alvritshai on either side, but the crush of bodies was too tight. More of the scattered Legion had joined them, answering the horn bearer's call, surging up from behind. He was being shoved under the horse, where he knew he'd be trampled. In desperation, he reached up and seized the dead Alvritshai by the collar of his armor and hauled him down from the saddle, then leaped and clawed his way into its seat. It tossed its head, snorting and biting at the humans before it, but Gregson jerked it to the side. Leont took a vicious cut to the throat and went down, Gregson stabbing the Alvritshai that had gotten him in the back. Then a sudden flight of arrows whipped into the Alvritshai that surrounded them, at least a dozen falling from their saddles, another half dozen screaming in pain as they clutched shafts protruding from arms, legs, and chest. In the reprieve, Terson and a few of his own Legion seized their chance and commandeered their own mounts, cursing as the horses fought them.

Gregson scanned the battlefield. The Legion now outnumbered the Alvritshai and one of the gray-skinned giants was down, the other bellowing in rage as it tore into the GreatLord's forces at the heart of the battle. More Legionnaires were headed their way, most on horseback. One contingent struck, cutting swiftly through the Alvritshai in a huge swath, like a sickle through grain.

Gripping his sword tightly, Gregson kneed his new mount forward, swinging left and right with his sword, his eyes fixed on the GreatLord's position. He drew breath and shouted, "Temeritt! For Temeritt and the Autumn Tree!" the cry taken up on all sides by the GreatLord's forces. The Horde's left flank fell beneath the onslaught, the second giant going down under a hail of arrows. The GreatLord's unit rallied and shoved forward, meeting Gregson and his men in the middle. They cut down the Alvritshai separated from their own forces—

And then the remaining Alvritshai broke, spinning their mounts and galloping toward the safety of the trees and the hills beyond. The Legion harried the retreat until a horn blared, calling them back.

Gregson turned, a triumphant cry rising from his own men, elation burning hot and tight in his chest. Terson clapped him hard on the back as he passed, his horse falling into step beside his as they approached the GreatLord's men.

Kobel's eyes widened when his forces parted and he saw who led the unit. He nodded and held out his hand, still encased in mail, then grinned ruefully and let his hand drop. "Temeritt thanks you," he said, "as do I. But we need to get as many men as possible inside the walls. The Horde is not far behind."

"I understand."

Kobel considered him for a long moment, his horse fidgeting impatiently beneath him. He controlled it with one hand on the reins, then said, "I believe you do, Lieutenant."

Then he turned away and began barking orders, the entire Legion moving instantly into action.

They rode hard to Temeritt's gates, passing stragglers on the roads and in the fields. Nearly all turned to watch them; a few cheered. They passed into the shadow of the Autumn Tree, Gregson staring up at its immense branches, at its fiery leaves, and then they rode beyond, the walls and gates of Temeritt rising out of the plains ahead. The roadways converged on the western gate, the crowds of people fleeing the Horde's destruction growing thick, but they parted before the blat of the GreatLord's horns.

And then, the sun nearing midday, Gregson and what

remained of his garrison and the fighting men of Cobble Kill passed beneath Temeritt's gates. He had no idea what had befallen Jayson, Ara, and the rest of those he'd protected for most of the march southward, but he vowed he would find out.

Four hours later, the gates of Temeritt were sealed shut. Any who remained outside its walls were left to fend for themselves.

Two hours after that, the reformed Horde appeared on the hills to the north and began its march on Temeritt's walls, a second darkness spilling across the plains as the sun began its descent to the west.

"Call for the Cochen," Quotl said tightly. "Call him now!"

To his right, the dwarren drummer began beating out a frantic rhythm, sweat dripping down his face. His mouth was lined, brow creased in concentration.

Quotl bit back a curse as he scanned the battlefield.

The plan had been simple. Confront the Wraith army on the flat beyond, engage them and hold them as long as reasonably possible. But there had been no intention of holding them there for long. It was indefensible and beyond the reach of the archers. But it would enrage the Wraith army, especially when they withdrew to the ditches, and give the Cochen and the two clans who rode with him time to get into position unnoticed.

The trenches wouldn't hold either, but the intent had been to try to channel the Wraith army toward the north, to where the ditches ended and there was nothing but flat, open land between them and the northern face of the Break. The ground to the south was open as well, but only wide enough to give the Thousand Springs Clan a narrow path for retreat. It wasn't wide enough to allow the attackers easy access to the landslide and the plain above. And

Shadow Moon stood on the cliffs, ready with arrows to further discourage them.

Quotl's heart had hammered in his chest as the Wraith army hit the ditches and split, part of the force heading toward the south, part to the north. A small group hit the dwarren in the ditches, but the Riders there defended their turf fiercely, driving the Alvritshai on horseback and the lizardlike orannian back. Only the lithe feline gruen were effective in the trenches, swarming over the dwarren at its far side.

But it was the orannian and a few Alvritshai attacking the southern forces that sent a spike of fear into Quotl. If the southern defenses fell, the entire plan would fall apart.

His breath quickened, and with it came the surge of power that had engulfed him before. It seethed through his arms, his chest; through it, he felt the earth beneath him shuddering with the tread of both armies, heard the cries and screams of the dying with a brittle clarity. He focused on the south, saw the line of Thousand Springs there falter, begin to break—

And then Shadow Moon hit the orannian with a hail of arrows so thick the air appeared black. Hundreds of the lizard-skinned men fell beneath the onslaught. More arrows launched from behind the lines arced over into the enemy, and Quotl breathed a sigh of relief as the Wraith force scrambled to recover. A piercing shriek from overhead forced him to duck as one of the dreun dove, extended talons raking through the dwarren and gaezels, the fleet animals panicking as the creature's shadow blanketed them. Shadow Moon shifted their arrow attack toward the fliers, the dreun crying out and banking left. Quotl squinted into the late afternoon sunlight to see most of the dreun circling out of range of the archers, then dropped his gaze back to the battlefield to find the dwarren of Thousand Springs rallying and pushing the orannian and Alvritshai back.

A moment later, the entire southern force spun and raced away, back onto the plains.

Thousand Springs roared in triumph and turned their attention to defending the ditches.

Quotl didn't allow himself to feel any triumph. The battle was far from over.

Reaching through his connection to the earth, testing its potential, its power, he listened. The ground trembled beneath the hooves and feet of the attacking armies, but faintly he could feel a new tremor, coming from the south.

He listened a moment longer, to make certain, then said to the drummer, "Have the northern forces fall back now. Lure the Wraith army in."

"But the Cochen isn't here yet."

Quotl spun on the drummer. Whatever the drummer saw made him flinch back, the orders already being relayed.

To the north, Painted Sands began to give ground, Clan Chief Corranu making it appear as if they did so grudgingly, drawing the combined orannian, Alvritshai, terren, and gruen forces with them. Those that had struck Thousand Springs to the south had joined them. As Quotl watched, he noticed a second group of figures near the back of the army, watching and directing. One of the figures was on horseback, dressed in the black and gold of the Alvritshai warriors.

The other was on a gaezel.

"Elloktu," he spat under his breath, anger boiling up within to replace his shock. The betrayal of the Lands was more bitter and vitriolic than with the other Wraiths, for the shorter figure on the gaezel was obviously one of the dwarren.

He had not thought one of the dwarren could so betray his people. Or his gods. He searched the Wraith's forces, but did not see any dwarren within their ranks. But even the betrayal of one enraged him.

Painted Sands had withdrawn behind the solitary plinth of stone that reached for the sky a hundred lengths from the Break. Quotl glanced toward the summit of the cliffs, to where he could see the archers of Claw Lake waiting. But none of them had fired on the Wraith army yet, except volleys shot into the air to keep the dreun at bay.

"Wait," he murmured, reaching out again to feel for the vibrations in the earth, searching for the Cochen. "Wait."

Painted Sands continued to draw back, the Wraith army surging forward into the opening.

The Cochen had almost arrived.

Drawing a steadying breath, Quotl said quietly, "Now."

The drummer didn't hesitate, began pounding out a different pattern that was carried along the back of the army up to the cliffs. Above, the archers—all two thousand of them—adjusted their aim from the dreun in the skies to the Wraith army that crammed the base of the cliffs below.

Quotl felt the release on the air, two thousand bowstrings humming at once, setting a vibration in his chest that was intensified by the power coursing through him. He gasped, even as the Wraith army recoiled under the onslaught. A second volley fell, Claw Lake firing as quickly as possible. The Wraith army began to pull back from the cliffs—

And then the Cochen arrived.

He led the combined forces of Red Sea and Broken Waters, the two clans charging across the plains from the south, a plume of red dust rising behind them. Quotl watched in silence as he and the Archon blazed past, circling the ditches, the members of Thousand Springs who guarded the southern entrance to the slide joining them.

They struck the Wraith army's flank, hemming the massive force between the cliffs, the deadly hail of arrows from above, and their own forces, Painted Sands suddenly breaking off their fake retreat and falling on them from the other side.

The Wraith army was hemmed in on three sides. The enemy forces seethed in desperation, the center falling under the arrows, unable to escape or fight back, the edges of the army hitting Painted Sands and the Cochen's clans hard. In the frenzy, Quotl saw many of the lizard-skinned orannian flare open hoods, swordplay giving way to lightning quick strikes with their fangs. Dwarren reared back at the unexpected attacks, some of the defense breaking in horror.

"Did you know they could do that?" the drummer asked softly, voice shaking.

"No, I did not."

Movement caught his attention and Quotl turned to find the two Wraiths—Alvritshai and dwarren—edging forward. The Alvritshai raised one hand to the sky and made a fist with it.

Quotl's eyes narrowed, and then he looked up.

Without warning, the dreun who'd been hovering out of the archers' reach plummeted from the skies, straight for Claw Lake.

Quotl cried out, took an involuntary and useless step forward.

A few of the archers saw the dreun coming, shots firing into the sky, but none of them struck. The dreun came at them from the upper plains, sweeping down and hitting the archers from behind, knocking them from the cliffs. Quotl cringed at the screams as bodies fell onto the battle below, the dreun flapping their massive wings once they passed the cliff face and pulling back up into the skies for another pass, some with dwarren clutched in their talons. Claw Lake scrambled to reassemble. The dreun swept by again, more dwarren plunging to their deaths, but this time a group managed to hit one of the leather-skinned fliers as it passed. It shrieked as it hit the edge of the cliff, stone breaking off in chunks as it scrambled for purchase, arrows sticking out from it like spikes. But it couldn't hold, one wing torn and crumpled to its side. Its scream as it fell cut into Quotl like a knife.

On the rocky field below, the Wraith army had regained its footing, no longer decimated from above. It dug in and began to push outward.

"It's not going to hold," the drummer muttered.

Quotl's jaw clenched. He wanted to backhand the Rider, but didn't. He'd seen the signs himself, had known it wouldn't hold.

But there was one last defense.

He turned to the drummer. "Have those in the ditches pull back to the base of the landslide."

He didn't wait for the order to be passed on. Turning, he swung himself up onto his gaezel and kicked it into motion, heading toward the slide at their backs. The power of the Lands thundered through him as he raced across the open area between the ditches and the ramp, then through the tents of the dwarren camp, the northern edge of the cliffs towering above him. He passed into their shadow for a moment, emerging into the lowering sun again as he began edging up the slide. Its slope was gradual enough that his gaezel only slowed to half pace, snorting with effort. Dreun shadows passed over him but he didn't glance up. More screams came from the cliffs to his right, steadier, fainter screams echoing it from the carnage below. It felt like an eternity before he reached the top and pulled his mount around so he could survey the battle.

The dwarren had been driven to the base of the slide, the ditches abandoned, the Cochen's forces now combined with Painted Sands and Thousand Springs into one massive throng of dwarren, the clans no longer separate. Those at the back were climbing toward the upper plains. Dwarren on foot and gaezels began swarming around him, both Claw Lake and Shadow Moon hitting the Wraith forces hard with arrows as they dodged the continued attacks from the dreun. Two more of the leather-winged creatures had fallen, leaving eight wheeling in the skies above. The dwarren clans were being driven up the slide, the cliffs to either side acting as a funnel.

The only clan not present was Silver Grass.

As the last of the dwarren fled the flatland at the slide's base, Quotl muttered to himself, "Now."

Nothing happened. He sucked in a breath, held it, his own blood pounding in his head, heightened by the power that filled him. The Wraith army began edging up the slope, orannian and Alvritshai at the forefront, the stone-skinned terren bellowing behind them. Quotl exhaled harshly. "Ilacqua curse you, do it now, Attanna! What are you waiting for?"

Half of the Wraith army was now on the slide, the rest on the flat beyond.

And then Quotl felt the earth shudder on the plains below. He closed his eyes and muttered a small prayer, body tense.

When he opened them, the earth shuddered once again —

And then a section of the plains below collapsed, the earth cracking in massive fissures as the clan of Silver Grass broke the supports of the warren that lay underneath and the system of tunnels there caved in. The fissures crazed the rocky plains, snaking outward from the central chamber that lay a hundred lengths beyond the end of the slide like the frozen surface of a pond in winter giving way beneath someone's weight. The Wraith army that stood above that hidden chamber and the tunnels beneath were thrown to the ground, and then, with a suddenness that startled even Quotl, the earth gave way beneath them, collapsing inward with a grinding, hideous groan.

At least a thousand of the orannian, Alvritshai, and terren perished as a plume of dust rose. The dwarren who had volunteered to break the supports died beneath them.

But it wasn't enough. Too many of the enemy had made the landslide. Too many had survived the collapse of the sinkhole.

Quotl sank back into his saddle, a numbing despair washing over him. It had been their final defense of the Break.

Drums sounded, and dwarren began to withdraw from the Break's edge, racing back across the plains toward the entrance to the warren they'd emerged from a week before. Claw Lake and Shadow Moon were pulling back from the cliffs. The Wraith army now filled nearly the entirety of the landslide, the Cochen holding the mouth at the heights.

Azuka suddenly appeared from the chaos of fleeing dwarren, riding hard to Quotl's side. His eyes were panicked, but his voice was stern. "Quolt, don't you hear the drums? We need to reach the warren. Quotl!" He reached out, grabbed Quotl's arm, and tugged him toward the open plains behind.

Quotl jerked his arm out of his grasp.

Another voice cut through the chaos, cut through the numbness that enveloped Quotl. He turned to find Tarramic drawing his gaezel up short. "We've called the retreat, but too many of the Alvritshai have already reached the heights. You need to do something, Quotl. If we don't slow them down, we'll never reach the warren entrance in time to collapse it."

Quotl barked laughter, the sound raw. "What do you expect me to do, Clan Chief?"

Tarramic frowned at his tone, then said brusquely, "Do whatever it was you did before. Call upon the gods."

Quotl recoiled, as if Tarramic had slapped him. At the same time, the power within him surged.

Before Quotl could respond, Tarramic spun his mount and charged onto the plains.

Quotl glared out toward the slide, toward the fighting,

now so close he could see individual dwarren dying beneath orannian and Alvritshai blades.

"Call upon the gods," he muttered to himself, shaking his head. "That's the Archon's job."

"You did it once before."

He straightened in his saddle. He'd forgotten that Azuka was there.

He didn't know what he'd done before, but sighing, he reached out through the power flowing through him, sank into the ground at the height of the Break, felt the stone beneath him, the layer upon layer of sediment and rock. He traveled through it, searching. Desperation had driven him before. He'd acted on instinct, reaching out and twisting without thought, and stone had shattered. Could he do that again?

Through stone, through the Lands, he felt . . . a flaw.

He sucked in a breath, centered on the flaw, on the weakness. It lurked in the rock of the northern cliff face, deep in the earth. As he explored it, he realized that it was the remnants of the flaw that had caused the Break to give way hundreds of years before, creating the landslide where the dwarren and Wraith armies now fought. The earth had shifted and settled since, but part of the flaw still remained.

All it needed was a push.

Drawing a deep breath, exhaling slowly, Quotl closed his eyes.

Then he reached out and *shoved*.

Stone cracked, the sound louder than anything Quotl had ever heard before, shuddering in his chest and making him gasp, eyes snapping open. Gaezels and horses alike stumbled in a panic, veering away from the sound. Those fighting on the slope paused, stunned.

Then the northern cliff face above the slide gave way, slipping and falling as a single, solid wall of stone. It avalanched into the Wraith army, burying it as the base of the stone face struck and it began tilting outwards. Everything in its path—orannian, Alvritshai, terren, gruen, and a host of luckless dwarren—turned and ran. The wall of stone slammed into the landslide, vibrations setting off another avalanche down the slope, taking a significant chunk of the Wraith army with it and blocking the mouth of the slide with rubble. Beyond, the earth's trembling unsettled the plinth of stone enough that it began to topple, dust and debris rising in a choking cloud to obscure its last moments from sight. Dwarren swarmed from the mouth of the slide, gaezels out of control.

When the stone settled, Quotl turned to Azuka. The shaman looked shocked, his eyes awed, but tainted with fear. Any chance Quotl had of allowing the Archon to take responsibility faded. He could see it in Azuka's eyes. "The warren," Quotl said.

He pulled his gaezel about and streaked toward the distant warren entrance. The dwarren on all sides abandoned the Break, all of the clans heading west. As the sun sank into the horizon, Quotl caught sight of the Cochen and the Archon, the two surrounded by the mixed clans, and relief coursed through him. The Archon could order the warren's mouth collapsed as soon as they arrived, Silver Grass already headed toward the two smaller entrances north and south with orders to seal them before rejoining the gathered clans underground. The Wraith army could not be allowed to reach the Sacred Waters and the Summer Tree. The dwarren had done what they could at the Break.

Now it was up to the Shadowed One.

23

ERAETH GLANCED TOWARD SIOBHAEN, who nodded, and then, as if they'd planned it, both sheathed their swords and pulled the bows the forest had gifted them from their backs. Feet planted at the supple wood's base, the two Alvritshai strung them in the space of a breath, Eraeth turning toward Colin, face taut and grim.

"You take care of Walter. We'll deal with the sukrael."

Neither waited for an answer, sprinting away from their location at the Source in two different directions, both reaching for the strange arrows the forest had left as they ran. Colin couldn't remember how many arrows each carried, but he hoped there were enough to kill all of the Shadows that surrounded them. He counted at least fifty, perhaps as many as a hundred.

"Use the bows as staffs when you run out of arrows," he shouted, brandishing his own staff. At the top of the steps, Walter drew a sword. "And remember that the sukrael perish if you can throw them over water."

He caught Siobhaen's first shot out of the corner of his eye, the shaft catching one of the Shadows and nailing it to the stone wall behind. Its supple, glistening blackness tinged with gold writhed and tattered as if it were cloth caught in a tempest—

And then Walter moved, slowing time, his form blurring. But Colin had been waiting for it. He reached out and seized time as well, used it to find Walter, the flows disturbed by Walter's presence, by his manipulations. Colin focused on the disruption and raced across the stone steps to meet his old tormentor from Portstown. Images of the abuse he'd suffered under Walter's hand flared across his mind—the beatings in the streets of the fledgling town, the humiliation of the penance locks, and his sly smile when both had thought Colin would hang at the gallows in the town square. All of it came rushing back as if it had happened yesterday, instead of decades ago. He'd allowed his hatred to seethe inside of him, unquenched and unsatisfied for so long. That hatred had driven him to halt Walter's awakening of the Wells, had taken him to battle against the other Wraiths and Shadows when they attacked the Alvritshai and dwarren afterward, had finally motivated him to create the Seasonal Trees to halt their destruction.

But all of that had been defensive. His hatred had not been sated. He wanted Walter dead, wanted revenge for the deaths of his parents, for the death of Karen and all of the others who had set out in that wagon train onto the eastern plains, driven there by Walter's father because of what Walter had done.

He let all of the frustration and rage that had accumulated over the span of nearly two hundred years out in a roar as he closed on Walter, the Wraith charging toward him with a twisted smile on his face. Raising his staff diagonally overhead, he brought it down with all of his strength.

It cracked into Walter's blade, the staff vibrating in Colin's hand as Walter lurched left under the force of the impact, but it didn't break. Without pause, Colin pulled back, shifted his grip, and swung the other end toward Walter's feet, but the Wraith danced back out of range, sword snicking in toward Colin's fingers. Colin hissed and pushed forward, aiming for Walter's hands and arms now, trying to knock the sword from his grasp, but Walter was too quick, slipping back and forth through time, slowing and speeding up, just enough to remain out of reach. Colin matched his pace, keeping them in synch, the effort causing sweat to break out on his face and slick down his back. They shifted up and down the steps, circling the Source, its blue pulse deepening as dusk began to descend.

Around them, the battle between the Shadows and Era- eth and Siobhaen proceeded in juttering spurts as the two humans danced with time, but Colin couldn't watch, didn't have the time or energy to spare. The two Alvritshai were on their own. Walter's actions were too quick, his strikes too sudden. Colin couldn't afford to look away.

He hissed as Walter's sword cut a smooth line across the back of his hand, blood welling even as Walter smirked, spun the blade in his grip, and brought it sharply across Co- lin's exposed throat. Colin seized time as he lurched back with a gasp, the blade slowing a moment, giving Colin a fraction of a second longer before Walter compensated, the sword tip passing within a finger's breadth of his neck, so close he felt its passage beneath his chin. He swallowed down the bitter taste of fear, stepped back, and tripped over a massive slab of the crystal debris that littered the floor, his back slamming to its surface with enough force his breath gushed from his lungs.

Walter shouted in triumph, leaping up onto the surface as Colin choked on air. Sword raised, the Wraith brought it down two-handed, attempting to plunge it into Colin's chest, but Colin rolled. The tip of Walter's blade caught the back of his shirt, the edge slicing a thin line down Colin's shoulders that *burned*, but Colin didn't stop moving. He tore free, the tip of the blade skittering across the crystal's face, nicking Colin again in the side as it jerked in Walter's hand before he drew it back. Colin swore, heard Walter laugh, the sound reverberating through the chamber—

And then he rolled over the edge of the crystal slab.

He hit the stone floor, felt grit, stone, and smaller crystal shards cut into his side, but flung out his arm to halt himself. His legs swung out over empty space and he sucked in a shaky breath. They'd somehow circled back down to the Source, the gaping, lipless mouth of the Well yawning to one side. His momentum and the weight of his legs nearly pulled him farther into the pit, but he jerked back, scrambling up onto the lip. He had a moment to catch his breath, leaning on one elbow, and then he heard Walter's feet grinding into the grit behind him.

He shoved himself up into a seated position, free hand slapping into the wood of his staff. He twisted and drove it hard into Walter's stomach. At the same time, he seized some of the Source's power—a power he could feel escalating toward its peak—and sent it through the wooden shaft.

Walter screamed and reeled back, hitting the same slab that Colin had stumbled over. Satisfaction surged through Colin as the smug expression on Walter's face contorted into a snarl of pain and hatred as he wheeled and fell. His sword clanged into the slab, jarred from his hand, and returned to real time, caught in mid-bounce. Walter swore and dragged himself to the far side of the crystal. His movements were slower, the clothing where Colin's staff had hit him in the chest scorched.

"You weren't expecting that, were you?" Colin climbed to his feet. He winced as he pulled himself upright with his staff, the blood from the cut on his hand trickling down his arm. The slice across his back stung with sweat. He grinned. "I've learned a few tricks since we last fought, there on the Escarpment."

Walter glared, pushing himself up into a low crouch. One

hand went to his chest, near the burn mark, hand cupped
strangely.

Then he smiled. "So have I."

He thrust his hand forward, palm out. Colin tensed, saw
a ripple on the air like a heat wave—

Then something slammed into his chest and flung him
backward. He crashed to the floor, scrabbled for purchase,
then felt himself slipping over the edge of the Well again.
His free hand grabbed at the lip. The fingers of his other
were crushed between staff and stone. His entire body slid
over and dangled against the edge of the Well, held only by
the arm holding the staff and his fingers. He tried to swing
his legs up to the lip, gasping with the effort, failed and
pulled himself up to his chest instead, keeping himself stable, the lip underneath both armpits. He glanced down, the
Lifeblood pulsing with bluish light not far beneath. It was
nearing the point where it would be full. If it awakened
completely, he wasn't certain he could reverse the process.

He was running out of time.

He snapped his attention back toward Walter, the Wraith
coming toward him with hand cupped to his chest again.
Walter paused long enough to return to real time and retrieve his sword, body stilling unnaturally for a single short
breath, then continued toward him, a malicious smile touching his lips.

Colin clenched his teeth and heaved himself up and out
of the Well.

Siobhaen drew and fired as she ran, the bowstring a consis-
tent twang in her ears, setting the wood in her hand humming. The sukrael streaked down from the sides of the
chamber, like black cloth blowing on a wind. Her first three
arrows took out four of the Shadows, snagging in their silky
folds and carrying them to the surrounding walls where

they were pinned to the stone, the third hitting two of them as they converged on her. A shiver of surprise ran through her that the arrows didn't shatter against the stone, but punched through it as if it were wood. She smiled in cold satisfaction when the sukrael began to writhe and tatter beneath the shafts as if being torn to shreds by a tempest.

To one side, she caught Shaeveran and the other Wraith blurring in and out of focus as they fought, their figures jumping from step to step, vanishing and appearing again twenty paces distant, sword and staff thrusting and lunging back and forth, until the disjointed fight began to make her head ache. Sounds of the fight intruded as well, oddly distorted as a grunt or shout began before fading or cutting off sharply as they disappeared.

She shoved their battle aside and focused on the Shadows with grim determination. She reached, pulled, and fired one last arrow, the creatures getting too close, then swung the bow in a sweep across her body. She felt the wood catch in their forms, the bow jerking in her hands as those closest were caught, but she solidified her stance and flung them out over the emptiness of the Well at her back. They fell into the pit, a high-pitched keening piercing through Siobhaen's head, but she didn't watch to see if they died. She dodged left and sprinted around the Well, trying to put some distance between her and the others.

As she ran, she felt a surge of power from the Source, the light throbbing like a heartbeat, the power within pushing against her skin. Beneath that massive force, she felt another power, recognized it as Aielan's Light, the white fire burning deep within the earth here. She reached for it unconsciously as she ran, drew it into her body as she had done at the Well in the White Wastes. But there the pool of white fire hadn't been as strong. She had been forced to dig deep, to root herself in ritual learned as an acolyte at the Sanctuary in Caercaern. It hadn't come easily, and she'd only been able to draw upon it enough to create the wall of fire that had protected them from the Wraith and the sukrael that had attacked them.

Here, the white fire came willingly. It filled her, burning beneath her skin. She exulted in its power, the emotions of her first immersion in Aielan's Light deep within the mountains beneath Caercaern smothering her. She cried out at their intensity, laughed as they seared her inside and out. She halted and spun, arrow placed and fired before any of the sukrael behind her could react. On the far side of the Well, she saw Eraeth doing the same, his face twisted into a snarl. But the sukrael were too fast, coming in from too many sides. They couldn't cover their own backs, and there was nothing in the chamber they could use—

Except themselves.

She grimaced in distaste, but shouted, "We need to cover each other!" even as she pulled and fired again and again, spinning on her heels.

Across the Well, Eraeth grunted. "Agreed."

He broke off his attack and ran, leaping up onto chunks of the crystal and jumping to the stone steps, weaving a path toward the opposite side of where they'd begun, where Shaeveran and the Wraith were still fighting. Siobhaen risked a glance in that direction, saw the Wraith appear long enough to snatch his blade out of the air as it fell, then blur away. She shot three arrows in succession and then bolted toward Eraeth.

They met in the middle of the steps, the sukrael streaking after both of them, perhaps forty remaining. Positioning themselves back to back, but with enough space between them to make drawing arrows easy, they began picking off as many of the sukrael as they could. Siobhaen listened to Eraeth's breathing as she focused her attention outward, adjusting her stance left or right as Eraeth shifted. They were keeping the sukrael at bay, and distracted from

Shaeveran, but it wouldn't last long. Desperation crawled up from Siobhaen's gut as she fired, her mind frantically searching for a solution.

As if reading her thoughts, Eraeth said, "We can't keep this up much longer. I'm running out of arrows."

"So am I."

"What's our strategy?"

Before Siobhaen could answer, light pulsed up and out of the Source, so intense she saw flashes of darkness on her vision even though she hadn't been looking at the Well. She swore and blinked rapidly, catching one of the Shadows as it reared up before her. At the same time, the power of Aielan's Light flared up inside of her, as if reacting to the pulse from the Source. Her heart surged at the sight of the Shadow so close, adrenaline sizzling through her skin, tingling in her arms. Without thought she released the arrow already nocked.

The arrow and the flare of the fire in her gut coincided. As the bow's string hummed, the arrow burst into white flame and streaked toward the Shadow. It shrieked as it was caught, then burst into a fiery white conflagration, the arrow carrying it away like a shooting star. Where its flames touched the other sukrael, they also burst into white fire, flailing as their shrieks joined the others.

Siobhaen sucked in a breath in shock. She had never called Aielan's Light without the use of a ritual before, but she had never felt so saturated in the Light before either. Whatever lay beneath the ground in this wasted, ruined city, it was more than simply a source for the Lifeblood of the Wells. Aielan's Light resided here as well, a more powerful conflagration than what lay beneath Caercaern.

"What happened?" Eraeth shouted from behind her.

"I called on Aielan's Light."

"I meant what happened to the Source?"

She felt her shoulders prickle at the derision in his tone,

but turned her focus on the Well, keeping one eye on the Shadows. The sukrael had halted their attack on her, hovering a short distance away as those caught by the white fire writhed in their death throes on the stone steps. Eraeth continued to fire arrows on his side.

The Source's light pulsed from within the Well, brighter and faster than before. She could see the Lifeblood within now. It had risen nearly to the surface.

Her chest tightened in horror. "I think the Well is almost awake."

Eraeth grunted. The twang of his bowstring halted. She turned.

"I'm out of arrows," he said.

She reached and grabbed all of hers that remained, handing them over. "Take them," she spat when he resisted. "I'll use Aielan's Light instead."

He nodded once, then grabbed the arrows and shoved them into the quiver on his back. There weren't many left.

She spun, reaching deep down inside herself, reaching deep inside the earth as well, down toward the source of Aielan's Light beneath the city.

Then she called it forth.

~

Colin jabbed his staff into Walter's stomach and unleashed a burning pulse of power as it connected, even as Walter brought his sword down across Colin's chest and threw a wave of power from his other hand. The sword nicked Colin's chin as he jerked his head away, cut into his arm on the downswing, and then the power hit him full force and flung him backward. Walter screamed as Colin's blast burst from the end of the staff before disengaging. Both of them hit the floor and scrambled to their feet, breathing hard. Walter was covered in scorch marks—on his chest, stomach, arms, and back—his clothing seared and smoking. Colin's entire body ached with bruises from the energy punches Walter had flung at him. Scores of nicks and cuts riddled his body. They glared at each other across the debris of the crystal dome, night sky above, the chamber lit only by the heartbeat of the Source at its center.

That heartbeat pulsed through Colin's blood, seethed through his skin with its urgency. The Well was filling; it was nearly awake.

Walter leaped across the distance separating them and dove at Colin with an overhead swing. Colin barely caught it with his staff, the force of the blow driving Colin and Walter to the ground. Colin's back slammed into the debris, stones and shards of crystal biting into his back, but he heaved upward with the staff and flung Walter up and over his body using all of his strength. As soon as Walter's weight lifted off of him, he rolled into a crouch. He heard Walter grunt as he hit the ground, turned in time to see the Wraith slam into the side of one of the chunks of crystal, and then he pushed forward with his feet, bringing his staff up and around.

It cracked into Walter's wrist. Bones crunched, and Walter screamed as he lost his grip on the blade again. But Colin didn't back off. Before the sword had halted in mid-fall, his staff pounded into Walter's chest, into his side, his legs, his shoulder. He pummeled his age-old nemesis, primeval pressure building in his chest, escaping in a wordless cry of pent-up frustration riddled with childhood fears, with the rage of youth, with grief and nearly two hundred years of hatred. Through the tears coursing down his flushed face, he beat at Walter's head, pounded the staff into the bully's body, seeing the youthful Walter who'd kicked the shit out of him in Portstown. He saw the blurred image of an older Walter, face swirling with blackness and speckled with blood, after he'd slaughtered the Tamaell of the Alvritshai in the parley tent at the Escarpment. He vented all of the stress of searching for him in the years since, following in the Wraiths' footsteps as they awakened the Wells, trying to catch them, to destroy them, only to have them slip away, as insubstantial as the Shadows that had tainted them.

And then he heard Walter laughing through his own strained and shortened breath.

Colin jerked back, breaking off his attack, his breath coming so fast and so short that he felt light-headed. Weakness shook his arms, his body, and he coughed harshly, trying to seize control of his hyperventilation. His skin was flushed and he felt hot and nauseous, his whole body trembling. The sensation was familiar, and he suddenly realized that this was how he'd felt after attacking Walter and his cronies with the sling back in Portstown, when he'd been only twelve years old.

And still Walter laughed. Face bloody and bruised, bones cracked, he still sucked in breath after breath and laughed. From his crumpled position against the slab of crystal, the Source's light pulsing blue against his black-swirling, blood-spattered skin, he watched Colin, his grin cutting into Colin like a knife.

Colin straightened as Walter's laughter faded into chuckles. When Walter tried to shift and grimaced in pain, Colin could see his teeth were stained red with blood. But still he chuckled.

Colin frowned in confusion. He stepped forward, stood over Walter, the Wraith staring up at him from where he'd collapsed.

"Why are you laughing?" he asked, although the question wasn't for Walter. He didn't expect the Wraith to answer, was surprised when Walter did.

"Because you're too late," Walter said, choking on blood as he spoke. He swallowed, face twisting in pain, and yet he grinned his bloody grin, saying more forcefully, "You're too late."

The Source suddenly flared with light, Colin turning as it pulsed upward and out, surging up through the floor and through Colin's body. The heartbeat that had been escalating reached its height. Partially blinded, Colin could still make out the Lifeblood that had nearly reached the lip of the Well. At some point, while fighting with Walter, or attempting to beat him senseless, he'd let his hold on time go. They were in real time now, and as they fought, the process that Walter and the Wraiths had started had neared completion.

The Source stirred from its slumber.

With a sickening twist of rage, Colin realized it had all been a ruse. The entire fight between them had been nothing but a distraction. Walter had simply been keeping Colin occupied while the Well continued to fill.

Colin snapped his attention back to Walter to find the Wraith watching him.

"You can't kill me," Walter said. "We can't die."

"No," Colin said, shifting his grip on his staff. He felt something deep inside him harden. "Not yet. But I can hurt you."

Fear flickered for a brief moment across Walter's face as Colin lifted his staff and then drove its end into Walter's chest two-handed, releasing the power of the Lifeblood that coursed through him through the living wood in a flood. He held nothing back, the shame that had caused him to halt his attack with the sling in Portstown and had sent him staggering from Walter here in this ruined city a moment ago burned away. Walter screamed, louder than anything Colin had heard before, the pain in the sound reverberating in Colin's head, in his bones, and yet he ground the staff harder into Walter's chest. Walter writhed beneath the onslaught, arms juddering against the floor and crystal slab, legs kicking, heels drumming a staccato rhythm against the stone.

When the scream died, Colin jerked his staff away, Walter's

body arcing on its side as residual energy coursed through it, then collapsing back to the floor, the Wraith unconscious. Beneath the blackened and charred circle where his staff had connected to his body, Walter's chest still moved. He still breathed.

Colin nearly drove the staff into him again, but wrenched himself away from the body and stalked toward the edge of the Well. The Lifeblood lapped within a few inches of the edge of the stone, but it had not fully awakened. There might still be time.

He raised his arms, staff in one hand—

And then sank into the power that coursed around him, into the eddies and flows of the Lifeblood, down and down into the Well, diving deep into the reservoir and the Source beneath. He let the Lifeblood fill him. Through its power, he felt a sudden flare, although it was distant and removed. He tasted it, recognized it as Aielan's Light, and relaxed. Siobhaen must have called it. She was the only one he knew of in the chamber besides himself who could control it.

He wondered briefly why she'd needed it, but then shoved that concern aside. He didn't have time. The Well was almost full, almost awake. Its power had escalated and was reaching its crest. It would peak within moments. He needed to halt it, or he would never be able to stop the attacks on the Seasonal Trees. If the Wraiths managed to solidify this power, they would be able to use it for years against the three races, decades perhaps. It might take him that long or longer to bring the rest of the Wells into balance enough that he could protect its power from the Wraiths.

He searched the Source for a way to halt the awakening. Lifeblood surged from the reservoir below into the Well, the currents of the underground lake and the surrounding streams that fed and stemmed from it forcing the water higher. He knew from his attempts to balance the Wells to the west that cutting off the flow along one branch or widening it along another would affect the entire system. It had taken him years of experimentation to figure out how it had worked. The introduction of the reservoir had complicated that system immeasurably. Yet he had only a few minutes to figure out how to stop it now.

He paused his frantic search of the currents and focused on the Well in the ruined city. Trying to calm his thundering heart, heightened by the pulse of the awakening, he let himself sink into the flows beneath the city. The Lifeblood coursed through a maze of tunnels and chambers, like those the dwarren used beneath the plains. Those corridors lay everywhere, connected to the lake far beneath. All he needed to do was find which currents would ease the pressure on the one filling the Well and then divert them.

He tried to calm his breathing, tried to relax.

There.

Excitement cut through him, but he forced it back, focused on the one channel he'd chosen and then began pouring power through himself into the flows there. He pushed them to one side, tried to divert them into a new passage, as if he'd taken his hand and plunged it into the edge of a stream to affect the currents.

The Lifeblood reacted, swirling around him as if he were merely a stone, creating new eddies, but not blocking the main channel feeding the Well. The stream was too large. He needed more power.

Opening himself up further, he let more of the power of the Wells course through him, felt his presence expand in the stream, but it still wasn't enough. He needed more. Shaking with the effort, he opened himself wider, and wider still, felt his control of the power trembling in his grasp. He had never extended himself this far, had never absorbed and held this much within himself, had never allowed so much of the Lifeblood to flow through him. He shuddered in ecstasy, on the verge of allowing it to carry him away, tasted its coldness to his core, the scent of ice and loam and earth overwhelming him.

And it wasn't enough.

"I can't," he murmured, trying to push himself further, to block the flow of Lifeblood. "It's too far along. I'm not strong enough. I can't stop it."

His voice drew his awareness back to his body, drew him back to the edge of the Well, the Lifeblood a finger's breadth away from the top now. He felt Aielan's Light burning around him, felt Siobhaen and Eraeth's presence on the far side of the Well, heard Siobhaen shouting something, her voice thick with warning.

"I can't," he whispered, trying to answer her, despair beginning to wash through him.

The Wraiths were going to succeed. Walter was going to win. They'd planned everything too well, Colin and Aeren and the dwarren reacting too late.

Then pain punched through the despair, a white-hot, ragged pain that began in his back and erupted from his chest, searing through his body as it arched, someone grabbing hold of his shoulder to keep him steady as the pain widened, gripping his entire chest, sending sheets of fire into his arms and legs. He glanced down as blood gurgled up in the back of his throat, coating his mouth, and saw the end of Walter's blade jutting out of his chest.

Walter's breath blew hot against his neck as the Wraith whispered, "You never did open yourself completely to the Lifeblood and all it offered as I did, did you?"

~

The white fire of Aielan's Light leaped from Siobhaen's hands in an arc, burning into the outer ring of sukrael instantly, setting them afire. Their shrieks filled the blue-lit chamber as Siobhaen pushed the fire outward, the Shadows twisting and writhing as they tried to escape. Eraeth had an arrow nocked and ready to shoot, sight trained along its length as he swung it back and forth, searching for any of the sukrael that might break free, but there was no need. Siobhaen could *feel* them through the fire as it seethed through her, knew where to direct the tendrils of flame. They were like voids in the living world around her, pits of emptiness.

She filled those pits with fire.

There were over twenty of the sukrael left and they all died within the space of ten heartbeats. Their black bodies flapped in the white furnace that Siobhaen called forth, burned to embers as the Light flowed through her. She found herself murmuring prayers to Aielan, litanies from her youth coming to her lips without thought. She prayed to her ancestors, to the flames beneath Caercaern, to the fire she drew upon now, and when the last Shadow had ceased to exist she felt that fire taper off and die within her.

Weakness shuddered through her and she collapsed to her knees, then back onto her heels.

"Siobhaen!"

She turned toward Eraeth's voice, removed from her body, hollowed out and burned to a cinder. She tried to smile in reassurance. "It came too easy," she said, and her voice trembled. "I couldn't control it."

"You controlled it enough to kill the sukrael."

She shook her head. He didn't understand. "I could guide it, but I couldn't control its power. It was too much. It burned me out."

She could tell by his scrunched up look that he still didn't understand.

Then movement caught her eye. Movement on the far side of the Well.

Shaeveran stood at the water's edge, arms raised, staff in one hand, but his eyes were closed, his face tense with concentration. To her burnt-out senses, he appeared to be throbbing, as if he were greater than he appeared, filled to bursting. The bluish light of the Well washed over him, casting him in strange shadows.

But the movement came from behind him and to one side.

"Eraeth," Siobhaen said in horror.

The Protector spun at the warning in her voice, bow already rising, string creaking as he drew the arrow back, fingers near his ear. But the Wraith had already risen, had already slipped behind the oblivious Shaeveran.

The human's eyes flickered. His mouth moved, as if he were speaking.

Siobhaen couldn't have moved if she'd wanted to, too drained by Aielan's Light. But she could still talk.

She drew in a deep breath and screamed, "Shaeveran! Behind you!"

And then the tip of a blade burst from Shaeveran's chest. He arched back, but the Wraith's hand clamped onto his shoulder and held him as the blade twisted and the Wraith murmured something in Shaeveran's ear.

With a jerk, the Wraith withdrew the blade and let Shaeveran fall to the side.

Siobhaen couldn't breathe. Her chest had constricted, her throat locked shut, mouth open. Horror tingled through her body, paralyzing her.

But not Eraeth.

She heard the twang of the bowstring, saw the first arrow streaking across the now completely full Well, the shaft shimmering with light from the water beneath. She felt it sink into the Wraith's chest as if it had struck her own instead. She jerked, drawing air through the constriction, something painful tearing deep inside. A second and third arrow were already speeding across the Well after the first, the sound of the bow somehow amplified in her ears. The

Wraith's body had twisted, the force of the first shaft throwing him back. The second arrow hit him high in the shoulder, kicking him in the opposite direction, the third taking him in the throat.

The fourth took him in the eye.

He fell, Siobhaen so attuned to the chamber she heard his clothes rustle, heard the thud of the body hit the stone. Then Eraeth's hands were under her armpits, heaving her up and slinging one arm across his shoulders so he could support her. She instinctively pulled away, not wanting his help, disgusted at the presumption, but when she dragged her feet under her, they would not support her weight.

"Come on," Eraeth growled. "I don't know how long he'll stay down." He began hauling her around the edge of the Well, heading toward the bodies. She noted he unconsciously veered around the blackened ash where the sukrael had died.

"He isn't dead?" she asked, her voice dry and ragged.

"No."

Stunned, she let Eraeth carry her for a moment, then began struggling to regain her footing, her legs tingling as the bloodflow returned to them. She hissed at the sensation, but by the time they'd reached Shaeveran's side, she could stand on her own.

Eraeth let her go and dropped down beside Shaeveran, rolling him onto his back.

Siobhaen sucked air through her teeth.

The hole in Shaeveran's chest still leaked blood, a large pool of it already surrounding his body, his clothes plastered to his side, his hair matted with it. More blood than Siobhaen had ever seen. Some of it had reached the edge of the Well, curling red-black in the water before dispersing. Shaeveran's face was ashen, his hands pale, his lips blue. And yet he breathed. If she hadn't seen his chest moving, she would have known by the bubbles of blood that formed at the hole in his chest. But his breathing was slow, perhaps one breath for every three of Siobhaen's.

"Is he alive?" she asked.

Eraeth gave her a scathing look. "Of course."

Siobhaen tensed at the derision, but Eraeth had already dismissed her, was digging through his satchel. He pulled out one of the waterskins, uncapped it, and upended the water onto the ground.

Siobhaen lurched forward. "What are you doing? We need that! We're in the middle of a desert!"

He thrust the skin into her hands. "Fill this with water from the Source as best you can. He may want it when he awakens. Don't touch the water. Don't even touch the waterskin where it gets wet. And for Aielan's sake, don't drink any of it."

He didn't wait to see if she obeyed him, turning back to Shaeveran instead, ripping the bloody shirt apart over the wound and beginning to clean it, not being gentle. As soon as he cleared it, the wound filled with fresh blood. Dark blood, rich and vital. Eraeth swore and continued working, motions frantic.

Siobhaen shuddered and turned away. Shaeveran had told her he couldn't die, but she hadn't believed it until now. He shouldn't still be alive. Any Alvritshai with a wound like that would have died before he hit the floor.

She gripped the waterskin in her hands, then made her way to the Well, stumbling only once on her weakened legs before kneeling. She made to dip the entire skin into the water, then remembered what Eraeth had said. Gritting her teeth, she held the skin along one edge and dipped the mouth beneath the smooth surface, the Well still pulsing with bluish light. Air bubbles escaped and rose to the surface, but she couldn't get much of the Lifeblood into the skin, not without reaching into the water.

She tried a few more times, then swore and pulled the

skin from the Well, holding it as if it were made of glass, letting the liquid drip down one side. She could feel the power of the Lifeblood, as if she held her hand out to a fire. It smelled of earth and loam.

When she turned back, she caught sight of the Wraith.

He'd fallen on his back, the four arrows jutting up from his body—chest, shoulder, throat, and eye. She grimaced at the last as she moved to stand over him. The sword that he'd thrust through Shaeveran's body lay next to his limp hand, slick with blood. She kicked it farther away, afraid to touch it. Then she knelt down beside the body.

Unlike Shaeveran, the Wraith's skin roiled with darkness, like ink. Blood stained his clothes as well, seeping from around the strange wooden arrows. His chest rose and fell in the same slackened pace as Shaeveran's, but somehow it seemed more unnatural to Siobhaen. She reached her free hand toward the end of the shaft that had sunk into the Wraith's eye socket, but couldn't bring herself to touch it.

She stood abruptly, spitting a vitriolic curse at the body, then hurried back to Eraeth's side.

"The Wraith isn't dead," she reported. "He's still breathing. Even with that arrow through the eye."

"It will take more than an arrow to kill them, even one given to us by the Ostraell. Be thankful that it's hurt him enough to knock him unconscious." Eraeth stood, staring down at where he'd bandaged Shaeveran's chest, the cloth over the wound already stained red. He glanced toward the Well, then Siobhaen, narrowing his eyes. "We need to get him out of here."

"What about the Source?"

"Without Colin, there's nothing more we can do. And I don't want to be around when the Wraith wakes."

"But—" Siobhaen turned to stare at the Well, at the bluish light that was beginning to dim.

Eraeth gripped her shoulder. "We won't go far. We'll find

someplace in the city to rest until he heals enough to tell us what needs to be done."

"Can anything be done now?"

Siobhaen's heart lurched with pain at the grim expression that flickered across Eraeth's face. Despair washed through her and she suddenly wondered if events would have turned out differently if she had turned on Vaeren before they had reached the Well in the northern wastes, if she hadn't wavered between her duty to the Sanctuary and Lotaern and her duty to Aeilan's Light and what she'd felt in her soul was right.

The thought that they would have, that Shaeveran would not be lying at her feet, his heart's blood staining the stone beneath them, sickened her.

Eraeth squeezed her shoulder, then glanced down at the waterskin she clutched in one hand. It was still damp with the Lifeblood.

He snatched up his satchel and opened it. Siobhaen dropped the skin inside and he cinched it closed and threw it over his shoulder. He motioned toward Shaeveran. "We have to move. Now. Help me with him."

They each took one of Shaeveran's arms beneath a shoulder, the human surprisingly light, and began dragging him up the steps away from the Source toward one of the openings that led to the outskirts of the building. Behind, the bluish light of the Well continued to recede, night reclaiming the broken dome's interior.

At the top of the steps, they paused to look back, the water of the Source placid, the light within as faint as moonlight now, washing the stone debris and the cracked walls of the chamber. The Wraith's body lay still and shadowed.

Siobahen's stomach suddenly clenched and she turned toward Eraeth, Shaeveran's body between them, head sagging forward. "What about the dwarren? And the humans to the south? What about the Seasonal Trees?"

The same pained, grim look flashed through Eraeth's eyes.

He didn't answer.

~

"Is that the last of the Cochen's forces?" Quotl asked. His voice still sounded odd to his ears, throbbing deep in his chest, and many of the dwarren who rode past gave him strange looks. Nearly all of them reached for the totems woven into their beards, some muttering prayers and raising them to their mouths to be kissed. Even those wounded, covered in blood and battle-weary, paused a moment before being ushered on by the shamans who tended them.

Quotl tried to ignore them, as he had ignored the reactions of Azuka and the others on the battlefield. But it was becoming increasingly difficult to brush the looks aside.

Azuka nodded. "The last of those in the main group have entered the cavern, including the Cochen, the clan chiefs, and the Archon." Azuka shot him a sidelong look as he mentioned the Archon, which Quotl also chose to ignore.

"Then seal the warren."

Azuka opened his mouth to protest—the order should have come from the Archon or the Cochen—but stopped himself, casting another glance at Quotl before nodding and kneeing his gaezel forward through the throng of dwarren toward the main entrance. Quotl remained behind, his gaze sweeping over those that filled the wide tunnel without really seeing them. A sense of inevitability enfolded him, numbed him. The power that had suffused him on the battlefield had waned, but his connection to it had not broken. It had merely subsided into the background.

He didn't know what had happened, didn't understand what it meant, but he was beginning to think it was more than simple chance. He'd overheard some of the rumors that were already threading their way through the dwarren ranks. Whispers that he'd been touched by the gods, that Ilacqua worked through him, even that he'd become a god himself.

He'd snorted in contempt at that last. But it was a troubled snort.

From far down the tunnel, he heard a rumble of stone that escalated and grew. He reached out to touch the wall beside him, his gaezel fidgeting beneath his weight as it felt the rock trembling. The roar of falling rubble increased, then peaked. As it began to fade, a cloud of dust and grit suddenly engulfed the entire corridor, moving swiftly past all of the gathered dwarren, the Riders crying out in alarm and breaking into fits of coughing. Torches guttered in the gust of air, a few sputtering out. Gaezels shifted restlessly. Quotl held his breath as long as he could, then sucked in a lungful of air, tasting the dry dust of stone in the back of his throat a moment before his lungs protested and he began coughing as well. As soon as the cloud of grit passed, it began to settle, everyone covered in a light gray-white film. Riders brushed themselves off and the hacking and wheezing faded.

"Who ordered the collapse?"

Quotl winced at the outcry, the voice instantly recognizable, a sour taste twisting his mouth into a grimace. He straightened, ran a hand down his dust-coated face, and prayed, wishing fervently for his pipe.

"I did," he said, raising his voice to be heard even though the Riders that were within range had fallen silent. "I called for the collapse of the entrance."

He turned to face the Archon.

On the far side of the tunnel, at least a hundred strides away, Kimannen spun in his seat, face contorted in rage. He stood with the Cochen, the clan chief covered in blood, his arm held out to the ministrations of one of Red Sea's shamans. Two of the other clan chiefs—Corranu of Painted Sands and Asazi of Broken Waters—flanked the Cochen and the Archon, also wounded.

"The sealing of the warren is the Archon's responsibility," Kimannen spat. He dragged his gaezel around and headed toward Quotl, the Riders between parting before him, their gazes flickering back and forth between the two.

Quotl stiffened, reaching forward to still his gaezel when it snorted in defiance. "You were preoccupied with the Cochen and his wounds, although I see that one of your shamans has seen to them."

Kimannen glared at the mild rebuke, halting a short distance away. "You overstep your bounds, Quotl. You always have."

At the threat that underlay the words, the Riders surrounding Kimannen stirred, a grumble of discontent rumbling forth. The Archon did not appear to notice.

Quotl's eyes narrowed. "Would you have left the warren open?"

"Of course not. We cannot allow the Wraith army access to the tunnels, to the Confluence."

"Then I have merely anticipated your orders."

"That is not the point!" the Archon shouted, trembling slightly. But when the murmur of dissent rippled among the Riders at his tone, he shot dark looks to either side. Confusion passed across his face, and he drew his gaezel back at the looks the dwarren were giving him, looks as dark as those he'd flung at Quotl.

He returned to face Quotl, the glare becoming a glower of hatred, of resentment.

He edged his gaezel closer, so that they stood side to side. His features smoothed, the anger draining away, although this close Quotl could still see it simmering deep in the Archon's eyes. He drew himself up to his full height and said, "You wielded the power of Ilacqua I sent you well on the battlefield today. I can feel it inside of you still. I see now that I was mistaken. It was Ilacqua who guided you in sealing the warren behind us, yes? As it was Ilacqua, through me, who guided you at the Break?"

All eyes were on Quotl. Doubt had crept into the murmurs of dissent from the Riders, doubt Quotl knew he could crush with a few words. He could challenge Kimannen here and now, seize the Archon's position before all of those gathered. It was not how the Archon was chosen, but this was the Turning. The world was slipping toward chaos, and perhaps that was the best reason to wrest control from Kimannen. They needed a strong Archon now more than ever.

But they also needed stability, especially among the clans. Kimannen hadn't kept control for so long because he was powerless. He had allies among the clans, knew how to manipulate them to get what he wanted. Most of the shamans knew that a few were more powerful than Kimannen when it came to Ilacqua's blessings, knew that Kimannen's personal communion with the gods had been slipping recently. But they couldn't afford a dispute among the shamans at this time. Not after the battle.

Quotl allowed himself to relax, his hand moving to calm the gaezel he rode. "Ilacqua guides me in all things, Kimannen, here and on the battlefield."

Kimannen's nostrils flared at the use of his name, rather than his title, but he answered, "As I suspected." His gaze raked those watching. "The warren is sealed by Ilacqua's will! Prepare to depart!"

Then, attention back on Quotl, leaning forward, so that only Quotl would hear, he said coldly, "You are not the Archon."

He jerked his gaezel's head around and headed back toward the Cochen. Oraju and the other clan chiefs had remained silent, but watchful. Corranu caught Quotl's attention and nodded, the motion subtle but laden with respect. Oraju's expression was impossible to read.

As soon as Kimannen turned his back, Quotl sighed. Tension in his shoulders drained away.

"Kimannen did not send you Ilacqua's strength on the battlefield," Azuka said from behind him.

Quotl started. He hadn't heard the shaman return. He frowned at him, as if his inattention had been Azuka's fault. "Who is to say? The Archon was distant. Perhaps he appealed to Ilacqua to aid us."

Azuka's penetrating stare didn't falter. "The shamans know. And most of the Riders on the field. *They saw you.*"

A queasy unease ran through Quotl's gut at the intensity in Azuka's voice and his hand twitched toward his pipe. He waved his hand in frustration. "What did they see? I am nothing but a shaman, an old one at that, well past my prime."

Azuka smiled. "True. But you've changed."

"How? How have I changed?"

Azuka's eyes widened. "You can't see it, can you?"

Quotl answered with a heated glare and Azuka settled back in his seat. His brow creased in thought.

"It's hard to explain. I'd have said that you glowed, but that's not accurate. You appear the same, and yet there's *more*. More life, more energy, more *you*. I can sense you even when I cannot see you, and what I feel emanating from you is..." He groped for a moment, then sighed, shoulders sagging. "What I feel is hope."

Quotl remained silent. Azuka's words made him uncomfortable, the stares of those Riders around him were worse. Throughout the chamber, dwarren began to pick themselves up and remount, those who were being attended by the shamans now finished. The clan chiefs were issuing orders, preparing to ride back toward the Confluence. They would need to discuss strategy, need to decide which of the

warren entrances would have to be collapsed to keep the
Wraith army at bay. Patrols would have to be established on
the main routes in the east, a warning system put in place,
supplies organized and all of the clans coordinated in the
defense of the Confluence and the Lands.

The amount of planning and preparation staggered
Quotl.

"You have been touched by the gods, Quotl, whether
you like it or not."

Quotl would have protested, but realized he couldn't.
Not when he could still feel the power he'd found on the
battlefield coursing through him. Not when he could still
feel the Lands beneath his feet.

~

Gregson stiffened, his heart aching, his throat hot and tight.
He stood on the third wall of Temeritt in the darkness, the
night sky open above, the stars brittle and clear. He'd been
on the walls for hours, weary from the fighting, from the
long, arduous march from Cobble Kill, the horrifying collapse of the Legion's defenses near the Northward Ridge
and the flight to Temeritt. But he could not sleep. He'd
come here seeking solace, the familiarity of the Legion, the
camaraderie of men who'd trained in the barracks here in
Temeritt, beneath the GreatLord's eye, in the shadow of the
Autumn Tree.

He would not find any solace tonight. No one in Temeritt
would.

The Legion manned the walls to either side, armored,
with spears and pikes held straight at their sides. Between
them stood other men—some of them no more than boys,
really, ten or twelve, but men now—clad in odds and ends,
with whatever armor they could find that would fit them,
carrying weapons that were unfamiliar and unwieldy at
their sides. A gasp had run along the length of the wall mo-

ments before, some men shifting forward, others back. Some had fallen to their knees while others signed themselves with Diermani's skewed cross and muttered prayers beneath their breath. A few were weeping.

They all watched what Gregson watched, what all of the citizens of Temeritt watched, even though he couldn't see them in the city below. He knew they were there, standing at windows, or lying on rooftops. He could *feel* them in the city that sprawled to either side and behind. He could smell their fear, like rank sweat, could smell their horror.

For below, on the low hills that surrounded the city, the fires of the Horde's camp flickered. Thousands upon thousands of fires.

At the center of the Horde's army lay the Autumn Tree. And the Autumn Tree burned.

Part IV

~

Threads of Darkness

24

AEREN STORMED INTO HIS ROOMS in Caercaern and flung the ceremonial House sword onto
his desk. "How is he controlling the Evant?" he
raged. "How is it that every vote on every issue ends up
swinging toward his own agenda? Who are his allies?"

He crossed the room in a minimum of strides and halted
before the lone table that held the artifacts of his House, a
dagger that was once his brother's, a pendant that his
mother had worn, the swath of cloth from one of his father's
shirts, stained with his father's blood. They rested on top of
the blue-and-red folds of a Rhyssal House banner draped
across the table. It had once held the House sword as well,
until he'd taken to wearing it whenever he left—not only to
attend the Evant, but even for an excursion to the market.

Caercaern no longer felt safe.

He leaned forward onto the table and bowed his head.
Behind him, he heard Hiroun murmur something to the
rest of the Phalanx, then close the door. Footsteps moved
into the room, but halted a discreet distance away, close, but
still leaving Aeren a sense of privacy; he could ignore the
guard if he wished.

Eraeth would have rounded the desk and come to
Aeren's side.

Aeren sighed and pushed back from the table, faced Hiroun, the Phalanx guard straightening slightly.

"Well?" Aeren demanded.

Hiroun's eyes widened before settling into a studied blankness. He'd obviously thought the questions were rhetorical, and he was not yet as astute at hiding his thoughts as Eraeth would have been.

He shifted, glanced toward the table beside Aeren, then back toward his lord. "It is difficult to tell. There are no Lords of the Evant who have voted consistently in Lotaern's favor. Every lord has voted for and against him at some point in the past two months. I do not see a pattern."

"And yet somehow he has controlled the outcome of nearly every vote and manipulated the discussions in his favor. Even Lords Orraen and Peloroun continue to both support and deny the Chosen."

Hiroun nodded agreement. "The only other member of the Evant who has consistently voted against the Chosen's wishes recently has been Tamaell Thaedoren."

Aeren grimaced and began pacing. "Thaedoren knows of Orraen and Peloroun's alliance. Of course he opposes them. But Lotaern . . . Lotaern is more resourceful than I thought, than I ever suspected. Even with Thaedoren's help, we haven't been able to stop him, only slow him down. He has risen far in the Evant, in too short a time."

Hiroun said nothing, but Aeren felt his eyes on him as he moved about the room. He massaged his temple with one hand, the headache that had begun at the beginning of the session of the Evant—that had plagued him at nearly every Evant since the beginning of spring—throbbed behind his eyes.

Still agitated, Aeren collapsed into the chair behind his desk. He frowned at the new missives stacked there. "Have the servants bring hot tea with honey."

Hiroun issued the order at the door, then closed it and

stepped to one side. Aeren reached for the letters. Most were reports from the magistrates of the various holdings of the House, forwarded by his son from Artillien, some with notes from Fedaureon, who had looked at them himself before sending them on. A new trade agreement between Rhyssal and the human Province of Rendell caught his attention and he broke the seal to see if the changes both sides had requested had been made and that no other portions of the language had been altered, then set it aside to be signed later.

Then he noticed Moiran's handwriting and he smiled. He pulled the thin letter from beneath a slew of others and broke the seal, a faint scent of lavender drifting up from the page as he unfolded it. It brought an instant image of Moiran's small sitting room overlooking the lake. An ache awoke in his chest, but he quashed the urge to return to Artillien immediately. There were only a few more weeks before the summer intercession, when the Lords of the Evant could return to see to the progress of their own lands. He could wait that long at least.

He began reading.

Within a few sentences, he stiffened, his smile dropping away. Something clenched at his heart, squeezing it tight.

On the far side of the room, Hiroun grew tense. Out of the corner of his eye, Aeren saw the Phalanx's hand drop to his cattan, heard the rustle of cloth as the guard shifted, but he did not look up.

He read the letter to the end, then read it again.

He let the parchment fall to his desk, hesitated, and finally glanced up toward Hiroun.

"Ready the Phalanx, all of them, and prepare the rest of House Rhyssal for an immediate return to our House lands. Do so quietly, but swiftly. I want to be outside the walls of Caercaern and as far west as possible by nightfall tomorrow."

"What has happened?"

Aeren regarded him steadily, then said darkly, "The Chosen, through the Order of the Flame, is planning an insurrection in our own House lands. I intend to stop it."

"But what of the Evant? Will you leave it to Lotaern?"

Aeren bowed his head, rubbed his eyes with the fingers of one hand. He suddenly felt weary, his age settling over him like a cowl.

He let his hand drop and reached for parchment and ink, spurring himself into action before the weariness could catch hold.

Tamaell Thaedoren must be informed immediately.

Without glancing up, he said harshly, "I have fought Lotaern in the Evant for months and achieved nothing. I cannot save those who do not wish to be saved. I will focus on saving my own House—my own family—if it is not already too late."

Hiroun did not respond, but as Aeren dipped a quill into ink and began to draft a missive to the Tamaell, he heard the door open and close.

A moment later, booted feet thundered in the corridor outside as the Rhyssal House prepared to flee Caercaern.

~

Peloroun and his two escorting Phalanx guards entered the Sanctuary at dusk and were led by one of the acolytes toward the Chosen's personal chambers deep inside the temple. Peloroun did not pause at the massive ritual basin in the main rooms, did not kneel and pray as was proper, and he ignored the disapproving look the accompanying acolyte gave him and his guards. He disliked being summoned by Lotaern mere hours after the closing of the Evant, the message arriving in the middle of his meal. And he hated being called to the Sanctuary. If any of the other lords became aware of this meeting, or learned that he had made a personal call on the Chosen at such an odd hour, their entire alliance would be exposed. Did the man have no sense of propriety? Of subtlety?

The acolyte knocked on the Chosen's outer door and, at a command from within, opened it to allow Peloroun and his guards to pass, closing it behind them.

Peloroun had never been to Lotaern's private chambers. The room was covered from floor to ceiling in plants, most of them in bloom. Vines climbed and wove among trellises and lattices overhead. Miniature trees grew from pots scattered on all sides. Tables strewn with smaller pots were set against the walls, a large desk set near the back. The room reeked of earth and the cloying scent of flowers and citrus.

But it was those already assembled that caught and held Peloroun's attention. He scowled as he stepped forward, his guards a pace behind. Chairs had been set out, Lord Orraen seated at one of them, his guards behind him. Peloroun halted a few steps away from where Lotaern leaned forward onto his desk, two members of the Order of the Flame flanking him.

"Are you insane?" he growled. "Why is Lord Orraen here? Why have you risked exposing us? Anyone who hears word of this will know of our alliance!"

Lotaern regarded him calmly, hands clasped before him. Behind, one of the members of the Order of the Flame shifted threateningly, Peloroun's guards responding in kind. The tension in the room mounted as Orraen's Phalanx also bristled.

Then Lotaern stood, and for the first time Peloroun noticed the strange wooden knife sitting on the unfolded chain cloth before him. The knife gleamed in the glow from the candles and lanterns that filled the room with warm light.

"The time for secrecy has ended," the Chosen said.

Peloroun's anger faltered. He shot a wary glance toward

Orraen, but the other lord had frowned, clearly as confused as he was. "What do you mean?"

Lotaern smiled. "The Autumn Tree has fallen. It's time to put all of our plans into motion. It's time to bring the Tamaell and the Evant to its knees."

The *Mary Gently* docked in the bustling town of Trent at midday. Tuvaellis stood on the deck and listened to the captain bellowing orders, watched the crew scramble, shirtless and sweaty in the heat. Her own cloak and cowl covered her in shadow, her black-stained skin hidden beneath its folds. The journey across the Arduon had been mostly uneventful. She'd remained in her cabin, venturing up to the deck only at night. None of the crew had bothered her, after the first who'd tried to rape her had ended up with two broken hands. She scoffed as she recalled how he'd waited for her beneath the stairs that led to her rooms, reaching out to snag her and drag her into the shadows with him. She'd smelled him from the deck before she'd descended. For a brief moment, she'd considered spilling his blood across the narrow hall, but decided that would bring too much attention to herself.

He'd been lucky she'd stopped with his hands.

If he'd managed to see the mottled Alvritshai skin beneath her cowl, she wouldn't have stopped there.

Now, she turned her attention to the port city, the air humid and thick. The land rose sharply from the crystalline waters, the whitewashed buildings practically stacked one on top of the other. The roofs were tiled, windows wide and arched at the top, colored shutters and doors open to catch the breeze from the ocean. The wharf and the visible plazas were thronged with people, carts, wagons, and horses. The docks reeked of fish and brine.

On the heights above, the land leveled out and she could

see vineyards and orchards and groves of olive trees interspersed with buildings. Columns supported open porticos
with cloth hung overhead for shade. Aqueducts like those
her own Alvritshai used wove through the fields. A large
manse surrounded by a low wall presided over it all.

"So different from the human Provinces," Tuvaellis muttered to herself. She could feel the age of the stone and of
the city, not unlike the abandoned cities of the Alvritshai to
the north of the Hauttaeren Mountains. Yet even with that
age, Trent felt cleaner than Corsair.

Perhaps that had to do with the way the sun glared on
the white stone of the buildings. Corsair used granite.

Behind her, something crashed to the deck, followed by
a hissed curse. She turned, still absorbed with her thoughts
of the city—

And found one of the crew standing over the trunk from
her rooms.

She reacted on instinct, rage enveloping her. She stepped
forward and backhanded the man, already reaching for the
hilt of her sword. The blade snicked free as the man reeled
back from the blow and fell to the deck. Its tip settled on his
neck before she managed to control herself.

"Who told you to enter my cabin and retrieve my
trunk?" she snarled.

The man froze in shock, his skin pale, blood trickling
from his nose. His eyes were locked on hers and he was
hyperventilating.

Hurried boot steps sounded and Tuvaellis shot a glance
to one side, saw the captain trotting toward them, his hands
held up in a calming gesture, as if she were a spooked horse.
Her eyes narrowed.

"Calm down," he said as he approached. His face was
beaded with sweat. "It wasn't Devid's fault. I saw you on
deck and sent him to get your trunk, figuring you'd want to
be off the ship as soon as possible."

He came to a halt out of the reach of her sword, his eyes imploring.

"Devid's a good hand," he added.

Tuvaellis said nothing, but after a long moment withdrew her sword from the terrified man's throat.

Both Devid and the captain heaved sighs of relief.

She glanced toward the trunk, scowled as she realized one of the corners had splintered, even though it was protected by brass, an edge of burgundy-colored cloth peeking through. A thread of fear swept through her and she nearly jerked the trunk open to check the contents, to make certain nothing had been disturbed, but she caught herself.

Unable to dampen her fear, she spun on the captain. "I need rooms in the city, and two crewmen to carry my trunk to them. Carefully." She glared at Devid, who flinched.

"Of course," the captain said. He did not look happy, but his need to see her off of the ship as soon as possible was evident. He motioned to two other crewmen who were watching the altercation to one side. "Take the trunk and the lady to The Painted Vine. Tell Irina I sent you."

The men grimaced but stepped forward, grabbing the leather handles of the trunk and lifting it. Tuvaellis' heart stuttered when she heard something shift inside, but she said nothing. They preceded her down the plank to the dock and into the crush of people along the wharf, winding their way up the switchback streets into the city beyond. Tuvaellis kept her attention on the trunk, distracted only once by the passage of a group of armored men in the colors of the Bontari Family. But the soldiers were not interested in her or the trunk. She watched the sun-gleaming figures vanish in the crowd, then motioned the two crewmen on.

It took half an hour to reach The Painted Vine. The wrought iron gate opened onto a small courtyard with a fountain at its heart, the water gurgling as they walked the cobbled path past a few sculpted fruit trees to the shade of a porch. A woman with skin a shade darker than most of those Tuvaellis had seen outside stood by the door, summoned by the chimes that had sounded when they opened the gate. Her mouth was screwed up into a tight frown, her arms crossed over her chest. Her gaze swept over the crewmen, then settled on Tuvaellis.

"Who are you?" she asked bluntly. "I do not service anyone off the street."

"Captain Escalli of the Bontari Family asked us to escort her here," one of the crewmen muttered.

She eyed Tuvaellis up and down, then snorted. "I'll show you to your rooms."

She led Tuvaellis and the crewmen to two rooms with a veranda overlooking the harbor. The crewmen set the trunk down in the sitting room, while the dark-skinned woman opened the lattice doors to the bedroom beyond. As soon as they were able, the crewmen fled.

"If there's anything you need, please let me know."

Tuvaellis ignored the disapproving look laced with curiosity. "Very well."

The woman hesitated, then departed, closing the front doors behind her.

Tuvaellis moved instantly to the trunk, flinging open the top and pushing the silky folds of cloth aside. Even in her haste, she was careful to keep from touching the object nestled within. She could feel its power, subdued but potent, and she didn't want to waken it accidentally. It would not have the desired effect if it were released here.

If it hadn't been damaged already.

She found it shifted to one side, only a few folds of cloth padding it from contact with the wood of the trunk. About the size of her fist, it looked like a smoothed chunk of marble, veined with streaks of green and flecks of gold, but as she sat back, she could see a steady light throbbing deep inside it. Occasionally, a thread of light would trace its way around the stone's edge.

She searched the stone for any cracks, any signs of damage, but saw none. The tension in her shoulders relaxed and with a relieved sigh, she stood.

She would need to find another container. The trunk was too heavy for her to carry alone; it had only been transported in the trunk to protect it from potentially rough seas. Now that she was in Andover, she could find a smaller case, something light and unobtrusive.

And then she would have to find a way to get it to the Rose.